ABOUT THE AUTHOR

From an early age, Martin was enchanted with old movies
from Hollywood's golden era — from the dawn of the talkies
in the late 1920s to the close of the studio system in the late
1950s — and has spent many a happy hour watching the likes
of Garland, Gable, Crawford, Garbo, Grant, Miller, Kelly,
Astaire, Rogers, Turner, and Welles go through their paces.

It felt inevitable that he would someday end up writing
about them.

Originally from Melbourne, Australia, Martin moved to Los
Angeles in the mid-90s where he now works as a writer,
blogger, webmaster, and tour guide.

www.MartinTurnbull.com

This book is dedicated to

Paul Patience

because old friends don't come along every day.

ISBN-13: 978-1506024615

ISBN-10: 1506024610

SEARCHLIGHT AND SHADOWS

a novel

by

MARTIN TURNBULL

Book Four, the *Garden of Allah* novels

CHAPTER 1

Gwendolyn Brick's head throbbed like a son of a bitch, but she didn't care. The traffic thundering along Sunset Boulevard was bordering on painfully loud and the midday sun shone so bright it hurt to open her eyes. But that didn't bother her, either. All that mattered was her brother's telegram. She clutched it in her hand as she waited for him on the sidewalk outside the Garden of Allah Hotel.

"I can't sit here anymore!" she declared, springing to her feet, but it made her head throb even harder and left her breath jagged. She sat down again.

Kathryn Massey yawned. "Aren't hangovers the worst?"

Gwendolyn had never been much of a drinker — which made her a rare bird at the Garden of Allah — until the Japanese attacked Pearl Harbor. Her brother was stationed there and the navy had listed him missing in action. As the grim days that followed blurred into wretched weeks, Gwendolyn made up for lost time by downing whatever booze lay at hand. At the Garden, there was always something within reach: champagne, gin, punch, brandy, martinis, daiquiris, manhattans. She kept it up through a dismal New Year's Eve, but Western Union brought her bender to a halt.

> AM ALIVE BANGED UP BUT RECOVERING STOP
> MEET YOU GARDEN OF ALLAH SUNDAY NOON
> STOP

The two women sat on the low brick fence next to the red and black pansies whose smoked-honey scent Gwendolyn usually enjoyed, but today found annoying. "Maybe they hit traffic?"

"It's all of three minutes past twelve," Kathryn said gently. "I'm sure he'll be along real soon."

They said nothing more until a black Cadillac with shiny chrome trim slowed to a stop opposite them. In the back seat, a young bride wrapped in a veil sat next to a handsome young man who was beaming in his army uniform.

"I guess we'll be seeing a lot of that now," Gwendolyn commented. She watched the Cadillac head east into Hollywood. "Do you think either of us will be married before the war ends?"

Kathryn started to say something, but cut herself off. "Is that a jeep?"

A fatigue-green vehicle, roofless and doorless, bounced up the boulevard toward them. Two men in white sailor caps were up front, but that was all Gwendolyn could see. She clutched Kathryn's arm and pulled her to her feet.

It wasn't until the jeep came to a stop that Gwendolyn could be sure it was her darling, damaged Monty. She raced to the curb, unaware that she was crying until Monty's grinning face blurred and wobbled. "It really is you!"

His driver, a beefy Italian, jumped out with a pair of crutches in his hand. "Don't even think of trying to help," he told her. "Mister Independent don't like that."

It took all of Gwendolyn's self-control to let her brother climb out of the vehicle under his own steam. He took the crutches from his buddy, hooked them under his arms, and swung himself onto the sidewalk. "See?" he declared. "Almost good as new."

The tendrils of Gwendolyn's hangover unfurled. She felt lighthearted and clearheaded as she wrapped her arms around Monty, crutches and all, and let her tears soak the shoulder of his dark blue uniform. He hugged her back as best he could. "Honest, sis, it ain't that bad. These here crutches? Just for show, mainly. More like an insurance policy."

She took a half step back and studied his face. A graze across his forehead was still healing, as well as some purple bruising down the left side of his neck. But most noticeable of all was a deep slash carving a line from under his right ear, across his cheek, to the middle of his chin.

Monty looked past Gwendolyn. "Hi, there. Kathryn, isn't it?"

Gwendolyn broke her hold on her brother to let him shake hands with Kathryn, then noticed that his ride had driven off. "Come on," she said, "let's go inside and—"

Monty pulled back. "I've been cooped up in that dang hospital for weeks. Can't we go out?"

"Got somewhere in mind?" Gwendolyn asked.

"Yeah, but you're not going to like it."

"Anywhere you want—it's your big day."

"Anywhere?"

* * *

The girls slid into a booth and watched Monty pitch himself unaided onto the seat opposite them.

"I know we told you anywhere," Gwendolyn said. "But—here?"

C.C. Brown's ice cream parlor on Hollywood Boulevard was just down from Grauman's Chinese Theater, and was famous for inventing the hot fudge sundae. Last time they were there, Monty confronted a guy who was bothering

Gwendolyn. It would have been gallant had it been anybody but Bugsy Siegel. Monty neither knew nor cared who that was, but Gwendolyn and Kathryn did, and so did their friend Marcus. They'd fled out of Brown's with their hearts in their throats and hadn't been back since.

"Hey!" Monty swiped a hand through the air. "That meatball left you alone, didn't he?"

Siegel had eventually taken the hint; not because of anything Monty did that day, but Gwendolyn let her brother think he'd come to her rescue.

After they ordered a round of sundaes and coffees, Gwendolyn faced her brother. "Your telegram said you got banged up, so I've been picturing the worst. You seem to be mobile." She flickered her eyes toward his crutches. "When you pulled up—"

He laid a hand on top of hers. "Sis, I'm okay," he said quietly. "I won't lie, it was touch and go for a while. There was a serious infection and—ah, skip it. You don't want to hear about all that."

"But I do," Gwendolyn protested. "All I got was one lousy telegram. Honestly, Monty, you could have taken the time to scribble a note, just to let me know."

"If I'd been conscious, sure I could've written you. Maybe even called."

"Not conscious?" Kathryn butted in. "How serious was this infection?"

"There was talk of losing a leg—"

"MONTY!" Gwendolyn squeezed her brother's hand.

"—but it didn't come to that. Once they got me stateside, the quacks down there in Long Beach tried something else. It worked and I'll be as good as new." He shrugged away the rest of his story.

"I bet it was mayhem after the attack, huh?" Kathryn asked.

He flinched. "I ain't got the words to describe what it was like. Destruction on that kind of scale," he shook his head slowly, "it's like nothing you can imagine. The noise! You shoulda heard it. On second thought, nobody should have to hear them sounds."

Gwendolyn leaned on her elbows. "I can't even imagine what you've been through. I'm surprised you've held onto your sanity."

Monty started to chuckle.

"What's so funny?"

He laid down his spoon and grinned at her. "I thought I was going to be able to get away with it, but I guess not."

"Meaning . . . ?"

He took suspiciously long to reply. "I was — er, when the Japs hit, I was in the brig."

"In *jail*?"

"I had a two-day liberty pass, so I tied one on. Got into a bar brawl with some other seadogs. I don't recall much of anything after about twenty-two hundred hours, but someone told me the MPs arrived and I took them on, too. Landed in the brig sometime before midnight. The first thing I knew of the attack was when the brick wall of my cell started crumbling and the tin roof pinned me to the bunk."

The waitress arrived holding sundaes piled high with vanilla ice cream, smothered with hot fudge and crushed peanuts, and crowned with a cherry. Monty dug in, cramming as much as he could into his mouth.

Gwendolyn shook her head. "Oh, Monty. The things I've been imagining."

He pointed his chocolatey spoon at her. "That drunken bar brawl saved my life. If I was sober and awake that morning, I'd have been supervising hull maintenance on the *Arizona*."

A thousand soldiers had lost their lives on that battleship, which now lay shattered at the bottom of the harbor.

They ate their sundaes in silence until Monty said, "Truth is, I'm ashamed I wasn't with my buddies. That two-day drunk may've saved my life, but it's wrecked my pride." His sky-blue eyes lost their focus for a long moment. "Can we just leave it at that?"

"Mo-Mo, I'm so sorry—"

"How's about you, Googie? Did you get your job back at the Cocoanut Grove?"

"Oh, heavens, no. I'd been slinging tobacco around that place too long. I need something new."

"Like what?"

Gwendolyn watched an old guy in gray overalls paste a *For Lease* poster to the front window of an empty store across Hollywood Boulevard. "All I've done is sell cigars and cigarettes since I got to LA. I don't know what else I'm good at."

Kathryn's burst of gunfire laughter took Gwendolyn by surprise. "What else you're good at?" she asked. "Are you kidding?"

"What?"

"You're the best damn seamstress I know." She turned to Monty. "You should see the dresses she makes for me. I get compliments everywhere I go." She slapped Gwendolyn's wrist. "If the studios knew what you were capable of, they would be falling all over themselves."

Gwendolyn resisted the urge to wrinkle her nose. Between the cattle calls, her disastrous screen test for *Gone*

With The Wind, and her two so-called big breaks in A-list movies, she hadn't had the best luck with the studios. They were the last place she wanted to work.

She scooped up the last of her sundae and slipped it into her mouth, savoring the warm fudge that was so thick and gooey it was almost chewable. Her eyes drifted back to the empty store across the street. The early afternoon sun was shining over the roof of C.C. Brown's and directly onto the spacious display window. It wasn't a large store, but it was opposite Grauman's and three doors down from the Roosevelt Hotel, which was a great location.

Best of all, it was available.

CHAPTER 2

Kathryn Massey never thought of herself as the moody type. As the *Hollywood Reporter*'s gossip columnist, she liked to think of herself as Gumption Girl. Hadn't she been the first to foresee the commotion Orson Welles caused over *Citizen Kane*? She'd tried to warn him against wading into Hearst-infested waters, but of course he didn't listen. He wouldn't have been Orson Welles if he had. The point was, she was the first one to see it coming, and that never would have happened if she was some wallflower.

Back then, when the *Kane* missiles were flying, she'd never have guessed her stance would lead her to the envelope in her purse. Back then she was sure of who she was and what she believed, and she wasn't afraid to stand up in public—or in print—and say so. But now she had an envelope whose contents made her question everything. She'd felt compelled to keep it close in case she was taken with the urge to look at it again. And she was often taken with that urge.

Kathryn's desk sat on the periphery of a vast room that housed the battalion of journalists, editors, and photographers who toiled to produce the *Hollywood Reporter*. Ignoring the gibbering typewriters and clanging telephones, she reached for her purse and pulled out the contents of the envelope.

*AS REQUESTED CONFIRM BIRTH DETAILS FOR
KATHRYN JANE MASSEY BORN 8.37 AM ON*

*JANUARY 24 1908 STOP MOTHER FRANCINE
MARY MAE CALDECOTT STOP FATHER NOT
APPLICABLE STOP*

I don't know why you care so much, she told herself.
You've done perfectly fine your whole life without Father,
dear Father Not Applicable. Who cares if he wasn't married
to your mother? That single, long-buried fact has no bearing
on the woman you are today.

"Father not applicable." The words blurred as her eyes
burned. *If only I could believe that.*

"Ahem? I said, excuse me?"

Kathryn smelled Chantilly perfume, the five-and-dime
scent whose bargain price and woody notes appealed to
spinster librarians and suburban housewives with budgets
as limited as their worldviews. Like most cheap perfumes, it
didn't stick around very long, which meant someone had
doused herself less than an hour ago.

The woman standing rigidly at Kathryn's desk was
dressed in a conservative two-piece suit of dark beige tweed;
a simple gold crucifix hung from her neck.

Kathryn got to her feet. "Can I help you?"

"You're Miss Massey?"

"That's right." Kathryn extended her hand, but the
woman regarded it with disdain.

"I am Mrs. Quinn." She fixed Kathryn with a stony look.

Kathryn forced herself not to blink or swallow or show
any sign that she wanted to run screaming from the
building. For nearly ten years, she'd been having an on-
again-off-again-on-again affair with a stuntman. By the time
she figured out he was married, she'd fallen for him. *It's not
my marriage*, she'd told herself. *It's not my problem.* Kathryn
never asked about Roy's wife and Roy rarely mentioned her,

except to say that she was deeply Catholic, so divorce wasn't an option.

"I see," Kathryn said softly. She doubted Mrs. Quinn could hear her over the cacophony of typewriters. "Would you like to take a seat?" *I suppose you have every right to make a scene, but not here at my office.*

"Please understand how difficult it was for me to come to you."

"You'll be more comfortable if you're seated."

Mrs. Quinn lowered herself into the chair in front of Kathryn's desk.

"Is there something I can do for you?"

"You can tell me where my husband is." The statement came at Kathryn like a sharpened bullet.

The intercom next to Kathryn's telephone buzzed. It was her boss' secretary, Vera. "Mr. Wilkerson would like to see you." The "immediately" was assumed.

Normally, Kathryn would be on her feet before Vera got off the line, but she stayed in her chair. Vera called her name again, but Kathryn didn't move. When the intercom went silent, she said, "Your husband is at Fort Williams in Maine."

Mrs. Quinn closed her eyes and rubbed her forehead with a gloved hand. "No," she said, "he is not."

"Then I'm sorry, but—"

"He hasn't responded to any of my letters or telegrams, so I called long distance. I talked my way up to the fort commander; all he would tell me is that my husband is on special assignment." She braced herself with a forced smile. "I figured if anyone knew where Roy was, it would be you."

"Mrs. Quinn," Kathryn said, "I've scarcely heard from him since—"

"Miss Massey, I am pregnant."

The din of telephones, typewriters, office chatter — even the stink of stale coffee — fell away, making Kathryn feel like she was sitting in the hushed eye of a twister. In that moment, she realized she'd been deceiving herself for ten years.

She dropped her eyes to a copy of the *Los Angeles Herald Examiner* that was open to an article about plummeting real estate prices in the Pacific Palisades after Pearl Harbor. Mrs. Quinn's news made her realize she'd been fantasizing that one day Roy's wife would consent to a divorce, and perhaps they could afford one of those houses overlooking the ocean. Kathryn had met Roy on the day of the Long Beach earthquake, so it always felt to her that their meeting was fated. But now she knew it was a deluded fantasy. She felt like one of those girls who read romance novels, dreaming that her prince would appear amid swirling mist. "Roy is a good guy stuck in a rotten situation" had been her refrain for so long she'd come to believe it.

Kathryn Massey, she told herself, you are one first-class dope. You have no right to feel like your boyfriend has been cheating on you. The woman in front of you is his wife; you were just the mistress.

Kathryn laid her palms flat on her desk and looked Roy's wife directly in the eye. She wanted to say, *At least your baby isn't illegitimate. At least it'll know who it is and where it came from.* But the buzzer cut her off.

"Kathryn, are you there? Mr. Wilkerson would like to see you." Mrs. Quinn raised her eyebrows; Kathryn shook her head. "Kathryn!" Vera barked. "I can hear you breathing."

"I'm in the middle of something," Kathryn shot back. "Tell Mr. Wilkerson I'll be there as soon as I can." She waited until Vera cut the line. "Mrs. Quinn, I had to pull strings leading all the way up to Louis B. Mayer to learn where Roy was stationed. I'm willing to pull those strings again to see if I can find out where he is now. Would you like me to do that?"

Mrs. Quinn fidgeted with the clasp on her handbag. "I didn't know what else to do. Thank you, yes, I would be greatly indebted."

Kathryn watched the woman's padded shoulders drop a full inch and thought, *You're the one who's done me a favor.* "How can I reach you?"

"I'll be at the Town House Hotel on Wilshire until the end of the month." Mrs. Quinn stood up, expressed her thanks, and left the pressroom.

As she watched her lover's wife recede from view, Kathryn felt the bonds tying her to Roy begin to wither. She picked up the telegram and started to fan herself with it. "The end," she said out loud. "Oh, Jesus, the boss!"

She was more than halfway down the corridor when she realized she still had the telegram in her hand. She slipped it behind a bra strap as she walked into Vera's office. Vera waved her past.

Wilkerson was seated amid the relentless tidal waves of paperwork that advanced and retreated across his desk, his attention trained on the distant Hollywood Hills beyond the broad windows that overlooked Sunset Boulevard. As she approached, her eyes fell on a single sheet of paper at the center of the detritus. Kathryn squinted and tilted her head. It was a list of people who worked at the *Hollywood Reporter*. The list had a title, but it was obscured by a red pencil.

"You rang?"

Wilkerson swung around to face her. "We need to talk, Massey."

Normally, she loved hearing Wilkerson address her that way; it showed he saw her as one of the guys. But discussions that started out with "We need to talk" never seemed to end well. She felt a rough patch of chipped nail on her right middle finger and dug it into her thumb. As Wilkerson reached for a fresh cigar, he brushed aside the red pencil to reveal the list's title: *LAYOFFS*.

She braced herself. "Talk about what?"

"Circulation."

She had to force herself to keep her eyes from skimming the list for her own name. "What of it?"

He pulled a ledger from a pile of paperwork. It was covered in columns of typed numbers. "Looks like people are more interested in war news than Hollywood news — even the people who work in the movies."

"You can't blame people for caring more about America's next move against Japan than what Abbott and Costello's next picture is going to be."

"Tell that to my bottom line."

"Boss," she said, "are we in trouble? Financially?"

His eyes turned flinty. "We need to do something to boost circulation."

Oh, I see. It's like that, is it? The subject of these layoffs is not up for discussion. She snapped her fingers to dispel the tension that had ballooned between them. "What about a color spread?" she suggested. "There's that new picture with Carole Lombard and Jack Benny, *To Be Or Not To Be*. It's set in Warsaw after the Nazis invaded, so it's topical, war-related. And it's Lubitsch plus Lombard, so it's bound to be a smash. I'm pretty good pals with the publicity honcho over at United Artists."

"You need to think bigger, Massey."

"Bigger — how?"

"Radio."

"You want to advertise on the radio?"

A look of testiness flashed across his face. "We need to get *you* on the radio."

"ME?!"

"Your readership is pretty much limited to LA. If we could get you on the radio, your audience could go nationwide. Take a moment to picture that."

Kathryn didn't need a moment. The thought of raising her profile to a national level was beyond thrilling. What she needed instead was a moment to digest the fact that she evidently wasn't on Wilkerson's layoffs list. "Sounds great," she hedged, "but how would I get on the air?"

"That's for you to figure out." He picked up a stack of papers and started to straighten them — his sign that the meeting was over. "Let me know what you come up with."

Feeling lightheaded, Kathryn was still walking back to her desk when she felt the telegram tucked into her brassiere scrape against her skin.

Oh, Lord.

If she were to get on the radio, more people would know of her, and would want to know *about* her. It was Louella Parsons who'd led Kathryn to discover her bastard past, and she had promised to keep the information to herself. But what about Hedda Hopper? Or Sheilah Graham? Or God only knew who else might stumble across this information? And if they did, what might they do with it?

CHAPTER 3

Marcus Adler peered into the empty grave dug that morning for Hugo Marr and found he couldn't see the bottom. "Where do they plan on burying him?" he asked out loud. "China?"

Kathryn joined him at the edge. "The priest told me it's a family tradition. They go twelve feet down."

Marcus looked around. The Hollywood Memorial Park Cemetery was deserted except for the small group gathered near the rectangular hole carved into this lonely corner. "It's pretty sad, isn't it?"

"This whole situation is sad. There are no winners here."

"When it comes time to bury me, I'd like to think more than ten people would show up."

"Hopefully you wouldn't have to compete with Carole Lombard."

It had been five days since the news of Lombard's death had punched America in the gut. Her funeral on the other side of town promised to be the biggest in years.

"Speaking of," Marcus said, "aren't you supposed to be there?"

"Yuh-huh."

"And when your boss realizes you're not?"

"He won't be happy." Kathryn penetrated him with her mahogany eyes. "But I wanted to be here."

Marcus raised his eyebrows. "Aren't you the thoughtful one. Honestly, though, if you need to go to Forest Lawn, I'd understand."

Kathryn shook her head. "If Wilkerson has a problem with me being here, he can lump it. We're at war now. Priorities change."

"Thank you." Marcus grabbed Kathryn's hand and kissed it, then sighed. "Poor old Hugo."

Seven weeks ago, before Pearl Harbor made the world feel like a darkly different place, Marcus' friend and fellow MGM screenwriter, Hugo Marr, had called him to his apartment to confess a tearful litany of sins before pulling out a gun and shooting himself. Hugo had screwed up his own suicide — the bullet shot through his cheek and didn't touch his brain — and he'd teetered for six weeks before succumbing to his wounds.

A teal Hudson rolled through the shadows of the palm trees slanting across the lawn, its tires scrunching on the gravel until it came to a stop near the silent group. Two men in dark gray suits got out: Jim Taggert, Marcus' boss at MGM, and his lover, Vernon, a screenwriter at Columbia who everybody called Hoppy.

Taggert took in the dozen or so people milling around. "This is all he gets?"

"Not even his dad's shown up," Marcus said.

"He's here," Taggert said. "We passed him on the way in."

"And looking pretty soused," Hoppy added. "I suspect we may be waiting a while." He took in a guy in the shade of a nearby oak tree, dressed in full Scottish Highland regalia, a set of bagpipes tucked under his arm. "I hope they're not paying him by the hour."

Taggert shot Marcus an unsettling look. It wasn't a stink eye exactly, but it was a close cousin.

The four of them stood at the grave in awkward silence. Hoppy broke it when he urged them into a huddle. "You know what I've just noticed? Excluding us, there are eight people here. How come four of them are from Paramount?"

What Taggert and Hoppy didn't know was that before he shot himself, Hugo confessed to Marcus that he'd been spying on MGM. Hugo wasn't sure who'd been paying him, but suspected it was Paramount. The only people Marcus had told were Gwendolyn and Kathryn. Kathryn was looking at him now, locking him in with those sharp eyes of hers.

"Are you sure?" Marcus asked Hoppy.

"The guy without his hat is from legal. The one with the checked tie is in security."

"You might have a point," Kathryn added. "I've met the one with the Durante honker; he's in production design."

"The tall one with the wavy dark hair standing by himself, I know him," Taggert said. "He runs the team that reads magazine short stories and gets galleys of new novels."

Marcus checked out the chap standing alone and felt a flicker of recognition. "I've met him, too," he whispered. "But not from the studios. Something social, a while ago."

"He used to be the slimiest kind of journalist," Taggert said. "Real muckraking type, a studio PR's worst nightmare. Then something must have happened, because suddenly he was at Paramount."

Hoppy cocked his head to one side. "Here comes Hugo's father."

He pointed to a sky-blue Pontiac Opera Coupe that was dented with rust spots. It spluttered along the gravel until it came to a stop behind Taggert's Buick. The driver hurried around to the passenger side, but Edwin Marr pushed him away with his cane and heaved himself to his unsteady feet. His desiccated skin was stippled with liver spots and sun blemishes, and stretched tautly over his cheeks and knuckles.

The Hollywood Memorial Park Cemetery butted up against the Paramount studio lot, and Hugo's gravesite was positioned two rows from the weathered fence between the two. In the distance, Marcus heard someone shout, "And . . . ACTION!" as Marr staggered toward them, scrutinizing the small gathering around his son's grave.

"This isn't right," Marr griped. "No parent should have to bury his child."

With Bible in hand, the pale-faced priest chose this moment to approach the plot, but Marr pulled him aside to berate him about the tombstone.

"Oh, sweet Jesus, come on," Taggert muttered. "Some of us don't have all day."

Taggert flashed Marcus that odd look again. It definitely wasn't a stink eye — there was an air of apprehension to it, Marcus decided. *Something must have happened.*

As Hugo's father hissed and wheezed at the priest, Marcus snuck a sideways glance at the slimy Paramount guy, and a long-forgotten memory detonated in Marcus' mind. About six or seven years ago, he'd been invited to one of George Cukor's Sunday brunches. All the guests were homos, including a scattering of sailors. Marcus discovered that one of the sailors was a yellow journalist in disguise who'd managed to sneak inside. Marcus overheard him on the telephone to his editor, and he immediately told Cukor. He now tried to think of the skunk's name. *Cliff? No — Clifford something. Starting with W, maybe?*

They watched Edwin Marr harangue the priest some more, then Marcus felt Taggert pull at his elbow and lead him away from the group.

"This might go on for a while," Taggert said, nodding to Hugo's father, "and I've got a ton of things to attend to when we get back to the office, so I might as well break the news to you now."

"Does this have anything to do with the fish eye you've been giving me since you got here?" Marcus asked.

Taggert grunted. "I had a meeting early this morning with Mayer and Mannix. *Pearl From Pearl Harbor* was on the agenda."

Pearl From Pearl Harbor was Marcus' next writing assignment, a vehicle for Judy Garland. Everyone from Louis B. Mayer down had been excited about it, but after the attack on Pearl Harbor, it hardly seemed the right setting for a musical comedy. It wouldn't be hard to relocate it, though, so Marcus wasn't worried.

Taggert eyed Marr for a moment. "Turns out Mannix lost a nephew, a cousin, and the sons of two boyhood pals in Pearl Harbor." A roughly hewn ex-bouncer from a New Jersey amusement park, Eddie Mannix was MGM's vice president, Mayer's right-hand man, and almost without equal in power.

"Obviously we can't set the movie there anymore," Marcus said. "Cuba could work. Maybe *The Cutie From Cuba*. No, that's horrible. I just need a couple of days —"

"The project's been scrapped."

A mournful note from the bagpiper hovered over their heads.

"The central story is strong," Marcus persisted. "We just need to —"

"Mannix is superstitious. He thinks any movie set in Pearl Harbor is jinxed, even if we reset it someplace else. He argued and badgered until L.B. canceled the whole thing. Sorry, Marcus, but *Pearl Harbor* is history."

* * *

Marcus could feel Kathryn's eyes on him.

"You're upset," she observed, "but not about Hugo."

Marcus stared at the back of the taxi driver's head. "*Pearl From Pearl Harbor* is off the books."

"Tough break," she said, "but that can't have come as a surprise."

"I was going to be writing the next Judy Garland picture and now I've got nothing."

He felt Kathryn's hand grasp his. "They pay you too much these days to let you sit around on your keister."

"I didn't realize how much I was banking on it."

She nudged his shoulder as the taxi turned onto Sunset Boulevard. "Don't sell yourself short. You'll have a whole bunch more brainwaves before you're done. Look at *William Tell*—talk about a great idea."

"Yeah, until Hugo buried it and gave it to Paramount."

"Hmmm, about that." Kathryn's sly tone took on an arresting edge. "Speaking of Paramount, I was on the lot the other day. They're doing a third *Road To* movie; Morocco this time. At any rate, one of the PR guys was shuttling me around, and there was a delay on set. We got to chatting about upcoming productions, so I asked him."

"Asked him what?"

"I said, 'Got any dirt on this *William Tell* picture I've heard about?'"

Kathryn's moxie never failed to surprise Marcus. "You sneaky little — what did he say?"

"He'd never heard of it. So he called some pal in production planning and the guy hadn't heard of it either."

"But it was Hugo's job to bury our ideas and slip them to Paramount." The gears in Marcus' mind started to rotate. *Pearl From Pearl Harbor* was good, but *William Tell* was a winner.

Kathryn wagged a finger at him. "All I'm saying is if you want to try refloating *William Tell,* you ought to make sure Hugo didn't do his job. Before a movie gets the go-ahead, where does it live?"

Marcus took off his horn-rimmed glasses and polished them with his necktie. Gestating story ideas was the domain of the writing department and he'd just learned that at Paramount they came under the jurisdiction of a skunk called Clifford. Marcus shook his head. "Of all people."

"Right," Kathryn said. "If you want *William Tell* back, you need to find out if that slimeball's got it."

"How? By breaking in?"

The smile on Kathryn's face swelled from sly to wily. "I had something a tad more legal in mind. You know our new downstairs neighbor?"

"The assistant director?"

"I did a favor for his girl. She's a big Jimmy Stewart fan, so I arranged for her to accidentally-on-purpose meet him at Ciro's."

Marcus put his glasses back on and Kathryn's face resumed its sharp features. "So now he owes you one."

"Did you know he works for Preston Sturges?"

"And the Sturges unit is at Paramount."

"Now you've got it. Sturges writes all his own movies, but his scripts have to be approved by the Breen Office, just like everyone else's. He needs someone to liaise between him, his writers, and the Breen Office, and that liaison is our downstairs neighbor."

The taxi pulled to the Sunset Boulevard curb outside the Garden of Allah. Marcus paid the driver and they both got out. "So you think your neighbor would be willing to snoop around the Paramount writers' department?" he asked. "That's a mighty big favor."

Kathryn cracked open her handbag and pulled out her gloves. "Apparently his girl was very — ahem — *grateful*. He told me that his loyalties are with Sturges, not Paramount, so there's a good chance he'll be amenable."

Marcus' hand lay on the brass doorknob of the front door of the Garden of Allah's main building. The smoothly polished metal felt cold to the touch, but it shone in the January sun like an Oscar statuette. "Miss Massey," he said, "I like your thinking."

CHAPTER 4

Gwendolyn was still furious as she strode toward the front doors of the Bullocks Wilshire department store. What a condescending little twerp, looking down his stubby nose at me like I'm some character out of a Russian novel, all grubby and downtrodden. "We don't lend money to women. Especially single women. And certainly not single women who want to open up their own business." In other words, "Wouldn't your time be better spent looking for a husband?"

She'd wanted to upend the little toad's coffee cup all over his fanatically neat desk, but she reminded herself that she was a lady in a man's world and gracefully withdrew from the office before she soiled the smart deep-turquoise suit she'd sewn specifically for the loan interview.

It's all quite out of the question, Miss Brick.

She pushed open the heavy glass door and let the store's refined atmosphere calm her. She always felt so peaceful there. Not that she could ever afford it, but it didn't cost anything to dream.

It also didn't cost to check out the merchandise, examine the stitching, feel the cloth, and analyze the construction. *It's all in the name of inspiration,* she told herself. If Chez Gwendolyn was going to be a success, she needed to fill it with the best designs.

In the women's evening wear department, a series of eight mannequins stood in a row. A particularly striking floor-length gown in a deep violet tulle caught Gwendolyn's eye. She held the material between her fingers; it was like stroking moonbeams. Twenty-nine ninety-five was an outrageous amount to pay for a gown, even one as beautiful as this. Gwendolyn figured she could duplicate it for five or six bucks — seven at most — and sell it for fifteen, maybe even twenty if it came out real well. Her heart quickened.

"Would Madame care to try this on?"

The query came from a redhead as tall as Gwendolyn and roughly her age — the unfortunate side of thirty. Her engraved nametag read *Miss Delores* but her frozen smile said, *You can't afford this dress anymore than I can.*

Gwendolyn shook her head. "I can tell the waist is too low."

Miss Delores gave Gwendolyn's suit the once-over. "Our in-house models can present anything you see here on the floor. All you need do is ask."

Gwendolyn thanked the girl with a smile, then moved onto a strapless calf-length gown of purple silk so dark it was almost licorice black. Its full skirt was made for sweeping and swirling on the dance floor of the Hollywood Palladium, but the bust seemed tricky. She ran her finger along the inside seam of the décolletage to get a sense of the stitching. She could barely feel where one panel ended and the next one began.

Stepping back for a better view, she murmured, "Oh, yes, I could whip you up in an afternoon." She opened her purse and pulled out the tape measure she'd started keeping with her. A girl never knew when she might encounter the muse.

As Gwendolyn measured the waist to the bust line, she saw an odd little fellow staring at her from the other side of the gallery. The lighting in Bullocks Wilshire was judiciously indirect; much of it glowed from inside giant clamshells sculpted into the pillars, and this guy stood below one of them, observing her closely. He was in his mid fifties, possibly older, and not very tall, barely five foot four. He was balding — he had only a third of a head of hair — and he peered at her through round spectacles, but he was nattily dressed in a pressed gray suit and a black-and-red-dotted necktie.

Gwendolyn snuck the tape measure back into her purse and offered the little gentleman her sweetest smile. *Time to leave.*

She strode down the center aisle, her heels clicking on the marble floor so loudly they all but drowned out the gentle chamber music playing over the PA. She realized she'd entered the perfume section when she walked into a cloud of Chanel No. 5. She slowed her pace to breathe in the jasmine, rose, and sandalwood. She'd never been able to afford it, so she soaked it in whenever possible.

When Gwendolyn opened her eyes again, she realized the little man in the gray suit had followed her. She picked up her stride but found herself passing a display of nylon stockings, and Monty's advice came back to her.

"If I were a dame," he said that day at C.C. Brown's, "I'd be buying every pair of stockings I could lay my hands on. Nylon is real versatile. The military uses it to make ropes, tires, tents — the list is endless. It'll be one of the first things they'll ration. Mark my words: go out and buy every pair you can afford. They might be the last you'll see for a long, long time."

She doubted she could afford even the cheapest pair, but she wanted to throw the chap off her trail. She bent over the glass cabinet and studied the artful layout.

"Hello again." It was Miss Delores. Her knowing smile lingered. "These start at seventy-five cents a pair, and go all the way up to fourteen dollars."

"Fourteen?" Gwendolyn gasped. "For one pair of stockings?"

"Japanese silk."

"I can't imagine you sell too many of those."

"Since Pearl Harbor, nobody wants anything to do with Japanese merchandise. I'm surprised we still bother to display them."

The odd little gent edged his way into Gwendolyn's peripheral vision, hovering like a suspicious seahorse under one of the clamshells behind the scarf counter.

"I'll take three of your seventy-five-cent pairs."

The redhead withdrew three sets of stockings from a drawer behind the counter, carefully folded them in white tissue paper, and enclosed them in a flat box. By the time Gwendolyn had paid, the gent was two clamshells nearer and closing in. She thanked Delores and hastened for the door.

"Oh, miss! MISS?"

Gwendolyn ignored him and marched through the door to the portico. A magnificent art deco mural on the ceiling over her head glowed greens, blues, and reds.

The man dashed around to stop her. "I'm sorry," he panted, "but do you have a moment?"

Gwendolyn eyed him warily, allowing him a brusque nod.

"Thank you so much." He spoke in a mid-Atlantic accent, the type usually adopted by people of good breeding back East as though they'd been raised in Britain. "My name is Dewberry."

His handshake was surprisingly manly, and reminded her of one of the few pieces of advice her mother gave her about the opposite sex: Only trust men who shake your hand with confidence.

He nodded toward the store. "I'm sorry if I appeared to be hunting you back there, but I wanted to be sure my instincts were spot on. I'm Bullocks Wilshire's senior women's-wear buyer. I like to think I know well-crafted apparel when I see it."

He clearly wasn't upset about her tape measure. "I'm sure you do," Gwendolyn murmured.

"This suit you're wearing." He waved his hand up and down her outfit. "It has the most excellent lines. I'd bet my last dime you didn't buy it in California."

She glanced down at her turquoise suit. "No, I didn't."

His eyes widened. "I knew it. Europe, am I right? Schiaparelli?"

"As a matter of fact, Mr. Dewberry, no. But I'm flattered you think so." She pulled at the bottom of her jacket to straighten out its silhouette. "I made this myself."

Dewberry's self-satisfied smile faded. He crossed his arms. "Using whose pattern?"

"I don't use patterns." Gwendolyn couldn't hold back the proud smile blooming onto her face. "I've never really needed them."

"Extraordinary." He reached toward her, then checked himself. "I'm sorry, do you mind if I feel the underside of the lapel?"

Gwendolyn had lived at the Garden of Allah long enough to know a come-on when she saw it, but she sensed only professional admiration. *Good golly,* Gwendolyn thought, *Elsa Schiaparelli!* She leaned toward him and watched him run his fingers down the left lapel of her jacket. She silently thanked heavens she'd taken the time to line it with satin.

"May I ask your name?"

"Gwendolyn Brick."

"Miss Brick, I don't suppose you'd be interested in coming to work here at Bullocks Wilshire?"

It was all Gwendolyn could do to stop her mouth from falling open. Lately, the newspapers had switched from reporting how Angelenos were abandoning the area, to how the cost of housing in Los Angeles was bound to leapfrog with the influx of workers needed to fill the factories that were being converted to wartime requirements. Rumor was rife that rents at the Garden of Allah were about to jump.

"What sort of job?"

"What do you do now?"

Gwendolyn decided it wouldn't hurt to stretch the truth just a little. "Cigarette girl at the Cocoanut Grove."

Dewberry's face lit up. "So you know how to sell. Excellent!"

Gwendolyn wasn't sure what a floor girl's hourly wage was, but surely seamstresses earned more. Every extra dollar she could sock away would put her into Chez Gwendolyn that much sooner. "But Mr. Dewberry," she said, "you've seen my handiwork. Surely I could be of more value to Bullocks than just standing behind some counter."

He shot her a not-so-fast-there-missie look. "Strict company policy. All staff members commence on the floor. That way you learn the business from the ground up." He pulled a card from the breast pocket of his jacket and handed it to her. "But after that? Why, anything's possible."

CHAPTER 5

Monty stood at the front door of Kathryn and Gwendolyn's villa, looking striking in his white linen uniform with epaulettes, gold buttons, and a black-rimmed cap. He was off his crutches now and the bandages no longer showed through his pants. The only sign he'd been through anything was the scar on the right side of his face.

Kathryn's eyes drifted over his uniform. Did he have to wear that? Tonight? I'm still recovering from this afternoon.

"Something wrong?" Monty asked.

"I—er . . . " The rest of her sentence drifted away like a soap bubble.

Kathryn hadn't meant to leave the telegram on the kitchen table for her mother to find. She *knew* Francine was coming over for tea; she *knew* the telegram was something she needed to approach with tact and delicacy; and she *knew* the information she was after wouldn't come easily.

Four or five hours weren't enough time for Kathryn to forget the way Francine had held up the telegram by two fingers as though it carried the bubonic plague — *You want to explain this?* — before letting it fall to the table.

Kathryn had served tea and cupcakes, but everything sat on the table untouched. She realized if they were going to have this conversation, she was going to have to start it.

"I got curious," she told her mother, "about my past, my father. It's only normal to want to know about that kind of stuff."

Silence.

Kathryn motioned to the telegram sitting between them. "Most people take that information for granted, but I realized that I knew nothing about my past, so I went looking. That's as far as I got."

More silence.

"So, if your maiden name was Caldecott," she persisted, "where did Massey come from? Was that his name? Come on, Mother, you've got to give me something. Anything. Please?"

Francine made a have-it-your-way tsking sound. "I was on the train heading out here, and I was thinking how I needed a new name when the train passed one of those signs: 'You are now leaving the great state of Massachusetts.' The name Massey popped into my head; it seemed as good as any."

Kathryn felt let down. Her name didn't belong to anybody—it was just made up. *No wonder we ended up living in Hollywood.* "So," she prodded gently, "if Massey wasn't my father's name, what was it?"

"I don't see the point of all this," Francine's voice was rising in pitch with every word. "It was all so long ago and has no bearing who you are tod—"

"Mother, please. Throw me a bone here, will you?"

Francine took a very long moment to sip her tea. Just when Kathryn thought she was going to have to insist, her mother said, "I can't tell you what his name was. The fact is I never did know it."

Kathryn absorbed the shock of her mother's admission. "Never?"

Francine clasped her hands together in front of her. "It happened at the Boston Cotillion. I was a debutante. It was all very grand, very exciting. I noticed him immediately. Terribly handsome in his military uniform, all white linen and gold braid. We flirted and flirted until he coaxed me outside with the promise of a cigarette. This was back when women smoking were considered indecent, and we all felt so grown up that night."

Francine halted her narrative, her eyes on her interlaced fingers. "I think the cigarette was laced with something. Opium, I suspect."

"OPIUM?!" After everything she'd seen in Hollywood over the past twenty years, Kathryn had come to doubt that she could be scandalized by anything or anyone, let alone her own middle-aged mother.

"My dentist used it all the time," Francine said matter-of-factly. "At any rate, I was feeling all floaty and dreamy. One thing led to another, and before I knew it, my lovely dress had grass stains and the handsome boy in white had disappeared. Two months later I found I was pregnant. That's all I can tell you, Kathryn." She glanced at the telegram next to the cupcakes. "That's the most succinct description I can think of for your father: Not applicable."

Monty's discreet cough brought Kathryn back to her front door.

"You—what?" he prompted.

Get yourself together. You're supposed to be showing the guy a night on the town. "I was just wondering where I put my handbag."

She disappeared inside, scooped up her purse, and rejoined Monty on the landing at the top of the stairs. "Shall we?"

* * *

35

Kathryn's second sense about a breaking story was triggered when she heard from one of her tipsters — a room-service waiter at the Ambassador — that the newly hitched Mickey Rooney and Ava Gardner were back from their honeymoon and planning a big entrance at Ciro's.

As it happened, Ciro's was where Kathryn had promised Gwendolyn she'd take Monty out for a night on the town while Gwendolyn was stuck at work doing her first inventory check. It couldn't have been more perfect. Plus, she wanted to take advantage of her Ciro's expense account while she could.

The whole staff was still reeling from the layoffs Wilkerson announced a couple of weeks after her meeting. Twenty staff members — most of whom Kathryn had worked alongside for the past seven years — were let go. The cuts had left a bleeding swath across the office — journalists, photographers, typesetters, advertising sales. Nobody at the *Hollywood Reporter* felt safe anymore. Kathryn feared it was just a matter of time before her boss sold Ciro's, too.

The maître d' showed them to Kathryn's favorite table, one in the corner that afforded a good view of both the stage and the crowd. Ciro's lighting shone from upward-facing lamps, from behind tall banquettes, and hidden in the curved ceiling. The only people who stood in direct light were the performers; everyone else glowed in the most complementary illumination on the Sunset Strip.

They ordered a couple of drinks — whiskey for him, a sidecar for her.

"You can't go wrong with the veal scaloppini, or the coq au vin bourguignon," Kathryn said. "I bet you don't find either of those in the mess hall."

"Sure is a whole lot better'n what I'm used to." Monty reached over to light Kathryn's cigarette, then lit one for himself.

"I can't imagine you're in any great rush to get back."

He shrugged. "Fact is, I kinda miss it."

"But you barely escaped with your life." Kathryn took in the gold braiding looped around Monty's shoulder and thought about her father.

Monty cracked a shy grin that must have melted the hearts of half the girls between Guam and Manila. "I miss my buddies, the camaraderie, you know? And now that we're at war for real, it makes all that training and discipline mean something. For guys like me, it gives us a reason to get out there and fight the way we've been trained. I was all ready to hightail it up to Santa Barbara!"

All week, the papers had been screaming reports that a submarine had surfaced off the coast of Santa Barbara and fired a couple of dozen shells at a nearby oil refinery. They hadn't done any damage, but it made already jittery Californians paranoid that they were next.

A wave of hushed whispering washed through the crowd. Kathryn looked at the maître d's podium to see Mickey and Ava pausing at the door. Mickey wore a grin so wide it just about split his face in two; Ava was a vision in soft pink ruffles and pearls. But Kathryn wasn't expecting the couple standing beside them: Louis B. Mayer with a rising actress/dancer named Ann Miller.

Miller had built a name for herself in a series of low-budget musicals at Columbia, and yet here she was making an entrance on the arm of MGM's head honcho. Kathryn felt her possible scoop swell into a double. She watched the foursome wend their way through the thicket of tables.

"Those two couples important?" Monty asked.

"One of them runs the biggest studio in Hollywood."

"The short one? Or the really short one?"

Kathryn playfully slapped his arm. "Oh, come on, even you know Mickey Rooney when you see him." The orchestra started playing "In The Mood." Kathryn asked, "You any good on the dance floor?"

Monty's smile pushed his scar out of sight. "I'll let you be the judge of that."

Ciro's floor soon filled with couples, including the famous foursome. Kathryn figured if they were close to Rooney and Gardner when the music stopped, she could say hello. Maybe she could suggest they swap partners so she could get some sort of scoop out of Mickey. Or if they were close to Mayer and Miller, she could squeeze him for insider gossip about MGM poaching the dancer from Columbia. Either way, she might dig up something her biggest rivals — Louella Parsons, Hedda Hopper, and Sheilah Graham — hadn't found.

But when "In The Mood" came to an end, they weren't anywhere near either couple. The band started an up-tempo version of "Take The A Train," and Monty took advantage of the full skirt of the purple silk calf-length gown Gwendolyn had recently made for her. He swept and swirled, spun and dipped her like a pro.

"Say, you're pretty good at this," Kathryn said.

"Googie gave me lessons. Told me girls can't resist a guy who can hold his own on the dance floor."

"How about you maneuver us over to the guy with the glasses cheek-to-cheeking the gal with the black hair. You see, he's married and—"

She felt Monty's body stiffen and his black patent leather shoe scuff her ankle. He scowled at her with his eyebrows knitted together and chin jutted forward: exactly the same puss she'd seen on Gwendolyn.

"You want to sit down?" Kathryn suggested.

Back at the table, their waiter appeared. Monty didn't care what they had, so Kathryn did the ordering. It wasn't until the waiter departed that Kathryn felt the awkward silence chilling the table.

"What's the matter?" she asked him.

"You always like this?"

"Like what?"

"Is it always work, work, work with you? Don't you ever go out to a nice joint and just enjoy yourself?"

"Of course. It's just that—"

He went to light a cigarette but stopped himself. "I guess places like this just ain't my speed." He dropped his matchbook onto the table without offering to light the cigarette she withdrew from her own packet.

Kathryn executed a quick survey of the room. Rooney and Gardner were back at their table, hand in hand, their faces so close together they were practically touching. Mayer and Miller were still dancing; Miller was doing her best to keep Mayer's eyes on her. Kathryn had all the information she needed.

"I owe you an apology," she told Monty.

"You got a job to do; I get it."

"I wanted to give you a memorable night on the town, but I never thought to ask what *you* wanted." She leaned in. "How about we eat our dinner, then ditch this ritzy joint for a spot that's probably more your speed?"

* * *

The shimmering lights of Los Angeles spread out in front of them until they met the blue-black ink of the Pacific. They blinked in the crisp February night air as the low hum of traffic rose up the sides of the canyon.

Monty leaned against the hood of his jeep. "This is more like it."

Kathryn could hear the smile in his voice.

He pointed to a cluster of lighted buildings a couple of miles away. "What are they?"

"Hollywood Hotel and Grauman's. The ice cream place we went to is next door."

Monty gazed at the half dozen cars spaced to their right along the Mulholland Drive overlook. "Popular spot."

"This isn't where the natives go to neck, if that's what you're thinking. Pecker's Point is the next clearing along."

"That's not what I was thinking."

"You're my best friend's brother," she pointed out. "There are some things which aren't appropriate." *Says the girl who just broke up with a married man.*

It had taken some doing, but she'd tracked Roy to Washington, DC. He was on a team of army personnel helping the government plan for the country's wartime needs. It was all very top-secret hush-hush, but she passed it along to Roy's wife. Mrs. Quinn's thanks had been cool, but it didn't take a genius to read the woman's mind: *At least they haven't sent him overseas yet.*

Monty took in a lungful of eucalyptus. "This is the sort of memory I can look back on when they tell me to report for duty."

Kathryn tightened her cashmere wrap to ward off the chill. "Did you get your orders yet?"

"Nope, not yet—hey!" He took a step toward the shoulder and stared at a shaft of light pointing into the night sky. "What's going on there?"

"That's one of those searchlights they use at movie premieres. I'm surprised there's only one. They usually come in pairs, or more often four, or even six." A second shaft appeared, followed quickly by a third, then a fourth. "See?" She looked at her watch. "Usually they switch them on before the premiere. It's midnight now, so I guess the crowd must be getting out."

"Look!" Monty pointed to a pair of searchlights lighting up farther west. "Another premiere?"

"No one schedules those things on the same night a rival studio holds theirs. Especially not on a Tuesday."

As though on cue, all the search lights started aiming toward the same patch of clouded night sky. Kathryn joined Monty at the edge of the gravel overlook. "I don't think those lights are for any premiere." A third set, originating from the Echo Park area, joined the others. Now nine searchlights were strafing the sky. "It's like they're looking for something."

With a start, Kathryn thought of the submarine off the Santa Barbara coast. With her hands pressed to her chest, she turned to Monty, but he was already racing back to the car. He switched on the radio. "This is a military frequency, so don't tell anyone I let you listen in."

A deep, authoritative voice burst through the crackling in the speakers.

"Dammit, Major, collect yourself. Can you see the outline of aircraft? If so, how many? Over."

"Negative, sir. Just individual lights. I don't know, maybe eight? Ten? The searchlights, they're — they're making it hard for us to — to make out anything for sure. Over."

A volley of gunfire cracked the night air. Kathryn gasped. Another volley followed, then a third, each one louder than the last.

"MAJOR!" the commander bellowed through the radio. "Was that you? Have we started firing? Or have *they* started firing on *us*? Over!"

More shafts of light joined the others, some trained on a specific area of the sky while others wildly swung from one end to the other.

"Is it the Japs?" Kathryn asked.

She gripped the edge of her wrap with shaking hands. Gwendolyn should be home from work by now and Marcus hadn't planned to go out. They'd both be at the Garden of Allah, but were they safe? Would the Japs bomb Hollywood to take out the best propaganda machine the US had?

"It's hard to say." Monty kept his eyes on the radio. "While I was still laid up, they asked me to be on the team to put together defense plans for the West Coast. Half the details are still in my head; I'm going to have to hightail it back to base."

Kathryn's heart started pounding like a jackhammer. "Can you drop me off back at the Garden?"

Monty clamped his hand on her arm. It gripped her tightly but she could feel it tremble. "If we're under attack, the safest place you can be right now is up here."

More shots punctuated the air and he revved the jeep's engine. "Combatants are trained to aim where the lights are brightest. Up in these hills, it's mostly dark. Until you know you're safe, my advice is to stay put. Sorry, but I gotta go."

Monty threw his vehicle into a tight U-turn and disappeared down Mulholland Drive in a spray of gravel. Kathryn waited until his red taillights were out of sight before she dug around in her purse for her cigarettes. She stood on the shoulder's edge and smoked while she watched the searchlights crisscross the sky like grasping fingers. By the time she was done, the other three cars nearby had taken off as fast as Monty had. She realized she was never going to find a taxi where she was, and figured maybe she could hitch a ride with one of the couples parked down the road.

The last thing she expected to hear at Pecker's Point was her name being called out.

"Kathryn? Is that you?"

None of the cars parked along the side of the road looked familiar, but an almost full moon slipped out from behind a bank of clouds and she saw a hand waving from a Studebaker Champion that gleamed silver in the moonlight. It was Alla Nazimova, the Garden of Allah's original resident. She lived in a bungalow near Kathryn and Gwendolyn's when she wasn't touring the country in Chekhov or Ibsen. She held out her hand for Kathryn to grasp.

"Madame, this is a surprise." Kathryn took Nazimova's warm hand in hers.

"Pang and I often come up here. You've met Franklin, haven't you?" She leaned back so Kathryn could see her escort. Franklin Pangborn was a comedic actor who'd made a career out of playing sissified butlers and fastidious hotel clerks. He and Madame had been pals for years.

"It's probably warmer in here," Franklin offered. "Climb in the back."

She pulled the chrome handle and slid onto the rear seat's soft leather upholstery.

"What on earth are you doing up here by yourself?" Alla asked.

They watched the searchlights zigzag the sky while Kathryn gave them a rundown of her evening. By the time she was done, the anti-aircraft gunfire peppering the sky had fallen silent.

"Perhaps it's over already?" Franklin asked hopefully.

"I can't imagine it'll be over until they switch off those —"

In the far distance, an extended machine gun volley burst to life and the searchlights lurched across the sky. The barrage lasted a few minutes, then stopped as abruptly as it started. The poles of light staggered wildly across the sky for another few minutes, but gradually calmed down to a lazy sway.

Eventually Kathryn asked, "Do you think that's it?"

"If it is," Nazimova said, "I do believe it was too short to be Pearl Harbor part two."

"I don't mind telling you," Franklin admitted, "for a while there, my heart was in my throat. All I could think was Hollywood is done for! Shall we return to our picnic?" He flicked on the cabin light and opened the wicker basket between him and Alla. He pulled out a handful of green gingham napkins and some sandwiches wrapped in waxed paper.

Kathryn took a bacon and mayo on rye. "And what, may I ask, are you two doing all the way up here in the middle of the night?"

"Every week, we pack a picnic and drive up here to take in the view and listen to *The Pepsodent Show*."

Bob Hope's show was one of the most popular programs on the radio. Half the country tuned in each week to hear Hope clown around with some of the top names in show business.

"He was going to have Humphrey Bogart and Frances Langford on tonight," Franklin said. "However, NBC preempted them once this craziness broke out. But the news department was clearly in an uproar, a lot of so-called 'unconfirmed reports,' which I'm convinced is code for 'Damned if we know what's going on.' So we turned the radio off and watched the light show, trying not to imagine the worst."

"Turn it back on, Frankie," Alla commanded. "Perhaps they're broadcasting again."

Kathryn settled into the back seat and savored the tang of the crisp bacon in her sandwich while Francis Langford's smooth vocals filled the automobile with "You Are My Lucky Star."

"Do you listen to this show?" Alla asked Kathryn.

"If I'm home."

"Did you catch it a few months ago when Hedda Hopper was on?"

"No, I didn't."

Franklin harrumphed. "She was awful. Every joke fell flatter than a phonograph record. Even her report was old news."

"You know who could have done a far better job?" Nazimova fixed Kathryn with an unblinking stare. She didn't say anything more, but as one of the silent screen's foremost actresses, she didn't need to.

Kathryn leaned back until her face was cloaked in shadow. *Pepsodent, huh?*

CHAPTER 6

The week leading up to the Academy Awards was always a nutty time around Tinseltown. Beauticians, dressmakers, dieticians, limousine drivers, jewelers — everybody ran around like the Keystone Kops.

Until now, Gwendolyn had been largely unaffected by Oscar week, but now that she was a regular working girl at one of LA's classiest department stores, she was caught up in the commotion. Society matrons, private secretaries, pretty starlets, and established celebrities swarmed her counter for perfume, stockings, and lingerie, rarely stopping to ask the price. The men were all the same, whether they were old-money gentlemen bankers or new-money studio executives: they bought perfumes for their wives and lingerie for their mistresses.

The novelty was fun at first, but as Oscar week plodded on, Gwendolyn's energy wore thin. The day before the ceremony, she arrived at her counter and looked at her watch. Nine hours to go. She looked up to find Mr. Dewberry gathering together the staff from other departments: jewelry, clothing, furs, and millinery. Gwendolyn joined her coworkers in the middle of the floor.

"Ladies and gentlemen, I have an announcement," Dewberry declared. "We are on track to break the sales record for any month outside of December in the entire history of our store. Firstly, thank you for all your hard work. Secondly, in an effort to set a new record, management has authorized an incentive. Each staff member who posts the highest sales figures in their department today will receive an in-store credit for twenty-five dollars."

Gwendolyn thought of the nylon stockings filling half her counter and did a quick calculation. At seventy-five cents each, she could buy at least thirty pairs. If she made each pair last two weeks — not easy, but not impossible — she'd have stockings to last a couple of years. Surely the war would be over soon, now that the US was in the fight?

Then she thought of Delores. The statuesque redhead had been working in department stores for as long as Gwendolyn had been schlepping tobacco around the Cocoanut Grove, which meant she knew her stuff. She'd been friendly, but not entirely welcoming; professional but guarded. Gwendolyn's years at the Cocoanut Grove had taught her how to size people up. She knew a competitive achiever when she saw one.

Gwendolyn spotted Delores on the edge of the group and could see the gears already churning in Delores' mind, calculating how many bottles of Chanel No. 5 she was going to have to hard sell.

It wasn't hard to see why Delores was so successful at her job. She possessed the grace of a ballerina, the polish of a duchess, and the sophistication of a finishing-school graduate, and topped it all off with a mane of shimmering cinnamon hair. However, she lacked one essential: an impressive bosom. God knows she'd tried every trick in the book — plumping, padding, lifting, squeezing — to negligible effect. Gwendolyn took solace in the fact that in the battle of the bust, she would always emerge the victor.

As it happened, today Gwendolyn was wearing one of her showier outfits, a dark pink dress with a rose petal pattern that hugged the important curves in just the right ways. If the old-money bankers and new-money yes-men outnumbered the society matrons and *haut monde* flirts, the new girl on the Bullocks block might well nab the prize from under the queen bee's nose.

Ladies, start your engines.

* * *

It was almost lunchtime before Gwendolyn had a chance to check her order book. She was running up a mental tally of the morning's efforts when Delores glided over to her.

"I've just sold Soir de Paris to Arthur Freed's wife," she declared. "I think she's his wife. At any rate, she bought three bottles!" She checked her flawless makeup in the mirror on Gwendolyn's counter. "Now, I ask you: who needs *three* bottles of the same perfume? And so *expensive*. How have you been doing?"

Delores' eyes were brown, but not the warm brown of fudge, more like an unforgiving shade of petrified wood. The girl used them to intimidate; it was like she could go for hours without blinking. A sale of three bottles of Soir de Paris alone meant she was already ahead.

"I've been busier than a one-armed bricklayer," Gwendolyn replied airily. It was true, but there'd been too many matrons and not enough bankers.

"It's nearly lunchtime," Delores said. "You want to take the early break?"

For a girl like Delores, "lunch" meant black coffee. Gwendolyn had never actually seen her coworker eat, which probably explained her nineteen-inch waist. Gwendolyn could feel the twenty-five-dollar store credit slipping from her grasp and almost volunteered to take lunch first, if only to get away from that unflinching gaze. But a split second before she opened her mouth to reply, Gwendolyn spotted a familiar silhouette wandering toward the lingerie counter on the far side of the marble hall.

"Why don't you go?" she told Delores. "I can hold off."

Gwendolyn hoped the clicking of her heels on the store's marble floor didn't give her away until she was ready to pounce. Fortunately, her quarry was preoccupied with lacy teddies until she reached him.

"Why, Mr. Flynn! How delightful to see you!"

Errol Flynn's handsome face lit up in genuine surprise. "Well, cut off my legs and call me Shortie! Gwendolyn, my love, I didn't know you worked here. What happened to the Cocoanut Grove?"

Gwendolyn swept a hand down the long marble hall glinting with lights that made jewels sparkle, gloves shine, and lace gleam. "Better hours."

She took a moment to drink Errol in. The dashing bachelor had been moving in and out of the Garden of Allah for years; sometimes between marriages, sometimes because he forgot to pay the mortgage elsewhere. Over that time, Errol and Gwendolyn had toyed and teased each other with their respective charms. Back in December, the night before Pearl Harbor, they'd gone as far as smooching in the shadows, and an overdue scamper to the bedroom had seemed inevitable, but they were interrupted.

He looked professionally put together: a new gabardine pinstripe suit, a honey-colored cravat folded perfectly around his neck. She could smell the citrusy cologne used by the barbershop upstairs. His skin shone with the radiance of a steam bath.

Gwendolyn subtly pushed out her chest. "Shopping for lingerie? Someone's a lucky girl."

Errol glanced down at the teddies. "More like looking for ideas."

Gwendolyn pulled out the most expensive one and laid it out on the glass counter. It was made of peach silk and matching lace, and weighed next to nothing. "A girl never feels sexier than when she's wearing one of these beauties."

He ran a finger along it. "I didn't know they made them so —" He stopped at the crotch and looked up at her. "Brief."

"Most materials are going to be in short supply, so there'll be a lot more female flesh on display. You know, for the war effort."

"We must all make our sacrifices." He studied the contents of Gwendolyn's counter. "And what about suspender belts?"

"Would you like to see some?"

Those come-to-bed Errol Flynn eyes were back on Gwendolyn. "I'm only interested in the ones you'd wear yourself."

"You mean if money were no object?"

"I've always admired the way you dress. You have a poise that can't be taught."

"Oh, Errol!" As a thank-you, Gwendolyn leaned over the counter to withdraw some satin garter belts, pushing her breasts together just enough to make them strain the material. She heard him groan quietly as she laid out two sets of belts — one black, the other red. "I'd be more than happy to wear either one of these." *Please pick the red one. It's three bucks more.*

"Are you wearing either of them right now?"

Gwendolyn flashed her green eyes at him, feigning shock. "That's an awfully private thing to ask a lady."

He traced his finger up the satin stripe and didn't stop when he got to her hand. He trailed it along her finger, and by the time he reached her wrist, she could feel herself going all tingly.

She pressed her hips against the sliding door of the display case and tilted them back and forth. "Is there anything else you'd like to see?" She tried to keep her voice from shaking, but the throb around her own skin-toned garter belt made it difficult.

"There's a lot more I'd like to see," he said quietly.

The harsh *ka-ching!* of a cash register on the other side of the hall hacked through the light strings of a Strauss waltz playing over the store's PA. Delores was back from lunch.

Gwendolyn looked at the merchandise arranged on the counter. *If I can get him to buy all of this, and perhaps a few pairs of our best stockings . . .*

But then the throb in her crotch ratcheted up a notch and she realized that what she really wanted was to put an end to a decade of flirting with one of Hollywood's biggest hound dogs. Half the pretty girls in town had succumbed, so why not her, too?

"Follow me."

She led him away from Delores' hawkish eyes to the small chamber where staff could exhibit lingerie for customers on one of the in-house models. The walls were decorated in salmon-pink flocked wallpaper, and the lighting was set to a muted glow designed to replicate a bedroom.

Gwendolyn locked the door and pulled the cravat away from his neck.

"You don't know how long I've wanted this," he panted, pulling off his jacket.

"I've got a fair idea." She guided his hand under her dress.

He breathed in sharply. "Oh, my sweet baby."

She turned around to face the wall and splayed her hand across the wallpaper. "Unzip me."

As he unhooked the top of her dress and ran the zipper down past her waist, he started to kiss her neck, lightly at first, but harder as his fervor intensified. "Why has this taken us so long?"

Her dress slipped down her body. He reached from behind and cupped her breasts and started kneading them gently. He let out a husky groan each time he thrust his swelling hard-on against her. His mouth found hers and he kissed her every bit as deeply, urgently, and passionately as she'd imagined. Then suddenly he pulled away.

"I'm going to the Oscars tomorrow night," he said.

She froze, disoriented.

"I want you to go with me." His mouth was on her ear, his breath heavy and rasping. "Be my date and blow every other woman out of the water."

"I — er, I just —"

"Pick out anything you need: dress, shoes, handbag, fur. You can charge it to my store account."

Gwendolyn turned around so that she could see Errol's eyes. "Are you telling me that the day before the Academy Awards, Errol Flynn doesn't have a date?"

His hazel eyes crinkled up as a smile broke out across his face. "I do now, don't I?"

The remaining air in Gwendolyn's lungs escaped in a whoosh. Errol took it for a "Yes!" and hitched her up onto his hips.

CHAPTER 7

Marcus strummed the dark wood tabletop and wondered if perhaps he should have chosen a booth closer to the door.

The Garden of Allah's Sahara Room was one of the most dimly lit bars on Sunset Boulevard. The management liked it that way: it encouraged clandestine tête-à-têtes between people who ought not be tête-à-tête-ing. If the couple decided they needed a room for the night—or just an hour—the hotel could kill two birds with one cocktail shaker.

But Marcus wasn't there for that sort of meeting. He wasn't even sure what the guy looked like. He might arrive, peer into the gloom, not see him and walk out. Marcus picked up his cigarettes and lighter and moved to a booth closer to the doors. Six booths of dark wood and even darker burgundy upholstery lined the west wall, and ten tables formed two columns leading up to the bar. Booths felt more private somehow; not that it mattered. None of the booths nor any of the tables were occupied.

Marcus pulled out a cigarette and found it was his last. He slid out of the booth and approached the bar. "Hey, Seamus, you got any Chesterfields?"

The bartender set the last of five bottles onto the glass shelf behind the bar, all of them Glenfiddich single malt whiskey imported from Scotland. It was top-of-the-line stuff, and as far as Marcus knew, the Sahara Room had never stocked it. Those five bottles represented nearly fifty dollars' worth. "What's with the Glenfiddich?"

Though American by birth, Seamus considered himself a Scot down to the marrow. He had the palest skin of anyone Marcus knew, and a thatch of copper hair, bright as a new penny and cropped military short. The guy's jaw was set into an uncharacteristic frown. "Both my sons, one of my nephews, and my cousin's two lads all signed up last week. Three for the army, two for the navy." He jutted his head toward the bottles. "I told them that when each of them comes back, we'll break open one of these babies to celebrate." He dropped his eyes, but only for a moment. "And if they don't, it'll be a hell of a wake."

Marcus pushed his glasses back up his nose while he thought of an appropriate response. "I'm sure they'll all come through it okay."

"God willing." Seamus pulled a pack of Chesterfields from underneath the counter. "I could start a tab if you're planning on spending all night here."

"Not sure," Marcus said. "I'm meeting someone and I—"

"Is that him?"

A slim figure in a three-piece suit hesitated in the doorway, hat in hand and wavering like a stalk of corn.

Marcus walked down the line of empty tables. "Quentin Luckett?" He extended his hand and introduced himself. It wasn't until they'd settled into the booth and ordered drinks that Marcus could take stock of the man with whom he was about to take an unnerving gamble.

Kathryn's downstairs neighbor, the assistant director for Preston Sturges, had been more than happy to furnish her with Luckett's name. The fact that Luckett so readily agreed to meet Marcus without knowing why seemed too good to be true, and Marcus had learned long ago that when things seemed too good to be true, they usually were.

Marcus smiled. "Thanks for coming."

Luckett was one of those baby-faced guys whose age was hard to peg. Marcus guessed anywhere between early twenties and late forties. He had the unlined skin of someone who spent too much time indoors reading. He narrowed his eyes and lit a Camel without looking at his hands. "Why, exactly, am I here?"

Marcus clasped his hands together and pressed the knuckles of his thumbs to his chin. "I have something I need to talk to you about. A matter of some delicacy."

"Sounds juicy."

"I'm a screenwriter at MGM—"

"I know," Luckett admitted. "I did my homework."

"Did you ever meet a guy by the name of Hugo Marr?"

Luckett shook his head. "Heard about him, though. We're talking about the one who offed himself right in front of some poor sap, right?"

Seamus arrived with their drinks. Marcus waited until he receded into the shadows again.

"Yeah, well, that sap was me."

Luckett nearly chocked on his bourbon. "That must have been—how was that?"

"Let's just say it's nothing like how we show it in the movies." Marcus let the image of Hugo shooting himself settle into Luckett's mind. "Did you know that Paramount was paying Hugo to spy on MGM?"

Luckett's eyes flared like a lit match. "I did not."

"But that's not why I asked to meet with you." Marcus kept his voice steady, his words low and even. "There's a particular project—"

Luckett's eyes flared again. "*William Tell?*"

Until this moment, Marcus wasn't completely sure that Hugo had stolen *William Tell*, or that Hugo's spy story was even true. He grasped now that he'd been giving Hugo the benefit of a doubt he didn't deserve.

"You've seen it?"

Luckett swirled the bourbon in his glass. "We have a system. Scripts, outlines, synopses—they each have their own format. So this outline lands on my desk and right away I see something's not quite right about it. I figured someone was slacking off, but now that you tell me about Marr—"

"Where is it now?"

Luckett shunted the little brass lamp with the dark green shade to one side, casting half his face into shadow. "Sitting on my desk at work."

He pulled out another Camel, so Marcus picked up his lighter—the one with the brushed chrome and the fancy French insignia. He used it if he wanted to impress someone, and even in this low light, it was hard to miss Luckett's double take as he leaned in to ignite his cigarette.

"I get it." Luckett was nodding now. "You want me to slip your *William Tell* out from behind the people who pay me, and give it to you so MGM can go produce what has all the markings of a great movie."

"So you think it's good?" Marcus countered.

"It's one of the best outlines I've read in a long time."

"If it was yours, wouldn't you fight for it?"

Luckett didn't respond. His eyes fell to Marcus' chrome lighter. Marcus decided to change tack.

"You work for Clifford Wardell, don't you?" Luckett nodded. "Has he seen my outline?"

"Who do you think gave it to me?"

Dammit.

"Mind you," Luckett sniffed, "Wardell seeing it and Wardell reading it are two different things. Picking gems from over the transom is my specialty."

"The whole picture is in the title," Marcus pointed out. "Surely he at least saw that."

"If it was on top, maybe. But it was in the middle, so probably not."

Inwardly, Marcus started applauding. "What would it take for you to remove *William Tell* from the pile altogether?"

Luckett studied Marcus, apparently weighing his options while he hung onto the cigarette smoke in his lungs, then let it out slowly, smoothly, before he spoke. "And why would I do that?"

Marcus ached to pound the table and yell. Because I wrote *Strange Cargo*, one of MGM's biggest pictures last year! I should be writing *A Yank At Eton* for Rooney or *Mrs. Miniver* for Garson, but instead I'm stuck on *Tarzan's New York Adventure*. I came up with *William Tell* and I deserve to have it back!

But instead he said, "Because it's the right thing to do."

Luckett acknowledged Marcus with a nod, but said nothing more.

"Look," Marcus pressed, "there are two ways I could have gone here. I could've told my boss about the theft. They would take it to Mayer, who'd explode like a firebomb. There would be lawsuits and counter suits flying all over Hollywood, and in the end everybody would be suspicious of everybody else, and nobody would trust anybody anymore about anything. That's not good for Hollywood, especially at a time when we're all expected to pull together for the war."

"Excellent point."

"But I chose instead to talk to you, writer to writer, and see if we could find a way to resolve this situation among ourselves."

Luckett fell back against the upholstery and withdrew his lighter from a pocket. It was the exact same brushed-chrome lighter Marcus had.

"You get that at Maxim's on Hollywood Boulevard?" Marcus asked casually.

"Uh-huh." A faint smile slipped out between Luckett's lips.

Ah, we have arrived at common ground. "I've always found they have a fine selection," Marcus said.

"One of the best haberdashers in the city."

"Did you ever treat yourself to a hot-towel shave in the barber shop down the back?"

"With Jean-Jules, he of the famous gentle hands?" Luckett arched an eyebrow. "You should try his foot massage."

"I have," Marcus replied. "Mr. Luckett—"

"Call me Quentin."

Marcus let out a long breath. "So, Quentin, how about it? Will you help me get my *William* back?"

"I could do that."

"Without your boss knowing?"

Quentin let out a *pfft.* "I'm just waiting for Wardell to hang from his own noose so I can nab his job. The half-wit can go screw himself, as far as I'm concerned."

Marcus wanted to jump up and do a back flip. "I can meet you anywhere, any time. Or you could mail it." He grabbed a matchbook and reached inside his jacket for a pen.

"Hold on there, cowboy," Quentin said. "This isn't charity. It's a quid pro quo type situation."

Of course it is. Why would it be anything else?

"What did you have in mind?"

Quentin didn't reply straightaway. Instead, he leaned an elbow on the table and rested his chin in the palm of his hand. "You're real cute." He let his eyes wander down one side of Marcus and up the other. "The kind of cute who doesn't know how cute he really is."

Marcus blinked with the deliberation of a safecracker. "I thought only pretty actresses were subjected to the casting couch."

"I've got something you want, and you've got something I want."

"So . . . " Marcus took his time finishing his drink, "in order to get *William Tell* back, I have to sleep with you?"

The question hung between them like a snowflake until Quentin said, "Hooray for Hollywood."

CHAPTER 8

Orange and pink fingers of dusk were just beginning to stretch across the sky over the Garden of Allah as Kathryn screwed a pair of pearl earrings into place. She picked up her handbag and gloves and made her way downstairs as a burst of booze-fueled laughter reached her from across the pool. Robert Benchley was back in town and holding his usual all-night cocktail party.

She paused at the bottom of the stairs next to a tangle of blooming jasmine whose scent was so powerful it almost made her giddy and put on her gloves, glancing through Benchley's living room window. It was the typical crowd: Algonquin Round Table refugees, down-on-their-luck actors, and a theater critic or two. At the center of the room stood Dorothy Parker—in town for the premiere of *Saboteur*, the new Hitchcock she cowrote—with her arms raised like a double-barreled Statue of Liberty. Kathryn had participated in enough rounds of Benchley Charades to recognize when one had gone awry, and this had all the earmarks: everybody laughing to the point of crying and Dorothy stamping her foot in frustration.

"They've been playing for two solid hours."

Errol Flynn stepped out of the shadows and into the fading light, wearing a casual shirt with no tie and too many buttons undone. His hair was mussed and he hadn't shaved for a few days. On the patio table behind him, she spotted a whiskey bottle and two tumblers, both empty.

"I hadn't heard you were back –" She caught herself. "Nor do I care. I'm not talking to you."

"Join the club," he sighed, and leaned up against a cedar tree.

"Lili giving you a hard time again?" Kathryn asked, but before he could answer, she cut him off. "Whatever reason your wife has for kicking you out this time, you probably deserve it."

He threw her a pained look. "You women are going to be the death of me." He inflicted expensive cigar breath on her, spoiling the scent of the jasmine. "Can I at least ask why you're not talking to me?"

"Because of Gwendolyn."

Errol seemed genuinely surprised. "You mean that day at Bullocks? I don't know what her version of the story was, but let me tell you, I didn't have to convince her to do anything."

"I'm not talking about that." When Gwendolyn came home from work that day, she'd been breathless and giggly. By all accounts, Mr. Flynn lived up to his roguish reputation – and then some. But Gwendolyn was thrilled to the point of feverishness at the thought of attending an Oscar ceremony. "Do you remember what you promised her that day?"

"Promised?"

Kathryn planted her hands on her hips. "The Oscars . . . ?"

Errol got as far as drawing breath to make his denial, then gulped. "Oh, shit."

She stepped forward into the light spilling out through Errol's window, and jabbed him in the chest. "Yes, Errol. Oh, shit. Do you know how much trouble she went to that night?

You want to take a guess at how long she sat there and waited, and waited, and waited for you to show up?"

"I—what can I say? I got caught up in the heat of the moment."

"And then?"

He threw out his arms like Jesus on the cross. "And then forgot."

"You don't ask a girl to escort you to the Academy Awards and then not show up!" She slapped his shoulder with her purse. "How could you have been with so many women and still not know how to treat them?"

The violins of a gloomy Russian melody floated over them from Alla's place a couple of doors away.

Errol returned to the patio table and helped himself to a couple of fingers of booze. "I feel terrible, just terrible."

"You should." When Kathryn came home that evening, Gwendolyn was still sitting at home in her pale magenta gown. Errol hadn't put in an appearance at the ceremony, or he and Kathryn would have had this conversation in the middle of the Biltmore Bowl with all of Hollywood's heavy hitters looking on. "You need to do the right thing and make it up to her."

"With perfume? Roses?"

"Jewelry!" Gwendolyn could thank her later. "You can't go wrong with Harry Winston."

Errol nodded thoughtfully, his eyes on his drink. "Bracelet? Necklace? Brooch?"

Kathryn sat down on one of the patio chairs and held out the other tumbler for Errol to fill. "If it comes in a Harry Winston box, all will be forgiven."

Another explosion of laughter burst from Robert Benchley's villa, but it didn't seem to register with Errol. He played with the dead cigar in the ashtray next to his whiskey. "Lili and I hit a brick wall this week. She's suing for divorce."

Kathryn had never seen him this serious. The last of the violet dusk left the evening sky and the only light now came from the lamp in his window. Even in this half light, Kathryn could see he was struggling to keep his head above the emotional tide washing over him. "It's probably for the best," he said finally.

"You two did fight an awful lot," Kathryn pointed out.

"But making up was always so magnificent!"

Kathryn waved away his rationalization. "That sort of thing is fine for affairs, but I've yet to see a marriage survive that sort of battleground. Just ask Humphrey Bogart." Over the past few years, Bogie and his wife, Mayo Methot, had earned their nickname, "the Battling Bogarts," by erupting into drunken brawls in nearly every bar and restaurant across Los Angeles.

"You're probably right. You usually are. I admire that about you, and yet at the same time, find it thoroughly annoying." He said nothing more, and Kathryn began to lose herself in a rabbit hole of thoughts about Roy. She tried not to think of him anymore, but every now and then he let himself in through the back door and sat around for a while.

"So how come you're not over at Benchley's charade-a-thon?" Errol asked.

Kathryn glanced at her wristwatch and thrust her glass toward him. "I'm off to a broadcast of *The Pepsodent Show*. My boss has got himself all riled up over increasing circulation. Told me it would benefit the paper greatly if I found a way to raise my national profile, but it's my problem to figure out how."

When Kathryn brought up the idea of getting on *The Pepsodent Show*, Wilkerson loved it. But when she suggested he might pull a few strings with his high-falutin' radio network exec pals, he admitted glumly that at a recent radio convention at the Ambassador, he'd gotten blackout drunk and ended up telling the network heads they were all "cheap-ass whoremongers who worked in radio because they were too damn ugly to work in pictures." While Kathryn resisted the urge to stub out her cigarette in her boss' face, he declared, "It's only me they hate, not the *Reporter*. They know how important my paper is to their standing in Hollywood. They wouldn't dare pull their advertising. You'll need to go door-knocking on your own, but be smart about it. Be a lady."

"So," she told Errol, "I'm hoping to talk my way onto the show as their resident Hollywood reporter."

"Pepsodent, huh?" he said. "They were after me last year for a magazine campaign to coincide with *They Died With Their Boots On*."

Kathryn couldn't recall seeing any ads featuring Errol in a Civil War getup while holding a tube of toothpaste. "Didn't work out?"

Errol chuckled. "They were real gung ho until they learned I played General Custer. They tried to hit the brakes, but I had a pay-or-play contract. It was the easiest twenty grand I ever made."

"Any pointers on who I should target?"

"You're wasting your time with the network boys. You need to go after the sponsors. The guy you want is Pepsodent's West Coast VP, Leo Presnell. He took me out on epic drunken sprees. Lord love a duck! Half the time, I didn't even remember getting home."

"Big drinker, then, huh?"

"He's a big everythinger. Big expense account, big appetite, big wardrobe, big thirst."

After living at the Garden of Allah for fifteen years, Kathryn was no stranger to heavy drinkers, but her experience was largely with writers and actors. Thirsty business executives were a whole different bottle of bourbon. "The executive sleazeball type, huh?"

"Quite the opposite. We're talking strictly Ivy League."

"Any fatal flaws I can use as a foot in the door?"

"He's a smooth one, I'll give him that. If there's a fatal flaw lurking in the shadows, you'll have to dig deep."

A classy executive? Kathryn's pulse quickened. She might be able to pull off this plan after all.

"Wilkerson needs to boost circulation?" Errol yawned. "Can't say I'm surprised."

"Why?"

"I heard he was going broke."

Kathryn sat up in her chair. "Where did you hear that?"

"More like overheard it. Greg Bautzer's office."

Bautzer was her boss' lawyer. "What did you hear?"

"I was running early that day—very unlike me, as you can imagine. I was cooling my heels in reception when an argument erupted in Greg's office. It got very, very heated, very, very fast. They started yelling about a night at the Clover Club when a poker table got upturned. That's when my ears really pricked up."

"Why?"

"I was there that night. Your Mr. Wilkerson was flinging down hundred-dollar bills like they were Kleenex. He got so sore at one point that he turned over the poker table. You should have heard the cussing."

"Drunk, I suppose?"

"Drunker than I'd ever seen him. So anyway, I'm sitting in Bautzer's outer office listening to Wilkerson yell at Bautzer that he had no right to tell him how to live, and Bautzer yelling back that he couldn't afford to go on living like this, not when he was four hundred grand in debt."

Kathryn stared out into the perfumed darkness and listened to a bee buzzing through the air.

"There's four hundred grand, and then there's four hundred grand," Errol stated, with a logic that only made sense to someone who earned two and a half thousand a week. "If he owes that kind of dough to his poker buddies, that's okay. But if he owes it to his bank? They're not quite so understanding."

"This argument you overheard, I don't suppose they mentioned Selznick? Or Zanuck? Or Hughes?"

"Not unless one of those guys recently changed his name to the Bank of America. Listen," Errol said, his voice softer now, "you might want to brace yourself for layoffs."

The honeybee's droning stopped suddenly. "We've already had those."

"I'm talking about a second round. And pay cuts." When she shot him a look of alarm, he raised his hands. "I'm only telling you what I heard."

Suddenly, the scent of the jasmine felt suffocating. Kathryn got to her feet. "This Presnell guy, what did you say his first name was?"

"Leo."

"How will I know him?"

"Just look for the most expensive suit in the room."

"Thanks. And I'm sorry to hear about you and Lili."

Errol shrugged. "Bound to happen sooner or later."

Kathryn leaned over the patio table and stuck her face close to Errol's. "Harry Winston. Necklace, ring, brooch, just as long as you don't go cheap."

CHAPTER 9

It turned out that sleeping with the guy from Paramount was more of a bed-half-full pleasure than the bed-half-empty chore Marcus expected. Quentin Luckett was a bit more pale and freckly than Marcus would have liked, but he was trim from twice-weekly swims, and his skin proved buttery smooth. He was a good kisser too, and took his time running his hands over Marcus, alternating between strong, tender, passionate, and gentle.

At first, there'd been some awkward button fumbling and twitchy eyeballs not knowing where to look. But after clothes were shed and covers flung, getting down to business quickly lost its morally dubious motivation, and an unexpected chemistry saw things to a satisfactory conclusion.

And Quentin was true to his word. Later that week, he couriered *William Tell* to Marcus, who then pitched it to Jim Taggert with a beefed-up romance angle: the love interest was now the daughter of the villain. By the time Marcus got his linens back from the Chinese laundry, Mayer had approved *William Tell* as an A-list movie.

But when a missive on "Q.L." monogrammed notepaper arrived nearly three months later asking Marcus to meet with him, Marcus didn't know what to make of it.

The Retake Room was a small neighborhood bar downwind from MGM. Weekdays, it was packed with stars and workers unwinding after a long day of conjuring dreams and spinning fantasies. But on a weekend? Marcus didn't know what to expect.

On that Sunday afternoon, the place was a skeletal incarnation of its midweek self. The door from Washington Boulevard opened on the diagonal to a square room with a dozen tables arranged checkerboard-style on black-and-white tiles. Barely a quarter of the tables were filled, and three booths along the south wall were empty. In one corner stood a battered upright piano on the edge of a dance floor with room for a half dozen slow-dancing couples. Along the eastern wall were seven dusty posters of MGM movies: *Another Thin Man, Strange Cargo, Love Finds Andy Hardy, San Francisco, A Tale Of Two Cities, Camille,* and *Forty Acres And A Mule.* Marcus stared at the last one. A huge hit during MGM's pre-talkie era, *Forty Acres And A Mule* had been directed by Edwin Marr, Hugo's tyrannical father.

A flash of daylight filled the bar as the front door swung open, and Quentin circumnavigated his way around the tables. He thrust out his hand as he approached. "Nice to see you again." He motioned toward the bartender for a beer, removed his homburg, and sat down. He pulled out a pack of Camels and offered Marcus one.

Marcus already had a cigarette going. He picked it up from the glass ashtray and took a drag. "I wasn't expecting to hear from you."

Quentin ducked his head from side to side. "Fact is, I kind of need you."

"It's nice to be needed," Marcus replied evenly. This guy had helped him get his career on track, but a growing suspicion that he was being used made Marcus squirm.

"I believe congratulations are in order. *William Tell* is in preproduction."

Projects in preproduction were movies not yet officially announced to the industry. They were treated like military secrets lest a rival studio get the jump and announce a similar project.

"You must have a very good source."

Quentin bared a knowing smile. "Everybody knows somebody."

Marcus nodded silently while the bartender deposited their drinks on the table. Quentin braced himself with a swig of beer; a rather large swig, Marcus noted. "Here's the thing. The other day, my boss asked me about a certain treatment he'd seen around the office."

"But you told me —"

"I know, I know."

"What did you say?"

"I scratched my head like an absentminded professor and made a bunch of noncommittal noises until he lost patience and told me to go find it."

"You think one of the higher-ups has been asking for it?"

"I'm thinking that whoever was paying Hugo to spy for them remembered your treatment and wanted to see it."

"But —"

"But all of this goes away when MGM announces their own *William Tell*. Once MGM goes public, Paramount will abandon the idea and everything's hunky dory." Quentin leaned in conspiratorially. "So we need to nudge this one along."

There's always some loose end waiting to trip you up.

Marcus realized they might have more in common than he first suspected. Like Marcus, the guy sitting opposite him was keen to get ahead, and evidently willing to partake in whatever horse trading it took to put him within reach of the next rung. "Are we here because you've already formulated a plan?" Marcus asked.

"The key is casting," Quentin said in a low voice. "When a studio secures the perfect person for a role, the publicity department gets involved, stories get planted in magazines, and the train pulls out of the station."

Marcus crossed his arms. "You have someone in mind."

Quentin nodded like a kid with his hand caught in the jellybean jar. "You won't believe how perfect this guy is. Ever heard of Trevor Bergin?"

"Should I have?"

"For the past six straight years he's been the US champion."

"Of what?" A cuckoo clock chimed inside Marcus' head. "You mean archery, don't you?"

"You should see what this guy can do with a bow and arrow. It's astounding."

"But can he act? Does he even want to?"

"Yes and yes."

"He's actually told you that?"

"We sort of run around in overlapping social circles."

"What sort of social circles would they be?"

Quentin grinned his jellybean grin again. "The fruity kind."

"He's queer?"

"Yuh-huh."

"How does he come across?"

"Straight as one of his arrows."

"Good-looking?"

Quentin gave a low wolf-whistle. "And how."

Over the loudspeakers, a symphonic movement—the sort of arrangement usually heard playing in the background of a Gable-Crawford love scene—filled the place.

"Tell me something," Marcus said. "When you found my *William Tell* in your slush pile, why didn't you just keep it?"

For the first time, Marcus saw Quentin's unassailable confidence take a dive. "Studio politics. You know how that can be."

"I want to know why you didn't keep *William Tell*," Marcus said flatly, "and I don't want any bullshit."

Quentin paused, appearing to turn conflicting agendas over in his mind. "Ever come across Anderson McCrae?"

The name tripped a wire, but Marcus couldn't place it. "Sounds familiar."

"He used to run the casting department at RKO before he jumped ship to join us."

Ah, yes. Marcus remembered now. Anderson McCrae was the guy Gwendolyn once threw herself at in the effort to get a job, only to discover he was queer and not the slightest bit swayed by her ample charms. "What of him?"

"Late last year, things got hot and heavy between us. I didn't see it coming but boy, when it arrived, ker-pow! But then an ex-flame of mine landed in town and asked me to meet him for a drink to chew over old times. One beer led to a whole bunch, which led to him suggesting we go upstairs for old times' sake. The guy's about to go off to war, so I figured this could be his last hayride."

"So you did?"

"And had a mighty fine time, too. It never occurred to me that Andy would have a problem with that, but brother! You should have seen the stink he kicked up. I didn't get it. Still don't. The whole thing blew up into a screaming yelling fighting punching brawl that lasted all afternoon, and ended up costing me a side table, a rocking chair, and three of my best brandy snifters."

"Ouch."

Quentin winced. "I really wanted to help Trevor get the role, but obviously any casting influence I might have had at Paramount is out the window. I'd almost given up and then your *William Tell* landed in my lap. So, what we need to do is — "

"Whoa, Nellie," Marcus interrupted. "You're right: casting is everything, but we lowly writers — "

The bar's front door let in a flare of daylight. Quentin shot his hand into the smoky air above their table and waved. "Brace yourself," he murmured, and vaulted to his feet.

Marcus felt compelled to stand, and soon found himself shaking hands with a man so handsome that it vaporized his ability to form a coherent sentence.

The guy stood six foot three and held himself with the ramrod posture of a ballet dancer. Topped with a thatch of brown hair so dark it was almost black, his face was defined with the type of chiseled jawline that studio lighting guys waited their whole careers for. Marcus could already see this face projected onscreen amid a chorus of lovelorn sighs radiating from the balcony of every movie house in the country. Trevor thrust out his hand toward Marcus, offering a smile as warm as a summer bonfire.

Marcus took the hand and almost wilted under its strength.

Quentin ordered a round of bourbon. Marcus and Quentin retook their seats and Trevor grabbed the one facing the door.

It was obvious to Marcus what was going on here: Quentin wanted to land this guy between the sheets and the best way to do that was to land him in the movies. Marcus smiled to himself. *You must have cracked an instant hard-on the moment you came across* William Tell.

"So," Quentin said, "Floyd Forrester. You know him?"

"I know *of* him," Marcus replied. "He's MGM's casting director in charge of pirates, conquistadors, vestal virgins, Egyptian high priestesses—anything historical."

"Including Swiss bowmen from the Middle Ages?" Trevor asked.

"Sure," Marcus replied. "Why?"

Quentin lowered his voice. "Because—and don't look around—he's sitting in one of the booths right now."

After Trevor's entrance, Marcus hadn't noticed the flares of sunlight that lit the bar whenever someone walked in. He must have missed Forrester's entrance while he was gazing into the dreamy face of MGM's soon-to-be New Exciting Find.

"So-o-o-o," Quentin purred, "why don't you pop over there and introduce yourself. Then find a way to weave into the conversation that the perfect person for the role of William Tell is sitting just a few feet away, and is *very* keen to meet him."

Trevor's smile made it quite clear that this ambush had been planned. "And," Trevor added, "is willing to do whatever it takes to get an audition."

Marcus glanced at Quentin, then back at Trevor. "Including . . . ?"

Trevor nodded. "You don't get to be the US champion for six years in any sport without being prepared to do whatever is necessary. You can quote me on that to Mr. Forrester."

"And remember," Quentin put in, "we need to get this project going before any more questions get asked back at Paramount."

As a screenplay writer, Marcus' stock in trade was characters: what they looked like and how they thought and behaved. He wended his way around the checkerboard tables to Forrester's booth and tried to surreptitiously snatch glances of the guy in an attempt to assess who he was dealing with. But the light in the Retake Room was too murky for Marcus to get a firm grip on his prey. Gingerly, he approached Forrester's booth.

"Excuse me, but you're Floyd Forrester, aren't you?"

Forrester looked up from his *Hollywood Citizen News*. It was opened at the story Marcus had read that morning about the sixty-two bars deemed officially off-limits to all personnel. Unofficially, they were known as H&H bars: hookers and homos. Forrester regarded Marcus' outstretched hand with a measure of curiosity before shaking it limply.

"My name is Marcus Adler and—"

"I know who you are." Forrester motioned to the other side of the booth. "Take a seat."

As Forrester lit a fresh Gitanes cigarette from the end of the one he'd just finished, he studied Marcus with amusement. "*William Tell* is going to make a hell of a picture," he said. "A fine feather in your cap, I must say."

Marcus nodded appreciatively and watched the guy suck in such a deep lungful of smoke that it burned through half his cigarette. His vest buttons strained against a heft they weren't designed to contain and a second chin swelled against the collar of his white shirt, sitting on the knot of his lavender tie like a Christmas goose. For all his wheezing bulk, Forrester looked like he had the personality of an ice pick. He lifted a tumbler of bright yellow liquid to his lips.

Marcus smelled aniseed. "What's that you're drinking?"

"A French liqueur, Pernod. I'd offer you a glass but Europe's going up in flames, so it might be years before I can get my hands on another bottle." He ran his eyes over Marcus. "It's one of my few remaining pleasures in life, and it's about to become as scarce as edelweiss in the Sahara."

Marcus held up his hand as though to say, *That's quite all right.* "Can I assume you'll be casting *William Tell*?"

"You can."

"Have you started putting together a list of possible actors for the lead?"

"I have."

"May I throw in a suggestion?" Marcus knew he was crossing borders. "Ever heard of a guy by the name of Trevor Bergin?"

"The champion archer?"

Forrester kept his face immobile and his hand at rest. Marcus couldn't tell if he'd overstepped his mark, or if he'd genuinely piqued the guy's interest, but he'd gone too far by now to back off. Marcus nodded in the direction of Bergin's table. "He's sitting right over there, very anxious to meet with you. In fact, he told me just now that he's keen to do anything necessary to be considered for the role. If you catch my meaning."

But Forrester didn't turn to look at Bergin. He lit his third cigarette since Marcus approached and smiled to reveal two rows of crooked teeth stained with nicotine. "What's your angle? You just being the screenwriter and all."

Marcus deepened his voice half an octave. "This picture could be the making of my career, so it's in my interests to see the best man cast in the lead. Not only is Trevor Bergin a matinee idol in the making, he's the best archer in the country. And he's very willing—"

"There is such a thing as 'too handsome.'"

"*Too* handsome?"

"In my book, there is. I don't trust 'em." Forrester's green eyes turned hard as jade. "Life comes too easily to them. Personally, I prefer fair-haired, round-faced, apple-cheeked types. Horn-rimmed glasses. Sensitive. Clever with words." The thick eyebrows rose and furled again while Forrester's meaning sunk in.

Marcus craved the smooth burn of expensive bourbon and the calming power of a Chesterfield. First I have sex with somebody to get my picture back, and now I have to do it with this lump of donuts to ensure it stays here?

Doing it with Quentin was one thing. The guy was a kindred spirit, honest about what he was doing, and reasonably attractive, too. But this guy? With his sausage-skin tweed and his horrible teeth, his French liqueur and stinking cigarettes? *Oh no, no, no, no, no. I'm willing to do a lot, but not that. Leastways, not with this smarmy jerk.*

Marcus slid out of the booth. "I get now why they just want the writers to write and the casters to cast."

Forrester shrugged. "*Quel dommage.* Trevor Bergin would have been perfect for the role."

Marcus lingered for a moment, trying to summon a stinging riposte, but nothing came to him. Instead, he shot the guy a withering look and turned back toward Quentin and Trevor's table. But he found he couldn't face them, either, so he headed for the door.

Outside on the sidewalk, the sun had sunk below the horizon. Marcus felt *William Tell* slipping through his fingers yet again. And for the slimmest, narrowest sliver of a moment, he considered marching back in and taking Forrester up on his offer. But then he pictured those teeth and that smug smile, and he knew he couldn't go through with it. *Even us whores have standards.*

CHAPTER 10

Gwendolyn was happy she'd taken the job at Bullocks Wilshire, and not just because she got to handle luxurious lingerie, perfume, and accessories. Slow days left her free to examine the construction and patterns of outfits, storing them up in her bank of ideas for Chez Gwendolyn.

She'd even learned to unchain her envy of the women who frequented the store. They wandered aimlessly, with no significant purpose or real reason for getting up in the morning. Chez Gwendolyn may never see the light of day, and if it did, it might not amount to much, but it had come to instill a purpose in Gwendolyn, and she loved the feeling it gave her.

As far as she was concerned, there was only one problem, but it was overwhelming. At her current rate of pay, it was going to take her thirty-three years to save enough money to open her store. By that time, she'd be sixty-five and ready for the old folks' home. She needed to make more money.

As she waited for the store to open, she polished the lingerie counter's glass top and thought about the breathtaking diamond choker that Errol — almost incoherent with shame — had presented her with. He'd impressed her with the effort he made by going to Harry Winston's and selecting a spectacular way to declare his mea culpa. Dazzling though it was, it didn't stop her from calculating the rate of interest she might get if she hocked the necklace and invested in war bonds. She was tallying figures in her head when Mr. Dewberry approached her counter.

"Good morning, Miss Gwendolyn," he said. "We need to talk about Miss Delores."

Gwendolyn glanced at Delores' deserted perfume counter. "It's not like her to be late."

He fiddled with the gold stickpin in his burgundy necktie. "It seems Miss Delores has left us."

Gwendolyn gave a start. "She quit?"

"She sent a telegram this morning giving her immediate notice. It appears she's taken a job at one of the new munitions factories down in Long Beach."

Delores always arrived at work with every hair in place, her face precisely made up, each accessory cherry-picked to complement her ensemble. Gwendolyn could scarcely picture her toiling in a noisy, smelly—not to mention dangerous—munitions factory. She tried to imagine herself in shapeless overalls, her hair fastened with a grimy scarf, bent over a production line filling missiles with explosives. Not for three times the pay could I do that, she decided. Not even for Chez Gwendolyn.

"I suppose she won't be the first staff member we'll lose," Dewberry said mournfully. "I do hope we shall not be receiving the same sort of telegram from you, too."

"Oh, Mr. Dewberry," Gwendolyn giggled, "can you really see me working in a munitions factory?"

"I can't picture Delores doing it, but here we are." He had a point. All Gwendolyn could do was nod. "At any rate, we're expecting next month's shipment of gloves, stockings, and garters today. The man should be here about eleven. Have you taken deliveries before?"

"No, sir. Delores always did that."

"There's not much to it. Just count the number of boxes to ensure what's on the delivery invoice is what's been delivered, then stock them on the storage shelves accordingly. I'll get Myra from the Saddle Shop to cover you when it arrives."

At eleven, Myra appeared and Gwendolyn let herself into the stock room tucked away on the store's western side. It was a long room with two aisles of shelves. At one end was a large table next to a wide set of gray double doors that led out to the delivery dock.

Gwendolyn sat at the desk leafing through a magazine until the delivery man walked in pushing a dolly loaded with two dozen shiny pink boxes labeled *The Gorgeous Gams Company*. He looked like a Brooklyn street-wise version of Mickey Rooney, and stared at Gwendolyn with a mixture of surprise and suspicion, all the while chewing manically on spearmint gum.

"Delores out sick, or su'um?"

Gwendolyn extended her hand toward the guy's clipboard. "She left us for better-paying pastures. I'm Gwendolyn." She squinted at the name patch sewn to his breast pocket. "Lester, is it?"

Lester screwed his eyes tightly. "Son of a bitch!" He popped them open again and scowled at her. "Where did she go?"

Gwendolyn wondered how it was any business of his where Delores went. Was he her boyfriend? "The boss said she took a job at a munitions factory down in Long Beach."

"The hell she did." Lester leaned against his boxes. "A girl like Delores? Getting all dirtied up in a factory? I can see you don't buy that story anymore than I do."

"No," Gwendolyn confessed, "it does seem out of character."

Lester read her nameplate, rolling something over in his mind. He looked around to check that they were alone. "She told me if she ever disappears, you're the one I should talk to."

"About what?"

"She said you were solid. You could keep a secret."

"If it's a secret worth keeping."

He looked her up and down. "It is."

As he worked his gum some more, Gwendolyn studied him anew. He didn't seem the dangerous type. More like a fresh-faced kid off some Midwest corn farm by way of Flatbush Avenue.

"Delores was my best distributor," he said quietly.

"Of what?"

"Nylons. You know, black market."

She looked, bug-eyed, at the stack of pink boxes behind him. "These are black market stockings?"

"Nah. These are legit. But in my truck out back I got others. Three dozen pairs. Every bit as good as Gorgeous Gams, guaranteed."

"Where do you get black-market—?"

"I deliver these babies once a month. You pay me the going rate, then sell them for whatever you can get."

Over the past six months, more and more commodities had been rationed: rubber, gasoline, sugar. Just as Monty predicted, when nylon was added to the list, panic stabbed at the heart of every well-dressed American woman.

"I see." Gwendolyn wondered why Delores had never offered her any. "You think this has got something to do with why she quit?"

"You bet your sweet patootie it is," Lester said sourly. "Delores was good at it because she was ambitious. She told me she wanted the money to go into business. Wanted to set herself up as a freelance secretarial service for traveling businessmen who come into town and need a typist or whatever. Did you know that broad can type sixty-five words a minute and speaks four languages?"

Good for you, she told Delores silently. "I guess she made enough to do what she wanted."

"Nah. These past few months she's been selling so many, I think she got greedy. And in this business, if you get greedy, you get careless. That girl sold to the wrong person."

"The cops?"

"Could be."

"Do you think the cops would care much about a shop girl selling black-market nylons?"

"Who knows?" Lester spat his chewing gum into a trashcan under the delivery desk. "There's money to be made and the rules are easy."

Gwendolyn knew exactly how she wanted Chez Gwendolyn to look. The front display would have two mannequins in the window: one dressed in formal wear, the other in casual. The name of the store would be in the same sophisticated French lettering she'd seen on the label of a gown in the couture department upstairs, and a little brass bell over the door would jingle every time a customer came in. "What are the rules?" she asked.

"There's really only one," Lester said. "Never sell to anyone you don't got no connection to. Family — fine. Neighbors — fine. Friends — fine. Friends of friends, and even friends of friends of friends — fine. Famous people or anyone with a public profile are okay, too. But not strangers. Nobody you can't track down. I'll bet my last plug nickel that's what Delores did. And now she's gone and I'm stuck with a stack of merchandise."

Gwendolyn could already see the formal mannequin dressed in lilac chiffon with a mint green fleck, strapless with a sweetheart neckline. "How much?"

"Twenty-five cents per pair."

"What did she sell them for?"

"A buck fifty, maybe two."

"At one fifty per pair, that's a dollar twenty-five profit. Multiplied by three dozen, that's —" She did a quick calculation. "That's a profit of forty-five dollars. So six dozen pairs mean nearly a hundred bucks profit, even more if I charge two dollars!"

"Nylon's only going to get scarcer the longer the war goes on," Lester pointed out.

"So if I can move five dozen a week, and if the war goes on for three years, that's fifty-two times three, times five dozen stockings a week at a profit per pair of a dollar twenty-five . . . " The numbers tumbled through Gwendolyn's mind like a stock-market ticker. "That's nearly three grand by the end of the war!"

"You figured all that out in your head? Without pencil and paper?"

Gwendolyn peered at Lester. "It's only numbers," she said. "So you have three dozen pairs at twenty-five cents a pair, that means you'll let me have Delores' stock for nine dollars?"

"Are you saying you want in?"

Gwendolyn thought of Errol Flynn's diamond choker and wondered how much she could get for it. She felt her fingers start to tremble.

CHAPTER 11

A clod of damp soil walloped Marcus in the side of his head. Ineffectively suppressed giggles followed.

"I say, Marcus!" It was Robert Benchley, of course. "It appears you've got a wee spot of schmutz on your mug."

Marcus left the dirt plastered to the side of his face. "Something tells me you're about to get a whole pile of schmutz in your lemonade vodka."

Dorothy Parker covered the top of her glass with her hand. "All I ask is that none of it ends up in mine."

Even planting a victory garden was an excuse for a party at the Garden of Allah.

Marcus swiped the dirt off his face, then sniffed it. He nudged Kathryn's shoulder with his. "I haven't smelled something like this since I left Pennsylvania."

"I don't think I ever have." She dug her fingers into the soil. "It's cooler than I expected."

It was Madame Nazimova who first suggested the residents dig a victory garden. Food was starting to be rationed, and posters had appeared around town encouraging people to start growing their own food. Nazimova pointed out that the fifteen-by-twenty-foot plot of grass outside her apartment received a lot of sun, and on the first weekend in September, eleven people showed up for the inaugural working bee to plant beets, lettuce, cabbage, and radishes. Each resident arrived with some sort of gardening implement in hand, and since it was the Garden of Allah, a drink in the other.

"Of course the soil is cool." Alla joined the other two on her knees. "If you were expecting it to be warm, like fresh bagels, it is time you reconnect with Mother Earth." She scraped at the soil with a trowel. "Back in Russia we planted our own potatoes and cabbages. Wait till you see what I do with these!"

A devilish glee lit up her lined face. Marcus realized that he'd seen her smile more often since her return to the movies. Last year she made her mark in a Tyrone Power picture over at Fox in a Valentino remake, filling the screen with her remarkable presence. After that, a role in a Norma Shearer vehicle at MGM gave her movie career a second wind and put a bounce back in her step.

"Well, now!" A cultured voice rang out across the victory garden. Nobody needed to look up to see who it was, but everybody did anyway because they knew the view would be worthwhile. Errol Flynn stood at the other end of the plot, a bottle of champagne in each hand. "When nobody was sitting around the pool," he announced, "I knew something was up."

"Refreshments we have already," Alla told him. "An extra pair of hands is what we need."

Flynn deposited his contribution on the table next to Benchley and accepted one of the hoes offered to him by new resident Bertie Krueger.

Bertie was an heiress to a canned beer fortune who'd decided that life at the Garden of Allah offered more appeal than the stuffy Garden Court Apartments on Hollywood Boulevard. She'd recently moved into what used to be Nazimova's own bedroom in the main house.

The girl had an unfortunately horsey look about her: widely spaced teeth, thick eyebrows, an unruly mop of hair she dubbed her Wild Man of Borneo, and a pair of hips that Reubens would have killed his grandmother to paint. But she was kindhearted, generous to a fault, and fun to have around. For a girl who'd never worked hard at anything, she'd taken to the victory garden with gusto.

"Marcus," Errol said, "I hear your *William Tell* starts shooting soon."

"Rehearsals begin Monday." Marcus took out a cabbage seedling from a little paper envelope and pushed it into the ground with his thumb.

Errol dug the hoe into the earth with a grunt. "My boxing instructor on *Gentleman Jim* tells me he has a pal who specializes in archery and jousting. He was hired by MGM for your picture, but there's nothing for him to do. Bergin doesn't need any help hitting the bull's-eye."

After he fled the Retake Room that day, Marcus had mentally prepared himself to hear that *William Tell* was dead in the water. But before the month was out, MGM's PR department started heralding it as one of their biggest, most expensive, and most exciting pictures for 1943. And to ensure the story was told with accuracy and panache, they'd cast Trevor Bergin in the lead. "I guess Forrester was bluffing," Marcus had later told Kathryn.

Moreover, Jim Taggert took Marcus aside last week and told him that Mayer was so happy with Marcus' script, he planned to lobby for a Best Original Screenplay nomination.

"The studio has high expectations all around." Marcus watched Alla for a moment to make sure he was planting the cabbage seedlings correctly, then continued. "If they have half the success Warners had with your *Robin Hood,* they'll be as happy as — "

"ROBIN FUCKING HOOD!"

Everyone turned to look at the figure slouched against the acorn tree.

The guy was a far cry from the virile example of American sportsmanship Marcus had seen at the Retake Room earlier that summer. This version looked like he'd slept in his clothes for a week and hadn't shaved in at least that long. His eyelids hung like broken window blinds.

Marcus scrambled to his feet. "What brings you here?"

The guy stood shuddering in the breeze for a moment, then laid a hand against the bark to steady himself. He fixed Errol with a stare, hostility radiating out of him. "All I ever hear is Robin Hood! Robin Hood!"

"Steady on, old boy." Errol tried one of his disarming smiles.

"I'm so sick of hearing about you and Robin Hood, and how this movie has to be better and bigger than yours. What I want to know is, why didn't they just hire you for the job and leave me the goddamned hell alone."

Marcus took a step toward Trevor. "Hey," he said, "how's about you and I go back to my place. We can make some coffee, I could probably scrounge up some donuts —"

"I didn't come here for coffee!"

"Then why are you here?" Alla was on her feet now, a Russian scowl wrinkling her forehead.

"You got me into this, Adler, you gotta get me out of it." Trevor's words escaped from him like air from a punctured balloon. His hands curled into fists.

"What was it you said to me that day?" Marcus asked. "You don't get to be the US champion without being prepared to do whatever's necessary."

"That's what Quentin told me to say."

"You don't want to be in the movies?" Bertie asked. "With your looks? Are you nuts?"

Trevor regarded Bertie sadly. "It all happened so fast, got my head all turned around. I don't know what I want anymore."

Benchley struggled to his feet with a filled tumbler in his hand. "This is half lemonade, half vodka. I think you need it more than I." Benchley's red face and extended belly were the consequences of several decades of heavy drinking. His own hand shook as he pushed the glass into Bergin's and gently prodded it toward his mouth.

Trevor took a couple of heavy swigs and braced himself as the vodka hit his system. "And then there's Melody Hope."

Marcus looked at Kathryn, who shrugged, then at Bertie. Melody Hope had quickly become one of MGM's more popular—and valuable—performers. For a few years, she'd been Bertie's neighbor at the Garden Court Apartments. Bertie shrugged, too.

Marcus strode forward, grabbed Trevor by the arm and started frog-marching him away. The guy reeked of days-old booze. Over his shoulder, Marcus jutted his head at Kathryn and Bertie. Nobody said anything until they were all inside his living room.

With little effort, Marcus prodded Trevor onto the sofa. "What's Melody Hope got to do with any of this?"

"Maureen O'Hara is out."

"Since when?" Kathryn was in the kitchen making coffee, but had ears the size of megaphones when a scoop loomed on her horizon. She was desperate for an exclusive now that her boss had announced a twenty percent pay cut for all *Hollywood Reporter* staff at the start of summer. And they were the lucky ones—twenty-three more staff members had been let go that week. Now more than ever, Kathryn needed to prove her worth.

"Since Fox decided to keep her for Tyron's new pirate movie."

Marcus could easily picture Melody as the virginal Lady Gwendolyn in a romantic clinch with Bergin. He sat beside Trevor. "And why is Melody a problem?" Hesitation filled Trevor's eyes as they lingered on Kathryn and Bertie. "It's okay," Marcus assured him. "You can trust them."

"Melody was the last girl I was with before I faced the fact that girls don't—that they're not what I'm looking for. The last time we were together, I couldn't—perform."

Kathryn crossed into the living room with oatmeal molasses cookies and four cups of strong coffee. "How did she take it?"

"Somehow, I gave her the impression that she was the one responsible for turning me into a fag."

Bertie grimaced. "Ouch."

Trevor nodded. "She started throwing things and screaming at me like a longshoreman."

"Sounds a bit extreme," Kathryn observed, "especially for Melody."

"I'm guessing it's been a while since you talked to her?" Bertie snapped off a chunk of cookie. "There's a reason I no longer live next door to Miss Melody Hope." She turned to Trevor. "I was at home, sitting on the other side of Mel's living room wall, the night you two had that fight. When she threw that lamp—"

"Damn near busted my fist!"

"I decided she'd become too much of a handful. You're lucky to be rid of her."

"But I'm not rid of her!" Trevor protested, his face reddening with frustration. "I'm supposed to be acting with her — in love scenes! — knowing she hates my guts and would gladly slide a knife between my ribs given half a chance."

"I'm sure she's calmed down since then."

"She hasn't," Trevor insisted. "I stopped by her dressing room last week."

"And?"

"She threw a vase at me." He started patting his pockets for cigarettes. Marcus leaned over the coffee table and opened a black lacquered box George Cukor had brought back for him from Hong Kong. He offered it to Trevor, who gratefully took a Chesterfield and lit it. "And anyway, that's only half of it. The studio's got a fortune riding on this movie. I've never acted before. What if I completely blow it?"

Marcus lit up a cigarette of his own. Is there a point at which a project becomes too damned difficult? And if there is, did I just pass it? He thought of Cukor's cigarette box; his head shot up.

"What if I convince George Cukor to coach you?"

Trevor seemed to sober up a notch. "You can do that?"

"I can try."

"But didn't I read somewhere that he joined the army?" Bertie asked.

"There's Regular Joe enlisting in the army, and then there's George Cukor," Marcus said. "He's going to be directing training films and probably won't be going any farther than Redondo Beach." He turned back to Trevor. "I can't guarantee anything, but I'll only ask him if you promise you'll give it your all."

Trevor nodded. "But what about Melody?"

"You leave Melody to me."

* * *

Melody Hope opened her front door and immediately slurred, "Come on in . . . close the door behind you . . . join me in a lil drinkie . . . they're so refreshing on a lonely Sunday afternoon."

When Marcus telephoned her, Melody had spoken with the softly rounded vowels and dropped g's she'd used in her most recent movie, *Sutter's Hill,* about the start of the Californian gold rush. She'd portrayed a displaced Southern belle with such warmth and humor that the movie was an instant hit. But by the time Marcus got to Melody's front door, her vowels had the same hard edge as her mouth. "What's up? Like I can't guess." She flopped onto her Chinese silk sofa.

Marcus joined her. "It's about *William Tell.*"

"No," she corrected him. "It's about Trevor Bergin."

Years ago, Marcus wrote a movie called *The Pistol From Pittsburgh* that gave Melody her big break, and she'd always been grateful. He was counting on that now. "You know I only have your best interests at heart, right?"

She yawned. "I know this is Hollywood."

He positioned himself on the sofa so that their shoulders were touching. "Lady Gwendolyn is a great part, and a big opportunity for you."

"And for you," she taunted him. "I've heard what Mayer promised if it turns out great."

Marcus maintained his indulgent smile. "It's time to be professional," he told her gently, "even if you still resent the guy."

She grabbed up her tumbler of gin. "Okay," she said from inside the glass. "I'll play nice."

Marcus resisted the urge to squint. *I'm here ten minutes and she's already rolling over?* She finished her drink and held out the glass for a refill.

Marcus took it and approached the chrome and mirrored wet bar against the wall. There were brown blotches the size of half-dollars on the white carpet at his feet. *That's a lot of booze over a long time,* he thought as he fixed weaker drinks than Melody was probably expecting. He joined her on the sofa. "What's going on with you?"

She pulled back. "What do you mean?"

"When we met, you were a sweet young preacher's daughter, a teetotaler, and — I presume — a virgin."

Her smirk looked jarringly out of place on her rosy-cheeked ingénue face. "But look at me now, boozing it up in the middle of the afternoon."

"Your affair with Mayer." Marcus caught the *harrumph* flashing through her eyes. "It was the worst-kept secret at the studio."

"What about Mannix?" she asked. "Did you all hear about that one?"

"You had an affair with Eddie Mannix, too?"

"Not so much 'had an affair' as 'had an affair thrust on me.' Let's just say that if I wanted my career to really take off, I wasn't offered a range of choices." Melody shrugged like none of it mattered. "I'll tell you this for nothing: what Mister Eddie Mannix lacks in movie-star handsome, he makes up for in enthusiasm. Boy, can that guy go."

No wonder you're sitting here socking it away. Marcus laid a hand on her arm. "Melody, you should have said — "

She yanked her arm away. "If you think that's why I'm drinking all on my lonesome on a Sunday afternoon, you're way off the bull's-eye. I'm here because my father's disowned me."

"He's what?"

She raised her glass as though in salute. "Yep, dear old Dad, the God-fearing preacher man, no longer recognizes me as his daughter because I'm a — let's see if I can get this word-perfect — a 'sinful, lascivious succubus willing to stop at nothing in order to become queen of the Hollywood Jezebels.' How do you like them apples?"

"What about your mom?" Marcus said. "Have you tried asking her to intervene — ?"

"My mother is the daughter of a Methodist pastor married to a Methodist pastor. How do you think she feels about lascivious Jezebels?"

"But you're her daughter — "

"I can't do anything about what my parents think, but I can do *this*." Melody raised her glass again. The ice tinkled in the still of the room. "Which brings us to the end of this well-intentioned discussion of my private life. Let's get back to the matter at hand." She crossed her chest. "I hereby solemnly promise that I shall be the epitome of the professional Hollywood actress during the production of MGM's greatly anticipated *William Tell*."

Marcus searched the girl's face for signs of mockery or insincerity, but saw only unblemished candor. "You will?"

"For you? Sure." She paused, then added, "For a favor."

Marcus closed his eyes and pictured himself standing in a grave deeper than Hugo's. "What sort of favor?"

"Now that your *Pearl From Pearl Harbor*'s got the ol' heave-ho, they're talking about putting Judy Garland into something called *For Me And My Gal*."

Marcus couldn't bear to look at her. He focused instead on a still-life hanging on the wall opposite them. "I heard that, too."

"The rumor is they're going to be casting this new up-and-comer. Some hot stuff Broadway dancer, Gene Kelly. I want that role, Marcus. I want it real bad. Floyd Forrester is casting *For Me And My Gal*, so all I need you to do is go see him and . . . do what you do."

"Melody, honey, I didn't write that picture. And even if I did, you know that writers have no say in casting."

"You got Trevor Bergin cast in *William Tell*, didn't you?"

He shook his head. "Nope. I tried, I failed, he got cast anyway."

A smirk spread across Melody's face like a rash. "That's not what I heard."

"What exactly did you hear?"

She posed like a coquette. "That you approached Floyd at the Retake Room. You got him drunk on French booze and made it clear you'd do anything — ANYTHING — to help Trevor win the role. So don't go pulling the Virgin Mary act with me. We've all done it." She was stage-whispering now. "It's no big deal. Really, it isn't."

"But that's not the way it happened."

A shrug so slight it barely registered. "If you say so."

"Floyd said if I wanted Trevor cast, then *I* was the one who had to put out."

"And did you?"

"No!"

"Well, then," Melody said with saucer eyes, "you need to know that the rumors flying around the studio say you're willing to do anything with anyone to get ahead. You've got yourself a reputation, buster, and it's not the sort that would make your mama proud."

CHAPTER 12

Kathryn looked up over a mountain of provolone and ham sandwiches and surveyed the barn. "I'm surprised it's not busier."

Bette Davis gave a snort. "Don't speak too soon. Every night it's been the same since we opened. One minute we're barely a third full, the next they're hanging from the rafters and we're all drowning in testosterone!" She surveyed their handiwork. "This should hold the boys until the next shipment of bread arrives. Oh, and thank you." Bette touched Kathryn's forearm lightly. "I know you're a busy girl with a busy job."

"It's not like yours is any kind of slouch," Kathryn insisted.

When Bette Davis and John Garfield came up with the idea of opening a place to give military personnel on shore leave somewhere to go, they'd recruited battalions of entertainers, musicians, set decorators, publicists, and all manner of studio craftsmen to volunteer their time to build the Hollywood Canteen into something special. It hadn't taken long for word to spread among military personnel that if they were on leave in Los Angeles, they ought to hitch a ride to the Hollywood Canteen on Cahuenga Boulevard. Not only would they be made to feel welcome, but if they ever wanted to meet a movie star, it might be their only chance.

The Hollywood Canteen was a large, squarish room done out in roughly hewn wood. Along the eastern and western walls were murals depicting Hollywood's version of what life on the farm probably looked like. The refreshment counter ran along the southern wall and overlooked bunches of circular tables where guys could eat their sandwiches and donuts and drink coffee. Along the northern wall was a stage with space for five or six musicians and a couple of singers. From the ceiling hung several chandeliers made of hurricane lamps suspended from wagon wheels.

"I hear *Now, Voyager* is your best work yet," Kathryn said.

The two women had encountered each other at movie premieres and award ceremonies over the years, but had never spoken. Bette offered up an unassuming smile Kathryn had never seen her use on screen. "If I send you tickets to the premiere, will you promise to attend?"

"Absolutely."

"Terrific! Now, if you'll excuse me, I have to spruce up before the NBC guys get here."

Kathryn's ears prickled. "NBC?"

"They're broadcasting *The Pepsodent Show* from here tonight."

Errol's advice to attract the attention of Pepsodent's Leo Presnell had proved tricky to execute. Over the past months, Kathryn had been to several *Pepsodent Show* broadcasts but was rebuffed every time by security guards. She'd requested an interview with Bob Hope, but between his movies, radio show, and gigs entertaining the troops, Kathryn couldn't get anywhere. She'd approached Presnell's office and pitched an idea for an article about the life of a hit radio show sponsor, but never heard back.

It was nearly four o'clock when Kathryn finished arranging sandwiches, and the next time she checked her watch, it was twenty to five and she was serving food as fast as the kitchen supervisor, Mary Ford, could replace it.

With Monty's help, Kathryn was learning how to distinguish navy from army, captain from colonel, ensign from admiral. But what hit home that first night at the Canteen was the forlorn look in the faces of the men she encountered there. They were lonesome for their hometowns and regular lives, but excited to see Los Angeles with its Pacific Ocean, wide boulevards, and palm trees. The possibility of seeing a movie star—and maybe even getting to dance with one—was suddenly and thrillingly real. But she could also see their anticipation and fear. They were about to ship out into a theater of war to fight an inscrutable enemy, and they might not come back.

She tried her best to welcome them with a jovial "How ya doin', fella?" Maybe she'd help assuage the uncertainties clouding their futures, or maybe nothing she did would make a dent, but she tried nonetheless.

It was after six when she felt a tap on her shoulder. Mary told her she'd earned a break, and that there was sherry in the office if she wanted a reviving sip.

Kathryn pointed to a team of technicians crowding the stage. "Are they from *The Pepsodent Show?*"

Mary nodded. "After tonight, everybody in America will know about the Hollywood Canteen."

"I don't suppose you know who is in charge?"

"Leo Presnell?" Mary giggled.

"Why is that funny?"

Mary pressed her fingers to her mouth. "I shouldn't laugh; it's really quite a serious matter. My husband just made a short military film called *Sex Hygiene*." Mary's husband was director John Ford. "It's a cautionary tale about fellows who visit prostitutes and catch venereal disease. Before production commenced, Mr. Presnell came over to the house several times. Somebody enlisted the help of Unilever because they make all sorts of hygiene products, as well as Pepsodent toothpaste."

"Is he here tonight?"

She pointed to someone standing on the side of the stage watching a pair of men connect wires to a microphone.

Kathryn picked her way along the side of the crowded dance floor and approached Presnell with the stealth of a deer hunter.

Leo Presnell carried himself with a confidence harvested from uninterrupted generations of old money. His midnight-blue suit hugged his shoulders and draped his torso so effortlessly that it had to be tailor-made. His barbershop shave and slickly manicured nails were just as Errol had described. He reached for Kathryn's outstretched hand.

"I wanted to introduce myself," she told him. "I'm Kathryn Massey with the *Hollywood Reporter*." She waited to see a flicker of recognition, but got only a practiced veneer of gloss. "You're not an easy person to reach."

"I'm not?"

She'd been expecting a dodge and a quick escape, but was confronted with a six-foot-two wall of overwhelming masculinity. She thought of Bette's comment about drowning in testosterone. Maybe that's what she was feeling — the escalating urges of the three hundred males behind her whose pent-up cravings saw no imminent release.

No, she decided, it's got nothing to do with the guys on the dance floor. "I've been to a number of broadcasts and tried to talk to you, but didn't get very far."

For such a well-put-together man about town, Presnell's lopsided smile was unexpected. "I do have an overprotective secretary," he admitted, "with whom I shall have a stern word."

"I wrote to you, too, but didn't get a response."

"Did you know we moved offices recently?" he asked. "It was a rough transition, and a number of things—" He cut himself off. "You have my full attention, Miss Massey. How may I help you?"

The earthy combination of sailor sweat and sawdust blew across Kathryn like a Santa Ana wind, and she strained to recall her pitch. "Well, you see, Mr. Presnell—"

"Please, call me Leo." He took an almost imperceptible step closer to her.

"The thing is—Leo, your show is in its fourth year now, and it strikes me that it could do with some revamping."

"Is that so?"

"Of course, this is just my opinion, but I think you need to break things up, not just with a song or two, but perhaps a five-minute Hollywood report from someone in the know."

"Like what Louella Parsons used to do on *Hollywood Hotel*?"

"Yes, that's right."

"But preferably someone with a bit more class?"

She nodded.

"This is really quite remarkable," he said. "Just the other day, I had a meeting with my marketing guys. Evidently, their research agrees with your assessment. They came up with a list of suggestions, and the one I liked the most was to include more Hollywood content."

It was too much of a coincidence. Kathryn suspected he was just telling her what she wanted to hear for reasons she couldn't yet fathom.

"Is that something you'd be interested in doing?" he asked.

Kathryn fought the urge to yip, but before she could form a response, a technician approached them. "Mr. Presnell, there's a call for you in the office. Something about Mr. Hope stuck at the studio. Sounds kinda urgent."

Presnell thanked him, told Kathryn he'd be in touch, and rushed offstage toward the Canteen's back office.

Kathryn bounded down the stairs and headed for the ladies' room, realizing rather belatedly that she ought to have performed a makeup check after working the sandwich line. It was a bit late for that now, but she began to fix her hair anyway. She was still at the mirror when Greer Garson walked in.

Kathryn had met Greer over the summer at a press screening for *Mrs. Miniver*. Kathryn thought the movie was superb and had praised it at length in her column. It had gone on to become an enormous hit, propelling Greer to stardom. The woman exuded every bit of the warmth and compassion in person that she evoked on the screen.

"I don't know why we bother," Greer said with a laugh. "Those boys are all so cross-eyed with excitement, I doubt they'd notice if we had rotten tomatoes dripping from our heads, bless their dear little faces."

Kathryn pulled out her hairbrush. "Did I hear right? You're doing that Madame Curie movie next?"

"If they offer it to me."

Kathryn started running the brush through her hair. "Poor woman. Who knows what she could have accomplished if not for all that radiation. What a shame we're not blessed with hindsight."

"Oh, but risk-taking makes life worth living. Haven't you noticed that since the war started, it's a way of life? I see people making decisions in moments that they would have thought about for months." She pointed through the doorway. "Any of those boys out there could be dead a month from now."

"So you'll take the role?"

"Abso-damn-lutely. My mother said, Never knock back a death scene. I'll get that role if I have to sleep with Mayer to do it!" Her mascara hovered in midair. "Oh God, can you imagine?"

Kathryn thought about what Marcus was going through with *William Tell* and the trouble it'd caused him. Fortunately, he'd managed to work things out to everybody's satisfaction. He convinced Cukor to coach Trevor, and talked Melody into slowing down on the booze in exchange for having a word with Floyd Forrester. Even more impressively, he somehow managed to get Floyd to stop telling people Marcus was a good-time Charlie. The idea that Marcus was some sort of floozy made Kathryn laugh every time she thought of it.

"The casting-couch option must be one hell of a hurdle," Kathryn said.

"I only *wish* I knew how that felt!" Greer declared. "It'd mean someone saw me as a woman, not their saintly mother—or worse, their respectable aunt. Mind you, I truly doubt there'll be much casting-couch cha-cha going on in the near future." She dropped her mascara and lipstick into her purse. "Not with what's happened to Errol."

A jolt of panic mule-kicked Kathryn in the chest. "Errol? Flynn? Why, what's happened?"

"Haven't you heard? He's been charged with rape."

CHAPTER 13

As Melody Hope lifted the veil from her face, a key light was positioned to make her brown saucer eyes glisten with Technicolored adoration. "Oh, William," she said breathlessly, "let's turn our back on the past. From this day forward, we shall keep our eyes on the horizon of our future."

Trevor Bergin beamed a loving smile that was guaranteed to melt a thousand hearts every night for the next three months—maybe longer, in larger cities. "With you, my Lady Gwendolyn, the future is a place where all is possible."

As the camera pulled back to reveal a dusky orange sun setting behind chocolate-box-perfect Swiss Alps, the words THE END filled the screen, and the audience erupted into applause so loud Marcus could feel the vibrations ripple the floor beneath his shoes.

It had all been worth it—sleeping with Quentin, cajoling Cukor to become a drama coach, promising Melody she'd get a shot at *For Me And My Gal*—or at least a chance to get into Forrester's good books.

Next to him, Nazimova almost had to shout to be heard. "Wonderful, my boy! WONDERFUL! You are so talented! I am so proud!"

As they made their way up the aisle, Marcus felt a strong hand clamp his shoulder. The scent of popcorn still lingered on Jim Taggert's fingers. "I think it's safe to say Mayer liked what he saw. It might be a wise career move to remind him of his promise tonight."

Though the prospect of an Academy Award nomination had been the gleaming reason Marcus put himself through all that maneuvering, he hadn't allowed himself to believe Mayer would make good on his promise. But now that his script had resulted in such a beautifully realized motion picture that was every bit as worthy as *Mrs. Miniver* and *Ziegfeld Girl,* Marcus permitted himself a flurry of excitement.

Taggert murmured, "Follow my lead," and strode ahead.

As a nod to wartime restraint, MGM had foregone the lavish celebration that typically followed a big premiere for a less formal party at the theater. The round, teak-paneled lounge was decorated with Corinthian columns, and at its center was a bronze Roman god plucking a lyre. Around its base tonight were tables loaded with desserts, including an ambitious display of donut holes dipped in bright red frosting to look like William Tell's apples, each skewered with a peppermint candy stick shaped like an arrow.

Marcus and Taggert had just joined Hoppy, Kathryn, Gwendolyn, and Nazimova in front of a huge painting of Napoleon Bonaparte on horseback when Charlie Chaplin came striding toward them with his arms outstretched.

"My darling Madame!" He beamed and enfolded Nazimova in his arms. Chaplin was still on a high since his latest movie, *The Great Dictator,* had been topping the box office for most of the previous year. Now in his fifties, the man was still charismatically handsome in spite of—or perhaps due to—his graying temples. Although he'd lived in America for decades, his British accent was still pronounced. "How *are* you, my dear? So *delightful* to see you here! And how *wonderful* you were in *Blood And Sand*! I'm sure the offers are *pouring* in now!"

Nazimova kept opening her mouth to speak, then closing it again as Chaplin continued to hog the spotlight. When she managed to get a word in, Nazimova explained that she was here because Marcus had written the movie he'd just seen.

Chaplin's face lit up as he told Marcus how impressed he was. When a roaming studio photographer happened by, he made a grand fuss about clearing everybody from the Napoleon portrait. "It makes for such an *interesting* backdrop, and it's always best to pose in front of an engaging setting in case the photograph doesn't turn out so flattering. You can at least deflect attention to what's *behind* you." He insisted the photographer take several shots of him with Marcus, declaring, "More takes, less worry!"

The fact that *William Tell* was remarkable was reward enough for Marcus, but being fussed over by such a titan of the industry left him almost giddy.

Chaplin moved on and Taggert pulled Marcus aside and pointed out L.B. Mayer. As per usual, L.B. was at the center of a Gordian knot of yes-men, hangers-on, and sycophants. Tonight's orbiting cluster included his right-hand man, Eddie Mannix. Not usually much of a smiler, Mannix was grinning wider than a shore-leave sailor at a whorehouse on someone else's dime.

"Walk past Mayer, but don't approach him," Taggert whispered. "You want your face to register. He'll see you, he'll recognize you, he'll remember that you wrote this picture, then he'll remember his promise. That's not to say he'll keep it, but the goal here is to connect your face with tonight's success. Just walk past him a couple of times. Make it look like you're going to fetch some of those apple donuts." Marcus felt Taggert's hands press against his back. "Ready, setty, GO!"

Marcus did his best to amble around some bejeweled and bedecked movie folk en route to the dessert table. When he spotted Mickey Rooney and Ava Gardner huddled near the

Mayer brigade with Trevor and Melody, he headed for them.

It was Melody who saw him first, and she introduced him to Rooney and Gardner, then slapped him on the back with the strength of a Canadian lumberjack. Her eyes were already bloodshot. "Here's the man we have to thank!"

During the shoot, Trevor had kept Marcus abreast of Melody's on-set conduct. She'd started out well and managed to stay professional for most of the shoot. But toward the end, she'd started to blow lines and miss cues. It got so bad that the director, Mervyn LeRoy, elected to take a calming walk around the soundstage rather than blow up in front of the crew.

"That was one heck of a screenplay you wrote, mister," Rooney exclaimed. "Wasn't it, honey?"

Gardner nodded agreeably. "Not that I know much about that."

Marcus hadn't yet seen Rooney's new wife in anything on the screen, but it was obvious that if she photographed as beautifully as she appeared in person, she could have a huge career ahead of her. In her strapless black silk gown, she was the most striking woman in the room. She flashed a mischievous grin. "But it's not my opinion that matters. There's only one person here whose approval means anything, and it looks like our illustrious Grand Poobah is trying to catch someone's attention."

When Marcus pointed to himself, Mannix nodded. Marcus arranged his face into a supplicatory smile.

"Adler, isn't it?" Mannix asked as Marcus approached.

He nodded. "That's right. Marcus Adler."

Mayer extended his hand. "Congratulations on a job well done. You crafted a fine motion picture."

It was a thorn in the paw of every screenwriter that Hollywood hierarchy pegged them to the bottom echelon of the studio food chain. It was almost as though they wanted to believe actors stood in front of the cameras and made up their lines as they went along, and the screenwriters simply took dictation. For someone like Mayer to go out of his way to publicly congratulate a lowly screenwriter was noteworthy.

"Thank you, sir." Marcus could feel the eyes of every person in the room drilling his back. He scoured his mind for something clever to say, but Jim's words came back to him: *He'll remember that you wrote this picture, then he'll remember his promise.* He bowed his head and took a few backward steps, then turned toward the Napoleon painting. His eyes landed on Alla, Kathryn, and Gwendolyn.

They were smiling and nodding. Jim stood next to them mouthing the word *perfect,* but then his smile dropped from his face like a trapdoor. Kathryn leaned closer to Gwendolyn, asking her a question. Before Marcus could do anything, a deep voice, gravelly and shaky, cut through the chatter.

"MURDERER!"

The hubbub in the room withered to a hush.

Edwin Marr, Hugo's father, stood ten feet inside the theater's front doors, glaring at Marcus like Lucifer himself. He was dressed in a tuxedo, but the fraying cuffs and faded satin lapels had seen cheerier days, and his walking stick, polished ebony with a golden grip, quivered under most of his weight. The man took another step or two and pointed with a finger gnarled with arthritis. "I know who you are," he croaked, "and we both know what you did."

The bystanders caught in Edwin's crosshairs cleared a path between them.

"Mr. Marr, I don't—"

"My son!" Edwin thundered. "My poor Hugo!"

Marcus risked a step or two closer to the old man, hoping to placate him. "I don't know what it is you think I've done, but Hugo was my friend. I was with him that night—"

Every wrinkle etched into the man's face deepened. "YOU DROVE HIM TO IT! I KNOW YOU DID!"

If anyone drove Hugo to suicide, it was you, Marcus thought. Edwin had made his own son feel he wasn't good enough. And it was Edwin who got himself so badly in debt he was forced to spy on MGM. There may come a time and place to air that sort of dirty laundry, Marcus decided, but this isn't it.

"Mr. Marr, I tried to stop Hugo."

Marr raised his ebony cane. "BAH! You tried to turn my son against me. I know what you're all about. I know what your type is like."

My type? Marcus felt the heat of a blush spread across his face.

"Edwin."

Out of the corner of his eye, Marcus saw Mayer break away from his pack. A whisper pulsed through the crowd.

"Edwin," Mayer said again, now pointing a thumb toward Marcus, "at lunch the other day, is this who you were talking about?"

Edwin pressed his lips together as though breathing in through his mouth might cause his head to explode.

Mayer didn't turn his head to look at Marcus, but instead slid his eyes to the right and studied him coolly.

Marcus sought out Kathryn's face. She and Mayer had been dance partners for years. It was quite possible she knew him better than most of the people now gawking at them. Marcus threw her a *What the hell is going on?* look, but she shrugged helplessly.

"I may be an old has-been," Edwin announced sourly, "but I know what I know."

Marcus wanted to reach out and grab Hugo's father by his shabby lapels and shake him until he confessed what he'd told Mayer, and then keep on shaking him until his scrawny old bones fell apart. But he stood nailed to the carpet, barely breathing, as he watched Nazimova march toward him with the dignified poise of a czarina.

She reached out and took his arm. "Clearly, the time for departure is at hand." A creature of the theater, Alla Nazimova knew how to launch her voice so that it projected to all corners of the room. She used it now to ensure that every onlooker knew Marcus Adler was not alone. "Let us continue tonight's celebrations elsewhere."

The individual people around him had all melded into a single amorphous haze punctuated with diamonds and black bowties but no longer distinguishable from each other. The murmuring Rorschach inkblots parted, and Nazimova led Marcus toward the front doors. He didn't blink until the biting October air slapped him in the face.

CHAPTER 14

Before Bullocks Wilshire opened for business each morning, the store filled with the chatter of its sales staff as they caught up with each other before stepping into their poised persona for the day. Every morning was a convivial review of their adventures among the cafés and nightclubs of a city flooded with dashing military uniforms, but when Gwendolyn clocked in on the first Monday in December, she sensed a solemn air. An entire year had passed since the attack on Pearl Harbor.

Once-complacent Americans now sat horrified in theaters watching *March Of Time* newsreels showing that the war in Europe wasn't going well. The initial declarations of "Now that we're in the fight, those Nazi bastards will be licked before you can say *sauerkraut!*" had been eaten away by nagging doubts. What if the British couldn't hold out? Would the war jump from the Continent to Britain, then to Ireland? What if it crossed the Atlantic to Canada? What if we can't fight off the Nazis like we bragged? People were starting to ask out loud the most horrifying conjecture of all: What if the Nazis win?

Monty had healed from his wounds, and was now back in Hawaii doing God only knew what. Gwendolyn posted a service star in her window to tell the world that she had a loved one fighting the enemy, but his letters were few, the details sparse. She decided she preferred it that way.

Meanwhile, she could barely believe she was selling nylon stockings on the black market. Nor could she believe the money she was making. Hocking Errol's diamond choker produced the cash she needed to launch her clandestine side career and begin amassing seed money for her Chez Gwendolyn fund, which was really an old pillowcase she kept hidden away.

She sold two pairs from her first shipment to Kathryn, two more to someone who worked with Kathryn, a pair to Bertie Krueger, and two pairs to Mary Ford at the Hollywood Canteen, where Gwendolyn now volunteered twice a week. For an outlay of twelve dollars she'd made a sixteen-dollar profit and still had one pair left. It was the easiest money in the world!

But it also made her jumpy, especially at work. One whiff of her black-market dealings and she'd be shown the door. So when Mr. Dewberry called her name, Gwendolyn gaped at him with what she suspected were guilty eyes.

"Yes, sir?"

"You've done some modeling, haven't you?"

"No, sir, I haven't."

He frowned, as though he was not entirely sure he believed her. "One of our VIPs wants to see some beachwear and has specifically requested you."

"She asked for me by name?"

"She told Mrs. Braithwaite your measurements are approximately the same as hers."

Mrs. Braithwaite ran the private modeling salon and looked after the store's in-house models and, by extension, acted as den mother to all the single salesgirls. She was the type of woman who'd found her signature look early in life and stuck with her pearls and taut bun for the next thirty years. She was a no-nonsense, all-business working woman, but sympathetic when crises befell her girls.

"Please report to Mrs. Braithwaite without delay."

Bullocks Wilshire had been the first store in Los Angeles to feature a private salon where shoppers could view garments on a model. The oval salon was similar to the one Gwendolyn had taken Errol into, but larger, with ample room for a model to turn and twirl across the muted green carpet.

Gwendolyn let herself into the anteroom and found Mrs. Braithwaite checking over a rack of beachwear: swimsuits, a blouse-and-shorts set, several straw hats, and a light cape.

"Ah, Miss Gwendolyn, get into that navy blue suit first. Pair it with the big straw hat and whichever pair of sandals fits you best. You need to be quick about it, the customer is waiting."

Gwendolyn slipped out of her dress and took off her jewelry, leaving on her corset and stockings. "Who is it, do you know?"

"Mrs. O'Roarke." The name meant nothing to Gwendolyn. "After you're done with the swimsuit, put on this sun cape with the green suit, then come out in the shorts and blouse. Don't forget the lace parasol."

Gwendolyn adjusted the broad straw hat Mrs. Braithwaite handed her and slipped into the first pair of footwear that looked her size. She stepped through a dramatic doorway that was topped with a pair of large sculpted scrolls, then paused in the light on the other side for a moment before taking three steps down to the salon's floor. In time to the dainty string waltz piped in over the loudspeaker, she crisscrossed the thick carpeting while Mrs. Braithwaite gave a running commentary about the comfort of the swimsuit's wool blend and its sturdiness against the rigors of lengthy exposure to sun and sea.

As she was making her final turn, Gwendolyn caught a quick glimpse of Mrs. O'Roarke and guessed that she was hovering on the cusp of handsome and matronly. Her starched hair was too uniformly brown to be natural, and her large bosom had a menopausal swell, but she was reasonably slim around the waist and sat on the loveseat with the upright posture of a ballroom dancer. She wore an approving smile but was not looking at the clothes. Instead, her eyes were fixed on Gwendolyn's face.

After two laps around the salon, Gwendolyn retreated into the changing room and switched into the ivy-colored swimsuit and satin-lined sun cape. Gwendolyn wished she had time to study the cape; it was beautifully crafted and was exactly the sort of thing she'd love to have in Chez Gwendolyn.

Out in the showroom, she took a couple of spins to show the cape's fullness, then heard Mrs. O'Roarke ask Mrs. Braithwaite if the model could come closer so she could feel the material. As Gwendolyn approached, she could smell the woman's perfume: gardenia, very expensive.

As the woman reached out to feel the hem, something brushed against the tips of Gwendolyn's fingers. Not soft, like skin, but smooth, more like — there it was again! Paper. She felt the women press something into her palm. The customer shot her a lightning-fast look — *Take it* — before turning to Mrs. Braithwaite. "Very nice," she said. "I'd like to see the after-sun ensemble now, please."

Back in the changing room, Gwendolyn unfolded the note hidden in her hand.

> *I have heard that you might be able to supply me with nylon stockings. I am willing to pay any price. If you can help me, give your chin a little tug and pat down your hair the next time you come out. My telephone number is Crestwood-2636.*

Lester's golden rule filled her ears: Only sell to someone you have a direct connection with.

She thought about how Mary Ford didn't question the three-dollar price tag when Gwendolyn handed over her nylons in the Canteen office. If this Mrs. O'Roarke could afford expensive clothes like these, she could afford three bucks a pop. Maybe even four.

No, no. Don't be greedy. Follow the rule.

She grabbed the parasol and thought about the wartime accommodation shortage, and how the residents of the Garden of Allah had been informed that their rent was going up significantly. It was going to bite into the cache she was socking away.

I'll decide when I go back out there. I need to see her face again.

Gwendolyn made her entrance and flicked open the lace parasol. Smiling blandly at the woman, she drew on her years of experience selling cigars and cigarettes at the Cocoanut Grove to size up this customer in one glance.

The woman returned a prosaic smile. She wore the conservative Chanel suit of a respectable socialite, but her eyes were sharp and etched with knowing. This was not a woman fooled by the silver screen.

Mrs. O'Roarke watched closely as Gwendolyn paraded back and forth, twirling her parasol over one shoulder, then the other. *But how do you know I sell black-market nylons?* This was all so unnerving. She hadn't seen this woman at the Hollywood Canteen, and she certainly wasn't part of the Garden of Allah crowd. *What to do? What to do?*

Gwendolyn started a third stroll past Mrs. O'Roarke when she heard Mrs. Braithwaite say, "Thank you, Miss Gwendolyn. That'll be all."

Gwendolyn returned to the doorway for a final pose. She risked a last-minute peek at the seated woman, whose knowing look had been replaced with a beseeching plea.

You may be a plant by management, she thought. You might even be an undercover cop. But I need to expand my market. This woman and her friends would pay three or four bucks, maybe even five.

Gwendolyn reached up and tugged her chin, then patted her hair before disappearing through the ornate doorway and withdrawing into the anteroom. She tossed the parasol to the side and sat down on the only chair in sight. She pressed her palms to her eyes and wondered what the hell she'd just done.

CHAPTER 15

Jim Taggert's office was spacious enough for a large desk, several brown metal filing cabinets, a bookshelf crammed with literary classics and history textbooks, a square meeting table with four matching chairs, and his own water cooler. But until he stepped into it on the last day of 1942, Marcus had never noticed how daylight filled it like helium in a hot air balloon; it was so bright that it almost hurt his eyes. *Then again*, he figured, *maybe I'm unusually sensitive right now.*

Jim looked up from the script in front of him. "Close the door behind you." He pointed with a freshly sharpened pencil to one of the seats at his conference table. "I've just come from an Oscar powwow with Mayer and Mannix about which flicks we want nominated." He bit into his lower lip for a moment. "*William Tell* is not one of them."

Marcus wasn't surprised. Not after that humiliating scene at the premiere two months ago.

"I went to bat for you," Taggert said, "but they didn't take the hint, or pretended not to."

Marcus smiled grimly. At least the waiting game was over. "Which ones are they going with?"

"*Mrs. Miniver* and *Woman Of The Year.*"

Miniver was an obvious choice — it was MGM's biggest success for 1942. And if the studio wouldn't back its number three grosser, his *William Tell,* Marcus was pleased it was *Woman Of The Year.*

The residents of the Garden of Allah liked to bask in a ray of that picture's glory. The previous summer, screenwriter Garson Kanin had holed up in his villa with his brother Michael, fellow screenwriter Ring Lardner Junior, and Katharine Hepburn, and cranked out the script in five days with the help of typists and food sent in from Chasen's. It cost the studio more than they'd ever paid for an original screenplay, but none of it would have been possible, Gardenites told themselves, if they hadn't restrained from throwing a party for *five straight days* to give the team the peace and quiet it needed.

Marcus got to his feet. "Thanks for letting me know."

"One more thing." Jim pushed an envelope to the edge of his desk. "Looks like it might be your first fan letter."

It didn't happen often, but from time to time the writers received mail, usually from some youngster who spent his small-town summers writing stories that were overly praised by an indulgent teacher. Marcus was the only screenwriter who had been with MGM for more than five years without getting one.

He picked up the envelope and headed for the door. His fingers were on the handle when he stopped. He stared at the return address, aware only of his own shallow breathing.

Jim's voice jolted Marcus. "Something wrong?"

"Did you notice the return address?"

* * *

Marcus filled his glass with whiskey, then propped the envelope against the bottle and stared at it while he sipped. The penmanship was methodical and deliberate. The paper, a very pale shade of pink, was weighty — she'd used the good stuff. The only jarring detail was the postage stamp — a white eagle emblazoned with the patriotic maxim "WIN THE WAR," affixed at a hurried angle.

There was a knock on the door. "Anybody home?"

He opened it to find Kathryn, Gwendolyn, and Alla standing before him. Unlike most New Year's Eves when they'd be dressed to the hilt for a night at Ciro's or the Mocambo, all three were wearing their scruffiest rags.

Kathryn looked him over. "You're not going like that, are you?"

Marcus looked down at his work clothes. "No—I just—something came up."

Gwendolyn peered past him to the letter leaning against his bottle of Four Roses. "Not bad news, I hope."

Marcus ushered the three women inside. "I haven't opened it yet."

Kathryn picked up the envelope and read the return address. "You didn't tell me you wrote to her."

"I didn't." Marcus tinkled the ice in his glass. "I started several letters, but always got stuck."

Alla eased herself onto Marcus' sofa. "May I ask who we are talking about?"

"My sister," Marcus told her. "Doris, the youngest one. She's tracked me down."

For a while last year, Marcus had kept seeing his sister in the faces of strangers. It was almost to the point of hallucination, which, Marcus kept telling himself, was ridiculous because he hadn't seen Doris in nearly fifteen years. She was ten when he slunk out of town on the midnight train without telling her goodbye.

"How come you haven't read it?" Gwendolyn asked.

Marcus plucked Doris' letter out of Kathryn's hand and tapped it against his knuckles. "Chicken, I guess."

"But the night of my party last year," Gwendolyn said, "you told us how much you miss your family."

"And I meant it. But now I'm not so sure I want to dredge up the past."

Alla grabbed his hand, then gently pulled him down on the sofa beside her. She studied him intensely with her violet eyes. "My boy, your sister cared enough to write. The least you can do is read it."

Marcus knew he looked like the Garden of Allah's village idiot for getting what he wanted, then no longer wanting it.

"You want us to clear out?" Kathryn asked. "Come join us at the victory garden planting party afterwards."

Marcus decided he was glad they'd come over. "How's about you all stay while I read it out loud?"

"Or we could do that." She deposited herself on his easy chair.

Marcus threw back what was left in his glass. While the smooth whiskey burned his throat, questions came lurching toward him like a gang of Frankenstein's monsters. Did Doris remember him? Did his parents ever tell her why he left? Did they know she'd written? Were they even alive?

He perched on the edge of the chair and pulled out the letter. It was only one page, and for a moment, he felt vaguely embarrassed. All that angst for a one-page letter?

"Dear Mr. Adler," he read out loud. "Either my name will mean something to you, or you are sitting there thinking, Who is this Doris Adler person and why is she writing to me? A couple of weeks ago, I went to see a movie called *William Tell* and I nearly went kerplunk when the credits came on and there, under 'SCREENWRITER,' was your name. I realize there's probably more than one Marcus Adler in Hollywood, but in case you're the Marcus Adler who was my most favorite brother in the whole wide world—"

Marcus stumbled over the last few words, then broke off altogether. He closed his eyes for a moment. When he opened them again, he looked at Kathryn, Gwendolyn, then Madame. Each of them wore the same tender smile.

" — in case you're the Marcus Adler who was my most favorite brother in the whole wide world, and who disappeared back when I was still a young girl, and who we've never ever heard from, I thought I would take a chance and write to you. If you are my long-lost brother, please write back and tell me how you are. And if you're not, thanks for a terrific movie anyway. You did a great job. Signed, Doris Adler."

He kept his eyes on the paper as he folded it over and reinserted it in its matching envelope. Gwendolyn was the first to speak.

"How old would Doris be now?"

"Twenty-five."

"And her return address, is that the house you grew up in?"

"Nope. Same town, though."

"She signed it Doris Adler," Gwendolyn pointed out. "She's twenty-five, not married, but no longer living at home. Sounds like a working girl to me. I like her!"

"What are you going to do?" Kathryn asked.

Marcus deposited Doris' letter on the coffee table and jumped to his feet. He felt like someone had sucked the air out of the room while he was otherwise occupied. "I'm going to get into my working duds and meet you down at the victory garden."

* * *

Since the night the Garden of Allah opened, parties — large and small, planned and impromptu — had always coalesced around the swimming pool. And it was a good thing, too, because Garden parties usually disintegrated into an unruly mess with at least one or two partygoers falling into the pool, drunk and often only partially dressed.

But since Nazimova started the victory garden a few months back, the parties had shifted to a patch of dirt where all sorts of vegetables sprouted through the earth. The residents, though, saw no reason why planting potatoes or picking peas couldn't be celebrated with a bowl of Dottie Parker's Pickled Party Punch and several trays of canapés. Furthermore, if a planting party should coincide with New Year's Eve, then so much the better. Even the National Victory Garden Institute couldn't argue with that.

When Marcus approached, the setting sun had departed, leaving behind a star-sprinkled sky. Thirty people had already gathered in and around the victory garden, most of them in dungarees or old clothes, kneeling in the dirt planting bulbs of garlic and onions and winter lettuce seeds. At each corner of the garden, someone had set up a table with a hurricane lamp, a bowl of punch, and a bottle of whiskey or bourbon.

A cluster of people standing off to the side burst into laughter. It was Benchley and his sidekick, actor Charlie Butterworth, and Charlie's girl, a knockout named Dusty. They were bent over laughing, something about one of the ingredients in Dottie's Pickled Party Punch. Behind them, Gwendolyn huddled with Bertie.

Marcus watched as Bertie pushed a wad of bills into Gwendolyn's hand. It was the first time he'd witnessed Gwendolyn conducting a deal, and he wondered what Kathryn thought about this whole scheme of Gwennie's. It was odd they hadn't spoken about it yet, and he decided to bring it up the next time they were alone. A little to the side, Marcus noticed Errol slumped in his chair away from the main gathering, staring into his drink.

It had been a hell of a year for him. He'd suffered a mild heart attack during the filming of his latest movie, *Gentleman Jim*. By the time it came out, Errol had been charged with statutory rape and audiences were snickering at his final line of the movie: "I'm no gentleman." It was the third Warners movie in a row to gross more than two million, but he didn't seem to care. Even the formation of a support group called the American Boys' Club for the Defense of Errol Flynn — ABCDEF for short — did little to lift his spirits. He was normally one of the first of the Garden residents to show up at a party and one of the last to leave, but the Errol Flynn slouched in Nazimova's patio chair was not that person.

"Yoohoo!" Nazimova was kneeling in the middle of the garden next to an aluminum watering can. "I could do with a helper here." A significant blotch of dirt matted her hair.

Marcus joined her on the ground and wiped off as much of the dirt as he could. "What do you need me to do?"

"After I bury a bulb, you water it — but not too much."

She pushed at the rolled-up sleeves of her raggedy men's flannel shirt, leaving a trail of mud up each arm. "That was a lovely letter from your sister." Marcus poured some water into the little hole she had just filled in. "It would be a shame if you didn't write her back."

He followed her up the garden another foot. "Who said I wasn't going to write her back?"

She frowned that very Russian frown of hers, managing to look sternly maternal. "You don't know which version of your life you want to share with her, do you? The authentic one or the version approved by the Breen Office."

The Breen Office was the organization tasked with the job of enforcing the Motion Picture Production Code. It was a long list of do-this-but-don't-do-that commandments to which the studios must conform or risk being denied approval for distribution. It ensured that no American movies contained direct references to sex, drugs, nudity, extended kissing, or ridicule of the clergy. Their rules forced the studios to present American life in its sunniest light, regardless of whether that bore any resemblance to reality.

Marcus scooped up a mound of freshly turned earth. He brought it up to his face and inhaled deeply. The smell — so fresh, so raw — reminded him of his family's yard back in McKeesport, of mud-pie summers and leaf-burning autumns.

"I don't want to lie to her," he said. "But how do I explain why I left town so abruptly? She doesn't need to know that our father railroaded me in the middle of the night because he caught me with the mayor's son. Or that I never married because I prefer to be with other men. She'll have a hundred questions and I'll have no answers." He watched as Benchley and Butterworth tried to coax Errol out of his chair, but they were waved away.

Nazimova pointed to the last onion bulb she'd just planted. He watered it, then followed her to seats on the edge of the victory garden where they accepted cups of punch from Alla's lover, Glesca. She was around Marcus' age and possessed a wide-open face and an infectious laugh and could match any Gardenite drink for drink. She and Alla had been together for more than a dozen years now; Marcus liked her a lot.

"Look at him," Alla commanded Marcus.

Errol was on his feet now. David Niven had succeeded where Benchley and his cohorts had failed. Errol and Niven had been notorious rascals, checking in and out of the Garden over the past decade while in between girlfriends, wives, affairs, houses, or contracts. Marcus was surprised to see Niven here now that he was married, but he seemed to have cheered Errol up. Errol was telling an animated story, something about Norway, the setting of his next movie.

"I like Errol," Alla said. "He's handsome, talented, generous, very good-natured. However, he lives his life with too much dissipation. Burning the candle from both of the ends with no thought for tomorrow. No thought for consequences. These accusations he now must face, these are the consequences for a man who confuses love with sex."

Dorothy Parker's punch was mainly vodka, infused with some sort of berry. Blueberry? Blackberry? Marcus wasn't sure. "What does Errol have to do with me?"

Nazimova tipped the rest of her punch into his cup. "You are not like him. You have a deep well of love inside you. You tried to give it to Ramon, but Hugo thwarted it for his own sad reasons. You are a kind, loving person. It would be a criminal shame if you did not share everything you are with your sister."

Marcus could feel a sheen of tears building up. "Even the nance bits?"

She smiled slyly and took his hand in hers. "You are entitled to keep your private life private. You are not entitled to keep a loving sister from her brother. This you may not do."

Her eyes were filled with such playful mischief — *Madame has spoken!* — that Marcus couldn't help but laugh. He wrapped an arm around her shoulder and felt the bones beneath her shirt. *When did she get so thin?*

"I have recently come to a conclusion," she told him. "Life and love are the same thing, and we must say yes to both. Always."

CHAPTER 16

When the Andrews Sisters launched into the opening notes of "Bei Mir Bist Du Schön," Kathryn leaned into Marcus' ear. "At a fundraiser for the USO, do you think maybe they could have opened with a song whose title wasn't in German?"

Marcus snorted into his martini.

"I just think," she continued, "maybe 'Beat Me Daddy, Eight To The Bar' may have been a better choice."

She lit a cigarette and looked around the nightclub Preston Sturges built next to the Chateau Marmont for entertaining his pals. He called it The Players and despite the gentleman's club décor — dark blue-and-brown-checked wallpaper, green velvet drapes, models of sailing ships in glass-framed shadow boxes — it was the sort of joint a guy could take a girl on their first date. Classy enough to impress, but relaxed enough for having a good time without worrying about fancy manners.

When Kathryn's boss came up with the idea to hold a USO fundraiser, she cajoled her downstairs neighbor into soft-soaping his boss to donate The Players for the night. The arrangements were made within a week, and two weeks after that, there they all were. But Kathryn couldn't shake the feeling that there was a hidden agenda at work somewhere in the crowded room.

Earlier that week, Wilkerson's wiry accountant, Ira Chalke, flagged her into his office like he was a member of the French Resistance and she'd just parachuted in behind enemy lines. She'd scoffed when he told her Wilkerson was going to make a fool of himself the night of the fundraiser and that she needed to thwart him, but she stopped scoffing when Chalke confided that Wilkerson's expenses were already at $230,000, and it was only the third week of January. By "expenses," Chalke meant "gambling," and by "make a fool of himself," he meant that the $50,000 check Wilkerson planned to present at the party would bounce. "The USO is a government entity," Chalke reminded Kathryn, "and you don't renege on Uncle Sam — especially not during wartime."

Kathryn spied the gold clock over the nightclub's bar and realized it wouldn't be long before Wilkerson made his speech, which was really just a prelude to the song-and-dance he intended to perform when presenting his whopper of a check. As the Andrews Sisters segued into "I'll Be With You In Apple Blossom Time," Kathryn scanned the room for her boss.

"You've got your working face on," Marcus commented. He'd pushed his glasses onto the top of his head, and now blinked drowsily at her.

"You might want to slow down on the martinis," she replied. "Aren't you supposed to be writing up this clambake for the USO newspaper?"

Frustrated at his being knocked back by the navy for poor eyesight, she'd been glad to see Marcus jump at the chance to do his bit for the war by joining a new organization, the Hollywood Writers Mobilization. Their job was to craft articles, pamphlets, and speeches that would bolster America's efforts with the most flowery and overblown language they could muster. The group's chairman, a Twentieth Century-Fox screenwriter named John Lawson Howard, had tasked Marcus with writing up glowing accounts of the USO's efforts to heighten morale among the military. Kathryn thought much of it bordered on propaganda, but she could see that it satisfied her friend's need to contribute. *And besides,* she told herself during her more jaded moments, *what I do can be considered Hollywood propaganda, so who am I to judge?*

Kathryn watched Lana Turner make a big entrance amid a flurry of white fur. On one side was her new husband, Stephen Crane, and on the other stood Leo Presnell. Kathryn hadn't seen him since that night at the Hollywood Canteen when he'd hinted she might be right for a role in a restructured *Pepsodent Show.* They'd gone ahead with the new format, but brought in a syndicated columnist from New York whose scratchy voice sounded like an out-of-tune violin. She was hardly God's gift to radio.

"Oh, for crying out loud, go find your boss! There's Quentin Luckett," Marcus said, jabbing the air with his Camel. "He's with Trevor Bergin and Melody Hope, and if that blonde with her back to me is Veronica Lake, so much the better. I'll be with them if you need me. Apparently there's another bar thataway." He jabbed the air in the opposite direction. "I'll lay you twenty to one your Mr. Checkbook is in there."

* * *

The bar at The Players was decorated with forest green curtains and crowded with leather sofas arranged for large parties of eight or more. Kathryn walked into it just as Greg Bautzer was leaving. Bautzer was Wilkerson's lawyer, and as suave and savvy as Hollywood lawyers got.

Kathryn nodded hello. "Have you seen my boss?"

Bautzer pointed to a lone figure at the end of the bar.

She drew alongside Wilkerson just as he was throwing back the last belt of his scotch. "Got a moment?"

"Let's talk after I've—"

"I'll walk with you." She held her tongue for a few steps before she pounced. "Listen, boss, would I be right in guessing you plan on making an impressive donation tonight?" He eyed her as he pulled a sheet of paper from inside his tuxedo. "I'm here, as your most devoted staff member, to tell you I think that would be a mistake."

Wilkerson's raised eyebrow told her to get the hell away.

They were in the main room of the club now, skirting the perimeter toward the stage. She made a playful grab for his elbow. "Look at this place! Lana Turner . . . Harry Cohn . . . I'm surprised there's enough room for all these egos. And I'm sure they've come with their checkbooks ready to write out some big fat ones so people like me can report it in tomorrow's edition."

"I'm sure they have, and I'm sure you will." His face had taken on a steely look.

"Let these big egos make their big public donations to the big worthy cause," she said. "You don't need to—"

Wilkerson looked away from her. "I wouldn't let any of my wives tell me what I can and cannot do with my money. What makes you think I'll let you?" He'd never spoken to her so coldly before.

"I'm sorry. You pay me to stick my nose into other people's business. I guess I just assumed—"

"OTHER people's business."

Yeah, and now you pay me twenty percent less to do it. Kathryn wouldn't have minded if the pay cuts were for the war effort, but now she felt like she was helping fund her boss' gambling habit.

Wilkerson sent her a withering sideways glance. "Now if you're done telling me what I ought to be doing, I have a speech to give."

She watched him mount the stage, but couldn't bear to watch her boss put his whole livelihood — not to mention hers — into such dire circumstances. She looked around for an escape.

The south wall of The Players' second floor was an enclosed balcony with waist-to-ceiling windows overlooking Sunset. Kathryn leaned against the glass pane, an unlit cigarette in hand, and watched the daisy chain of red taillights heading west. For ten o'clock on a Saturday night, traffic was light. Gasoline rationing made getting around town easier for those with enough coupons.

She'd never seen her boss so defensive before. He had the desperate look of a bank robber who'd gone too far to turn back. The gun was in the air and everyone was facedown on the floor. She tapped the end of her cigarette against the glass with a steady beat. *He's entitled to detonate his own career — but not mine.*

A roar of applause and exclamations of "Bravo!" surged from the main room onto the balcony. Clearly, Ol' Moneybags had just made his announcement. She puckered up her lips and kissed her career goodbye.

"It's not going to light itself." Leo Presnell held up a gold lighter, his thumb on the trigger.

"Oh, hello." Kathryn tried to cover her embarrassment — *Did he see me do that?* — by holding out her cigarette toward him. "I caught your big entrance with Lana."

He cracked a smile that showed off his teeth, baking-soda white against a Palm Springs tennis tan. "You're the only one who did. When you walk in with Lana Turner, you're rendered invisible." He lit both their cigarettes and pocketed the lighter. Together, they watched the traffic below them. "Last time we talked, I asked if you'd be interested in a slot on *The Pepsodent Show*."

"You were called away to the telephone before I could give you my answer."

"What would it have been?"

"That's a moot point, isn't it?" She kept her eyes on the traffic. "You went out and found what's-her-name from New York."

He groaned. "She was a mistake."

"But only if you want to put her on the radio." She faked a sympathetic shudder. "That voice of hers. Ouch!"

"I won't be making that mistake again."

"But aren't you stuck with her?"

"Fortunately, no. We only signed her to a three-month provisional contract."

"And when is that up?"

"End of this month." The glossy smile was gone now; a slicker version was in its place. Less teeth, more oil. "So? Interested? Available? Should I be speaking with your boss?"

"No!" Kathryn blurted out. That was the last thing she wanted. "I'm quite capable of making my own decisions."

"Glad to hear it. Did I mention the pay is a hundred?"

"Per week?" With an extra hundred bucks in her pocket, Kathryn would barely notice the pay cut she'd been forced to take. A cluster of three couples burst onto the balcony, mid laugh. They lined up along the window overlooking the Strip while one of the men filled their glasses from a magnum of champagne. Kathryn wished she had one of those glasses; she licked her dry lips.

Presnell lowered his face until his mouth was close enough for her to feel his warm breath. "Did you know there is a secret passageway from this place over to the Chateau Marmont?"

"No, I did not." *I should have, though*. Her closed-lipped mother was the head telephone operator at the Marmont.

"Sturges had it built so his guests could come and go without prying public eyes."

"How very cloak-and-dagger of him."

"I was thinking we might use it. I booked a suite over there."

As Presnell's meaning sank in, Kathryn pulled back, looking at him from the corner of her eyes. She'd have found his knowing smile attractive in a different set of circumstances.

"We're both adults, aren't we?" he said. "Unattached. Capable of making our own decisions."

It was the way he threw her own words up at her that made Kathryn's stomach lurch. She wanted to laugh out loud. *First Marcus, and now me? Since when does the casting couch extend to screenwriters and columnists?*

For a fleeting moment, Kathryn might have said yes. After all, this Presnell guy was really quite debonair in a way that held a considerable measure of appeal. He certainly looked like he knew his way around a hotel bed. She told herself she ought to be flattered—and hell, a hundred bucks was a hundred bucks. But then she thought of Marcus, what he'd been through with *William Tell* and that unctuous casting director, Floyd Forrester, and how he had to deal with a reputation he hadn't earned. Suddenly, Mr. Pepsodent didn't look quite so appealing.

"Thank you for the light." She left him standing in his expensive tux and slick smile and went back inside.

Marcus was sitting by himself at their table nursing a fresh drink. "What happened to Veronica Lake?"

"They had some Paramount soirée to go to. Billy Wilder's birthday or something."

She dropped into her seat and stole a mouthful of his martini. "Did you know there's a secret tunnel between here and the Marmont?"

"No. Is that where you've been?"

"I just found out about it. I'm surprised my mother never mentioned it."

"There are a lot of things your mother never mentioned." He turned toward the doorway out to the balcony to see what Kathryn was eyeing. "What is it?"

"Tell me. Were you ever tempted to say yes to that guy from casting?"

Marcus nearly choked on his martini. "You wouldn't be asking me that if you met him. Why? Jesus, don't tell me Floyd Forrester's out there on the balcony!"

"No, but I suspect a Floyd Forrester by any other name is still a Floyd Forrester."

CHAPTER 17

Charles Laughton couldn't croon like Bing Crosby or dance like Fred Astaire, nor could he clown like Donald O'Connor, but he wanted desperately to entertain the servicemen at the Hollywood Canteen. "How about I recite the Gettysburg Address?"

Bette doubted it was enough to hold the attention of the Canteen's raucous crowd, but she hadn't counted on Laughton's ability to fill a room with the majesty of his voice. Every time he took the stage and recited Lincoln's speech, the attention of three hundred servicemen turned to him, and him alone. He never failed to bring down the house.

By the beginning of 1943, Gwendolyn had heard Laughton perform it enough times to know when to slip her shoes back on.

She wasn't supposed to take them off at all. On their first night, the volunteers were handed a copy of the *Canteen Hostess Rulebook*. None of the rules were unreasonable, and all were geared toward leaving the servicemen with a perfect memory of an unforgettable night; pretty girls without their shoes on was not what management had in mind.

But her shoes — black leather pumps with a Cuban heel — were brand new, and after two uninterrupted hours of dancing were no longer as comfy as they'd been at the May Company shoe department. She nudged the hostess next to her, a petite redhead from Paramount Gwendolyn thought was cute enough to be on camera instead of stuck in the typing pool.

"This is our shoe cue."

The redhead ducked behind Gwendolyn and reshod her swollen feet. "I'm happy to dance to dawn for these boys," she said, "but gosh, oh my, it'd be easier on the tootsies if we could get decent nylons. I suppose you get yours at Bullocks?"

Gwendolyn had three pairs of stockings in her purse, but she'd just met this girl and Gwendolyn couldn't remember her name. Arlene? Doreen? Maureen? *You're not always going to be as lucky as you were with Mrs. O'Roarke.*

It turned out the customer who'd handed Gwendolyn that note was married to Clem O'Roarke, head of security at Warners, which meant she wasn't breaking Lester's golden rule: *Never sell to someone you can't track down.* It also didn't hurt that Mrs. O'Roarke ordered twelve pairs at four dollars each without balking at the price tag. Then Mrs. O'Roarke started volunteering at the Canteen, making things as convenient as they were lucrative.

When Gwendolyn declared to Kathryn that making money this way was so easy it was criminal, Kathryn reminded her that it *was* criminal. If it had been tougher to pull off, Gwendolyn might not have stayed in business, but a 325% markup was too hard to walk away from.

Gwendolyn nodded to Arlene-Doreen-Maureen and let her think she got her nylons at work. Technically, it was true — she just didn't *buy* them there.

When the house band jumped into a lively version of "He's 1-A In The Army And He's A-1 In My Heart," Gwendolyn hunted through the throng. She was still getting used to the integrated crowd at the Canteen. On the day it opened, Bette declared that if colored men were good enough to fight for Uncle Sam, they were certainly welcome at the Hollywood Canteen—no separate doors, no separate bathrooms or drinking fountains. It was the first time in Los Angeles that a prominent gathering spot had declared a policy of complete racial integration. It caused a small wave at the time, but people had come to accept it as part of the Canteen's charm.

Normally, the boys weren't shy to ask hostesses for a dance—they knew they'd never be refused. But some of them hung back, so Gwendolyn made a point of seeking out the hesitant ones. She soon spotted one. He was leaning against the far wall underneath "Cowboy Heaven"—a mural painted by volunteers from the Motion Picture Illustrators Guild to make the rural lads feel more at home. This guy had the sunburned face of someone who's spent most of his life pushing a plow. He had a bad case of the fidgets, alternately tucking his hands in his pockets and hooking them in his underarms. His eyes started to bulge as she approached.

"This is a heck of a good song to dance to," she pointed out. "How's about you and me go for a spin?"

The Canteen Hostess Rulebook encouraged the girls to contribute to the festive atmosphere by dressing colorfully. Hostess rule #6: Feel free to wear bright colors as an antidote to the drab grays and browns of their day-to-day military life. Gwendolyn had sewn an outfit especially for her nights at the Canteen—bright yellow with a snugly sashed waist and a full skirt made for spins. As an extra bonus, the décolletage put her bust on discreet but full display.

This kid couldn't have been more than twenty, and was kind of cute in his olive green private uniform. The pants were a touch too short and the sleeves of his pressed shirt a little too long, but she told him it suited him well. He nodded his thanks and took her in his arms with surprising confidence and merged them into the dance floor traffic. He picked up the beat of the music quickly.

"What's your name, Private?"

His smile was quietly unassuming. "Pete."

"You're hot stuff when it comes to this dance floor business."

"I come from a real big family and there ain't much to do at night. Mama plays the fiddle, and Uncle Jack, he's pretty good on the banjo. The rest of us dance."

His eyes took on a distant look, so she let the conversation drop. She'd learned when to talk and when to just give a serviceman the pleasure of holding a woman in his arms.

After a couple of laps around the dance floor, she felt his grip tighten. She saw a hand tap Pete on the shoulder. It was a tow-headed sailor in the same black and gold seaman's uniform she'd seen Monty wear.

"Sorry, sailor," she told the guy, "there's no cutting in unless it's a tag dance."

Pete let her go. "That's okay. It's been a pleasure, miss."

Before Gwendolyn could say anything, Pete melted into the churning crowd. She turned to the sailor. When she opened her arms to allow him to scoop her up, she saw that he had no left hand.

Hostess rule #9: Don't talk about a guy's injuries. Engage in conversation, but stick to cheery topics like where they're from and what is his mother's best dish. But this was the first time Gwendolyn had danced with an amputee, and she hated herself for staring at his arm as long as she did.

"Battle of Midway," he said matter-of-factly. He picked up the rhythm and propelled them on their way.

"What's your name?"

"Fitzy." She could see the spray of freckles across his face now, speckled all the way to each ear. "I'm sorry I had to barge in like that, but I got me a bus to catch. Leaves at midnight." Gwendolyn glanced at her watch; it was ten thirty. "I got married just before I shipped out. I haven't seen my wife in two years and she'll be picking me up at the bus depot tomorrow morning."

"You must be looking forward to seeing her."

"Yes and no. I ain't told her about my injury. Couldn't work up the nerve."

"I see." Hostess rule #4: Let the guy talk as much as he wants to or needs to. Your job is to listen.

"It's going to come as a shock to her. So I got to figuring if maybe I could bring her back something she'd appreciate, then maybe it'd soften the blow."

"That's very considerate of you, Fitzy." Hostess rule #2: Use his name as often as you can.

"That's when I heard about you."

Gwendolyn's spine stiffened. "What do you mean?"

Fitzy leaned in. She could smell antiseptic ointment. "You're the nylons girl, right? The one with the black-market nylons for sale." Gwendolyn looked across the dance floor to the snack bar where Mrs. O'Roarke was setting out a tray of coconut cake.

"One of the orderlies at the military hospital told me about you. He said, 'Keep an eye out for the knockout in the yellow dress.'"

Gwendolyn did her level best to keep a low profile when selling her stockings. Always to someone she knew, always when nobody else was around, always asked her customers to keep it to themselves. *Some orderly is telling sailors about me?*

"Can you help a guy out?" Fitzy pushed. "I gotta leave here in a few minutes so as I don't miss my bus."

It wasn't hard for Gwendolyn to picture the small-town sweetheart this guy left behind. She was probably a Betsy or a Wanda and right this very moment was probably pressing her favorite outfit in excited anticipation of greeting her war-hero husband at the depot. She pictured Fitzy stepping off the Greyhound bus, his face filled with the fear of what her reaction was going to be.

"Give me five minutes," she whispered into his ear. "Go out the front, turn right and when you get to the parking lot, turn right again. You'll see a door marked *Stage Entrance*. Walk past it so you're not in the light. This is completely against the rules, so don't do anything to attract attention."

Although Hostess Rule #19 forbade fraternization with the servicemen outside the Canteen, the girls tended to look upon it more as a guideline than a rule. Wartime was different. The certainty of a future everyone had taken for granted during peacetime had given way to a feeling that nothing could be counted on anymore. Everyone had thought the Battle of Midway was as bad as things could get, but then Guadalcanal happened and they lost more than seven thousand men. People were learning that "here and now" was all anybody really had.

A couple of people lingered in the pool of light outside the stage door. Gwendolyn could make out a few silhouettes idling in the shadows, not all of them alone.

"Pssst! Over here!"

Gwendolyn joined Fitzy in the darkness and opened her purse. She pulled out the three pairs she had and handed them over.

"How much?"

"I want you to have them, Fitzy."

The guy withdrew his hand. "I ain't no charity case."

"I wouldn't disrespect you like that," she insisted. "These are a gift. From me to — what's your wife's name?"

"Valerie." Emotion choked his voice to a whisper.

"Tell Valerie I hope she wears these the first time you take her out dancing."

"I don't know that we'll—"

"She'll be the envy of every girl in the place. You mark my words, Fitzy."

He dropped his head down onto his chest and tried to steady himself with a deep breath. Had he not done that, Gwendolyn wouldn't have noticed Mr. Dewberry walking out of the Canteen's back door. He'd mentioned to her once or twice about volunteering, but she wasn't aware he'd started. He was heading right for her.

She grabbed Fitzy by the wrist and pulled him toward her, sandwiching the stockings between them. She managed to squeeze out "Follow my lead" before pivoting him around so that he stood between her and Dewberry as he walked past. She pulled him closer and planted her lips to his. She could taste the bologna from the sandwiches Hedy Lamarr had been handing out all night.

She listened to Dewberry's footsteps on the gravel and heard them stop for a moment before continuing. A car door creaked open, then slammed shut. An engine purred to life, then suddenly they were drenched in the blinding glow of his headlights.

* * *

When Gwendolyn arrived at work the following morning, she was still cringing at how close she'd come to being caught by her boss, black-market stockings in hand and illicitly smooching a serviceman. How Dewberry had failed to see her in her bright yellow dress was a mystery.

St. Valentine's Day was less than two weeks off, and the regulars were starting to gather at the lingerie counter like locusts. *Sugar daddy* seemed a smidgen too vulgar a term for these gents, who took great care to select precisely the right expensive gifts for their mistresses and chorine girlfriends; Gwendolyn liked to call them sweetiepies.

She was just finishing up with one of the newest members of the sweetiepies club—this one wore an enormous handlebar moustache like a medal of honor and certainly knew his silks and satins—when Dewberry appeared. His indecipherable smile sent her into a dry-throated panic when he asked her to follow him to his office. She'd never been in his inner sanctum. The room was painted a startling shade of teal and lit by sunshine streaming through tall windows that overlooked Wilshire. By the time Gwendolyn sat down in front of Dewberry's desk, she'd promised to give up this whole black-market thing. It wasn't worth the strain on her nerves.

I'm going to have to find some other way to finance my store.

"It's about your job," he started. Gwendolyn clenched her hands together. "I always thought Delores was irreplaceable, but you've proven me wrong." Gwendolyn loosened her fists, but just a fraction. "You've probably noticed that we've lost more staff lately. All those war factories offering wages we cannot compete with. So management has decided to change things up a little, and we're creating supervisors for each department. It will involve more work, but in return, these supervisors will get a bigger staff discount, a say in hiring and firing, first choice of floor samples sold at a steep reduction, and free meals in the Tea Room."

Gwendolyn unfolded her fingers and pressed her palms into her lap.

"Miss Brick, I'd like to offer you the position of supervisor of perfume, lingerie, gloves, and scarves."

"Me?" The word popped out an embarrassing squeak.

"I saw you volunteering at the Canteen last night."

"You saw me there?"

His smile was indulgent like a favorite uncle. "You're doing your bit for the war; I was terribly impressed."

Gwendolyn stared at Dewberry while he stared at her. For several moments, neither one spoke a word, until Dewberry, frowning slightly, said, "Miss Gwendolyn, would you like me to fetch some water? You look like you're about to faint."

CHAPTER 18

The air in the courtroom corridor grew humid with apprehension. Kathryn started to fan herself with her notepad. "I never knew how interminable this waiting could be."

Gwendolyn nodded. "Imagine how Errol feels."

Through the whole of January 1943, Errol Flynn had been fighting for his freedom against three counts of statutory rape.

At the trial's outset, Kathryn wondered where her loyalties would lie. In spite of his rakish ways, she genuinely liked Errol and suspected that he — and not his pouting accusers — was the real victim in this mess. She put a lot of stock in the rumors that some of LA's less-than-sterling politicians had trumped up this dog-and-pony show as a warning to uncooperative studio heads whose kickbacks were less than lucrative. Kathryn didn't believe a star of Errol's stature would actually be convicted; if he was found guilty, the axis of power would tilt away from the studios, and nobody knew what that version of Hollywood might look like.

On the other hand, the allegations that Errol had drugged and raped these girls sounded like a harsh version of her mother's tale. Kathryn was far from convinced that Francine had told her the whole story of her conception — *Opium, indeed!* — and as Errol's trial ground on, she became less convinced that the girls' testimony bore anymore resemblance to reality than her mother's did.

Kathryn and Errol had been at a working bee last spring when he announced to a round of good-natured laughter, "I like my whiskey old and my women young!" Only a wolf as charming as he could get away with that, but it wasn't quite as droll in the harsh light of the superior court as it had sounded at a boozy party.

Kathryn's eyes drifted over to a banner, five feet across and three tall, with *ABCDEF* in big blue letters over *American Boys' Club for the Defense of Errol Flynn*. Errol smiled every time he caught sight of it.

"The jury foreman, Mrs. Anderson," Gwendolyn said without preamble, "she looks a lot like my biggest customer. I keep wondering if they're sisters or cousins."

Gwendolyn rarely talked about her side business. The crowd around them had spread along the length of the hallway, so Kathryn snatched the opportunity. "You're being careful, right? No unnecessary chances? You never did figure out how that one-armed sailor found out about you."

Gwendolyn nodded. "You know how much I've got stashed away? Nearly two thousand."

Kathryn figured Gwendolyn had made a few hundred bucks by now, but two grand? She wasn't sure what two thousand dollars looked like when stacked together, but she couldn't imagine she'd miss it sitting around their villa. "Where is all this loot?"

Gwendolyn leaned her head on Kathryn's shoulder. "You know how Bertie's living in Alla's old bedroom?"

"The room with the hidden safe?"

"Uh-huh."

"Just promise me you won't do anything nutty—"

"In the whole time you've known me, have you seen me do anything nutty?" Gwendolyn paused for a moment, then added, "With my money, I mean."

"No, of course not," Kathryn conceded. "It's just that—oh, don't listen to me. I need to be reminded that not everybody's like my pea-brained boss."

Wilkerson's plan to finance his $50,000 pledge to the USO fundraiser was to win it back at David Selznick's poker game the following weekend. According to Ira, he came close to pulling it off, getting as high as $43,000 before blowing it all—and then lost another $71,000 in a scramble to recoup. This morning, before she left for the courtroom, Ira pulled her into his office and told her that some recent stock-market gambles had also gone bad, and that his calculations put Wilkerson's debt at over half a million dollars. She thought about Presnell and his hundred bucks a week and his suite at the Marmont, and wondered for the five hundredth time whether she'd made the right call. Was it too late to change her mind?

Gwendolyn pointed to the bailiff at the door as the mob crowded back into the courtroom with sober expectation hovering like a thundercloud. Errol was already seated at the defendant's table next to his hotshot lawyer, Jerry Giesler.

A feverish voice several rows behind Kathryn called out, "We believe in you, Errol!" Errol turned around and forced a smile. He looked meticulously dapper in his dark blue suit, white shirt, and finely checkered tie, but his face was pale as a pallbearer's.

The bailiff asked everyone to rise as Judge Leslie Still—as sober and serious a judge as you'd find in any movie—entered the chamber and asked that the jury be shown in. One by one, nine women and three men filed into the room and took their seats.

"Mrs. Anderson," the judge said, "have you reached a verdict?"

Ruby Anderson was a stout woman who looked like she hadn't changed her makeup since Pola Negri was a star. "We have, Your Honor." She handed a slip of paper to a bailiff, who passed it to the judge.

Judge Still read the three verdicts and then handed them to the court clerk. "Read the verdicts, Mr. Averre."

As the clerk got to his feet, the weight of anticipation pressed the air. Kathryn focused on Errol's back; she watched his shoulders inch up. Averre read the words on the paper in his hand. "Not guilty, not guilty, not guilty."

The bubble of tension ruptured over the audience and applause filled the room. Someone shouted, "We knew you were innocent!," then someone else, "Justice is served!," but Errol didn't appear to hear them. He dashed over to Mrs. Anderson to shake her hand, then worked his way down the line of jurors.

Kathryn waved, trying to attract Errol's attention. Wilkerson had told her not to return to the office without "some sort of boffo quote. He's Errol Flynn—shouldn't be too hard." But Errol was too distracted by the racket around him. He nodded to Giesler and they plunged into the roiling sea of outstretched hands and press photographers' flashing bulbs.

Kathryn and Gwendolyn let themselves be swept up in the undertow that led to the sidewalk outside the courthouse, where dozens of people had gathered. A roar went up as Errol emerged into the cool February sunshine. A couple of reporters prevailed on him to say something.

Errol pushed back his hat and flashed his million-dollar smile. "Gosh!" he exclaimed. "I didn't become an American citizen for nothing." Like most good actors, he knew when to pause for effect. "The fair play I have received in this trial proves the value of my American citizenship. I want to thank all of those who stood by me."

The *ABCDEF* banner shot up over the head of the mob and Errol saluted it.

"ERROL!" Kathryn called. "OVER HERE!" She watched helplessly as Giesler hustled him into a Packard, which quickly merged into traffic on Grand Avenue.

Kathryn jammed her hat onto her head and considered the journalistic integrity of making up a Flynnian quote.

"Kathryn Massey?"

One of the bailiffs, a hairy-knuckled bear of a guy, handed her a note written on the back of an envelope: *I'm throwing a party to celebrate. My place – 7740 Mulholland. Any time after 9 P.M.*

* * *

Free from his rollercoaster marriage to Lili Damita, Errol had bought a parcel of land on Mulholland Drive and built a five-bedroom house he dubbed Mulholland Farm. The parties there were notorious and fueled rumors of secret passageways, spy holes, and two-way mirrors.

Gas rationing had made finding a taxi tougher and tougher, and it was well after ten o'clock before Kathryn and Gwendolyn pressed the bell at Errol's gate. The seven-foot iron gate slid to the left, revealing a gravel driveway that meandered to the right. They followed it up to the sprawling house's front door. Gwendolyn pressed her ear to it.

"I don't hear anything. He did mean tonight, didn't he?"

Kathryn pulled out Errol's note. "It doesn't specifically say."

The white door swung open to reveal Errol in a Hawaiian shirt scattered with yellow pineapples, and a pair of unpressed khaki trousers. He had the distracted gaze of a guy who'd started drinking early.

"Someone came!" He raised his hands, forgetting that one held a fresh martini. A couple of olives sloshed out of the glass and onto the brick steps.

The place was rustic, with lots of wood and exposed beams. Several rooms away, a radio was playing Dizzy Gillespie on trumpet, but it was the only sound in the place.

They followed Errol into a long, wide living room. At one end stood a buffet table crammed with food: oysters, shrimp, celery stuffed with crab, Swedish meatballs. Next to that, a bar was filled with several ration books' worth of booze. At the other end, tall windows looked onto a swimming pool. In the middle was a fireplace, and over the mantle hung a banner with the word CONGRATS spelled out in red slashes of paint.

"Made that myself," Errol commented. "Waste of time, as it turns out."

"It was so hard to get a taxi, I never thought we'd be the first to arrive," Kathryn said.

He held the corner of the banner between his fingers, but didn't yank it off the wall. "Ever had a recurring nightmare?" His eyes were fixed on the drips of blood-red paint. "I dream that I give a party and nobody comes. I sit in an empty room. Just me and the food, booze, music, all waiting for a bunch of people who never show up." He let go of the banner and draped an arm around each girl's shoulder. Kathryn noticed a dab of shaving cream in his ear. "I thought my worst nightmare had come true tonight." He pulled them closer. "I appreciate you showing up. You gals are the best."

Gwendolyn unhooked herself from Errol's arm. "There could be any number of reasons why people aren't here yet."

Kathryn followed suit. "This place isn't easy to find — maybe some of them got lost. Or have another place to go first — you did spring this party at the last minute."

His eyes, usually so full of mischief and confidence, were heavy-lidded and sour with resentment. "My life has been one shortsighted decision after another, and now it's caught up with me. I've got no one to blame but myself."

"Or," Kathryn chose her words carefully, "maybe everybody's just a little bit late."

He turned toward the bar, but turned back again, his eyes locked on Kathryn. "You're always first with the dirt around town. Give it to me straight," he commanded her. "Am I on the outs with Hollywood now? Is that why nobody showed up? I pushed my luck just that little bit too far, didn't I? And no one wants to be seen with me. That's it, right?"

Kathryn wondered if Errol was aware that more than just his personal freedom had been at stake in this trial. A guilty verdict would have loosened a thread that could have unraveled the movie moguls' control over this town, its politicians, and its judicial system. His not-guilty verdict was a close call for everyone with an interest in keeping the status quo. Maybe they'd stayed home to wipe the sweat from their brows.

"I don't believe for a minute we're the only people who'll show up," Kathryn announced. "You're Errol Flynn, for crying out loud. And if we're it, then screw 'em. Personally, I'd love a drink. One of those martinis would be great, but only if you can haul yourself out of your pity pool long enough to fix one for me, Mister I Didn't Get Sent To Jail For Ten Years."

She was relieved to see a roguish smile breaking through. As he crossed over to the bar, Kathryn told him that she couldn't go to work the next day empty-handed, and perhaps while they waited for the others to arrive, they could brainstorm a memorable quote for her article.

They sat on his sofa and spent the next hour getting tipsy on martinis—even Gwendolyn indulged—and bandied around phrases like "triumph of the American justice system" and "opportunistic moneygrubbers" while leaving unsaid the truth about why he'd had to endure such a high-stakes game of Chicken.

As ten thirty became eleven and eleven drifted toward midnight, the house slipped deeper into darkness, and Flynn grew more and more sullen. The slow recognition that nobody was going to show up ground the conversation into the carpet.

Kathryn cast around for a diversion. "You must have a hell of a view from the pool."

He escorted them outside, but it was barely worth the effort. With wartime dim-out regulations, the view was reduced to the odd pinprick of light between hefty blots of gloom. They fell into another silence until Errol piped up. "Say, whatever happened to Leo Presnell? Did he ever come across with an offer on *The Pepsodent Show*?"

Gwendolyn let out a martini'd giggle. "He sure came across with something."

"Oh, like that, was it?" Errol asked with a chuckle. "I always figured Presnell as being a member of the club."

"What club?" Kathryn asked.

"The type whose membership is prone to making decisions using a part of his body other than his brain."

Like my boss, Kathryn thought. Whatever he was using to make decisions, it sure wasn't his head. Anybody who could get himself into so much debt was a fool. "The Idiot Club?"

She felt her face burn in the moonlight as Flynn stared at her, his mouth hanging open. She scrambled to piece together a hasty apology; after what he'd been through, he didn't deserve a crack like that. But before she could muster a word, Errol drew in a sharp breath and burst into laughter. It was a belly laugh, sourced from somewhere deep inside, and erupted at such a force that he needed to lean on his diving board for support. It was a while before he regained control.

"I needed that more than you could possibly know." He kissed Kathryn on the cheek. "It's time to refreshen these drinks. Won't be long."

Gwendolyn declared she needed to find one of the four bathrooms Errol had boasted about, and followed him inside.

The image of Presnell's barber-shop-shaved, Palm-Springs-tanned face conjured itself in the dark sky above Kathryn. Presnell hadn't set a deadline, but it had been a couple of weeks and she guessed the offer was dead in the water by now. As flattering as it was, it wasn't like she'd ever intended to take him up on it. She went to finish off her martini but found the glass dry.

There's got to be a better way of getting what I want.

She wrapped her arms around herself for warmth against the winter wind blowing up the walls of the canyon below. She contemplated the pockets of inky shadow blotting the landscape below, then headed back inside.

CHAPTER 19

The tombstone read:

HERE LIES BILLY THE KID

KILLED BY PAT GARRETT

JULY 13, 1881

The image gave way to a vista of brush-dotted plains that led to hills scrubbed by clouds sweeping across a New Mexico sky.

As the landscape faded and the closing credits appeared, the lights in George Cukor's private screening room flickered on.

The first man in the room to speak was Adrian, MGM's most prominent costume designer. "I was expecting to see more of her tits."

"With all that fuss over the poster, you'd think that movie was wall-to-wall knockers," Marcus said.

"Was it just me," Cukor declared, "or would the relationship between Billy the Kid and Doc Holliday be more at home among this gathering?"

Taggert got to his feet and stretched. "If I were a cynical man, I'd bet that Hughes' PR stunt was just propaganda designed to camouflage the fact that he was really filming the first homo western."

The group headed into Cukor's living room, a large space decorated in shades of apricot: pale for the thick carpet, medium for the wallpaper and lampshades, and a darker tone for the upholstery. Along one wall stood a mahogany sideboard upon which George's houseboy had set out a late supper.

Donnie Stewart was a screenwriter who lived at the Garden of Allah and had written the recent Hepburn-Tracy reteaming, *Keeper Of The Flame*, which George had directed. "You've got to hand it to Hughes," Donnie said while loading cold cuts, crackers, and olives onto his plate. "I doubt there's anyone in America who hasn't heard of *The Outlaw*. I hear he's maniacal for detail."

Taggert grunted. "One of the guys at the Breen Office told me Hughes fought them for a month over a seven-second cut they demanded. And after all that, he's only going to let *The Outlaw* run for a month or two in San Francisco before he pulls it out of circulation."

Sydney Guilaroff, a lanky Brit who was the king wizard of hair at MGM, nearly dropped his plate. "He's what?"

"They've given up trying to figure what's going on in Hughes' head."

It was nice to be around George again. Marcus hadn't seen him since he joined the army. Naturally, George wasn't sent to an active front, but was placed in their filmmaking department. He'd recently completed a short film for the Army Signal Corps called *Resistance And Ohm's Law*. He assured the group it was every bit as dull as it sounded, but he was happy to be contributing to the war effort.

When George got to Taggert's glass, he said, "That guy at the Breen Office. His name wasn't Trenton, was it?"

"Oliver Trenton. You know him?"

George took a seat on one of the tapestry-covered Louis XV chairs and sipped his wine. "We tangled over *Her Cardboard Lover.*"

The movie was such a bomb that it prompted Norma Shearer to announce her retirement, and George had been tempted to follow suit. His previous movie, *Two-Faced Woman* with Garbo, had also flopped, and his next effort, *Keeper Of The Flame*, hadn't been the smash he'd hoped for. All in all, it was a difficult time for him. Marcus could relate.

Marcus had been consigned to the backwaters, too, even after penning a big success for MGM last year. He'd worked on some A-list projects like the new Garland-Rooney picture, *Girl Crazy*, but only to sharpen somebody else's dialogue. Once was bad enough, but he had to do it again for *Lassie Come Home* and *DuBarry Was A Lady*.

When he pitched a couple of ideas—one about the Wright Brothers' flight of the Kitty Hawk, and another about the American doughboys of the Great War—both were rejected. He tried again with an original love story inspired by a drawing of Londoners taking refuge in a tube station, certain that Mayer would go for it, and was shocked when it got nixed.

He couldn't shake the feeling that this stonewalling was connected with Edwin Marr's rabid accusations in front of MGM's executives and marquee names. But it wasn't like he could waltz into Mayer's office and demand an explanation, so Marcus resigned himself to hammering away at every halfway decent idea until he came up with such a sure-fire hit that Mayer was forced to forget Marr's accusations.

"Marcus," George said, his mouth quivering in uncharacteristic hesitation, "there is something I must share with you."

Marcus' eyes jumped around the room, but each face they landed on was blank. "And what's that?"

"I felt I should be the one to tell Mayer I was joining the army, so I went to see him. I wasn't in the chair five seconds before I realized he thought I was there to discuss my flops. I felt like I was starting to fight for my career, but then he said to me, 'Just be glad I didn't get you to direct *William Tell*.'"

Marcus tightened his grip around his wine glass. "But it was a huge hit."

George nodded. "I told him it was a very fine picture which added significantly to the prestige of the studio. He looked at me with those beady black eyes of his and said, 'Once the pinko bits were taken out.'"

"What?" Taggert jeered. "I read that script half a dozen times myself. There weren't any Communist—"

"Apparently there was a scene where William Tell makes a big speech. 'Today it is him with his bow and arrow, but tomorrow it will be the cobbler with his hammer; the day after that, the blacksmith with his furnace.' He said Edwin Marr had been to see him and told him you were responsible for Hugo's death and 'What else could anybody expect from a leftist pinko Communist sympathizer like Marcus Adler?'"

"Excuse me, but since when is being a member of the Communist Party a crime?" Sydney demanded. "Personally, I don't adhere to Communist political theory—I'm a capitalist through and through—but last time I looked, this is America, and in America we're allowed to believe whatever we want to believe."

"I've got five words for you," Taggert said. "House Committee on Un-American Activities."

"What have they got to do with anything?" Sydney asked. "The HUAC investigates citizens with Nazi ties, not pinkos."

"That's where it started," Hoppy joined in, "but then they decided to probe the Federal Theater Project when someone whispered in their ear that it was overrun with Communists.

In their bird-brained minds, it's a short hop from thinking if the FTP is overrun with Commies, then Hollywood probably is, too. Remember that thing with Humphrey Bogart and Jimmy Cagney?"

The summer before Pearl Harbor, some publicity-seeking member of the local Communist Party appeared before the HUAC's Dies Committee, purporting to crusade against subversives in the government. He stated publicly that Bogart, Cagney, and Fredric March attended secret meetings in Malibu where they gathered to read the doctrines of Karl Marx. His testimony landed all three actors in scalding hot water, and they had to scramble to extricate themselves from controversy. It was a hotly contested issue at the time, and the memory caused a reflective silence to settle on the gathering.

"Mayer thinks I'm some sort of un-American pinko?" Marcus started feeling overheated. "It's bad enough these days that I'm not in uniform."

"So then I thought," George continued, "Mayer knows that Edwin Marr's a broken-down old has-been, and nothing he says is worth listening to, and I said as much to L.B." He grimaced. "But timing is everything. The same day Edwin got into Mayer's ear, the script for *William Tell* returned from the Breen Office with several notes where they said the story reflected 'un-American principles.'"

"Kind of ironic," Hoppy commented, "considering he's from Minsk."

Marcus turned to Taggert. "Did you know about this?"

"I didn't know about the conversation with Edwin Marr. All I saw were Trenton's notes attached to the script and Mayer's cuts. I didn't say anything because you were fixing *Girl Crazy*. It was falling behind schedule, and I needed to keep you focused."

The ugly scene Marcus had endured that night at the Carthay Circle started to make more sense. Marcus wondered where that script was now, and if he dared ask Jim for it. He'd be opening a can of slimy, noxious worms for a movie that was over and done with, but Edwin Marr was someone he needed to take seriously.

* * *

A frigid wind blew down Western Avenue from Griffith Park. Marcus tried to ignore the matronly woman standing at the bus stop. Without looking at her, he could feel her scowl. He hated getting that look, so accusing, so judgmental: *Why aren't you in the armed forces? What's wrong with you?*

He took off his glasses and polished them with his handkerchief. I'm patriotic enough to join the Hollywood Writers Mobilization. Nothing's wrong with me. I probably wrote the speech that inspired you to buy ten more dollars' worth of war bonds.

It had taken some cajoling, but Marcus had convinced Taggert to dig out the Breen Office report on *William Tell*. He couldn't believe the notes in the margins.

UNAMERICAN INFLUENCES

UNPATRIOTIC STANCE

UNACCEPTABLE STATEMENT UNDERMINING AMERICAN VALUES

Ordinarily, Marcus would have passed it around the Garden of Allah and laughed it off over manhattans. But the timing of its arrival on Mayer's desk got him brooding about this Oliver Trenton guy. Had Marcus done something to him and now he was exacting his revenge by sabotaging Marcus' best chance at an Oscar nomination? Was he in cahoots with Edwin Marr?

He lifted his jacket collar against the wind. He knew he was breaking every rule in the book, but he was angry enough to punch a wall. Marcus had managed to wrestle a description of Trenton out of Taggert, and he was fully prepared to have it out with him — damn the consequences.

A minute after six, a huddle of conservatively dressed office workers exited the corner building, but none of them remotely fit Taggert's description. Marcus jammed his hands into his pockets for warmth and leaned against a telephone pole for shelter from the gusts.

"He looks like the kind of guy who has the neatest desk you ever saw and always cleans the peanut butter off his knife before he eats his sandwich," was how Taggert described his prey. "About your height, about your age, with a clipped Ronald Colman moustache."

Someone fitting that description exited the front doors and headed along Hollywood Boulevard. Marcus stepped in Trenton's path before he could second-guess himself. "Oliver Trenton?"

The man looked up as though he'd been expecting Marcus. "That's right."

"I'd like to have a word with you. My name is Adler."

"I know."

Marcus had been counting on the element of surprise, but Trenton's acknowledgment slackened his sails. Taggert was right: the guy in front of him did look like he had the neatest desk in the office. His face was composed of sharp-edged planes, as though he'd escaped from an old German expressionist film.

"It's about a picture I wrote," Marcus said.

"Could we get out of this wind, perhaps?" Trenton led Marcus into the doorway of a closed shoe store. "*William Tell*, right?"

The store light allowed Marcus to see this Trenton fellow more clearly. Taggert hadn't mentioned how the Colman moustache suited the angular contours of his face. His eyes were hazel flecked with green, and filled with a depth of kindness and understanding Marcus wasn't expecting. The inescapable truth was that this defender of the Hays Code was damnably attractive.

Marcus nodded. "It's just that I've seen your report on my script and I don't — that is, it came as a shock to — what I came here to say — "

"You really shouldn't be here." Trenton's voice was firm, but his eyes were smiling. "We ought not be having this conversation at all, especially not four doors down from where I work."

"I'm fully aware of that, Mr. Trenton. But it's import — "

"How about we discuss this over drinks?"

"You mean — now?

"I know this place, a bar. Low lighting, very private. Perfect for — " he looked Marcus up and down, " — our purposes."

"Sure," Marcus replied, more wary now. "Does it have a name?"

A smirk emerged, subtle but unambiguous, canny but not hostile. "It's called the Garden of Allah."

* * *

As Marcus approached the bar in the Sahara Room, he noticed two of Seamus' Glenfiddich bottles were missing. "Tell me it's good news."

Seamus shook his head. "Tunisia and Guadalcanal."

For the last couple of months, the war department had been touring a group of Guadalcanal survivors. At the Hollywood Writers Mobilization, Marcus had been asked to write a speech aimed at keeping up morale and reminding a wearying public that the need for war bonds was greater than ever. "I hear Guadalcanal was hell."

Seamus picked up an empty bottle of Glenfiddich. "Gone but not forgotten. What can I get you?"

"I'm meeting someone here, so I should probably — "

Seamus jutted his chin toward the door.

Oliver Trenton was making his way around the empty tables toward Marcus, that knowing smile still etched on his face.

"Four Roses okay?" Marcus asked. Trenton nodded.

Drinks in hand, they retreated to Marcus' favorite circular booth in the far corner where the murky light barely reached. Trenton slid in next to Marcus, closer than Marcus would have liked.

"I find it very interesting that you should pick this particular bar," he said.

Trenton nodded but said nothing.

Marcus swirled the liquor in his glass without breaking Trenton's stare. "You know I live here, don't you." What started out as a question ended up a statement.

Trenton blinked a slow, deliberate blink, as though to prove a point. "You have issues with my notes on your movie?"

Now that he had a couple of belts of Four Roses in him and was out of the bitter wind in a softly lit bar with a not-unattractive guy, Marcus felt suddenly self-conscious about the point he wanted to make. "I know this is going to sound ridiculously irrelevant now that the movie's out, but I saw your notes and they got me all bent out of shape."

Trenton seemed to take Marcus quite seriously. "And why is that?"

"All that business about my script being full of un-American influences. I assume it was the word *proletariat* that tied you up in knots? Well, it isn't the sole domain of Bolsheviks, you know. It means any working-class people."

"I know what *proletariat* means," Trenton said. "But here's the thing: We're not allowed to pass a script—any script from any studio—with no notes. Breen has decreed that we must find *something* wrong, declare *something* needs to be fixed."

Marcus had long suspected that the sort of censorship the Breen Office exercised over the studios was a game. A high-stakes game, but just a game, nonetheless. "Every single script, huh?"

Trenton's smile turned self-deprecating. "How else could we justify our existence?"

Marcus gestured to Seamus for another round and pulled a fresh pack of Chesterfields out of his jacket pocket. He offered one to Trenton, who declined. He lit up. "Yeah, well, the reason this whole thing sent me into a spin is that Mr. Mayer now thinks I'm a pinko. Not just from your notes on *William Tell*, but you didn't help."

"It's not illegal to be a Communist," Trenton said calmly.

"No, but we're fighting a world war against the forces of Fascism and Socialism, and in the minds of the powers that be, Communists are their kissing cousins. There are those who say the next war we fight will be against Communism. Who knows if that's true or not, but—"

"I hope you don't think I deliberately set out to sabotage your career."

Trenton's sincerity momentarily derailed Marcus' rant. For a long moment, the two men stared into each other's eyes. "No, I guess I don't," Marcus hedged, "but nevertheless, the hot water your notes got me into—"

"I had to write something." Trenton started drumming the wooden table top with a fingernail.

"You—what?"

The nervous tapping continued for a few seconds, then stopped abruptly. "You wrote one of the best scripts ever to come across my desk. The action, the love story, the triumph over the villain—it was all there. But I have rules to follow. I had to return your script with something. While we're at war, Hollywood movies need to wave the flag and beat the drum. They need to ignite patriotism. I was hard pressed to pick out any faults so I simply went with the obvious. We give our bosses what they want to see. I added those notes and sent it down the pipeline. But," he added with a smile and pointed finger, "it was tough to find fault with what you'd written. I mean that as a huge compliment."

The guy's smile was so disarming that Marcus found it impossible to dismiss.

"In case there are any lingering doubts," Trenton continued, "allow me to reiterate: if I had any idea my notes would land you in a jam, I'd have tried harder to come up with something else. However, I freely admit that I'm glad they got you so indignant that you came after me."

In the fifteen years Marcus had lived in Hollywood, he'd heard, witnessed, and used all sorts of pickup lines, but this was a first. "You are?"

"The studios provide us with a list of every writer who contributed to a script, no matter how slight their involvement. It's gotten so I can tell when a Marcus Adler lands on my desk; I don't even need to consult the submission. You are very good at what you do, Mr. Adler, so I got curious about you."

"What've you been doing? Following me around?" Marcus tried to laugh off his question. He feared he only partially succeeded.

"I was there at Ciro's the night Judy Garland made her debut. You were at the bar talking with George Cukor."

That was the night the inspiration for *Pearl From Pearl Harbor* hit Marcus like a battering ram. Roy Rogers could have been four feet away sitting atop Trigger and Marcus wouldn't have noticed.

"Ciro's was just a coincidence," Trenton went on, "but I hoped you'd be at *The Wizard Of Oz* premiere, so I wrangled a ticket. I was rather disappointed when you and Ramon Novarro snuck out after the movie started."

"You saw that, huh?"

"You and Ramon still have a thing going on?"

"Mr. Trenton—"

"Call me Oliver. May I call you Marcus?"

Marcus doubted the propriety of being on first-name terms with someone from the Breen Office—otherwise known as 'the enemy' to all studio personnel. *But we passed the point of propriety the moment he asked me to meet him for a drink.* Marcus stubbed out his cigarette. "That white elephant has been dead for quite some time."

"Ah!" Oliver clasped his hands together like a contemplative monk in prayer. A brief silence settled over them until he asked, "Does Mayer really think you're a pinko?"

"Evidently, but you're only partially responsible, so don't beat yourself up too much."

"Nevertheless, I'd like to make it up to you."

"How do you propose to do that?"

Oliver cocked his head to one side. "I was thinking we could start with going back to your place."

Under the table, Marcus felt the heat of Oliver's hand sliding onto his thigh.

The day of Hugo's funeral, Kathryn told Marcus that he looked "different somehow, more open." He didn't pay her much attention at the time. When he described the encounter with Quentin Luckett, her only comment was "See what I mean?" He'd shrugged that off, too, and thought no more about it. But now this guy was making his feelings very clear, and Marcus knew it was time he conceded her point.

"It's taking all of my will power not to lean over and kiss the cotton-pickin' dickens out of you," Oliver whispered. "You make my hands clammy, my knees weak, and my heart palpitate."

Until that moment, Marcus hadn't noticed what was playing on Seamus' radio. It was *The Abbott And Costello Show,* and just as Oliver finished his speech, the audience burst into applause. Thunderous, enthusiastic, unrestrained applause.

CHAPTER 20

Gwendolyn walked into the living room. "Zip me?"

Kathryn blew on her fresh nail polish. "Not till these babies are dry." She pointed to the newspaper on their kitchen table. "Did you see this?"

The *Times* screamed the same headline every newspaper in the country carried that day: *ROOSEVELT FREEZES ALL WAGES, SALARIES AND PRICES FOR DURATION OF WAR.*

Gwendolyn nodded. "It's not like a salary increase was in my future." She'd been supervisor at Bullocks for a couple of months now. It was a shame that a raise hadn't come with the promotion, but it would have been nice to get a little something in before Roosevelt froze everything like a New England snowstorm.

Kathryn tilted her nails toward the kitchen light to see if they were dry, then motioned for Gwendolyn to turn around. "I don't think the president's power extends to the black market."

"Yes. About that." Gwendolyn slipped on her shoes, whose soles were appallingly scuffed from dancing at the Hollywood Canteen.

"About what?" Kathryn stood up to thread a narrow black belt through the fancy version of a shirtwaist dress Gwendolyn made for her.

"The guy who supplies me, his number came up. Hello, army, goodbye, Lester."

"So that's the end of that, huh?"

"Unless you know a supplier."

"I have to say, I've been very impressed how you've handled it all."

"Turns out I have a head for numbers," Gwendolyn declared with a laugh. She started straightening up the mess of newspapers on the table.

"Do you have enough to open Chez Gwendolyn?"

Gwendolyn looked out the kitchen window for Monty, who would be coming down the path from the main building. To the left, she could see Marcus and Nazimova kneeling in the victory garden, pulling weeds and making each other laugh. The latest crop of cabbages, carrots, and string beans were starting to ripen, and it would be tomato-planting season soon.

Marcus had been so happy lately — almost glowing. Gwendolyn asked him about it during a particularly raucous farewell party for Dorothy Parker, who was heading back East with her husband. Gwendolyn hoped Marcus would confess, but he just shrugged.

"I'm not even close," she told Kathryn. "Maybe half of what I'll need."

"What are you going to do?"

She shrugged. "Beats me. I do hope Monty isn't late. Last week I saw Bette Davis bawl out that sweet little blonde from Technicolor. The poor thing left in tears."

Gwendolyn tried not to think of what lay ahead for her brother now that the navy doctors had deemed him fit for combat. Time with him was more precious than diamonds now, and she was determined that his last night in Los

Angeles would be fun—even if they had to start it at the Hollywood Canteen.

Kathryn and Gwendolyn were rarely rostered for duty on the same night, and it was a shame it had to be Monty's final one. Failing to show up was a big no-no, but they figured they'd take Monty along, do their shift, then head out to a lively nightspot and give him an evening to remember.

When a knock sounded on the door, Gwendolyn pulled it open. "You ready for a—?"

The man standing in front of her was not Monty.

He was in his mid to late thirties, and dark where Monty was fair. With black hair, pale skin, and blue eyes set deep under thick eyebrows, he had a narrow face that ended in a dimpled chin. He was as tall as Monty, but slimmer in the hips and more slightly built.

He looked past her to Kathryn, then back to Gwendolyn. "I'm Lincoln Tattler." He announced his name with such authority that Gwendolyn felt a little foolish for staring at him so blankly. "This is villa number twelve, isn't it?"

"Yes."

"I'm here for Gwendolyn Brick."

Gwendolyn peered over her shoulder to Kathryn, who shrugged. She turned back for a second assessment. In his expensive tuxedo and air of assured confidence, the handsome man didn't give off the air of a con artist.

"That's me. But—"

"I'm here to pick you up? For our date? Today's Thursday, right?"

"Mister—?"

"Tattler. Lincoln Tattler."

"Mister Tattler, I fear you're the victim of a practical joke. I can assure you we've never made any arrangement for a date."

"We didn't," he agreed. "It was set up through Leilah O'Roarke."

"Leilah O'Roarke?" The outburst came from Kathryn.

Tattler glanced down at his patent leather shoes that were polished to such a high sheen that they reflected the purple dusk of the sky. "This is awkward." He looked up. "She assured me she'd fix everything and all I had to do was knock on your door at the appointed hour." He looked Gwendolyn up and down, taking in her outfit with appreciation. "Seeing as how you're already dressed, perhaps we shouldn't waste a perfectly lovely evening?"

Monty's face appeared over Tattler's right shoulder, frowning but bemused.

Gwendolyn turned to the stranger. "Lincoln Tattler, this is Montgomery Brick."

Tattler's eyebrows bunched together. "Brick? You're married?"

"Monty's my brother. He's shipping out tomorrow."

Monty took in the expensive tux. "You Kathryn's date tonight?"

Tattler shook his head. "You obviously have a night planned, so I'll bid you all good evening." He stepped back to leave.

"We could do with a fourth," Monty said. "Why not join us?"

If Gwendolyn could have pulled Monty aside discreetly and told him, *Because we don't know who the blazes this guy is,* she would have. Instead, she explained that they were off to a shift at the Hollywood Canteen before moving on to one of the nightclubs, and pointed out that only servicemen in uniform were allowed in.

"What if I volunteer?" Tattler suggested.

"You'd be bussing tables and washing glasses," Gwendolyn told him. "In a monkey suit like that? I don't think so."

"If I take off the jacket and tie, I'll just be a monkey in a white shirt and black pants."

Gwendolyn doubted this Ivy Leaguer would know how to bus a table if his sanity depended on it. She could tell Kathryn was thinking the same thing. "It can be messy work," she warned.

"They give you an apron, don't they?"

* * *

Backed by the Benny Goodman orchestra, June Allyson and Gloria DeHaven were bringing their rendition of "Is You Is Or Is You Ain't My Baby" to an energetic close when Kathryn and Gwendolyn walked in the Canteen's volunteer entrance. The audience whooped and hollered until the electrified hurricane lamps dangling from the wagon wheels overhead shook.

"Is it always like this?" Tattler shouted into Gwendolyn's ear.

"Sometimes it gets crazy."

The supervisor was relieved to see a new busser. "It's a good thing you're tall, fella. You'll need all that height to lift trays over everybody's heads."

"Not quite the night you had planned, huh?" Gwendolyn said.

When Tattler smiled, he looked like Tyrone Power. "I'm only sorry I didn't think to volunteer here sooner. I assumed they only needed pretty girls to dance with starstruck boys. I was thinking we might all go to the Mocambo, but if you're about to spend the next hours dancing, perhaps—"

"How come you're not in uniform?" Gwendolyn hadn't intended the question to pop out of her like a torpedo—she knew how sensitive Marcus was about it—but it had been on her mind the whole drive over.

He tied the strings of the apron around his waist. "I would like nothing more than to do my bit, but—to quote the army doctor verbatim—I have 'the flattest feet this side of a flat-footed Boobie bird.' I told them I was willing to take the risk, but they showed me the door."

He hadn't looked her in the eye the whole time he was telling her this. It was time to change the subject.

"How do you know Mrs. O'Roarke?"

"Leilah?" The Tyrone Power smile was back. "My dad and her husband have been pals since college. Even before he became a cop."

"A COP?" Gwendolyn knew Leilah's husband headed up security at Warners, but this cop business was news to her. She felt her armpits go damp.

Tattler hoisted a tray onto his shoulder. "I can see the plates and cups piling up."

Gwendolyn watched him plunge into the churning sea of eager servicemen and smiling girls as she mulled over this new nugget. Surely Mrs. O'Roarke knew Gwendolyn's merchandise was black market. But had she told her husband?

It wasn't until Gwendolyn was halfway through a dance with a beanpole sailor from Racine, Wisconsin, that it occurred to her that whether or not Leilah O'Roarke had told her husband about Gwendolyn, she hadn't been arrested. Still, she'd been closer to the law than she realized, so maybe it wasn't an altogether bad thing that she was getting out of the black-market game.

* * *

It was ten o'clock before Gwendolyn took a break. By that time, she'd danced for two straight hours with every type of serviceman, from the terminally clumsy to the Astairean graceful. Whatever their skill level, these brave boys did their best and Gwendolyn loved them for it.

But there was a limit, and she needed a few minutes off her feet. Before another hopeful private or midshipman could catch her eye, she sneaked down the back and into the Canteen's office, which had a little space to the side where girls could take a break.

There was usually somebody balancing the books or juggling the next week's roster at one of the three desks that were crammed together, but when Gwendolyn walked in, there was nobody around. She plopped down on the battered sofa and kicked off her pumps.

"Bully!"

Gwendolyn knew who it was before she looked up from rubbing her feet. Bertie Kreuger was one of her favorite people who'd moved into the Garden of Allah since the start of the war. In a town filled with amply blessed girls, Bertie never seemed the slightest bit put out that she'd been dealt a meager hand in the looks department: broad face, mess of corkscrew hair the color of oleomargarine, widely spaced teeth, and eyes neither blue nor green but something in between. But she possessed a heart as big as the Gulf of Mexico. She also had a knack of giving everyone she met a nickname. Gwendolyn's was "Bully," as in Bullocks Wilshire.

Bertie flopped onto the sofa. "What a crazy night!"

"We get busier and busier every week."

Bertie nudged her. "But not so busy that I didn't notice you chatting with Junior."

Gwendolyn kneaded the ball of her left foot. "Did I tell you Monty ships out tomorrow?"

"I was talking about Tattler Junior."

"You know him?"

She juggled her head from side to side, sending her double chin to wobbling. "His dad's the tuxedo king."

"You mean Tattler Tuxedos?"

Tattler Tuxedos was the best-selling line of formalwear at Bullocks. They were beautifully hand-stitched from the finest wools and silks, and cost so much that only top stars and executives could afford them.

"Who did you think he was?"

"It didn't come up."

"His family and mine are both Johnny-come-latelies into the *Los Angeles Blue Book*. We're new money, but we've both got enough of it to qualify for the social register."

"I'm surprised you care."

Bertie barked out a laugh. "I don't give a diddly-damn about that, but my parents do, so they drag me to those tedious balls at the Biltmore and the Jonathan Club. That's where I usually see Linc."

Gwendolyn slipped her shoes back on. "They must sell a lot of tuxes to get into the Blue Book."

"Tuxes are the tip of the iceberg. They make all those fancy jackets and caps for the yachting crowd. And those whatchamacallits for polo players—jodhpurs. And morning dress suits, and chauffeur uniforms, and judges' robes. They make a lot of things. You still figuring on opening your own dress shop?"

"I hope so."

"If you're looking for brains to pick, you could do a lot worse than Lincoln Tattler. Play your cards right, he might even bankroll you."

Gwendolyn's mind started sprinting.

Bertie heaved herself up from the sofa. "By the by, I came in here to give you a message. Our commander in chief says it's okay if you gals cut out early."

Gwendolyn pulled open the door and the din of several hundred couples jitterbugging to "Minnie the Moocher" avalanched into the office. Lincoln wasn't hard to spot—he was the tallest guy in the room, and was holding a tray piled with glassware above his head as though it were made of cotton candy. She watched him thread through the maze of tables filled with lonesome soldiers and obliging starlets.

As he neared the kitchen, he lobbed one of his Tyrone smiles at her; more genuine than any she'd seen on the idle rich boys who shopped at Bullocks. She tapped her watch, then mouthed the words "thirty minutes."

He might even bankroll you.

Gwendolyn knew better than to count on a long shot like that.

CHAPTER 21

Marcus sprinkled as much cinnamon as he could spare into the cake batter and stirred it while he watched Oliver pull down a volume from his bookshelf.

"*Crime and Punishment*, huh? Did I ever tell you what I studied in college?"

Marcus stopped stirring. "I don't think so."

"I was a double major. English literature and Russian studies."

Marcus focused on his batter. "You're the Russia expert but I'm the pinko. There's irony for you."

Oliver fell silent and they listened to the cast recording of the latest Broadway hit, *Oklahoma*, as Celeste Holm told them how she cain't say no. Oliver walked into the kitchen and planted an unhurried kiss on Marcus' shoulder. "I never said you were a pinko, so if you're spoiling for a fight—" He ran his fingers through Marcus' unruly hair.

"Nah," Marcus said, "not with you, anyway."

"Then who?"

Marcus stirred the batter some more. "It still bothers me that Mayer thinks I'm a pinko."

"Are you sure he does? From what you've told me about Edwin Marr—"

"*William Tell* grossed more than *Yankee Doodle Dandy,
Road To Morocco,* AND *Holiday Inn.* Two thirds of our guys
with any know-how are in the service, which makes me one
of the most experienced writers we've got. And yet not only
has he knocked back every idea I've come up with since
William Tell, but what have they got me working on? *Maisie
Goes To Reno.*"

"Hey," Oliver protested gently, "I like those *Maisie*
movies."

"Me too, but it's no *Madame Curie,* is it?"

"Keep at it. You'll come up with something that'll knock
their socks off."

Oliver traced his hand from Marcus' hair, down his neck
and onto his chest. He leaned in for another one of those
languid kisses he was so good at. They left Marcus with a
sense of falling—but in a good way, like Alice down the
rabbit hole to a queer Wonderland. He'd thought he loved
Ramon, but now that he had the real thing, he could see he'd
been fooling himself. For the longest time, Marcus doubted
he was any good at this boyfriend business, and had almost
resigned himself to a monklike life with the occasional
encounter. But then Oliver came along, and his private life
became such an effortless oasis of tranquility that he
marveled at how he'd doubted himself.

After a deliciously long smooch, they broke apart like two
halves of an oyster shell. Oliver leaned against the counter
with his back to the window. The late afternoon sun
enveloped him like a veil.

"I do like your place."

The gang at the Garden of Allah was as open-minded as
any group of highly paid bohemians. Oliver could be an
opium-smoking circus freak-show reject and nobody would
bat an eyelid. It was an unspoken rule at the Garden that
once you moved in, you were family. That meant you were

free to be whoever you were, do whatever you wanted, sleep with whomever you pleased. No matter your vice — booze, pills, sex, racetracks — there was no judgment, no rejection. Dorothy Parker joked once they should put a plaque over the front desk: *Whatever transpires inside these Garden walls remains within.* On the outside, the queers played it straight, the boozers feigned sobriety, and the tramps exuded a virginal posture. But on the inside, you were who you were, and that was just fine with your neighbors.

However, Marcus strongly suspected that even the Gardenites would draw the line at one of their own dating the Breen Office. In the us-versus-them trenches of Hollywood, a studio screenwriter and a Breen Office censor were considered mortal enemies. So every time Oliver suggested they meet at the Garden of Allah, Marcus changed the subject.

Then Orson Welles moved in with his latest paramour, Lili St. Cyr. One weekend while working amid the tomato stalks and cabbage leaves of the victory garden, he announced that his *Jane Eyre* had reached the rough-cut edit stage, but he wasn't sure the picture worked. Could he bring everyone to the studio for a screening to gauge their reaction? Orson had neither directed, written, nor produced the movie, but it hadn't occurred to him that it wasn't his movie to screen.

Everybody said yes except Marcus. This was a rare chance for him to be home alone with Oliver without having to explain anything to anyone, including Kathryn and Gwendolyn — or even Alla.

It was five thirty, so they had at least a couple more hours. After the screening, Orson was treating the group to a smorgasbord dinner at Bit of Sweden restaurant.

Oliver peered into the mixing bowl. "What are you making?"

With its raisins boiled in cloves and lard, the batter looked like something Dottie Parker's dachshunds might puke up. "It's called war cake," Marcus said. "There's no butter, eggs, or milk, so I'm making no promises. But it came highly recommended." He indicated a recent *Saturday Evening Post* that featured a Norman Rockwell painting of a rather muscular woman named Rosie holding a hefty rivet gun across her lap.

Oliver dipped his finger into the batter and conceded that it tasted better than it looked. "I think your Hollywood Writers Mobilization can come up with a better name than that."

Marcus opened his oven door. "Why don't we just call it what it is: a poor-excuse-for-a-dessert-that'll-have-to-do-until-we-win-the-war-and-rationing-comes-to-an-end cake."

A voice from down near the pool called out, "Looks like he's home!"

It was Kathryn, and she wasn't alone. The stone pathway crunched under a dozen pairs of feet.

"MARCUS!" Orson Welles boomed through the open window. "We need every drop of Four Roses in your possession!"

Marcus' front door swung open and ten bodies lurched in.

Kathryn led the pack. "You said you wouldn't be—" She froze when she caught sight of Oliver in the corner, buttoning his shirt.

"I thought you all were going out for dinner afterwards," Marcus said.

"Haven't you heard?" Gwendolyn asked, her eyes on Oliver. "A bunch of sailors and marines are fighting with those Mexicans who wear the zoot suits."

"Something about the Sleepy Lagoon murder." Kathryn started pulling off her gloves. "Apparently downtown is a mess, so we figured we'd better hightail it back here. It's all over the radio — but I guess you were busy."

Oliver stuck his hand out and introduced himself.

There were now twelve bodies crowding a living room intended to comfortably fit a half dozen. Marcus' heart ratcheted up a notch while Kathryn shook Oliver's hand. "You're one of Marcus' screenwriter buddies at MGM?"

"Nothing as exciting as that." Oliver turned to Orson, offering his hand. "Mr. Welles, I count myself a big fan of your *Citizen Kane*. It deserved better treatment than it got."

Orson beamed and treated Oliver to his trademark two-handed shake.

Kathryn sidled up to Marcus. "Did we interrupt something?"

The smell of cinnamon and boiled raisins filled the air around them. "Just baking a cake."

Orson declared he'd come up with a new punch recipe based on a daiquiri Hemingway had served him once, and Marcus pointed to two unopened bottles of bourbon. Before Oliver entered Marcus' life, no bottle of Four Roses had gone unopened for long, but now one could sit there untouched for a whole week.

Lili spoke up. "Say, Oliver. Your last name ain't Trenton, is it?"

Oliver's response was slow in coming. "Uh-huh."

Marcus steeled himself.

"I know that name." Donnie Stewart was a fellow screenwriter at MGM. Marcus could see it registering in Donnie's mind like an electric sign flickering on one light bulb at a time. "From the Breen Office?"

"I knew it!" Lili exclaimed. "When I was dancing at the Florentine Gardens, someone pointed you out to me. Called you a snake in the grass. When I asked why, she told me where you work." She pulled her face into a sneer. "You old maids disapprove of everything."

Ten pairs of eyes turned to look at Marcus, daring him to explain.

"Actually," Marcus began with little idea of what to say next, "it's the damnedest thing. Oliver was the guy who evaluated my script for *William Tell.*"

"You mean he was the one who put the idea into Mayer's head that you're a Commie?"

The accusation came from Kay Thompson. As MGM's choral arranger, she was responsible for most of Judy Garland's vocals. She and her radio-producer husband, Bill, hadn't been at the Garden very long before she'd ensconced herself at the epicenter of the hotel's social life. Thin, blonde, and fully confident of her extraordinary abilities, Kay was one of those people who filled every room she entered. Not an easy feat to pull off in a room already crowded with the likes of Orson Welles and Lili St. Cyr.

"No," Marcus replied. "That was Edwin Marr. All Oliver did — "

Oliver stepped forward. "What Marcus probably won't tell you is that when he saw my notes on his script, he marched down to our office and confronted me."

"You didn't!" Donnie's round face was the picture of amazement suffused with admiration. He knew better than anyone else in the room the risk Marcus had taken.

Nazimova hadn't said anything at this point, but she took advantage of the shocked silence to speak. "Did you really do this?" Her weary eyes appraised Marcus in a way he'd never seen before.

Oliver nodded. "Bawled me out like a son of a gun."

Orson leaned up against the doorway into the bedroom. The same look of reevaluation in Alla's face filled his, too. "That takes guts."

"How very *Fruit Fight At The OK Corral* of you." Kay Thompson threw her hands up. "Don't get me wrong, pumpkin, but I hardly think I'm the only one here who draws the line at your doing it with someone from the Breen Office. If there's a snitch among us, I for one want to know about it."

"Hold on a minute, Kay."

Ogden Nash stepped out from behind Lili. Marcus hadn't seen the poet since he moved out of the Garden. Back then, Scott Fitzgerald and Marcus were writing a screenplay and Nash was working up a treatment for *The Wizard Of Oz*. Neither Marcus nor Nash got screen credit for their efforts and they'd clinked shots of commiserating whiskey. "I don't know that any of us have the right to go snooping into—"

Kay sliced a hand through the air like a horizontal guillotine. "I beg to differ, Nashie darling. One of the reasons Bill and I chose to live here was the Garden's reputation as a haven where us creative folk are free to express ourselves." She turned to face the antsy crowd. "Am I wrong?"

"Not at all." Orson had lost his look of fleeting admiration. "While some in Hollywood call the Hays Code and the Breen Office a necessary evil, I disagree. I consider myself an artist and am, quite frankly, appalled at how frequently I'm forced to defend my work against self-appointed moralistic bowdlerizers who have bestowed upon themselves the moral high ground." He thrust a finger toward downtown LA. "As far as I'm concerned, the Breen Office is no better than those zoot-suited hooligans."

"And I think you're all hypocrites," Oliver shot back.

The group drew in a collective gasp.

Marcus felt his heart sink to the soles of his bare feet.

Lili St. Cyr piped up. "Well, how do you like that? The Breen Office fairy is telling us *we're* the hypocrites."

Under different circumstances, Marcus would have laughed at the irony of a semiliterate stripper becoming the moral voice of the Garden, but—.

"May I speak?" Oliver asked. "Or have you already made up your minds before you hear me out?"

Marcus braved a glance in Kathryn's direction. It wasn't hard to tell what she was thinking: *You've certainly got a live wire on your hands, haven't you?*

Alla flickered an inscrutable look at Oliver. "Go ahead, Mr. Trenton."

"You people give me a pain!" Oliver stated. Several mouths dropped open. "Did it ever occur to you that maybe we're on your side?"

Orson released a caustic laugh. "No, Mr. Trenton, it never has."

"I guess I ought only speak for myself," Oliver conceded.

"Perhaps you should," Marcus urged quietly.

"Both my father and grandfather were preachers. It was assumed that one of my siblings would follow in the family footsteps and lucky for me, I had an older brother to shoulder that burden. It left me free to pursue a career in the movie business, and I knew exactly what I wanted to do. So I sent a letter to Joseph Breen and asked if there was an opening for me."

The tension in the room broke; several people scoffed.

"You *volunteered?*" Gwendolyn asked.

"I could see what they were trying to do, but felt they were going about it the wrong way."

"And what," Orson asked, "did you think the Breen Office was trying to do?"

Oliver clapped his hands together as though begging his audience to hear what he had to say. "The Greeks and the Romans had their gods; the Europeans, their kings and queens. Us twentieth-century Americans? We have our movie stars. It's like what Voltaire said: 'If God did not exist, it would be necessary to invent him.'"

Alla's lover, Glesca, stepped forward. She was a forthright woman given to speaking her mind, consequences be damned. Marcus would have been crestfallen if she took a dislike to Oliver. "Mr. Trenton, I feel reasonably sure that Voltaire was not talking about movie stars."

"Stars serve a purpose," Oliver rebutted. "Like gods and royalty, they fulfill a fundamental human need for heroes. What we do here in Hollywood is create role models for regular folks to emulate. They represent Americans at our finest, and inspire us to be like that, too."

"A very fine soliloquy," Kay said. "However, the point is, you work for the organization that seeks to clamp down on our freedom of speech. We don't take that light—"

"The Breen Office exists because the Hollywood studios have been charged with creating the American dream. When left unchecked, they allowed greed and lust to overtake all other considerations. And so we got the Hays Code with all its stringent rules and regulations enforced on us. The problem is, the Hays Code hasn't kept up with the times." This triggered a restless ripple through the room. "I have intentionally positioned myself as the voice of moderation within the Breen Office. I make it my business to suggest other—more modern—ways to look at things, more in keeping with the way American life is lived in the present, not the past."

Donnie Stewart broke into a shrewd smile. "You're telling us that you went to work at the Breen Office to change it from the inside?"

"Exactly."

"I tip my hat to you, Mr. Trenton. What you're doing is gloriously subversive."

"I wouldn't say that," Oliver responded.

"I would!" Orson stepped forward to slap Oliver on the back. He executed it with such oomph that Oliver had to catch himself from staggering forward. "All the more reason to celebrate with my Hemingway daiquiri punch!"

Marcus pointed Welles toward his mirrored cocktail cart, then started to pull glassware from his kitchen cabinet. He felt Kathryn slink to his side and nudge him with her hip.

"You little dark horse, you." They watched Agnes Moorhead and Nazimova lead Oliver out to the courtyard outside Marcus' front door, where Orson had pulled the cocktail cart. "Are you happy?" Kathryn asked. "Is he treating you well?"

"Very and very," Marcus replied. He handed her six glasses and said he'd follow her in a moment.

As she left, Oliver poked his head through the doorway. "I told them about your cake and they want to know how long it'll be."

Marcus curled a finger, commanding Oliver to join him in the kitchen. The light outside had faded into a deep dusk; shadows now fell across the sharp angles of his face. "How long have you been rehearsing that speech?"

"Since that day at the Atlanta railway station."

Marcus frowned. "I've never been to Atlanta."

"The one they built for *Gone With The Wind*."

Two years ago, Marcus volunteered as an extra on the day they shot the scene where Scarlett O'Hara picks her way through hundreds of wounded Civil War soldiers outside the Atlanta railway station. "You were there?"

"A buddy of mine was supposed to do it but he fell ill. He really needed the cash, so I did it for him. That was the first time I ever saw you. I know how screenwriters feel about the Breen Office, so I figured I'd better have my argument in my back pocket."

Marcus wasn't sure how he felt about this revelation. Flattered? Wary? "The Voltaire touch was very good."

Oliver started playing with the strings on Marcus' swimming trunks. "I hope your friends like me."

Marcus brushed his fingers up Oliver's arms. "You took a risk, but I think you've pulled it off."

"I'd hate to be the cause of any rift between you and—"

Marcus pressed his thumb against Oliver's lips. "How about we save the drama for the screen? I say let's cross bridges when we come to them. For now, all I'm really concerned about is that dubious bowl of gelatinous muck fermenting in my oven."

The air smelled of burning raisins. "You want me to take a gander?"

"No. My war cake, my responsibility."

"How about we chance it together?"

"I'm warning you, Mr. Trenton, this could get scary."

Oliver grabbed Marcus' hand. "I'll take my chances."

CHAPTER 22

From her center aisle seat halfway to the stage of NBC Radio's Studio D, Kathryn looked across a sea of hats awaiting the *Kraft Music Hall* broadcast to commence. "It's seven thirty," she muttered. "Cutting it a bit fine, aren't they?"

Marcus shrugged. "This is my first time at a broadcast."

"They're usually on stage by now," Francine said. "Except for the stars."

After Kathryn decided her mother's opium story was too hard to swallow, she'd hired a private eye to go through the society columns of old Boston newspapers for mention of a Francine Caldecott making her debut in 1908. He did find a listing, which punched a hole in Kathryn's baloney theory, but not a big one. She decided to include Francine in her life more, and hoped to spot opportunities to dig a little deeper.

Four microphones were evenly spaced at the front of the stage and the orchestra's seats were arranged at the rear. The sound effects guy's assortment of contraptions was laid out on a table to the right: brass triangle, coconut shells, miniature slamming door, kazoo.

Francine pointed out a trio of men huddled at the far left, talking over one another in forced whispers. "They don't look happy."

A teenage usher in a gold and purple uniform strolled past Kathryn and she flagged him down, betting that he was so wet behind the ears that he didn't know the rules yet. "I'm Kathryn Massey of the *Hollywood Reporter*. I'm here to cover Melody Hope's radio debut for a series of articles I'm writing on radio's contribution to the war effort." She let her credentials sink in. "I can't help noticing that nobody's on stage yet except for those three gentlemen." She could feel hesitation radiating off him. The series was still only an idea, and Melody's radio debut was just a cover story; her real motive was to see Anita Wyndham. "Is something amiss?" she pressed.

The usher's ambivalence endured only a few seconds longer. "We go live to air in thirty minutes, but half the musicians haven't arrived yet. And there ain't no sign of Miss Hope. There was talk of opening with Anita Wyndham's gossip spot, but she hasn't turned up, either."

When Kathryn turned down Presnell's shady offer, it was because she had a keen sense that it would come back to bite her on the behind. Why risk something like that leaking out when there were so many other radio shows?

Anita Wyndham was a nationally syndicated columnist in magazines like *Ladies' Home Journal* and *Collier's*. She'd scaled the mountain Kathryn was only just starting to tackle, so Kathryn had decided she needed to see Wyndham in action for herself.

The situation at work lately had been less than encouraging. The layoffs and pay cuts had made Kathryn realize she'd put all her professional eggs in a basket that was showing signs of breaking. She had no intention of leaving the *Reporter*, but what if the *Reporter* collapsed under the weight of Wilkerson's colossal gambling debts? She needed a backup plan, and a regular radio spot was the perfect solution.

"Why is everybody so late?" she asked the usher.

"There's a fire at Ciro's."

Kathryn pinched the boy's lapel and pulled him closer so nobody else would hear. "Did you say Ciro's?"

"It just came over the wire. Miss Wyndham lives in Brentwood, which puts the fire between her house and here."

Kathryn let his lapel go and read his nameplate. "Thank you, Sonny." The boy tugged at his cap and retreated down the aisle. Kathryn turned to Marcus and kept her voice low while she pulled on her gloves. "Ciro's is on fire."

"Literally?!"

"I should hightail it down there on the double."

"You could. Or . . ."

Kathryn took stock of Marcus' crafty smile. "Or what?"

"Or we could talk our way backstage, where you could find a telephone and call Gwennie."

"You cunning little so-and-so." She leaned across to Francine. "Mother, could you mind our seats?"

* * *

When Kathryn instructed the security guard to tell the show's producer that she had a solution to his crisis, the doors flew open like she was Ali Baba. A harried man with an intense scowl came running toward her. "I'm Wallace Reed, the producer," he said.

Within moments, Reed was pulling her along a corridor lined with photos of NBC radio stars that flew past her in a blur. He ushered her into his office and pointed out the telephone. Kathryn called the Garden of Allah and asked the operator to put her through.

Like most attractive, single women living in Los Angeles during wartime, Gwendolyn had more dates than she knew what to do with. Servicemen were constantly stopping her — on the street, at the movies, in stores. She said yes more often than not, so it was no sure thing she'd be home. Kathryn was relieved when Gwendolyn picked up.

In very few words, Kathryn told her friend to dash up Sunset, see what was going on, and call her from the apartments across the street. She hung up and turned to Marcus. "If it takes her four minutes to run to Ciro's, three minutes to take stock of the situation, two minutes to find a phone in the Sunset Tower's foyer, that's eight minutes, which gives us six minutes to spare."

That was an awful lot of ifs. At the very least, she'd come to the attention of the *Kraft Music Hall*'s producer, and that was no small thing.

"Gangway! Gangway! She's here!"

"That sounded like Bertie Kreuger," Marcus said.

They peered into the corridor to see Bertie and Melody dodging personnel and equipment. Bertie was in her usual getup: an ill-fitting dress that highlighted her wide hips and bulky arms. Beside her was Melody, awash in black chiffon. Bertie spotted them and waved with the anguish of a drowning person.

When they drew up alongside them, Bertie gasped, "Where can I hide her?"

Melody's head slumped onto Kathryn's shoulder and she let out a ferocious belch. "'Skuze me."

Kathryn guided them into chairs along a wall in Reed's office while Marcus scurried away in search of coffee.

"Ladies and gentlemen," said Bertie, gesturing toward the chair, "I give you America's wartime sweetheart."

As a way to compete with Betty Grable's skyrocketing pinup fame, MGM's publicity machine had labeled Melody "America's Wartime Sweetheart" after she scored a huge hit with a musical called *Singing On The Swing Shift*, in which she played an aircraft factory worker who falls for Gene Kelly's ace pilot.

"Why is America's wartime sweetheart smashed to the gills?" Kathryn asked.

"Because she's a mess," Bertie retorted, "and getting messier by the day."

Slumped in her chair like a sack of soggy potatoes, Melody peered at Kathryn through eyes hazy with booze. "She's right. Just call me Messy Bessie."

Kathryn glanced at the clock above the wartime sweetheart's head. Nearly six minutes had passed since she hung up on Gwendolyn. She pulled Bertie closer to the door. "What gives?"

"She's a nervous wreck. She's never performed live before; they haven't even rehearsed the number together. Not to mention the fact that Bing Crosby is a perfectionist. A sip or two of Dutch courage led to several shots, and here we are."

Marcus burst into the room holding a tray. "COFFEE!" He handed one to each of the girls, then sat down beside Melody and guided her hands around the cup.

The telephone jangled. Kathryn reached it in two paces. "Gwennie?"

"Oh my goodness, it's pandemonium!" Gwendolyn's voice was shaky and out of breath. "Traffic is blocked in all directions."

"What about Ciro's? Is it bad?"

"Bad enough for four fire trucks and at least nine police cars. The smoke is awful!"

Kathryn rustled through the producer's desk drawers until she had enough paper and pencils to make all the notes she needed. She thanked Gwendolyn and hung up, then turned to Bertie. "What song are they singing tonight?"

"That lovey-dovey duet from *Oklahoma*."

Marcus looked up. "'People Will Say We're In Love'?"

"Yeah," Bertie said, "that's the one."

"How well do you know it?" Kathryn asked Marcus.

"I pretty much know it backwards."

Kathryn cupped Melody's chin with her left hand and lifted her face up. "Honey," she said softly, "I'm so sorry."

"For what?"

"This." Kathryn walloped the side of Melody's face with the most brutal smack she could muster.

"WHAT THE—?" Melody's big brown eyes snapped into focus.

Kathryn would have preferred that the producer not choose that particular moment to march into his office, but suddenly he was standing next to her.

"Miss Hope!" Reed exclaimed. "Nobody told me you'd arrived—" He caught sight of the wild look on Melody's face. "Is everything all right? We're five minutes to air—"

"Mr. Reed," Kathryn said, picking up her notes. "I have all the information I need to give your show a breaking-news-as-it-happens report on the fire at Ciro's. Perhaps if I throw in some Hollywood tidbits from tomorrow's column, more musicians will have arrived to give Mr. Crosby and Miss Hope enough of an orchestra to get by."

The producer shifted his gaze from Kathryn to Melody and hesitated, knowing he'd walked into something, but they were mere minutes to air.

"Miss Hope, please remain here until I send an usher to collect you." He turned to Kathryn. "The orchestra is going to do an extra-long introduction, then Bing and the bandleader will do some shtick they're working up about his new movie, *Dixie*. I need you on stage and ready to go in one minute."

When Reed left the room, Marcus followed him to the doorway and signaled to the women when he was out of earshot.

"Melody, I—" Kathryn started, but the girl stopped her.

"I'm close enough to sober to get the job done. Let's hope so, anyway. Marcus, could you hunt around for the sheet music?"

Kathryn picked up her handbag. She'd spent months thinking about how she might bring about her radio debut, but hadn't put much thought into how she would feel when it actually arrived. She squeezed her kid gloves until her knuckles were white.

"Anita Wyndham's here," Marcus cut in from the doorway.

Kathryn threw her gloves onto the desk. "Just when I— OOOO!"

"Anita Wyndham?" Bertie asked. "What's she got to do with any of this?"

"She's the resident gossip columnist on this show," Marcus explained. "We're here because she hadn't shown up and we saw a chance for Kathryn to show what she can do on the air."

Bertie smirked. "You need me to head her off at the pass?"

"That wouldn't be ethical."

"It's not what I asked. We're both on the committee for this big fundraising shindig we're organizing for the Women's Army Corps. We locked horns, and I ended up battering her with my pocketbook."

"She's sixty feet away," Marcus reported.

"The minute she spots me," Bertie said, "that bitch will take a powder so goddamn fast you'll be tasting Max Factor clear through to next week." She marched into the corridor. "ANITA WYNDHAM! I WANT TO TALK TO YOU!"

"Move it," Marcus said. "She's got you covered."

Kathryn wished Melody luck, grabbed her notes, and headed for a doorway marked *STAGE*. She shouldered it open to find Wallace Reed and Bing Crosby in the wings. Crosby saw her first and stepped forward, offering his hand.

"Dottie Lamour says nothing but good things about you. I can't tell you how relieved I am that you're helping us out like this."

Kathryn wondered if he'd be so effusive if he knew Bertie Kreuger was cornering his resident gossipmonger like some poison-spewing Hydra. She nodded modestly and asked where she should stand.

Reed led her to the microphone on stage left. Crosby followed her amid a thunderous round of applause. The bandleader tapped his baton and a voice came over the loudspeaker. "Stand by. And five, four, three, two . . . "

A large red *ON AIR* sign at the back of the auditorium lit up, and the band started playing the *Kraft Music Hall* theme, a jaunty mix of sprightly violins and trumpets.

"Good evening, listeners." Crosby's voice was buttery smooth. "Welcome to what's become a night of drama and mayhem on the streets of Hollywood." Kathryn could hear the adrenaline pounding her eardrums. *Don't screw up! Don't screw up!* "And to tell us about it—" *I'm on? RIGHT NOW? What the hell happened to the shtick Bing and the bandleader were going to do?* "—is Kathryn Massey of the *Hollywood Reporter* giving us an up-to-the-minute bulletin."

Kathryn peered at her notes. Her scrawl was now just a blur of indecipherable scratches. Instinctively, she let the pages in her hand float to the floor and looked into the sea of expectant faces until she found her mother's. Francine was silently clapping her hands and mouthing the word "Smile."

"That's right, Bing," she improvised. "World-famous nightclub Ciro's on the Sunset Strip usually confines its excitement to the musical variety, but tonight it was at the center of its own pandemonium."

CHAPTER 23

Gwendolyn almost felt guilty going to a place like the Mocambo, whose Brazilian-themed décor was like nothing else in LA. Mounted on the walls and hanging from the ceiling was the craziest stuff: papier-mâché lambs holding pink and white parasols while balancing on trapeze wires, Siamese cats dressed as ringmasters in tall skinny hats of gray satin and orange silk sashes, lanky silhouettes of dark-skinned women in headdresses exploding with pink feathers and draped in gold mesh. All of this madness played out against walls painted cherry red and booths of olive green upholstery. Walking into the nightclub was like encountering a Mardi Gras parade every night of the week.

At any other time, Gwendolyn would have adored spending a gay night at a place that served extravagant, fruity cocktails that looked like something off Carmen Miranda's head. But this was wartime, and it seemed insensitive to have such fun while the boys overseas were fighting for their lives in unthinkably ghastly conditions. And, of course, she had one particular overseas boy in mind.

The last time she saw her brother was the night Lincoln Tattler turned up on her doorstep. The next day, Monty shipped out for some far-flung corner of the Pacific whose location he was not at liberty to reveal.

It was tough reading the newspaper reports about Japan's rampage through the Pacific. They were now in New Guinea and the Solomon Islands, virtually on Australia's doorstep.

Gwendolyn couldn't decide what was worse: knowing where Monty was, or knowing nothing. The only thing she knew for sure was that she'd have no rest until the war was over.

A crash of cymbals from the Mocambo's band heralded a samba, and two dozen couples on the dance floor hurled themselves into a frenzy of bouncing hips and jabbing kicks. Overhead, mini spotlights raked the dancers in shafts of blues and greens.

Gwendolyn felt Linc's arm slide around her waist and his warm breath in her ear. "We can leave if you'd prefer."

She thought of what Kathryn said when she voiced her hesitation earlier that evening. Those boys in the trenches and the submarines would be the first ones to tell you to get out and live life while we can. Isn't it what we're all fighting for? "Let's stay," Gwendolyn said. "We're here now."

Although she'd initially resented Mrs. O'Roarke for setting her up with a stranger and forgetting to tell her, Gwendolyn was soon glad she had. That first night, Linc took her and Kathryn to the Café Gala up on the Strip. When he dropped them home, he said nothing about contacting her again. She spent three weeks thinking about him and was delighted when he telephoned to ask her out on a date to Billy Berg's, a jazz club on Vine Street. Linc was smooth on the dance floor, tasteful in his clothing, generous with his money, and attentive in his conversation—it was no wonder they were sleeping together by their fourth date.

The Mocambo's maître d' showed them to a table next to the dance floor, where they ordered drinks and settled in to watch the dancers.

Gwendolyn accepted the cigarette Linc offered and waited for him to light it. "So how're things down at Tattler's Tuxedos?"

"Same old, same old, you know."

"No," she told him, "I don't. You so rarely talk about it."

Bertie's prediction had stayed with her: *He might even bankroll you.* She hadn't brought up the possibility because it seemed tacky; he might get the impression that she was only sticking around for his money. But he was never going to offer if he didn't even know her plan to open her own store. *Bring it up,* she told herself. *Let him get used to the idea.*

"There's not much to tell," he said. "Tuxes, cravats, jodhpurs, tie clips. Six of these yesterday, twelve of those today. It doesn't change much. But you know all about that, I expect." She was about to agree when he said, "By the way, what you're wearing tonight—is it new? One of your own creations? It's very becoming."

Her dress had been a donation from Kay Thompson: a royal blue moiré silk ball gown with a black sash and a necklace edged with pearls. Rationing dictated shorter hems for less fabric, so Gwendolyn revamped Kay's gown into a cocktail dress. She was satisfied with how it turned out, but what pleased her more was that she was dating a guy who would even notice.

"This one's more of a remodel. I love that you have the sort of eye—what are you doing?"

He was patting the pockets of his tuxedo jacket. "I have something for you." From inside his breast pocket he withdrew a slim package wrapped in cream tissue paper and tied with gold string.

"Is this some sort of anniversary?"

"No." He leaned over and kissed her hand.

Gwendolyn unfurled the wrapping paper until three pairs of nylon stockings fell onto the table. They were from Gorgeous Gams' ritzier line—even Lester had trouble getting his hands on these. The few times he did, Gwendolyn sold them to Mrs. O'Roarke for twice the regular price. "Where did you get these?"

"A couple of weeks ago I was helping you out of your dress when I noticed you weren't wearing any."

She picked up one of the stockings and held it to the light. It was so sheer she could barely see them. "Who did you have to hit over the head to get your paws on these?"

Linc's halfhearted shrug made it clear he wasn't about to divulge his secret.

She told him, "Come here and let me thank you properly."

She felt Linc respond to her lingering mouth—his hand slid up her thigh and would have kept on going had the waiter not arrived with their drinks.

Now that Ciro's was a burnt-out carcass of charcoal rafters and singed curtains, the Mocambo was the place to be. Despite the ambivalence she felt about going to the club, Gwendolyn thanked heaven for an oasis among the browns and blues of military uniforms and jeeps that seemed to pervade the city.

"Would you like to dance?" Linc asked. "I do like the way you rumba."

He led her onto the dance floor and pulled her into his confident arms. Together they swayed to the rhythm of the tune spilling over them from the orchestra pit. She snuggled in closer, pressing her face against the folds of his dress shirt, where she could feel the rise and fall of his chest.

They hadn't taken more than a few steps before the shattering of glass fractured the music, followed by a woman's voice shooting across the dance floor like a poisoned dart.

"SON OF A BITCH!" Another crash of exploding glass. "LOW-DOWN, NO-ACCOUNT, GODDAMNED BASTARD!"

Several hundred heads turned in the same direction, except Gwendolyn's. She kept hers pressed against Linc's chest. "Let me guess — the Battling Bogarts?"

Humphrey Bogart's distinctive voice opened fire. "SO NOW WE'RE DOING THIS IN PUBLIC? YOU DESPERATE LITTLE WASHED-UP LUSH, YOU THINK YOU CAN COWER ME BECAUSE WE'RE AT THE MOCAMBO?"

Gwendolyn jumped at the sound of heavier glass breaking against the floor. He'd upped the ante from wine glass to wine bottle. She looked up to see Bogie standing with the neck of a broken champagne bottle in hand; one of the lapels of his tux had been ripped away and now hung limply down his side. His wife, Mayo, stood several feet away in a white chiffon cocktail dress, unaware — or perhaps didn't care — that a dark stain blotted her right hip.

"I'D JAM THIS INTO YOUR CHEST IF YOU HAD A HEART," Bogie yelled.

Mayo went to lunge at him, but the Mocambo's maître d' caught her deftly by the elbow and pulled her back. He said something to them, but he was drowned out by the music restarting from the bandstand. Mayo yanked her arm free, grabbed her handbag, and started storming toward the front door like Sherman on the march. Bogie let go of the busted bottle, reached inside his torn jacket, and tossed a flutter of money onto the table. Gwendolyn watched the crowd part as he plunged across the dance floor.

Had she not been following Bogie's progress, she might not have spotted her friend, Ritchie Pugh, sitting in a booth against the far wall. He was the fifth wheel at a table filled with three thuggish bruisers in expensive suits and a strikingly handsome blue-eyed dreamboat with a matinee-idol smile, diamond-studded pinkie finger, and a nationwide reputation as the most dangerous mobster on the West Coast: Bugsy Siegel.

Gwendolyn met Ritchie when he was a waiter at the Vine Street Brown Derby, but he'd gotten into big trouble at the Santa Anita racetrack and soon found himself working for Bugsy Siegel and Mickey Cohen to pay off his debt. Then the FBI approached him to spy on the gangsters with the promise that they'd fund his freedom. Gwendolyn hadn't heard from him since long before Pearl Harbor and hoped he'd escaped his predicament by getting drafted.

Linc kissed her ear. "You don't actually know Bugsy Siegel, do you?"

Gwendolyn had had a couple of run-ins with Siegel and only just managed to extricate herself from his treacherous web, but that was the last thing she wanted Linc to know. "One of the guys at their table used to be my favorite waiter at the Derby. I'm just shocked to see him."

"You want to go over and say hello?"

"With Bugsy Siegel and Mickey Cohen sitting right there? No siree, Bob!"

The rumba came to an end and they returned to the table. Gwendolyn kept an eye on Ritchie. The guy had bags under his eyes, thinning hair, and hardened edges around his once-boyish face.

When he spotted her, Ritchie pulled out a notepad and wrote something on it, then folded the paper in half, then in half again, and then a third time. He said something to the guys at his table before sliding out of the booth. When he reached up to scratch his face, she saw he'd slotted the folded paper between his second and third fingers.

One of the Mocambo's many features was a glassed-in birdcage that ran the length of an entire wall. It contained dozens of bright green parakeets, inky blue macaws, and fuchsia lovebirds. She watched him walk past it and into one of the telephone booths at its far end. He didn't make a call, though. He stood facing the telephone for a moment or two, then exited the booth. He was halfway back when he reached up to scratch his face again—the paper was no longer between his fingertips.

"If you will excuse me," Gwendolyn said, placing her napkin on the table. "Kathryn isn't feeling very well tonight. I promised her I'd call to see how she's doing."

Thankfully, Ritchie's phone booth was vacant. His wad of paper was wedged behind the telephone.

> *What is it with you and shady types? You do know Lincoln Tattler is a black-market racketeer, don't you?*

Gwendolyn pressed the paper to her chest and wondered what a racketeer was. The word had been flung around during Prohibition, but what did it mean these days? Gangster? Hoodlum? Just someone who broke the law by selling on the black market? By that definition, she was a racketeer. *But that hardly makes me a hoodlum.*

She slipped the paper into her purse. *The Tattlers are rich as blazes,* she reasoned. Why would Linc need to sell on the black market?

She paused beside a six-foot-tall white painted bamboo cage. Inside was an enormous cockatoo with a magenta beak, huge blue eyes, and a crest of pink-and-red-striped feathers. Gwendolyn ducked behind it to observe Linc, who was eyeing the Siegel table with a grimness she'd never seen before. She hadn't figured him for the jealous type.

"Sorry about that." She dropped her purse on the table and took her seat.

Linc's face had resumed its usual carefree expression. "She's okay, I hope."

"Kathryn? Yes, much better." She reached over and squeezed his hand. "Thank you again for those nylons. You boys have no idea!"

Linc smiled. "I like to think I have some. While you were making your call, I got to thinking." He leaned in. "I want to tell you something I've never told anyone."

"I'm listening."

"Working for dear old Dad and the clothing business, it's okay, but my heart really isn't in it." His face lit up. "I've landed on something that really gets me going: electrical appliances, radios, and phonographs and the like."

Gwendolyn took a moment to chew over this information. "Phonographs? Like with records?"

"I love anything electrical, but radios are really my thing. I built my first ham when I was ten. In my last year of high school I built a shortwave radio and began listening to broadcasts from the BBC in London. Give me any broken electrical gadget, and I can fix it in a snap."

Gwendolyn grabbed his hand. "Aren't you a surprise?"

Linc nodded like a boy given his first BB gun for Christmas. "What I want to do is open a store that sells radios and gramophones to start with, but then I'll sell televisions."

"Televisions? What's that?"

"It's like radio, but with pictures. Like a small cinema that fits in the corner of your living room."

"In the corner of—really? Is such a thing even possible?"

"Trust me." Linc's face took on the same gravity she'd seen from behind the gigantic cage. "It's coming, and when it does, look out."

Gwendolyn rested her face on the palm of her hand. "We both want to open our own stores. I didn't know we had that in common. But what about financing all this? Do you think your father will help you out?"

"Parentasaurus Rex?" Linc scoffed. "Even if he offered—which he won't—I wouldn't take it. A man needs to stand on his own two feet, you know?"

Gwendolyn thought of Linc's elegant house on San Ysidro Drive north of the Beverly Hills Hotel, his gleaming silver Packard, and the hand-stitched suits he never seemed to run out of. Not to mention the fancy dinners and classy nightclubs he took her to. *That's all very well,* she thought, *but if you think you can have all your nice things by selling radios, you're in for a crash landing.*

"Selling overpriced tuxes to spoiled jerks isn't the only way I can make the money I need." He drained his champagne in a single swallow.

Gwendolyn looked across the dance floor to Siegel's table and saw Ritchie slumped in his seat, part of the group but not part of the conversation. Without warning, his eyes shot up to meet hers. He raised his eyebrows and, almost imperceptibly, started shaking his head.

CHAPTER 24

Kathryn slid a tray of bologna-and-cheese sandwiches onto the table and took a look around the packed barn. Marlene Dietrich and Deanna Durbin were on coffee duty and Lana Turner was tonight's hatcheck girl. Even Rita Hayworth had shown up, which wasn't especially unusual, but she and Orson Welles had just gotten hitched in a surprise ceremony. For Kathryn, the surprise was that Orson would get married at all. Kathryn and Orson had indulged in an affair before the war, and it didn't take her long to figure out that he was hardly the hitching type. She wished them lots of luck. They'd need it.

The throng around the stage whistled their appreciation for Jimmy Durante's "Inka Dinka Doo." As always, the servicemen couldn't get enough. Kathryn turned to her tablemate for the night. "Is it just my imagination, or is it particularly star-studded in here tonight?"

Betty Grable tucked a lock of white-blonde hair back into a light blue cap that matched her vaguely militaristic uniform, which Kathryn decided must be a studio creation. She doubted Grable had time to join the WACs or the WAVES. "We're expecting our one millionth serviceman tonight," Grable said. "They asked me to stick close by. When Mister Million comes through the door, I've been elected to bestow upon him the congratulatory kiss." She laughed. "Everything's a publicity opportunity, isn't it?"

Kathryn had never met Grable before being assigned to sandwich duty with her tonight. She was the biggest female star in the world these days, but it didn't seem to be going to her head. She seemed to know that all the attention and clamor would fade away eventually, but for now, it was on her shoulders to embody every wife, fiancé, and sweetheart each guy had left behind.

"You're going to give some lucky GI a kiss he'll never forget," Kathryn told her. "Especially if he saw you in *Coney Island.* You looked sensational."

Grable frowned. "Don't remind me. I'm still fighting with Anita Wyndham over that. Wouldn't you know it, she's here tonight."

Kathryn raked the crowd. "She is?"

"She gave it the big rah-rah on *Kraft Music Hall*—which is great, but she got everything wrong. She said I costarred with Robert Montgomery, not George Montgomery, and Eddie Cantor instead of Cesar Romero. I'm surprised she got the picture's name right. I caught your fill-in spot that night Melody Hope was on."

"It was all so crazy. Talk about flying by the seat of your pants."

"Oh, honey, you were terrific. They should give you that job. At least your heart would be in it. Anita's nice enough, but she's been doing such a slapdash job since the night of the fire."

A hoard of eager servicemen descended on Grable. She already had a pen in hand and smiled her famous smile as she signed the autograph books and magazines thrust in her face.

Kathryn got a dance hostess to watch the sandwich table for a while and worked her way down to the coffee stand. She only knew Anita Wyndham from the photograph that accompanied her byline, but the nest of black curls piled on top of her head made her easy to identify. Kathryn hadn't planned on saying anything, but just sniff around, but to Kathryn's surprise, Wyndham beckoned her over.

"It's time we met," she said. "I'm Anita Wyndham." She paused long enough for Kathryn to shake her hand. "I owe you a belated thank-you for saving my bacon that night."

Kathryn pictured Bertie cornering Wyndham like a rabid hippo. "I don't know that I saved your—"

"Oh, but you did! Even though I got to the studio in time, I was so frazzled I couldn't have put three coherent words together. Someone from the WAC committee waylaid me, and before I knew it, I heard your voice over the loudspeakers. I can't begin to tell you how relieved I was."

"Miss Wyndham," Kathryn began, but one of the guys from the kitchen interrupted them with a giant wicker basket filled with fresh donuts.

"Please, call me Anita. Can you give me a hand to stack these? They won't last long, but we're supposed to present them nicely." They started piling the donuts into a pyramid.

Kathryn had listened to the *Kraft Music Hall* every week since that night, and Betty Grable was right—Anita had been stumbling over her words, getting her facts wrong, and missing cues. "Things going well, I hope?"

Anita pouted. "Depends what you mean by 'well.'"

"Are they treating you okay? Are you happy there?"

"Absolutely yes to your first question. But the second?" Anita topped the stack with a final donut, and almost immediately, an undernourished Coast Guard plucked it off its perch. "I'm committed to a contract, so what does it matter?"

Kathryn's fantasy that Wallace Reed or Bing Crosby would call her to say they'd sacked Anita and wanted her had faded by the end of the month. But now a flutter of ambition quickened Kathryn's pulse. "I'm sure Bing, not to mention the gentlemen at *Kraft*, would be concerned if you're not happy."

Anita dusted sugar off her hands. "I suppose."

A roar of a hundred male voices filled the place as Marlene Dietrich took the stage and launched into "Lili Marlene." Kathryn took Anita by the arm and pulled her into a quieter corner.

"Contract or no contract, if you're not happy, there are plenty of columnists who'd be more than willing to fill your place. I'd give anything to have that job."

Anita shook her head. "No, you wouldn't."

"I would, yes." Anita shook her head again. "Is someone putting pressure on you to — well, you know, *do something?*"

Anita looked genuinely horrified. "No, no, nothing like that. It's just that when you get on the radio, you raise your public profile. A lot more people become aware of you." Anita's face grew hard with apprehension. "I'm surprised you haven't found that out already."

"Oh, but I have. You must have heard about my run-ins with Louella."

A few years back, at the height of the industry-wide conflict over *Citizen Kane*, Tallulah Bankhead and Agnes Moorhead got drunk at the Garden of Allah and made an effigy of Louella Parsons, then encouraged everyone to stick it with any sharp-edged implement they could find. When the story of that night flew around Hollywood, it was dubbed Kathryn Massey's Parson Piñata Party, and Louella hadn't spoken to her since.

Anita waved her hand dismissively. "Louella is the least of your worries. Have you met Nelson Hoyt yet?"

"I don't think so."

Anita let loose a snicker. "Between the Rhett Butler accent and that deep cleft in his chin, you'd know if you had."

"Which studio is he with?"

Anita flashed her a steely look just as a howl of cheers went up. Everybody in the Canteen started applauding.

A handsome army sergeant lingered at the front doors of the Hollywood Canteen, bewildered and startled. Betty Grable, standing out in her sky-blue uniform, hooked her arm through his as Lana Turner and Deanna Durbin looked on. Dietrich grabbed the microphone.

"Ladies and gentlemen, something very exciting just happened!" She consulted a piece of paper in her hand. "The Hollywood Canteen is very proud and excited to welcome First Sergeant Carl Bell with the US Army. He is very special to us because he is our one millionth guest!"

The whole place shook with a bellowing ovation while the Canteen's photographers captured Betty Grable planting a kiss on Sergeant One Million's cheek.

It was a while before the crowd subsided to its regular din and the band started playing a peppy version of Glenn Miller's "I Know Why And So Do You."

Kathryn turned to pick up her conversation with Anita but the woman had disappeared. She turned to one of the busboys. "Did you see where Miss Wyndham went?"

The busboy turned around and flashed a devilish smile. It was Gene Kelly. "Well, hello again!"

Kathryn had met him only once before, when he was fresh from his Broadway triumph in *Pal Joey* and relatively unknown in Hollywood. He was now a rising star at MGM.

"Mr. Kelly," she said. "I didn't know you were volunteering here."

"It's my first time." He jutted his head toward the lucky sergeant at the center of attention. "Looks like I picked a swell night." His smile revealed a small scar near his mouth that Kathryn assumed MGM would want fixed. It was arresting to still see it there. "You were asking about Anita?"

Kathryn nodded.

"Her shift finished as mine started. I saw her heading out to the parking lot."

Kathryn convinced Kelly to mind the coffee table for a few minutes, then she dodged the obstacle course of dancing couples, panting soldiers, and footsore sailors and beelined for the back door. The September air was still warm. She spotted Anita opening a white Cadillac and called out her name. "I wanted to finish our conversation."

"You want my job on the show, don't you?" It could have been an accusation, but Anita said it with surprising resignation.

"Only if you aren't happy, or no longer want it. Then yes, I'd like a chance."

"They were very impressed with you that night. The *Kraft* people, Bing — everybody."

"Are you saying you want to give it up?"

Anita's eyes turned to marble. "It might help if I can present my replacement, already approved and ready to take over."

"Just say the word." A spot on *Kraft Music Hall*? Wilkerson is going to flip!

Anita eyed her carefully. "I'll let you know." She closed the door and wound down the window. "You do understand that a job like this raises you to a national profile?"

Kathryn nodded and watched the white Cadillac pull into the Hollywood traffic. Raise me to a national profile? Isn't that the whole point?

CHAPTER 25

Alla Nazimova's Studebaker wasn't ideal for a long stakeout. There wasn't much legroom in the back seat, and the overhead light wasn't quite bright enough for four people to eat by. On the other hand, neither Gwendolyn, Kathryn, nor Marcus owned their own vehicle and Madame was more than happy to lend them hers, providing she could come along. "Which isn't to say that I approve of what you're doing," she added in her dowager voice.

San Ysidro Drive branched off Benedict Canyon just north of the Beverly Hills Hotel and cut an almost straight line up the Hollywood Hills. Every half dozen houses, a streetlight punctuated the dark. At 1137 San Ysidro, Linc's house sat halfway between Fred Astaire's and the one shared by Laurence Olivier and Vivien Leigh. It was a wide, two-story house with a thick chimney at one end and a deep front garden filled with flowering shrubs and miniature fruit trees.

As Gwendolyn bit into a pickle, Kathryn asked, "How long are we going to give this?" She said "we," but Gwendolyn knew the question was aimed at her.

Alla suggested midnight.

The lights were ablaze in Linc's bedroom, living room, and kitchen. His drapes were open, but there was no sign of anybody inside.

"Here's what I don't get," Marcus said, popping open a root beer. "If Linc has a poker game every Wednesday night, why aren't any cars parked outside his house?"

For as long as Gwendolyn and Linc had been dating, the one unbreakable rule was that Wednesday was poker night and therefore off-limits. She'd scheduled Canteen shifts for Wednesdays and never thought much about it, but now she found herself sitting in Alla's Studebaker at eleven o'clock at night, peering at Linc's house and wondering why the only car around was his silver Packard.

"Maybe Linc's poker buddies are all his neighbors?" Gwendolyn knew how improbable that sounded before the words even left her mouth.

"Or maybe," Marcus said, "there's more going on in the life of Lincoln Tattler than he's shared with you."

"I still don't believe it," Kathryn said.

"But Ritchie —"

"I'm just saying I find it highly improbable that Mister High Society Tattler works the black market."

Alla leaned forward from the back seat and clapped a hand on Gwendolyn's left shoulder. "Most people would also find it highly improbable that our lovely Gwendolyn works the black market." Gwendolyn laid her hand on top of Alla's, which was taking on a dry, papery feel. Until that moment, Gwendolyn had thought of her as ageless; this was the first time she realized Alla Nazimova was aging like a mere mortal.

"Why would the heir to the Tattler fortune need to deal in the black market?" Kathryn peeled back the aluminum foil from a slice of Marcus' dense, sticky war cake. It had become standard fare at Garden of Allah gatherings. "It just doesn't make any sense. Even though I don't doubt Ritchie's word, I still don't think it's enough to warrant this stakeout you've got us on."

"There's something I haven't told you all," Gwendolyn confessed.

The car went quiet.

"A couple of nights ago, Linc and I got home from a USO benefit at the Beverly Hills Hotel and his telephone was ringing. It was his father. There must have been some sort of crisis with the business because pretty quickly the conversation went from whispering to screaming." She took a deep breath. "I found out that everything Linc has—the house, the car—none of it is his."

"Linc owns nothing?" Kathryn asked.

"It's all in the business' name. From what I could gather, all bills go to his father, and in return Linc gets an allowance."

"It must be a heck of an allowance," Marcus said. "Those dinners and nightclubs? Not to mention those expensive corsages and all that champagne?"

"The point is, Linc feels like his father still treats him like he's twelve. It was a really awful fight, but that's not what I'm confessing. The next day when he went out for bagels and lox, I went hunting around for a soft rag to clean my shoes, and I found a stack of nylon stockings. Same as the ones he gave me at the Mocambo. I counted them—there were forty-five pairs, and right next to them was another box: eleven bottles of a perfume called Miramar."

"Miramar?" Alla exclaimed. "That's a Spanish perfume. Very expensive."

Gwendolyn sighed. "So that's why I insisted we come out tonight and see if anything happens."

The car fell into silence until Kathryn started to chuckle. "Look at us! Spying on what could be a big-time war profiteer. What are we, nineteen years old? This feels like the crazy sort of stunt we were pulling when we first moved into the Garden. We tried anything to get our foot in the door."

"Like when Gwendolyn fell off that dancing billboard?" Marcus asked.

"Or that security guard chased you all over the MGM lot like he was Ben Turpin."

Gwendolyn fell prey to an attack of the giggles. "What about the time I dressed up as Scarlett O'Hara and presented myself on David Selznick's doorstep on Christmas Eve? Where did I find the nerve?"

"Yeah, well, we're in our mid thirties now," Kathryn said, finishing off her cake. "In a few years we'll be forty, and that's middle-aged."

"Speak for yourself!" Marcus butted in. "I feel like I'm just getting going, so don't you drag me into the old folks' home just yet."

Alla cleared her throat in her best school-marm manner. "Speaking as someone on the north side of sixty, you are all still whippersnappers to me. I don't consider anyone middle-aged until their knees start aching in winter—oh! Look out!"

A pair of white headlights rounded the bend in the road and a woodie station wagon pulled into Linc's driveway. All four of them sank down in their seats and watched the driver get out. Instead of approaching Linc's front door, he walked down the hill and out of sight.

"That was odd," Marcus whispered. "Shall I go look inside?"

"What if Linc comes out?" Alla asked.

Nobody could come up with a remotely plausible story to explain why Marcus would be standing in Linc's driveway peering into windows.

A rectangular tile of light caught their attention. They watched Linc close his front door behind him, get into the woodie, and start the engine. He backed out of his driveway and headed up the hillside, in exactly the opposite direction Gwendolyn was expecting.

"I can't believe I'm going to say this," Kathryn said, "but Marcus, follow that car."

Keeping the headlights of Alla's Studebaker switched off, Marcus kept his distance to the top end of the street, then around a disorienting series of curves and corners until they turned onto Mulholland Drive. From there, Linc led them to Coldwater Canyon, where he headed down into the San Fernando Valley. Eventually they ended up in Burbank.

"Is he going to Warner Brothers?" Marcus asked.

Linc pulled up to a darkened stretch of the high wall that surrounded the studio. Farther down, a billboard featuring Bette Davis in front of a microphone advertised Warners' all-star wartime propaganda, *Thank Your Lucky Stars*. The rest of the street was thrown into shadow.

Linc opened the car's back door and pulled out a large cardboard box. He walked up to the fence and tossed it over the wall.

"He's done that before," Kathryn observed.

Linc jumped back into the woodie and drove out of the Valley, past the Hollywood Bowl, and to the eastern border of the Paramount lot, where the same scene was played out again.

"Those boxes don't look too heavy," Marcus remarked. "Like they're filled with something very . . . sheer."

They followed Linc to a side street adjacent to the Twentieth Century-Fox lot and watched him lob another box over another wall. Then they followed him farther west. With so few cars on the road, they might have been too easy to spot, so Marcus kept the Studebaker at a distance, sometimes too far back, almost losing him.

"He's going to MGM, isn't he?" Alla said.

"Yep," said Marcus.

"Does your pal Hooley still work the gate?" Gwendolyn asked.

"Yep."

"Will he get us in?"

"Yep."

Several years back, Marcus made friends with one of MGM's longest-serving security guards, who was an incurable insomniac and therefore the perfect night watchman. He and Marcus shared a passion for crossword puzzles, so from time to time Marcus would pick up a pair of football-sized hoagies and keep Hooley company for a few hours while they worked on a puzzle together.

Hooley was the stoic type, and didn't raise an eyebrow when Marcus turned up at one A.M. with three women in tow. Without questioning Marcus' request to borrow a flashlight, he allowed them through the gate with a sweep of his hand.

Gwendolyn had never been inside a movie studio so late at night. It was eerie, she decided, like an evacuated town, and they were the last four inhabitants left to roam through deserted streets.

They found Linc's box resting behind the railway station façade where countless romantic scenes had played out, tender goodbyes whispered between glycerin tears.

Gwendolyn knelt beside the box. It was tied with string.

Alla fished in her purse for nail clippers. They were a little on the dull side, so it took Gwendolyn several attempts before the string fell away.

Gwendolyn hesitated.

"Don't you want to see what's inside?" Kathryn asked.

"I think we already know," Marcus said.

Gwendolyn laid her hands on the box but kept them there. "It's just that," she started, but didn't know if she could reconcile the conflicting emotions battling it out inside her head.

"Go on. Open it." Linc stood a few yards away, his face frozen in the moonlight.

Gwendolyn stood up, unsure if he was angry, or surprised, or even bemused.

"Linc," she said, but it was all she could manage.

Marcus stepped in. "Did you know we've been following you all over town?"

"Let's just say you wouldn't make very effective private eyes." Linc eyed the box between them. "What do you think's in there?" he asked Gwendolyn.

"Stockings," she said. "Like the ones you gave me at the Mocambo."

He took a step closer. "So you've guessed my little secret?"

"Judging by the size of the box," Gwendolyn offered a tentative smile, "I'm guessing your little secret ain't so little. I don't know how you've been managing to get your hands on them, but if this box is filled with Gorgeous Gams, you've got yourself quite an operation."

He leaned back slightly, his face pulled into a questioning scowl. She decided to go for broke.

"If that box is full, there must be seventy-five to a hundred pairs. Let's round that off to eighty. If you're selling them for five bucks a pair, that's a profit of, what, three or four per? Times eighty pair, that's something like a three-hundred-dollar profit you've got in that box."

He jammed his fists onto his hips. "Hang me high! You're her, aren't you?"

Gwendolyn hoped her face was in shadow, hiding her uncertainty.

"What do you mean?" Alla demanded, suddenly maternal.

He clamped his hands on the top of his head as though to keep it from exploding. "All this time I've been hearing about the woman with the stockings. Good product. Discreet. Not greedy. No price gouging. Everywhere I went I heard about her, but nobody could tell me her name. It was always 'I know a guy who knows a guy who knows a girl who's heard of the girl with the quality merchandise.' And all this time she was right under my nose!" He let out a laugh. "Well, if that don't beat the cotton from the cottonwood tree!" He marched toward her and grabbed her hand. "My biggest competition, glad to meet ya!"

"I'm not your competition anymore," Gwendolyn admitted. "My source got himself drafted. The field's all yours."

"Nuh-uh!" Linc protested. "I've got more business than I know what to do with. This studio stuff is just the tip of the iceberg. Why do you think I've been trying to track you down?"

Marcus stepped forward. "You want to go into business with her?"

Linc kept his eyes on Gwendolyn. "Nylons are the backbone of the market, but then there's perfume, scarves, lipstick. They say this war could go on for another year, maybe even two. By then we'll both have saved enough to open our stores: Gwendolyn's Gowns and Tattler's

Televisions. Maybe we could get them side by side. Wouldn't that be neat?"

Gwendolyn pouted. "It's called Chez Gwendolyn."

She looked at Kathryn and Marcus. It wasn't like she needed their approval, but if she went into cahoots with Linc, she'd be stepping from the small time into the big time. Or the medium time, at least. Knowing they weren't completely against the idea meant the difference between telling Linc goodbye and letting him know that she was on deck.

Marcus' smile was so wide she could tell he didn't have a problem with this unexpected turn of events, but Kathryn's face wasn't readable until she stepped into the moonlight to join Marcus. "I'd kill for a decent lipstick."

Gwendolyn looked past Marcus and Kathryn to Alla. "And you, Madame? What do you think about all this?"

Alla stayed where she was. "Does it matter what I think?"

Gwendolyn moved into the gloom of the fake railway station. "Of course it does."

"We are in a time of war."

"So you don't think it's wrong of me to sell these things on the black market?"

"Right, wrong, good, bad, just, unjust. Rules are flexible. Opportunities present themselves. The only thing to avoid is regret." She reached up and stroked Gwendolyn's face. "Chez Gwendolyn deserves a chance."

CHAPTER 26

Marcus and Kathryn strolled out of the Egyptian Theatre and headed up the long forecourt toward Hollywood Boulevard. The night air was cooling now that Thanksgiving was around the corner. They stopped in front of the marquee and watched an usher perched on a ladder removing the letters: *Special RKO preview "Higher And Higher" starring Frank Sinatra*. The rest of the audience skirted around them as they exited.

Marcus took Kathryn's hand and folded it into the crook of his arm. He caught the faint whiff of the sweet carnation corsage pinned to her jacket. It smelled like Pennsylvania to him. *Or maybe Pennsylvania has been on my mind more than usual lately.* "What did you think?"

"Pretty good," she said, "seeing as how it's his first movie. He told me at Kay Thompson's birthday party last week he was anxious because if he didn't make a complete ass of himself, Mayer would approach RKO about buying out his contract. Apparently, Mayer cried when he heard Frank sing 'Ol' Man River.'"

They stood on the sidewalk on Hollywood Boulevard and watched a streetcar rattle past them. "You want to head home?"

Kathryn shook her head. "I'm wide awake. Let's amble."

They headed west toward Highland Avenue, crossed the boulevard, and were soon passing the Hollywood Hotel.

"Speaking of Mayer," Kathryn said, squeezing his hand with her elbow, "how're things at work these days? You don't talk about it much."

Marcus blew a long, wet raspberry. "I always thought that in Hollywood, you were only as good as your last movie. Well, *my* last movie was one of the top three moneymakers for the year, so there goes that theory."

"Maybe you should get into the black-market business with Gwennie," Kathryn suggested with a laugh. "She tells me she's making buckets of cash since she teamed up with Linc."

They stopped to let a black Mercedes-Benz sedan pull into the driveway of the Hollywood Hotel. It was the first one Marcus had seen in a while—most German cars had quietly disappeared since America entered the war. "I campaigned for both *Meet Me In St. Louis* and the one we're doing about Marie Curie, but got knocked back. Ditto that new horse picture, *National Velvet.* Then I really went all out for *Song Of Russia*, because that's our big contribution to pro-Soviet/anti-Axis relations. I figured if I could talk my way onto that picture, it'd prove to Mayer that I'm as red-blooded as any American. But all I got was '*nyet.*'"

"So what now?"

"New tactic: come up with my own flag-waving, patriotism-inspiring story." He furtively patted the letter in his breast pocket. He needed reassurance that it was still there before he showed it to Kathryn.

She pulled them to a stop. "Let's watch them turn off all the lights."

Theaters were now subject to a citywide dim-out. At ten P.M., they had to switch off every outside light. Angelenos no longer feared a surprise Japanese air attack, but until the Allied Pacific forces stormed Tokyo, everybody agreed: Why take a chance?

Marcus and Kathryn lingered on the sidewalk as Grauman's switched off their lights in four stages. It left them standing in a shadowy haze — the streetlights were still burning, but most stores followed suit and switched off their lighting, too. The only lit places were cafes, bars, and restaurants.

Kathryn pointed down the street to a crowd of several dozen gathered outside C.C. Brown's. "Something's going on."

By the time they reached the ice cream parlor, the mob had whipped themselves into a feverish state. "I wonder who's in there," Marcus said. "Must be someone big."

A girl with hair braided to military precision turned around, exclaiming, "It's Melody Hope!" in a breathless voice usually reserved for overexcited teenagers. "She's on a date! With Trevor Bergin!" The girl pointed toward the glass windows.

For someone who had been insecure to the point of paralysis before starting *William Tell*, Trevor had acquitted himself so well that MGM rushed him into a pirate movie — *Storm The Spanish Main*. It turned out every bit as thrilling as anything Errol Flynn was in for Warners or Fox was churning out for Tyrone Power. And Trevor was just as good playing a Flemish painter caught in the wake of Napoleon's army in *March to Waterloo*. It was hard for Marcus not to feel a snip of resentment that he was good enough to write *William Tell* but wasn't even considered for Trevor's follow-up movies.

He thought about Quentin. The last thing Marcus heard from Quentin was that he and Trevor were happily — albeit discreetly — shacking up in Quentin's apartment halfway between MGM and Paramount. Marcus wondered what Quentin thought about this public show of simulated romance.

A date between Trevor Bergin and Melody Hope had to be a studio thing, but Marcus couldn't find fault in it. A month before, the LAPD conducted a raid on the Open Door, a queer bar in Hollywood. Nineteen men were thrown into lockup, fingerprinted, and ID'd before being released the following morning, and the next day their names, ages, addresses, and employers were published in both the *Times* and *Examiner*—which meant all nineteen men had lost their jobs by the end of the week. Among them were workers from all six major movie studios, including four from MGM. For Marcus, it was a jabbing reminder that while anything goes inside the Garden of Allah, outside its walls, a harsher reality existed, and if he wasn't careful, it could sneak up and sock him in the jaw.

The teenager with the taut braids let out a squeal. "Here they come!" She waved her autograph book over her head and called out Melody's name as the two stars shouldered their way through the thicket of grasping hands and high-pitched squeals.

A black Plymouth rounded the corner and pulled up at the curb just as Melody and Trevor broke through. They climbed inside and sped off, leaving a trail of fans alternating between excitement at having seen a pair of real-life movie stars and disappointment that they had slipped away so quickly. Within the space of a minute, the crowd dispersed into the encroaching darkness.

"Got any ration coupons on you?" Kathryn asked. "We could get ourselves a sundae."

Marcus shook his head. "My cupboard's bare."

With so few taxis around these days, hoofing it home was the best option. Outside the La Brea Market farther up Hollywood Boulevard, they came across a gathering of a different type. About a dozen people were lined up in silent, patient pairs.

Marcus approached the two women on the end; their heads were bound up with cheap scarves and they wore no makeup. "What's going on here?"

"We've heard —"

"From a reliable source —"

"That they're getting in a shipment —"

"Of shoes!"

Marcus' war cake had proved that you could bake a cake without butter, eggs, or milk, and Kathryn's rosemary lentil casserole had shown that you could go without meat if you had to. But it was the rationing of shoes that most people found hardest to cope with. There were only so many times you could take your old shoes to the cobbler.

Tempting as it was to join the line, there was an eight-hour wait until La Brea Market opened its doors, so they moved on. Marcus was about to pull the letter from his pocket when Kathryn said, "I was just thinking the other day about war movies. They're all about soldiers at the front, but hardly any of them deal with the war at home, showing scenes where people line up in the middle of the night on a rumor they might get some new shoes or an egg."

"Funny you should say that," Marcus said. "I've been mulling over an idea I had a couple of weeks ago. I see it as an all-star movie about neighbors who all live on the same street, and how they each deal with the war and its effects on the home front."

"That's a great idea!"

Marcus jiggled his head from side to side. "Yeah, but I haven't got a villain yet. The Nazis and the Japs are all five thousand miles away, not in the house next door on Main Street, USA. So I still have some figuring to do."

"What if you have someone come swooping into town? Maybe someone who left for New York or Hollywood, and drops in, flaunting ration books or — " She snapped her fingers. "Or black-market goods? We know someone who could give you pointers."

They walked on for a few steps in silence until Marcus felt the time was right. "Speaking of dropping into town." He stepped into a pool of light from a streetlamp and pulled the letter from his jacket pocket.

Kathryn sniffed the envelope. "*Nuit de Paris,* if I'm not mistaken. Who's it from?"

Marcus counted to three. "Doris."

"WHAT?" A lone figure hurrying through the shadows on the other side of Hollywood Boulevard looked up briefly before continuing on his way. "She wrote back? What's it been, a year?"

"Nearly. I'd pretty much given up on her, but this came in the mail today."

"What did she say?"

Marcus started fanning the letter. "She wants to come visit."

Kathryn pulled him into a hug. "How wonderful!"

"Mmmm . . ."

She kept her grip on his shoulders but pushed him away to arm's length. "I clearly recall a certain farewell party in which you wailed over how much you missed your family. And now your favorite sister wants to come visit and all you have to say is 'Mmmm'?"

Marcus shrugged himself out of Kathryn's clasp and wrestled with the knowledge that what he was about to say might make him sound idiotic. "She's a small-town girl, daughter of the mayor, unmarried and therefore probably a virgin — "

"So?"

"So she comes to LA, sees where I live, sees *how* I live . . . " He let the sentence peter off.

She ran her hand down his arm. "Are we talking about how your sweetheart isn't a girl?"

"The fact is I'm thirty-seven years old and never been married. Back home we used to call those fellows 'confirmed bachelors,' but we all knew it was just a euphemism. That rejection was hard enough to take the first time; I honestly don't know that I could handle it again. Especially not from Doris."

"Then why did you write back to her at all?"

"I thought we could get to know each other through letters. It never occurred to me she'd come all the way out here."

"Ever heard of the Greyhound bus?"

"You're not helping." He started to walk away.

She hurried to catch up. "I'm sorry. Let me help."

He kept his eyes on the empty road ahead of him.

"Show her only as much of your life as you want to."

He slowed his pace, but kept his eyes trained on the sidewalk.

"Tell her there's a drastic shortage of accommodation because of the war — which is quite true — and that you couldn't get her into the Garden. We'll find her some nice place. We can take her to the Mocambo and maybe shock her a little with the floor show at Florentine Gardens. I could treat her to a facial at Elizabeth Arden, you give her a tour of MGM, arrange to bump into Melody or Judy Garland or someone. You fill her head with thrilling memories, and then put her on the Greyhound back to Pennsylvania. Fade to black. Closing credits."

Marcus stopped. "So just edit out the socially awkward bits?"

"Hasn't your work with the Mobilization taught you anything? It's all about how the message gets put across." She tilted her head to one side. "It's what you're doing with Oliver, isn't it? He's welcome at the Garden, but other places, you edit him out of your social life. It doesn't have to be all or nothing."

"What does that mean?" Marcus could feel the heat rising off his face.

"You're an all-in kind of guy. Look at how long you held that torch for Ramon. Most people would've given up long before."

"I thought I was in love with him."

"All I'm saying is that you're a very loyal person. Look at how it's been at work for you. They're such Indian givers: they love you, they hate you, they give you a raise, then they don't give you any decent pictures to work on. They hint at an Oscar nomination, then they back out. But do you give up? No! You're still in there swinging, doing your damndest to stay in the game. It's all or nothing with you. And in a lot of situations, that's terrific." She reached up to wiggle his ear and didn't react when he pulled back. "But with something like this visit from your sister, it's okay to be selective. And if we stage-manage it right, not so hard to pull off."

The apprehension of voicing his fears about Doris coming to visit had been weighing on Marcus like a yoke. "What would I do without you?"

She blew a raspberry. "You'd probably resort to hiring some frightful hooker and spend the entire week trying to explain to your virginal small-town sister why your pretend girlfriend knows every other guy she passes in the street. Now *that's* the movie you ought to write, if you ask me."

CHAPTER 27

Kathryn watched the rows of orange trees rush by her window. "Really," she told her boss, "you didn't have to come."

Wilkerson almost looked paternal the way he peered at her over his reading glasses. "The first time I went up, I damn near shit my pants."

It hadn't occurred to Kathryn to be nervous about her first flight. Excited, yes, but not nervous.

He returned to his newspaper. "You'll be in a DC-3, you know."

A sign reading *Lockheed Air Terminal – 2 miles* flashed past her.

"DC-3?" Kathryn pulled out her compact and checked her lipstick, some Argentinean brand Linc had snuck into the country. So silky, so moist. "Is that bad?"

"It's the same sort of aircraft Carole Lombard was in."

"WHAT?!"

"Relax. Hundreds of DC-3s fly around this country and hardly any of them crash. Statistically speaking – "

"UGH!" She threw the lipstick into her purse. "Why would you even bring up something like that?"

"You've got nothing to worry about," Wilkerson insisted. "From what I heard, Lombard's crash was human error, but

Howard Hughes will be in the seat today, and he's probably the best civilian pilot in the country."

Kathryn pulled at the edges of her chinchilla coat. It was sixty degrees in Los Angeles, but the weather for Seattle was predicted to hit the low forties. She sat in silence trying to banish thoughts of Carole's plane crash.

The chauffeur pulled onto the airport driveway. Ahead of them, a TWA plane sat on the runway, the early morning sun glinting on its unpainted silver body. A banner erected between two steel poles stood off to one side: *USO TOUR* in big white letters against a blue background. Along the bottom read the motto *UNTIL EVERY ONE COMES HOME*. The whole thing was surrounded with white stars and a bright red border.

They parked alongside several other expensive cars. Kathryn got out and waved toward the group of people milling around the stairwell. The first to wave back was Humphrey Bogart; he came striding toward her.

It struck Kathryn that he was more handsome in person than he was on the screen, perhaps because he always played cynical loners and world-weary heavies. Bogie smoked Chesterfields like every other guy, but on him they smelled more manly somehow, more reassuring. "Tyrone was telling me this is your first flight," he said. "Anxious?"

Kathryn glanced at the USO sign. Until every one comes home. She shook her head. "All ready to try my wings."

He stroked her chinchilla coat. "Nice," he said sardonically. "Now that you're this big radio star, I guess you gotta dress the part."

It had been nearly four months since Kathryn took over from Anita Wyndham on *Kraft Music Hall*, and she was still getting used to the idea that she was heard from coast to coast. Her first on-air reports were a bit shaky, but Bing had given her tips on how to steady herself: "Double-space your notes; short breath between sentences; cut out milk the day of the broadcast."

By the fourth week he was engaging her in banter, and two weeks later, she parried one of his good-natured digs. "Any more cracks like that, mister, and I'll be telling Zukor your next picture should be called *Road to Nowhere.*" The studio audience howled with laughter, Crosby gave her the thumbs up, and she hadn't looked back. When Marcus suggested she report on the USO's program for entertaining the troops, she started a series that unfettered an avalanche of fan mail and resulted in the USO inviting her on tour. Wilkerson sent around an all-staff memo saying the *Reporter*'s circulation was up by nearly ten percent, thanks to Kathryn.

Bogie walked her to the plane, where Judy Garland, Gene Kelly, and Danny Kaye were dancing an improvised time step to keep warm. Kathryn was thrilled to see Judy there. Rumors had been rife lately that she and her director on *Meet Me In St. Louis* were getting romantic. The movie had been an enormous hit, due in part, Kathryn thought, to the skillful way Vincente Minnelli guided Judy through a difficult shoot. Kathryn had only met Minnelli once and found him a quiet-spoken man of innate good taste, dripping with class. She hoped the rumors were true and sensed a big story.

"Thank God you're here!" Judy grabbed her arm. "I was afraid I'd be the only gal to keep these galoots in check."

Van Johnson protested with a stern "HEY!"

"You know we can hear you," Tyrone said. He looked dashing in his formfitting Marine Corps uniform. He doffed his hat and motioned toward the stairway that led up into the aircraft.

The cabin had six rows of double seats separated by a center aisle. Kathryn had hoped for a seat next to Judy, but Judy and Gene were singing "When You Wore A Tulip And

I Wore A Big Red Rose" from a long way down the stairwell. Kathryn stared at the portholes — barely one foot by one foot — and wondered if staring at the ground falling away from them was the best thing she could do to quell her nerves. She heard Bogie's voice behind her.

"For the first-time flyer, I suggest a room with a view."

She removed her fur and handed it to the blonde stewardess, then she and Humphrey clipped themselves into their seats. When Bob Hope spotted her in the front row, he broke out into a chorus of "I'll Take You Home Again, Kathleen." Judy threw Tyrone's Marine Corps cap at him. "It's *Kathryn*, you big dope!"

"If she'd signed on to *my* radio show, I'd have gotten her name right."

Kathryn wondered if he knew what his sponsor's price of admission was.

While the rest of the passengers — the USO band and a couple of backup singers — boarded and the crew settled everyone in, Kathryn looked out the window. She spotted Wilkerson and Howard Hughes standing together on the tarmac. Dressed in a gray flying suit and no hat, Hughes was shaking his head almost as vigorously as Wilkerson was nodding. They didn't seem to be arguing, but they weren't in agreement, either. Abruptly, Hughes walked away. Wilkerson cupped his hands to be heard over the propellers. He was still shouting as Hughes mounted the staircase.

This was the first time Kathryn had seen Howard Hughes up close. With his dark hair parted neatly to one side of his long face, and his intense dark eyes, Kathryn could see why he had such success with the ladies. The fact that he was worth a fortune that would make King Solomon blush probably helped. He did a double take when he spotted Kathryn and squatted down in front of her.

"Your boss tells me this is your first time up in the wild blue yonder."

Kathryn could barely hear him over the roar of the engines. "You'll keep it smooth, won't you?" She really wanted to ask him what happened on the tarmac.

"Perhaps once we're airborne, you might like to come forward and see the cockpit."

"I'd love that."

"It's a date, then." He shook Bogart's hand and disappeared behind the cockpit door.

The aircraft heaved forward and Kathryn felt every vibration and shock as they sped along the runway. She gripped the armrests as the plane heaved itself into the air, and didn't open her eyes until she heard Bogart's voice.

"I'll wager next month's pay you've never seen Los Angeles like this before."

She peered out the window and gasped. At ground level, the San Fernando Valley was so vast it was difficult to tell it was a valley at all. But at this altitude, the hills shaped the landscape clearly. As they climbed higher, the orange and lemon trees began to merge into a sea of green orchards flecked with tiny dots of color.

"Is it any wonder Hughes has a God complex?" Bogie said. Kathryn kept her eyes glued to the square porthole. "I can see why Ty joined the Marines. If I was only ten years younger."

"My friend Marcus tried to sign up even before Pearl Harbor, but they knocked him back on account of his eyesight. So he joined the Hollywood Writers Mobilization."

"Is that supposed to make me feel better?"

She clamped a hand on his. "My point is, we're all doing our bit."

"Gable's only a couple of years younger than me, and he joined up. Jimmy Stewart, too."

"Jimmy Stewart *is* ten years younger than you," Kathryn pointed out. "And as for Gable, yes, he signed up, and went to England and flew his five combat missions. But then what happened? Mayer pulled his strings and now he's back here with the Army Motion Picture Unit. And you're here with the USO to give our boys a much-needed respite. Seeing you in person will mean a lot to them. They'll be talking about it forever."

The stewardess appeared. "Mr. Hughes has asked if you'd like to come visit."

The cockpit was more cramped than she expected. There were two seats behind an incomprehensible console of gauges, dials, buttons, and levers. Hughes' copilot climbed out of his seat and offered it to Kathryn, then disappeared through the door as she climbed in beside Hughes. It wasn't until she was settled that she was able to fully take in the astounding panorama in front of her.

Her eyes followed Sunset Boulevard along the foothills until she caught sight of the stark white Los Angeles City Hall, its pyramid-shaped roof pointing into the clear January sky. She pressed her hands to her chest. "Everything's so tiny! It's like the world is just made of doll furniture. Look at those people at Sunset and Doheny! What are they, ants? Is it always this clear?"

"You've caught LA on a good day."

Far off in the distance, the blue Pacific sparkled in the sunlight. Kathryn pressed a finger against the windscreen. She could feel the thrum of the engines vibrate up her arm. "Is that Catalina?"

"Yep."

Hughes steered a wide curve to the right. Directly below them lay the Hollywood Hills dotted with the odd mansion, the sapphire of swimming pools scattered among the foliage. One pool in particular at the base of the hills caught her eye. "That's the Garden of Allah!" She couldn't see who was laying around the pool, but its grand-piano shape was unmistakable. From this vantage point, the rooftops' apple-red Spanish tile looked more vibrant than she had ever pictured. "This is astonishing!"

Hughes grunted. "Remember in *Casablanca* when Bogie said how the problems of people don't amount to a hill of beans?"

"Is the *Hollywood Reporter* building—OH!" She squealed like a six-year-old. "There it is! And look at Paramount. You'd swear it's the size of my dining table!" She wished she could share all this with Marcus and Gwendolyn. *How can a city I know so well look so foreign?*

"Miss Massey, I brought you up here for a reason."

"Yes?"

"There's something I feel I ought to share with you."

Hughes' change in tone arrested Kathryn's attention.

He straightened his steering wheel and pulled at a lever. "I understand that you and your boss enjoy a close relationship."

"I'm not sleeping with him, if that's what you're getting at."

"I only meant that he trusts you a great deal."

Kathryn shifted in the copilot seat so that she could face him more squarely. The glint of a smile had dropped away, leaving his mouth set in a line. "I'd say that's true."

"Miss Massey—"

"Please call me Kathryn."

"Kathryn, you need to know that your boss and I were part of a poker game at Zukor's house last night."

This didn't sound good. "Is that what your little tarmac tiff was about?"

"Last night, your boss won ninety-seven thousand."

Kathryn slumped back in her seat. Large gambling debts were part of life in Hollywood society. They showed that if you could afford to bet high, you were a major player and it garnered you great prestige. How these guys found the nerve to gamble such mind-boggling amounts was beyond Kathryn's comprehension, but at least this meant Wilkerson had started the year ahead of the game.

"Unfortunately," Hughes continued, "he went on to lose two hundred and fifteen grand."

Kathryn stared out the window, but she no longer saw the City of Angels spread out before her like a picnic blanket. It now looked like a pit of quicksand. "From what I understand, those kinds of numbers are fairly routine."

"They are. But last night was the third time in a row your boss has lost more than a hundred grand in one sitting."

"Why are you telling me this?" Kathryn kept her eyes on the horizon. "Don't get me wrong, I appreciate the tip-off. But it's not like *I* can cover his debts."

Hughes swung the plane toward the coastline. As Malibu came into view, turbulence started to shake them around. "I wanted you to see what the world looks like from up here. We get so caught up in the triviality of life. How am I going to seduce her? Who's making more money than me? How come her dress is prettier than mine? It's easy to forget what really matters."

"What really matters to you?"

"I like Bill. I like the way he thinks, and I admire what he's achieved. But he's getting himself deeper and deeper in the hole." A pocket of air jolted the cockpit. Carole Lombard's face flashed before Kathryn. "He can't see how badly he's risking everything he's built up. I've asked around and the consensus seems to be that you're the one he's most likely to listen to."

"We've already had one of those discussions," Kathryn told him. "It didn't go well."

"Then you need to try harder."

The Pacific coastline stretched before them as far as Kathryn could see. It was a gorgeous sight, but the turbulence was starting to punch at her stomach.

"Thank you," she said. "I appreciate you sharing this with me."

Hughes pulled back on his steering wheel, lifting the airplane higher. The jolting abated a little. "In return, I have a favor to ask."

Why do guys like you always have a motive? "Ask away."

"You're good friends with Melody Hope, aren't you?"

And why do your motives nearly always involve a girl? "I'd like to think we're friends."

"It seems I've gotten her in the family way."

Kathryn sighed. This guy has more money than the Federal Reserve, but he can't spend a couple of bucks on some French letters for protection? "Surely you have some sympathetic doctor on call who can take care of that problem?"

"Melody isn't listening to reason right now. It's not like I can shoot her with elephant tranquilizer, but I need her to see straight. I like the girl, but I'm not going to marry her. Will you talk to her for me?"

Kathryn watched the coastline unfurl like a giant zipper. "I'll give it a go. But I'd like a favor in return."

"I thought the information on your boss was the favor in return."

The turbulence started up again, this time heavier; the shudders piled up, one after the other. Kathryn started wishing she was back in her seat, Bogart holding one hand, a brandy in the other.

She was about to concede when Hughes asked, "What do you want?"

She gripped the armrests. "You have an in with the military brass, don't you? I have a friend. My roommate, actually."

"Gwendolyn, the blonde."

"She's got a brother in the navy. I was hoping maybe you could find out where he is. Just a general location, so that she knows. Can you do that?"

The aircraft pitched into a stomach-churning lurch; something on the other side of the cockpit door crashed to the floor. "You'd better return to your seat. Looks like we're in for a rough ride."

Kathryn waited for a few moments, hoping for a more definitive answer. When she didn't get one, she climbed out of the copilot's seat. Hughes waited until she had her hand on the door handle.

"I'll try."

She thanked him and staggered back to her seat. "Is it going to be like this all the way up to Seattle?" she asked Bogie.

"Hard to say."

Outside her window, the Channel Islands off Santa Barbara jiggled and wobbled. She closed her eyes. *Why did Wilkerson have to mention Carole Lombard?* "Tell me something nice to take my mind off all this."

"The *Sluggy*," Bogart replied.

"What's that?"

"My boat. Nothing relaxes me more than to take her out to sea."

"Does your wife like it?"

"Mayo don't like nothing that gives me pleasure."

"So you don't go sailing with her?"

"Not if I can help it. Betty likes it, though."

Kathryn pressed her hands against her stomach. "Betty? Who's that?"

"This picture I'm just finishing, *To Have And Have Not*. She's my costar. Real young, real raw, but she's got something, that's for sure."

"And her name is Betty?"

"Her real name, yeah, but Howard Hawks decided to change it."

Kathryn forced a swallow. "What did he come up with?"

"Lauren Bacall."

CHAPTER 28

The bus depot was a one-story building squatting on the east side of downtown LA amid a maze of nondescript offices and warehouses. The side wall featured a fifteen-foot greyhound sprinting against a dusty pink background, coated with exhaust fumes and peeling so badly it looked like it had measles.

Marcus got out of Bertie's DeSoto. In ten minutes, Doris' bus would roll around the corner, and he wondered if it was enough time for him to shake off his nerves.

"Thanks for volunteering," he told Bertie. With gas rationing, it was no small thing for her to drive them all the way into downtown.

"Don't you think twice about it, hon." Bertie swiped at the air dismissively.

They crossed Sixth Street and walked inside. Gray linoleum, dull cream walls, flat fluorescent lighting. They found an empty bench and sat down.

"Nervous?" Gwendolyn asked.

"I don't know that *nervous* is the right word," he replied.

Of course it's the right word! It's exactly the right word! So are anxious and apprehensive and tense.

"It's been a while since you've seen your sister, huh?" Bertie asked. "You know what she looks like?"

The passage of seventeen years had faded Marcus' memory like a photograph left in the sun, leaving him with frail vestiges of a once-happy time. Freckles. A high-pitched giggle. The knack of seeing the funny side of everything. But no, he could no longer picture her face. She said that she'd be wearing a silver brooch in the shape of an airplane on her jacket, but that was the only clue he had.

They felt the rumble before they saw it. An interstate bus with gray metal siding and a blue-and-white paint job momentarily filled the window before disappearing around the north side. Marcus stood up, wishing he'd snuck in a cigarette. In his peripheral vision, he saw Bertie get to her feet and then Gwendolyn pull her back down.

Disheveled travelers started to emerge. Rumpled clothes. Bleary eyes. Food stains. And suddenly she was standing there, ten feet from him, recognition filling her eyes. She dropped her brown valise and pressed her gloved hands to her mouth, straining to hold back tears. By the time he reached her, she'd lost the battle and he realized he had, too. They wrapped their arms around each other, and Marcus let himself dissolve.

Long-buried details of the life he'd left behind engulfed him. The tang of burning autumn leaves, January snow crunching against winter boots, chocolate birthday cake, his mother's clam chowder and his grandma's sweet potato pie, his father's custom-blended pipe tobacco, and the high-pitched crow of the neighbor's rooster. Marcus hadn't thought of these things in nearly twenty years, but the sight of his baby sister triggered a landslide of memories.

He wasn't sure how long they stood weeping onto each other's shoulders. Ten seconds? Twenty, maybe? When they resurfaced, he pushed his glasses back onto his nose. Doris had his broad face and apple-dumpling cheeks, and the freckles were still there, spraying her skin like tiny cherry blossoms. But it was her eyes, olive green, flecked with blue and quick as a flashbulb, that shot him back seventeen years.

"I'd have known you anywhere," she said.

He could see a swell of emotion cresting in her eyes. "I never thought I'd see you again." The words clogged his throat.

"I have so much to tell you!"

Marcus spotted a poster on the wall opposite them. It featured an army officer gabbing to a starry-eyed blonde while a Hitler-like man eavesdropped from behind his newspaper. The poster warned, *LOOSE LIPS SINK SHIPS!* Marcus became aware that they had plenty of time to talk, and standing in the middle of a busy bus depot was not the place to do it.

He sensed Gwendolyn and Bertie approach and introduced them as he picked up Doris' suitcase. "Bertie was kind enough to drive us downtown and drop you off at your hotel."

Outside, the sunshine caught Doris' hair, revealing it to be a Greer Garson shade of auburn. "I'm not staying with you?"

"Accommodation is hard to come by," Gwendolyn said. "This city's been packed to the rafters since the start of the war."

"But we found you a room at the Chapman Park Hotel," Marcus said.

In truth, there was a room available in the main building of the Garden of Allah, but as Marcus told Gwendolyn, it "was too close to too many people who were too drunk too often and therefore too likely to spill too many personal details that would be too embarrassing and too hard to explain away."

"It's right opposite the Brown Derby," he said, "and the Ambassador Hotel where the Cocoanut Grove is." Bertie turned her DeSoto onto Wilshire from Sixth Street and headed toward MacArthur Park. "Gwendolyn used to be the cigarette girl there, so I'm sure she can get us a good table."

"Absolutely," Gwendolyn said. "And your hotel is right near Elizabeth Arden. Kathryn and I plan to treat you to a facial. You'll adore it."

"Kathryn?" Doris asked. "She's the one on *Kraft Music Hall*, right? I can't believe you know somebody who knows somebody who works with Bing Crosby. That sure is something."

"She would have been here to meet you, but she had a Sunday brunch date with Judy Garland—"

Doris' eyes flew open. "You say it like it's an everyday thing."

"Kathryn went on a USO tour along the whole West Coast. Judy was part of the lineup and they hit it off. Kathryn's looking forward to meeting you."

"So we'll get you checked in and settled—"

"Ummm," Gwendolyn cut in. "Check-in isn't until four o'clock."

Marcus looked at his watch. It was only a quarter after eleven.

"We've got seventeen years to catch up on," Doris said. "I want to go everywhere, see everything, meet everyone. I want to see where you work, where you eat, where you go to the movies." She placed her hand on top of his. "But most of all, I want to see where you live. I want to see the Garden of Allah."

* * *

The fluid notes of someone banging out boogie-woogie on a piano down by the pool floated in the air while someone else encouraged a couple to dance faster. There were a few people sitting around the pool, but the February sun was still too chilly to tempt anyone into the water.

As Marcus led Doris through the Garden, he pointed out various spots: the window of the room he stayed in when he first arrived, the bar area, Errol Flynn's villa. Then Kathryn emerged from her door and flew down the steps.

"What happened to the Chapman?" she asked.

"Check-in's not until four," Marcus said.

"So I insisted we come here," Doris finished. "How was brunch with Judy Garland? Is she good company? She seems like she'd be fun to be around. Oh, listen to me! I sound like such a rube from the sticks, don't I?" She paused for a moment. "I guess I am, when you think of it." She turned to Marcus. "I'll try my best not to embarrass you. Can I see your place now?"

Kathryn looked at him. Her eyes said, *Chatty little thing, isn't she?*

Marcus was glad to keep her tucked away in his villa, where there was less chance that they'd be invited to the party on the west side of the pool. He turned to go but felt Kathryn tug him at the elbow. "Oh, and while I think of it, you asked me to remind you about the Bublichki photos . . . ?"

Oh, no.

A couple of weeks before, Alla and Glesca landed on Marcus' doorstep with the news that the two-year Siege of Leningrad had finally come to an end. When Kathryn suggested they celebrate it at the Bublichki Russian Restaurant up on the Strip, Alla proposed asking Oliver along.

It was Alla who'd advocated Marcus recruit Oliver into the Hollywood Writers Mobilization. "It will give you both the perfect cover if anyone questions you being seen together. You can say, 'Wartime makes such odd bedfellows, doesn't it?' and then change the subject." Oliver joined the Mobilization the next day, but that evening at Bublichki was the first time they tested Nazimova's theory. As it turned out, nobody batted a drunken eyelash.

At the last minute, Marcus grabbed his Brownie camera and snapped everybody in spiraling stages of sobriety. On the vodka-saturated stagger home, Kathryn took photos of the two men draped over each other in intimate ways not often exhibited by guys their age. Those photos were spread all over Marcus' dining table and were — quite literally — the last thing Marcus wanted his sister to see.

As he inserted his key, he explained that he wasn't expecting visitors, so his place was a typical bachelor mess. He swung the door open and directed Doris to the kitchen window. He pointed out the view with one hand — "Those are the Hollywood Hills!" — and with the other, he indicated that someone needed to shove the photos into the first drawer she found.

"So you'll be here a week, is that right?" Kathryn asked.

"And we've got a full week planned," Marcus said.

"As a matter of fact," Doris said, plucking her white gloves off finger by finger, "I might need some time to myself."

Kathryn glanced at Marcus. "Oh?"

"Back home, I work at a factory. Before the war, we made furniture. I ran the office, and that was fine. But the war came along and all the men left. Then the government ordered us to start manufacturing pilot seats. Within six months I was running the whole factory floor."

"You must be good at your job." Kathryn set out a plate of war cake on the coffee table.

Doris bit into a slice and chewed on it for a moment. "We got a commendation from the War Production Board, and so now I'm thinking ahead. When this war ends, the boys will return home and expect their jobs back."

"You can't blame them for that," Gwendolyn said.

"I don't, but at the same time, I reckon I'm better at their job than they ever were." Doris' face took on a serious expression that looked so much like Marcus' father that he had to lean back. "We make the cockpit seats for the aircraft our boys fly over the Pacific. Most of them go into the P-38s. Over at Lockheed, they think I'm the bee's knees. More than once they've said to me, 'If you're ever in Los Angeles and need a job . . .'"

Marcus found himself running short of breath. He gulped at the air until he could speak without his voice failing him. "I suspect they were just being polite."

Doris laughed. "Oh, I know. But then I started to wonder. What if they really meant it? I looked up Burbank on a map and saw it wasn't too far from where you live. So then I thought, seeing as how I'm out there, two birds, one stone. You never know. So I took two weeks off and here I am."

Doris caught the alarm on Marcus' face. "I'm not in the way, am I?"

"It's just that two weeks at the Chapman is going to run up quite a bill," Kathryn said. "If we'd known you were going to be here that long, we'd have found you a cheaper place."

Bertie snapped her fingers. "I've got the perfect solution! I live up at the big house in a two-bedroom. I've got plenty of space. Why don't you stay with me?"

Doris' eyes grew bright. "Are you sure I wouldn't be an imposition?"

"I've never had a roommate," Bertie beamed. "I'd love it! And hey! If you're going to be around for two weeks, you'll be here for the Academy Awards ceremony! Marcus, you're going this year, aren't you? You could take your sister!"

Marcus looked at Kathryn who looked at Gwendolyn who looked at Marcus. His carefully laid plans were unfurling like a ball of string.

CHAPTER 29

Gwendolyn held open the back door to the Hollywood Canteen and let Kathryn, Bertie, and Doris step into the night.

"Hot diggedy dog!" Doris exclaimed. "You certainly gave me a night to remember!"

Kathryn chuckled. "All we did was put you to work."

Doris jammed her little black velvet pillbox on her head and inserted a hatpin to keep it in place. "When that makeup guy turned Mickey Rooney into a miniature Clark Gable, I thought I'd die laughing! And besides, it's not work when you get to meet Eve Arden and Lucille Ball and Barbara Stanwyck and Red Skelton and Boris Karloff and — oh, my heavens, I'm going to have to write down all those names so I can tell everyone back home." She let out a high-pitched yelp. "I nearly passed out when Bette Davis thanked me — ME! — for helping out."

"It takes a small army to run a place like that," Gwendolyn said, reaching into her purse. "Bette told me personally how pleased she was to see what a hard worker you were." She handed Doris a flat package, wishing she'd hoarded prettier wrapping paper. The *Herald Examiner* would have to do.

"What's this?" Doris tilted the package toward a coming streetlight.

"A thank-you gift."

The contents of the package rendered Doris all but speechless. "Are—? These—? Real—?"

Gwendolyn nodded. "You're going to the Academy Awards, aren't you? I thought you could use a pair."

"I haven't had real nylons since I don't know when," Doris said, almost to herself. "How did you get your hands on these?"

Bertie saved Gwendolyn by hooking arms with Doris, pulling her into a huddle, and asking her what other stars she'd met. Kathryn and Gwendolyn fell a few steps behind.

"You and Bette were having quite the tête-à-tête in the office," Kathryn said. "What was all that about?"

Gwendolyn was still trying to figure it out.

It was Leilah O'Roarke who'd suggested approaching Bette Davis. Linc's black-market nylons were a step up from the ones Gwendolyn had been peddling. When she showed them to Leilah, the woman insisted on a standing order of ten pairs per month. From Leilah alone, Gwendolyn was making forty dollars a month. Between her other customers, plus the Miramar perfume, some South American lipsticks, and silk scarves, she was pulling in nearly two hundred smackers.

Like everyone else, she wished the war would end next week, but most theories suggested that both the Germans and the Japanese were prepared to fight to the death, so the war could easily last another year. If it did, Gwendolyn figured she'd have enough to open Chez Gwendolyn.

But four dollars per pair was a lot, even for nylons as heavenly as Linc's, and finding customers like Leilah O'Roarke wasn't easy. When Leilah suggested approaching Bette Davis, Gwendolyn was doubtful. Even though Davis was the highest-paid woman in America, Linc's supply to Warners meant she could get her hands on as many as she wanted. But Leilah explained that she gave them to her makeup guy and her cinematographer to give to their wives as a way of keeping in sweet with the men who made her look good on the screen.

When Gwendolyn summoned the courage to make her offer, the star was delighted, but her face darkened when Gwendolyn mentioned Leilah's name.

Bette waved a finger at Gwendolyn. "Power behind the throne, that one."

Gwendolyn had always taken Leilah as a professional Hollywood wife who knew how to use her husband's connections, but didn't throw her influence around like a grenade. And after all, it was Leilah who introduced her to Linc. "How do you figure?"

"Clem O'Roarke was just a barking drill sergeant when he came out of the army," Bette said. "He joined the police department after the Great War and was a beat-walking flatfoot until he nabbed the Warners job. There's no mystery how that happened. He served in the Fourteenth Field Artillery with Fletcher Bowron."

"The mayor? Of Los Angeles?"

"Trust me, those O'Roarkes are very well connected, and they put themselves first every time."

When Bette told Gwendolyn she'd take six pairs as long as they didn't cost more than five dollars each, Gwendolyn said the price was four. Bette was impressed and upped her order to ten.

It was nearly midnight when the four girls reached Sunset. They crossed to the north side and peered east in the hope they hadn't missed the last streetcar. There was hardly any traffic in sight—and certainly no streetcars—so they headed home on foot. For a bunch of girls still hopped up by a lively night at the Canteen, the Garden didn't seem so far.

Doris looked back at Gwendolyn. "Thanks again for the stockings. I've almost forgotten how they feel."

"Do you need a garter belt to go with them?"

Doris' mouth dropped open. "I didn't even pack one!"

Gwendolyn liked Marcus' sister very much. She had such spunk and was up for anything: a picnic on the beach, a rumba competition at the Cocoanut Grove, a game of charades with Dorothy Parker and Donnie Stewart. Gwendolyn had helped spread the word around the Garden that Doris was not privy to Marcus' private life, and — miracle of miracles — nobody had spilled any drunken beans.

Abruptly, Doris pulled them into a huddle. "There's this guy who's been following us since we left the Canteen. Right now he's standing about a block behind us, kind of just loitering there. You think he's a masher?"

They were at the Crossroads of the World shopping mall now. Towering over them was a quartet of white pillars topped by a globe of the world lit up in red, white, and blue neon. Although it was a busy shopping plaza by day, it was deserted at night.

"I don't see any cops around," Doris fretted.

Bertie sniggered. "I bet he doesn't even weigh one twenty."

A hundred-and-twenty-pound masher? Gwendolyn turned to take stock of him. "Oh, for gosh sake." She nudged Kathryn. "It's Ritchie!"

Ritchie Pugh was loitering just outside the circle of light cast by the neighboring streetlamp. When Gwendolyn called out his name, he approached them with an almost-sheepish reluctance. He was only a few feet away when it occurred to her that Siegel himself might be lurking in some parked car.

"Can we have a word?" Ritchie studied Bertie's and Doris' faces. "In private?"

Bertie took the cue and led Doris into a lap of the Crossroads of the World's quaint collection of European-style stores.

"I was driving home just now when I saw you walking," Ritchie said, "so I thought it was as safe a time as any."

"Safe for what?" Kathryn asked.

"To ask you if the name Valentina de la Veracruz means anything?"

"I don't think so."

"It's a name that's come up lately between Siegel and Cohen. They mention her a lot."

"In connection with what?"

"Your boyfriend."

Gwendolyn thought of that night at the Mocambo when they encountered Bugsy Siegel and Mickey Cohen. "What do they say?"

"It's financial stuff I don't glom onto so good. But the way they talk, I reckon Linc knows who she is."

"How do they talk about this Valentina woman?"

"Like they're in on some big state secret." He looked at Gwendolyn again. "Whoever this gal is, I think your Mr. Tattler would want to know that they know about her."

* * *

The ceiling over Gwendolyn's head stretched a good thirty feet and featured hand-painted scenes in the style of a Renaissance tableau. A pair of vast chandeliers radiated a soft shade of candlelight, transforming the Biltmore Hotel's Crystal Ballroom into a dreamland of love. What a shame, Gwendolyn sighed, that it's all a load of baloney. She knew everybody around her thought the same thing, but professional smiles were fixed on flawless faces and would be for the duration of the spectacle.

She felt Marcus draw alongside her. "This room has enough star power to catch fire before they serve the charlotte russe."

Every MGM luminary worth their weight in glitter had shown up. Judy Garland, Gene Kelly, Esther Williams, Fred Astaire, Katharine Hepburn — they were all there. And not just the stars, but even the producers like Arthur Freed and directors like George Cukor had been recruited.

"Talk about turning on the works," Gwendolyn said. "They must have conscripted everybody's ration coupons to throw this clambake." She noticed Kathryn had already darted off in search of some scoop or other. "Come on." She hooked her arm through Marcus'. "Let's see whose table they've thrown us on."

When George Cukor saw them approach, he broke away from his conversation with Adrian and his wife, Janet Gaynor. "Where's that handsome boyfriend of yours, Gwendolyn?" George asked.

"He'll be along. Some sort of necktie crisis." Earlier that evening, Linc called saying he'd have to meet her at the hotel. She wondered what sort of calamity could befall a necktie department at six o'clock on a Saturday night, but she'd said nothing, mainly because she had trouble believing it. This whole Valentina business made her edgy, and she knew she couldn't relax until she could ask him about her. A wedding reception for two hundred wasn't ideal, but she hadn't seen him all week.

A couple of champagne rounds later, a blast of trumpet fanfare filled the room and the newly wedded couple made a spotlit entrance to a hollow round of applause. Trevor Bergin seemed unable to summon even a bogus smile and his not-so-blushing bride, Melody Hope, looked as good as Hollywood's best makeup artist could manage, considering the toll that booze was starting to take on her. But photos could be cropped and airbrushed, and that's all that mattered.

Everybody was halfway through their seafood cocktails by the time Linc rushed in. "There was a fire in the storage room. Looks like we've lost forty percent of our neckties."

Gwendolyn waited until Linc had finished the last shrimp before she pulled him off his seat. She threaded them through the maze of tables, out through the ballroom's doors and into the Biltmore's ornate main corridor. But it too was filled with people; photographers, reporters, movie fans, and hangers-on. She spied a staircase leading up to the second floor and headed for it, hauling Linc in her wake.

The stairs led to a line of Juliet balconies that overlooked the wonderland of sparkling jewelry, forced smiles, and miniature rose centerpieces MGM's art department had concocted. Linc fell onto one of the seats in the first balcony he spotted. He was more than two champagnes' worth of drunk.

"Was there really a fire at your store?"

"Nope." He belched. "My dad and I haven't been getting along too well lately. I went to clear the air but things didn't go so great. Nothing you need to worry about." He waved away any more questions while Xavier Cugat's band started a waltz. "You want to tell me what we're doing up here?"

"I brought you up here to discuss Valentina de la Veracruz."

In the seventeen years Gwendolyn Brick had lived at the Garden of Allah, she'd never seen anyone sober up as fast as Lincoln Tattler did at that moment. He yanked her down to join her at the tiny table. "How do you know about her?"

Gwendolyn flattened her palms onto the tabletop to steady her nerves. "Who is she?"

"TELL ME—" He paused to collect himself. "How do you know about Valentina?"

"I have a friend who is close to Ben Siegel."

"You mean that beanpole we saw at the Mocambo?"

"He told me that the name Valentina de la Veracruz has been cropping up in conversations between Siegel and Mickey Cohen. He said that you know who she is and that you'd appreciate learning that Siegel and Cohen know of her too."

Linc ran his hands over his pomaded hair. "Got any cigarettes?"

"Linc, honey—" She struggled to push the words out. "Is this someone you're involved with?"

Linc sandwiched her hands between his. "No, my darling heart. You're the only girl in my life."

Gwendolyn wanted to believe him. "Then tell me who this Valentina is."

"She's a person I invented," he said. "In fact, she's not even that. She's a bank account. All the stuff we sell on the black market, it comes from South America—Argentina, Brazil, and Uruguay. I deal with one supplier in each country, and we transmit funds back and forth using a bank account in Buenos Aires under the name Valentina de la Veracruz. As far as I knew, only the four of us were aware of it."

"Apparently Siegel and Cohen know about it, too."

Linc slammed his hand against the table. "Dammit!"

"Nothing good can come from being someone Ben Siegel and Mickey Cohen are watching. Linc, what do you think all this means?"

"It means we've done our job so well that we've attracted the attention of the mob. They have to have done some mighty deep digging to find out about Val."

"So what now?"

Linc took Gwendolyn's hands again and squeezed them gently. "Baby, it's time you and I got out of the black-market business."

CHAPTER 30

Marcus and Oliver had a secret code. It was so simple and so innocuous that nobody ever noticed it. He hadn't even shared it with Kathryn or Gwendolyn.

Sometimes it was three knocks on a door or a table; sometimes it was replying "Yep" three times to a question; sometimes it was pretending to scratch an itch using three fingers.

Tap, tap, tap = I love you.

Yep, yep, yep = I love you.

Scratch, scratch, scratch = I love you.

Being a guy in love with another guy, opportunities for public displays of affection were scarcer than hookers in a nunnery. From the moment Oliver made his "collective American dream" speech, nobody at the Garden cared where Oliver worked. The Garden of Allah was Marcus and Oliver's sanctuary. But outside the walls was a different story.

Nights like the booze-soaked evening at Bublichki were rare, but not unique. There were times when the movie industry came together, and, not wanting to get on its bad side, invited the Breen Office's staff, then largely ignored them. On nights like those, Marcus and Oliver publicly declared their love with three tugs of a shirt collar or three faked sneezes.

The night of the 1944 Academy Awards coincided with Marcus and Oliver's first anniversary. Earlier that day, Oliver's present had arrived in the mail: a pair of gold cufflinks, each one imbedded with three tiny emeralds. The note attached read, "Wear these tonight and meet me at the bar, 7:30." Marcus was still hooking the links when he walked out of his bedroom; Doris was seated at his dining table in front of a *Los Angeles Examiner*.

"The Motion Picture Alliance for the Preservation of American Ideals," she read from the paper. "They sure sound like a riot, huh?"

Since the Alliance announced its formation a month before, the *Examiner*, in classic hysterical Hearst style, had ballyhooed the message pounded by the men behind its formation: Walt Disney, director Sam Wood, and MGM writer-producer James McGuiness, among others. They were convinced that Hollywood was infested with Communists and Fascists intent on perverting the movies "into an instrument for the dissemination of un-American ideas."

Most of Hollywood — and certainly everybody at the Garden of Allah — dismissed their grousing as grumpy-old-men paranoia. But this morning, the paper reported that the Alliance had set their sights on the Hollywood Writers Mobilization. They viewed the HWM as dangerously influential because of the progressive sentiments its members were writing for the screen.

"Since when does progressive equal Communist?" Marcus moaned to Alla earlier that week. It was bad enough that Marcus was still toiling away uncredited on one MGM picture after another, but now he was a member of the organization the Alliance had in its sight. That made two strikes against him.

Doris stood up and straightened the lilac organza ball gown Gwendolyn had donated for the evening. She fingered the amethyst necklace Kathryn contributed. "Is this on straight?"

Kathryn let herself in, pulling Jim Taggert behind her. "Look who I found lingering outside." Marcus had arranged for Taggert to be Doris' date.

"I bought you a corsage," Taggert confessed, "but I slipped on a champagne cork and now the cursed thing is floating in the pool."

Doris bunched her hands together and confessed, "I do believe I'm starting to get quite nervous! Humphrey Bogart will be there tonight, won't he?"

"He's nominated for *Casablanca*, so you can bet he'll be there," Kathryn said. "I'll introduce you to him if you like."

Doris started to fan herself with her purse and made little noises that sounded like a giggle crossed with a gasp. Marcus fingered his new cufflinks. "Oh, baby, you ain't seen nothing yet."

* * *

On Academy Awards night, Grauman's Chinese Theater was usually lit up brighter than the Fourth of July. But this was wartime, so the searchlights were in storage, the banquet was dispensed with, and the giddy excitement was noticeably subdued.

Marcus found a nook just outside the auditorium doors, where they watched Paulette Goddard, Mickey Rooney, Greer Garson, and Walter Pidgeon float past. He felt Doris' grip tighten when Bogie and Mayo appeared.

The Battling Bogarts now dispensed with anything resembling an everything-is-peachy façade, and instead ignored each other as they picked their way through the crowd. Only Bogart was smiling as he graciously acknowledged a succession of well-wishers. He looked relieved when he spotted Kathryn. Marcus felt his sister tremble as Kathryn introduced her to Bogart. He could almost feel her memorizing every last detail for the benefit of her friends back home.

Marcus and Doris hadn't talked about the folks yet. It was a conversation he'd wanted to avoid at first, but that was before he'd discovered that his pigtailed little sister had grown into an open and warm woman. Her small-town upbringing had left her naiveté untarnished, and yet she was far more astute than he'd anticipated. Now that her visit was drawing to an end, Marcus felt compelled to bring up the subject he'd most dreaded.

"I'm going to grab a quick drink at the bar," he told her. "Why don't you take a wander through the crowd? Gary Cooper's bound to be around here someplace." He was relieved when she nodded. "You have your ticket; I'll meet you inside."

He made his way to the bar through a crowd of servicemen the Hollywood Victory Committee had bussed in for the night. He smiled when he saw Oliver had lined up three dry martinis, each with three olives. They clinked their glasses three times.

Oliver said, "You have very good taste in cufflinks."

Marcus extended his arm so the emeralds twinkled in the light of the crystal chandelier. "They're my favorite." He glanced down at a specific point below Oliver's waist. "Are you comfortable?"

Marcus' gift to Oliver was a pair of silk boxer shorts he'd found at Desmond's department store. Against a background of alternating black and gray stripes, the number 3 was arranged in a pyramid formation. "Very comfortable, thank you for asking. I appreciate your interest."

Oliver tapped a cigarette on the bar three times and lit up.

"Your sister's visit is coming to an end soon, isn't it? Tomorrow, if I recall."

They'd agreed it was best if Oliver kept his distance while Doris was in town. Marcus ached to feel Oliver's arms around him again.

Marcus nodded. "Yep, yep, yep. The eleven o'clock bus."

"Shall we say your place? Three o'clock?"

The lights in the packed foyer dimmed for a moment. Marcus bowed. "Enjoy your evening."

"I expect to enjoy my afternoon more."

* * *

After the ceremony, when Doris suggested they walk back to the Garden of Allah, Marcus was glad to hear Kathryn declare her heels were too high for a twenty-block walk. They left Taggert and Kathryn in the line for taxis and headed west along Hollywood Boulevard.

Marcus took his sister's hand. "Was tonight everything you hoped?"

"Oh, Marcus!" Doris exclaimed. "When I came to Los Angeles, all I really wanted was to get to know you a bit. Yes, okay, and maybe look into job prospects with Lockheed, too. But I never dreamed I'd get to go to the Academy Awards. I can't begin to thank you for tonight. I'll never forget it as long as I live. Back home, nobody'll believe it!"

"That does bring up something I wanted to ask you," Marcus said.

"You mean about Lockheed? I don't know why I thought things would be any different out here. The guy was very nice, showed me all around the plant. When I bought up the possibility of coming to work there, he was all for it. But the next thing out of his mouth was, 'Until the end of the war.'" She shrugged. "I gave it a shot."

Marcus was surprised at how sorry he felt. He'd gotten used to his sister's bubbly laughter and spirited approach to life. They stopped at the La Brea Avenue corner.

"We haven't had the conversation I was hoping we'd have," he said evenly.

"You mean the one about the folks? How they are, and all that jazz?"

The lights turned green and they stepped off the curb. He nodded.

"Everybody's fine. Conrad and Jessica and Betsy, they're all out of the house with families of their own." Marcus caught his breath at the mention of his three siblings: he hadn't spoken their names in the seventeen years he'd been gone. "Pop still runs the show, so he and Mom rush around town playing Mr. and Mrs. Mayor. Banquets, meetings, you name it. Especially since the war. Mom's on seven different committees and heads up four of them."

Marcus could feel his hands clamming up and wished he wasn't holding Doris'. "So," he said with all the nonchalance he could summon, "do they ever mention me?"

When Doris spoke, her voice dropped a notch. "You're the big family secret nobody talks about. I never knew how to bring you up to the folks until that night at the movies when the credits for *William Tell* came up. I heard Mom give a little yip when she saw your name."

"And Dad?"

"Nothing. I waited until we got home and brought it up with them. But Dad left the room before I even finished the question."

"And Mom?"

"Mom just shook her head, like she was saying 'Don't even bother.' That's when I decided to write to you. I figured, Hey, you're my brother. I'm entitled to contact you if I want."

"I'm so glad you did."

Doris let out a nervous giggle.

"So when you told them you were coming to LA . . . ?" Marcus prompted.

"They didn't say anything. Maybe because I made out that it was really about a job with Lockheed." She pondered what she'd said for a moment. "I don't know about Dad, but I doubt I fooled Mom."

They walked on in silence as the stores on Hollywood Boulevard gave way to houses and apartment blocks. Eventually, Marcus said, "And when you get home? Will you tell anyone you saw me?"

"Are you nuts?" She hit him playfully with her purse. It was snakeskin, dyed black to match her shoes, neither of which really went well with her dress, but it was the best she could do. "I have a brother who writes movies at MGM. He hobnobs with stars and took me to the Academy Awards. Look at what you've achieved, where you live, your wonderful friends. You think I'll go home and *not* talk about that?"

"I meant are you going to mention all this to Mom and Dad?"

Doris stopped walking and looked into her brother's eyes. "Why did you leave?" she asked, unblinking. "No warning, no goodbye?"

"What did Dad tell you?"

She parked her rear end on a low brick fence in front of a weather-beaten bungalow. "He said you'd decided it was time you went out into the world, like it was *Pilgrim's Progress*." She watched the traffic snaking along the boulevard.

It had been a while since Marcus thought of that night, but he could still picture the horrified look on his father's face as he scrambled to pull up his pants. Seventeen years, and he could still hear the screaming and the cussing echo off the brick walls. He could still feel the outrage and disappointment radiating from his father as they sat in his car to the McKeesport railway station where Roland Adler silently bought his son a one-way ticket on the night train to Chicago.

"I always knew that McKeesport wasn't for me," he said. "I was made for big-city life."

She somberly studied his face for a moment or two. "It sure has its charms." She hooked her arm around his as she stood up, and pulled him farther westward. The night air was cooling noticeably and she pressed herself against him for warmth. "Who was that guy you were talking to at the bar before the show started?" He could smell the Miramar perfume Gwendolyn had lent her. "The one with the Ronald Colman moustache."

He'd assumed she was too distracted by the crème de la crème to notice. "Remember that organization I told you about, the Hollywood Writers Mobilization? He belongs to that, too. Why do you ask?"

"Some guy came up and asked me about the two of you."

"What guy?"

She shrugged. "Said he worked for the mayor."

"Mayor of Los Angeles?" Fletcher Bowron rarely made an appearance at the Oscars. If he had, Marcus would have noticed. "What did this guy look like?"

"Kinda rough around the edges. Like he knows how to throw a punch. Talked like a New Yorker, but not some Park Avenue sophisticate."

The man Doris described sounded like Eddie Mannix, assistant to Mayer. The skin across Marcus' back felt taut and prickly. "Are you sure he didn't say he worked for Mayer, as in Louis B. Mayer?"

"Maybe. At any rate, he caught me watching you from across the foyer. He came right up to me, complimented me on my dress. I told him I was your sister, and he asked if I knew who you were talking to."

"What did you say?"

"I recognized him from the photos you've got stashed in the drawer where you keep your playing cards and poker chips."

Marcus felt twitchy. "You saw those, huh?"

"I was looking for a pen to write some picture postcards. So I told this guy, he's a pal of my brother's." She noticed Marcus had slowed his pace to a sluggish stroll. "Did I say something wrong?"

Marcus fingered the three emeralds on his new cufflinks and wondered if their cover story about the Mobilization was sturdy enough to withstand scrutiny—especially now that the Motion Picture Alliance had decided it was a den of dangerous progressives.

"Nah."

He went to cross Fairfax Avenue and head down to Sunset when she pulled him back from the curb.

"What's his name?" she asked.

Marcus swallowed hard. "Oliver."

"He's more than just some pal, huh?"

Her face had taken on that same intense, unblinking gaze Marcus had last seen on their father. He nodded silently, then found himself overcome with a sense of relief he hadn't seen coming.

"So he's your . . . I don't even know what the right word is," she confessed with a nervous laugh. "*Beau* seems too way-down-South-in-Dixie. Boyfriend, maybe?"

"I guess you could call him that." It struck Marcus that the word *boyfriend* seemed too casual for what he and Oliver had.

"So, this Oliver guy, he makes you happy?"

Any idea that Marcus had about his sister being just a small-town girl evaporated at that moment. "Yes," he said, "very happy."

Doris jutted her chin out and gave her head a decisive nod. "That's all I need to know."

She squeezed his arm and pulled herself in closer for warmth. "Come on. It's time we both went home."

CHAPTER 31

When Bing Crosby walked to his microphone and said, "This one is for all our fellas on Utah and Omaha beaches," the atmosphere in Studio D became electric. Every joke, song, and piece of business and patter was met with tidal waves of hope and joy.

Well before the end of the show, the audience was on its feet, hollering so rowdily that Bing had to wait a few moments before he could point to Ginger Rogers. Their duet of "There'll Be A Hot Time In The Town Of Berlin" just about brought down the ceiling.

Kathryn had been on the radio for almost a year now, but she hadn't been approached by strangers until she participated in the USO bond drive last winter. It first happened in Eugene, Oregon, and Kathryn was so flustered she broke the fan's pen. Bogie and Judy Garland had laughed themselves silly. Fan mail started to arrive soon after; ironic, considering her first Hollywood job was answering Tallulah Bankhead's fan mail. But nothing had prepared her for the surge of adrenaline fueled by tonight's audience. She felt like she wouldn't sleep for a week.

She was taking a minute to wind down in her dressing room when Sonny the NBC usher appeared. "Miss Massey, there's someone in the foyer asking to see you."

Kathryn looked at her watch. She was already late for Cole Porter's birthday party. "Business or fan?"

"Definitely not business," Sonny said, "but no sign of an autograph book."

Kathryn checked the mirror. Her heart was still pumping, her cheeks were flushed.

"Oh, and Mr. Wilkerson said he'll be waiting in his car around the corner on Argyle."

Kathryn thanked Sonny and gave her hair a quick comb. She stepped back to check her dress: a calf-length hip-hugger in terracotta crêpe Georgette. Not quite formal enough for a party at Cole's, but it would have to do.

The main foyer of NBC's radio studios was a cavernous three-story atrium dominated by an enormous mural depicting a four-armed genie holding a portable radio that spit sparks in several directions.

The woman who stood by herself against one of the walls was instantly recognizable. Kathryn had met her only once, at her desk, two and a half years before. Her face was thinner now, more drawn—like so many faces these days.

"Hello," Kathryn said solemnly.

Roy's wife interlaced her gloved fingers. "I have news to share with you."

Kathryn took in the woman's outfit. From pillbox hat to low-heeled Mary Janes, she was dressed all in black. Kathryn felt her breath grow shallow. She focused on the onyx brooch pinned to the woman's jacket.

"Roy was at D-Day," Mrs. Quinn said calmly. "He was part of the Western Task Force that landed on Omaha Beach." Kathryn felt a cold sweat break out beneath her hair. "He wasn't supposed to land, but things got crazy and he went ashore."

"You're wearing black." Kathryn barely recognized her own voice. It sounded distant, unemotional.

"His body was identified two days later."

A broken "Oh!" shuddered out of Kathryn.

"I'll say this for them: they don't waste any time sending that telegram."

Kathryn dredged up the courage to meet Roy's wife in the eye. She saw there only a steely determination. *If she can get through this without crying, so can I.* "Thank you. I—I want you to know how very much I appreciate you going out of your way."

Mrs. Quinn made a vague shrug. "I like to think that this war has made us all a bit more compassionate. I realized if I didn't tell you, perhaps nobody would."

Kathryn heard footsteps echo on the terrazzo. "Miss Massey?" It was Sonny. "Mr. Wilkerson sent me to tell you he's waiting."

Mrs. Quinn turned to go.

Kathryn offered up her hand. "Thank you."

The woman eyed it for a moment, weighing up whether or not to shake it, and decided against it. "Goodbye, Miss Massey," she said, "and good luck."

* * *

Kathryn slipped into the rear seat of her boss' limo and prayed Wilkerson wasn't in a chatty mood.

"Damn, but you're good at this radio stuff, Massey," he declared. "Real smooth and professional, but not all high society like Sheilah Graham—or like Hedda wishes she was." He popped an encouraging punch on her knee.

She managed to nod her acknowledgment and let him yammer on about the effect D-Day had on newspaper circulation—even the *Reporter* had seen a marked increase.

Kathryn watched the Crossroads of the World's neon globe pass by. It made her think of Gwendolyn and how happy she seemed with Lincoln. *And why not? He's a nice guy.* So was Oliver, even if he did work for the Breen Office.

And I had Roy. Part-time had him, at any rate. She closed her eyes and tried to imagine Roy in his military uniform. I bet you looked marvelous, she told him. You must have had all those WAC girls falling over themselves, dreaming of marrying you one day, just like I did. She mentally slapped herself across the face. Married? You're not sure you even want to get married. Kathryn had often reflected on how disposable Hollywood marriages were — an endless carousel of I-like-him-I-want-him-I-love-him-I-marry-him-I-hate-him-I-divorce-him-I-like-someone-new.

"Did you hear me?"

Wilkerson's question pulled her back inside the limo. "What?"

"I was confiding something to you." His mouth was a thin pout. "Forget it."

"I'm sorry. I just got the wind knocked out — never mind." She angled her body toward him. "I'm listening."

Ordinarily, Wilkerson wasn't one for slouching in his seat, but he was now, his head resting against the back and his eyes on the padded ceiling. "I'm in debt. It's bad, Massey. More than six hundred grand."

Kathryn bit down on her lips to stop herself from making the same mistake she made at The Players. *Don't play the substitute wife. Be the good listening pal.*

She thought about how Wilkerson had been more and more absent over the past few months, handing over much of the daily running of the paper to the managing editor. "Maybe you should spend more time in the office. A big ship needs a strong captain."

"At Zanuck's last week, I was up four hundred grand at one point."

Kathryn wanted to tell him he was entitled to do whatever he wanted with his own newspaper — including run it into the ground — but dozens of people relied on him to make their living. But that's what a nagging wife would say, so she asked instead, "What's your plan?"

He rubbed his hands together like a villain out of *The Perils Of Pauline*. "I do have a plan, and it's a doozy."

"At the rate you're going, it'll have to be."

"I'm going to open a casino!"

That's like putting a dipsomaniac in charge of the distillery. Kathryn struggled to keep her voice on an even keel. "Gambling isn't even legal in California, so why complicate your life by opening a casino? Is that what you're going to do with Ciro's? Resurrect it as — "

"Nah! Forget Ciro's and forget California. I've got my eye on a town called Las Vegas."

"Where's that?"

"Nevada. I've been out there a few times lately. It's the perfect place to open a casino. Gambling's legal there, it's out in the middle of the desert where nobody will — "

"That's your plan?" She could see the *Reporter* folding within a year and her job evaporating in the desert heat. Her determination not to scold melted away. "A casino? In the middle of nowhere?"

"The middle of nowhere puts it beyond the long arms and beady eyes of the mob. You've got to think big, Massey. Places like Ciro's are chickenfeed compared to casinos. Those things are goldmines."

Kathryn's temples began to throb with exasperation. "Wouldn't it be easier to just stop playing high-stakes poker?"

Wilkerson let his head fall into his hands. "If it was easy as all that, don't you think I would?"

"Just don't go! Stay home and read a book instead. Why is it so hard—"

"Okay," Wilkerson cut her off, "I'll agree to stop gambling if you agree to stop breathing. Deal?"

She glared at him. Then it hit her; saying no to a poker game was quite a different thing for her than it was for him. "Oh," she said softly. "I see." Although she really didn't see at all.

They passed four or five blocks in a dense, suffocating silence until Wilkerson said, "Every place I've set up— Vendome, the Trocadero, Sunset House, the Arrowhead Springs Hotel, Ciro's—they've all been smashing successes. A casino is the next logical step." He was starting to breathe more heavily now. "This is what I'm good at."

Yeah, Kathryn thought, *that's exactly what Roy said to me in his telegram.* She'd read it so often she knew it by heart.

KATEY-POTATEY STOP I'VE SIGNED UP FOR THE ARMY STOP SHIPPED OUT YESTERDAY TO TRAINING BASE IN MAINE STOP WAR IS COMING AND I WANT TO DO MY BIT STOP BE HAPPY FOR ME STOP THIS IS WHAT I'M GOOD AT STOP

And look what happened to him.

Wilkerson's driver pulled onto St. Pierre Road, where Cole's ornate mansion was lit up like a movie set. Kathryn realized this was the very last place she wanted to be. She needed space and time. Time to think about how gambling could possibly be as fundamental as breathing. And Roy— she needed time to mourn him. She thought she'd expelled him from her system when she learned he was still sleeping with his wife, but it was clear now how ridiculous that was. *I'll go out of my way to say hello to everybody as quickly as possible, then sneak out.*

And maybe while she was at it, grab a champagne or two, because even if the world was at war, Cole Porter could always be counted on to serve the best.

* * *

Cole's house was the sort of faux chateau Kathryn didn't go for much: witch's hat turrets, sixteen-foot vaulted ceilings, stained glass windows, tapestries the size of a Duesenberg, and statues of lions and griffins dotting the yard. His parties were always loaded with fabulously dressed people whose conversation sparkled with the cleverest *bon mots* because they'd read everything, met everyone, and been everywhere. Three steps inside the door, Kathryn could see that this one was no different.

What a shame, she told herself. I'm hardly in the mood for any of this.

She shanghaied a waiter and relieved him of a pair of champagne coupes, then realized Wilkerson had already melted into the crowd.

"Kathryn, my sweet! You have a spare? How divine."

Kay Thompson was only five foot five, but with her pencil-thin body sheathed in a formfitting dress, she seemed much taller. She grabbed one of Kathryn's coupes and emptied half its contents before coming up for air. "Cole was just asking about you. A bunch of us sat around listening to your show tonight." She squeezed Kathryn's hand. "Spectacular!"

Kathryn was relieved she'd bumped into Kay. Laying claim to the position of chattiest person at the Garden of Allah was no small thing, but Kay Thompson was the current titleholder. Kathryn knew all she'd have to do is insert the odd syllable into the conversation and Kay would do the rest.

The champagne was crisp and chilled to exactly the right temperature. Kathryn let it bubble down her throat like a desert spring while Kay prattled on about her vocal arrangements for the new June Allyson-Van Johnson picture, *Two Girls And A Sailor*. When she could take no more, she asked Kay, "Where's Cole now?"

A congregation of gold bracelets clinked together when Kay pointed toward the piano room. "Last I saw him, he was being cornered by that Ann Miller dancer. Do you know her?"

"I know *of* her."

"Judy told me the other day that Mayer's about to dump that suicidal wife of his and he's already started in with Ann. Don't be surprised if she scores a nifty contract at MGM. I'd tell you to mark my words, but you didn't hear it from me."

The piano room was lit with lamps tactfully placed to soften and flatter. The shrieking laughter, glittering jewelry, and sharp-edged party-talk crowded the room, leaving Kathryn feeling besieged. She glimpsed Cole in his wheelchair, sleekly tuxedoed and pretending to smile. Ann Miller still hovered nearby but a couple of Marx brothers had shunted her aside. Kathryn caught Porter's eye and lifted a glass. His forged smile ripened into a genuine one.

A pair of wise-cracking Broadway chorus girls in overly-spangled getups of silver and red stepped between Kathryn and Cole, breaking their eye contact. By the time they'd moved on, Zeppo Marx had reclaimed Cole's attention.

Kay had inserted herself in some other conversation, leaving Kathryn free to show her face in the piano room, the Louis XVI dining room, and the glass-paneled conservatory before retreating toward the back.

As she headed for the kitchen, Kathryn encountered a spectacle she never thought she'd see in a thousand lifetimes: Louella Parsons and Hedda Hopper marching shoulder to shoulder like a set of Siamese twins. As the rival gossip queens of Hollywood, they rarely allowed themselves to be in the same room together; the sight of them glued Kathryn to the tiled floor.

"Kathryn," Hedda purred, "we've been waiting for you."

"You have?"

"Indeed," Louella said. She presented Kathryn with a hollow smile. This was the first time Louella had spoken to Kathryn in three years. "Let's find a quiet corner."

The two most hated women in Hollywood hustled her through the kitchen and into the maid's room. It was a small square holding only a single bed and table, and was devoid of personal effects save for a matching pair of cream Bakelite frames holding photographs of a couple of Negro children. As soon as Louella closed the door, the room felt stifling. Kathryn braced herself for a barrage about the Parsons piñata party.

"We want to know about Humphrey Bogart," Louella said.

Bogart? What the — ?

"We know all about how the two of you became great pals on that USO tour," Hedda added, "so don't give us the runaround."

It didn't take much gray matter for Kathryn to figure out what this was about. That day on the airplane when Bogie talked to her about his young costar, she could tell he was falling for her. When she spotted Bacall at the Hollywood Canteen a few weeks later, she could see why: the girl was striking. Kathryn's contacts at Warners started to report a gag flying around the studio. If Bogie's wife called, she got the same answer: "He's out with the cast." On the *To Have Or Have Not* set, the crew referred to Bacall as "the cast."

"You must tell us what you know about the Book of the Day," Louella commanded.

Kathryn stared at the women. "Book of the what?"

"Oh please, Kathryn," Hedda said, "you're much too smart for silly games. You must tell us about Bogart's connection to the Book of the Day."

"You mean the bookstore on Hollywood?" Kathryn asked.

Louella snorted. "We can stay locked in here all night if that's the way you want to play it."

"Humphrey has a finer appreciation for art and literature than most people give him credit for." Kathryn could have sworn the walls had inched inward. "Other than that, ladies, I really don't know what to tell you." She brushed past them and reached for the doorknob.

"You mean to say nobody's brought this up with you?" Hedda asked, her tone withering. "Not even Nelson Hoyt?"

Kathryn's hand lay on the doorknob. Somebody had mentioned that name to her, but she couldn't place it.

The way Louella shook her head reminded Kathryn of a condescending governess. "It's just us, Kathryn. Nobody else can hear you."

"Describe this Hoyt guy," Kathryn said evenly.

"The charming Southern Gentleman accent? The deep cleft in his chin?" Hedda started to tap her shoe. "You know very well who Nelson Hoyt is."

The name came back to Kathryn in a rush. Anita Wyndham mentioned him that night at the Canteen when she said that Louella was the least of her worries. But then the one millionth serviceman came through the doors and their conversation had broken off.

"See?" Hedda said to Louella. "I knew the FBI had gotten to her too. What was his approach?" she asked Kathryn. "Just show up at your desk? Or did he send a telegram?"

The word triggered the voice of Roy's wife. *They don't waste any time sending that telegram.* Had it only been an hour ago? *ROY IS DEAD!* It was like Mrs. Quinn was in the room with them, screaming in her ear.

Just then, the door swung open and a young black woman dressed in a plain blue uniform with a white apron stood gaping at them. A couple of rooms away, Kay Thompson's voice javelined over the hubbub. "Three cheers for the birthday boy!"

As the gathering erupted, Kathryn pushed past the maid and bolted from the room. The kitchen was deserted and she had a clear path to the back door. She rushed out into the twilight.

Roy is dead and I'll never see him again.

The back fence of Cole Porter's mansion was an eight-foot hedge. Near the northern end, a dark wooden gate lay between her and freedom. If it was locked, she was prepared to scale it like an escaped con.

Nelson Hoyt is with the FBI.

She closed her fingers around the iron ring and yanked at the gate. It opened without protest onto a service lane that curved to the right. Overhanging branches of oaks and elms stippled the lane with shadow. She laid her hand against the hedge, but it was rough and scratchy and offered no support. She realized she'd left without her handbag and gloves. Panicked, Kathryn knew she couldn't go back, so she stumbled over the cobblestones until she could no longer hear the laughter and music. There were no taxis in sight, but she needed the time it would take to walk all the way home.

She had a lot to think about.

CHAPTER 32

Linc turned his silver Packard onto Linden Drive. "Have you been here before?" he asked Gwendolyn.

She shook her head. "We either did our business at the Canteen or she sent someone to pick up her merchandise."

Eight hundred and two North Linden was nothing like the house Gwendolyn had envisioned for Leilah O'Roarke. She was expecting an elegant French Provincial with tapering columns and pristine topiaries, but Linc pulled up in front of a white Spanish Mission revival. It had two separate balconies on the second story and a very tall chimney reaching for the sky. A driveway stretched along the right-hand side, and on the left a trio of palm trees swayed as one in the June breeze.

"Remember what we agreed." Linc had his business voice on. Low and husky.

"I know, I know." She laid a hand on his leg to placate the jitters she'd put up with on the drive over. "We drop off the merchandise. Collect the dough. Leave. Minimum chitchat. We're in, we're out."

It'd been two months since they'd decided to get out of the black market at Trevor and Melody's wedding at the Biltmore. The timing wasn't ideal as far as Gwendolyn was concerned. She was still short the minimum needed to open Chez Gwendolyn, but quitting the game was better than working for the mob.

Then Leilah's telegram arrived announcing she was head of the Hollywood Victory Committee, whose eighty entertainment units toured the country and overseas. They were mounting a huge undertaking to England and needed a hundred pairs of nylons, regardless of cost. Between them, Linc and Gwendolyn had ninety-four pairs left in their stockpile. Ten bucks a pop meant Gwendolyn would net around four hundred dollars for what they were calling their "grand goodbye."

They got out of Linc's car and approached the front door. It was made of oak and curved to snugly fit the stone archway. Inside the house they could hear a doorbell chime, then a voice call out, "I'll get it, Mimi!"

The door swung open to reveal Leilah in a black skirt several sizes too small and a silk blouse as glaringly white as the outside of her house.

Leilah saw the large boxes in their hands. "My lifesavers! What I would've had to do without you doesn't bear thinking about."

She bustled them inside and told them to set their boxes down. "I'll pop upstairs and get your money. You've got time for a drink, haven't you?"

"As a matter of fact," Gwendolyn said, "we've got another stop—"

"One quick sherry!" She disappeared up the stairs.

They stepped into the living room. Like most Spanish Revival homes, it was built to keep the rooms cool; the walls were thick and the windows were small, letting in little light. A matching pair of standard lamps in opposite corners were placed more for mood than function. It took Gwendolyn a moment to realize someone else was there.

"I thought I knew that voice," the figure said.

Countess Dorothy di Frasso had been at the center of the city's social scene since before Gwendolyn moved to town. They first met outside Jean Harlow's funeral — Gwendolyn didn't have an invitation, and the countess arrived too late to get inside the crowded chapel — and became good friends for a while. They hadn't seen much of each other since the war started, so Gwendolyn was pleased — if surprised — to see her.

When they embraced, Gwendolyn could smell the custom-made rose-and-lily perfume that the countess commissioned for her sole use. "I wasn't aware you and Leilah knew each other," Gwendolyn said.

"We go all the way back to the New York speakeasies." The countess tsked. "Prohibition. It seems so long ago, doesn't it?"

Gwendolyn guessed the countess was in her fifties now, but she didn't look it. Gwendolyn took in the dark hair, the squarish face tipped with a pointed chin, and those lively dark blue eyes. She was glad to see her friend hadn't changed.

"Are you on the Victory Committee with Leilah?" Gwendolyn asked.

"My checkbook is," she said with a laugh. "Does that count?" She looked at Linc and extended her hand toward him.

"Linc," Gwendolyn said, "this is Countess Dorothy di Frasso. Dorothy, this is Lincoln Tattler."

Dorothy shook his hand. "Ah, so you're the Tattler boy? Leilah has—" She spun around and gaped at Gwendolyn. "You're Leilah's girl?" She clapped her hands together. "How priceless! I've been getting my stockings through Leilah, but if I'd known, I'd have shopped direct!"

"Catching up, I see?" Leilah entered the room, a thick envelope in her hand. She passed it to Linc on her way to a bronze liquor cart.

"Leilah, you might have told me Gwendolyn was your nylons girl."

"How was I to know that you were acquainted?" Leilah poured out two fresh sherries.

Linc had already adopted his let's-get-the-hell-out face. Gwendolyn was about to speak when the countess laid a hand on her arm. "It was Leilah who introduced me to you-know-who!"

The countess was loaded with charisma and money in equal measure, so the mental list of lovers Gwendolyn had to flip through was considerable.

"Remember? That day at Bullocks Wilshire?" Dorothy insisted. "At the perfume counter? You smelled Chanel No. 5 for the first time and I was telling you about my affair at your Garden of Allah."

Gwendolyn now stood at that same perfume counter, but she had never thought about that day when Dorothy told Gwendolyn how she was indulging in a red-hot affair with an East Coast businessman. It wasn't until much later that she pieced together the fact that Dorothy's paramour was Bugsy Siegel. Suddenly, the boundaries of Gwendolyn's world shrank.

Gwendolyn swirled the amber sherry around her glass. "I forgot about you and Ben Siegel. Didn't he run speakeasies back East?"

"Half the people I know can be traced to those New York joints. Benjy was one of the main suppliers; and Dorothy was—"

"One of the main consumers!" The two women burst into high-pitched laughter. "I never told you this," Dorothy continued, "but Benji really was the love of my life. And I like to think that I was his. At least that's what he told me, but considering what the man does for a living, it's hard to tell reality from hoopla, isn't it?"

Leilah smiled wistfully at her friend. "Guess who's rented the house three doors up from here?"

"Who?"

"Virginia Hill!"

"Isn't that Siegel's girlfriend?" The question came from Linc. He set his untouched sherry on a side table and then ran his finger around the brim of his hat.

Leilah pointed through the front window. "Across the street, three doors along. Ain't it something?"

Gwendolyn deposited her sherry on Leilah's quartz mantle. "I'm sorry, but we really do have to be going." Her voice came out high and squeaky, but she couldn't help it. She planted hurried kisses on the two women amid a flurry of lovely-to-see-you-agains, and scurried out of the house, saying nothing more until they were seated in the Packard.

"JESUS!" Linc hissed. "Please tell me you didn't know about any of that."

"All I knew was the countess and Siegel had an affair, but that was years ago. The rest of it was news to me."

"I nearly crapped my BVDs!" He turned the ignition and the vehicle roared to life. "She said the girlfriend lives three doors up, but which direction, do you think? I don't even want to pass it."

"Don't know, don't care!" Gwendolyn pulled off her gloves and started fanning her face with them. "For the love of Mike, just start driving!"

Linc pulled away from the curb and headed north but they'd barely gone twenty yards before a guy in a double-breasted pinstripe stepped into the street. He faced them, impassive and unmoving.

Linc hit the breaks. "This isn't good."

From the front porch of a one-story house to their right, another dark pinstripe reached the concrete driveway, where he stood curling his finger, beckoning them inside.

"I can't believe Leilah set us up like this!" Linc barked. "She's like an aunt to me. Her husband and my dad, they were college roommates."

Gwendolyn kept her eyes on the porch guy walking slowly toward them. "Let's not jump to conclusions."

"Clem O'Roarke took a lot of look-the-other-way bribes during Prohibition," Linc said. "He ended up with stacks of money he couldn't account for with the IRS, so he gave some of it to my dad to help him get Tattler's Tuxedos off the ground."

"Does Ben Siegel know all of this?"

"It's probably best to assume he does."

Porch Guy stood at Gwendolyn's window, making a circular motion with his hand. After she rolled down the window, he snarled, "Mr. Siegel would like a word with you."

Link parked the car outside Virginia Hill's house and they followed Porch Guy inside.

In contrast to Leilah's dark, chilly house, this one was filled with warm sunlight and furniture upholstered in a bright floral that Gwendolyn would normally have taken a moment to memorize. But this wasn't a normal moment.

Benjamin Siegel sat on the largest sofa. He wore a tweed jacket patterned in unusually large black-and-white checks, a white shirt, and a black necktie with a playing-card pattern on it. *It's a shame he chose a violent life,* Gwendolyn thought. *The guy's so good-looking he could be a movie star. No wonder the countess fell for him.* Seated next to him was his girlfriend, Virginia Hill, a broad-faced woman with dark shoulder-length hair who was a little on the plump side. Her carefully painted lips hinted at a sneer, giving her an air of unvarnished cheapness.

With practiced deliberation, Siegel drew a long breath from his cigar and slowly stubbed it out in the black ashtray to his left. He looked at Linc and said, "Thanks for saving me a trip across town. I didn't want to have to do this at your fine establishment."

"Do what?" Linc asked.

"Let you know that I'll be supervising your activities from now on."

"I'm sorry, Mr. Siegel, but you're too late. We just sold our last supply. We're out of stock and out of business."

Virginia Hill let out a scoffing sound and her crossed leg started to jiggle. Siegel laid his right hand on her knee to subdue the twitch. He made a point of inspecting his nails, which seemed unnecessary. From where Gwendolyn stood, she could see they'd been expertly manicured.

"That's not accurate, Mr. Tattler, and we both know it." Siegel's voice was measured and deliberate. His eyes were a deep aquamarine, but there was nothing beautiful about them.

"Look, Mr. Siegel," Linc said, "you obviously know what Valentina is, and where she is. We're walking away; she's all yours."

Siegel gave no indication he'd heard anything Linc said. "My own supply has just about shrunk to nothing, but Valentina's is better merchandise. The quality, I'm impressed. So from now on, you'll do what you've been doing, only I'll be supervising. For a cut."

Virginia Hill's leg erupted into manic jiggling again and her veiled snicker bloomed into barefaced scorn. Despite the warmth of the sun streaming into the room, Gwendolyn felt a film of clammy sweat blanket her forehead. She wanted to wipe it clean, but her arms refused to budge. The only movement in the room was Hill's kneecap. The atmosphere bulged with tension until Siegel finally spoke.

"You can go now," he commanded. "I'll be in touch."

"How will I—" Linc began, but the mobster cut him off.

"Trust me, Tattler, you'll know."

Linc seemed nailed to the carpet until Gwendolyn pulled at his elbow. Neither of them said a word until they were five miles down Sunset, and even then, all Gwendolyn could manage was "Holy crap."

CHAPTER 33

Marcus couldn't sit still any longer. He started pacing the length of Jim Taggert's office.

"How are we supposed to work with you being all Jumping Jehoshaphat?" Taggert asked.

"How are we supposed to work at all?" Marcus shot back. "Our troops are nearly there. By this time next week, Paris will be liberated!" Down the hallway, very few typewriters were clacking away. All Marcus could hear was low-volume chatter.

"*Might* be liberated," Taggert corrected him. "We don't know what's going to happen. But Paris or no Paris, this script needs to be finished by Friday."

"It's an Abbott and Costello movie. These things write themselves."

"Obviously they don't, otherwise we wouldn't be here trying to come up with a better ending. These movies are huge moneymakers; we're lucky to have wrestled them from Universal. I could have asked anybody to fix this turkey but I asked you."

Taggert's telephone rang, so Marcus kept pacing. The success of D-Day was one thing, but if the Allies can liberate Paris, surely that spells the beginning of the end?

Jim hung up and got to his feet. "We've got a meeting." He reached for his jacket. "Mayer's office. Right now."

"We?"

Taggert stopped halfway through donning his jacket. "When was the last time you spoke to Mayer?"

"Not since the *William Tell* premiere."

"We've been clashing a lot lately."

"Has my name come up?"

"Not till just now."

* * *

Mayer's desk was built on a platform so subtle that anybody sitting across from him was unconsciously intimidated, even though he was only five foot three. Consequently, Mayer was rarely seen in meetings anywhere but behind his desk.

The fact that Marcus' presence had been ordered was the first clue that this was no regular meeting; the second was how Mayer was leaning against the small conference table instead of sitting at his desk.

The mogul pitched himself forward, hands outstretched, smiling like a used-car salesmen. Eddie Mannix, followed suit, but pulled off the salesman routine less convincingly.

The third clue was the way both men babbled on about the hopeful situation gathering momentum outside Paris while they settled at the conference table. In Marcus' experience, neither man was much for small talk.

Something was going on, but Marcus couldn't make out what. Then, abruptly, it was time for business.

"Gentlemen," Mayer began, "we are in need of a great pro-war story. We released *Song Of Russia* earlier this year, and *Thirty Seconds Over Tokyo* will be coming out soon, but we need something else."

Mannix added, "Something along the lines of *Since You Went Away*." He turned to Marcus. "Did you see it?"

Surprised that Mannix would be interested, Marcus nodded—Alla had a small role in the movie. He wondered if Mannix would know that, but decided his paranoia was getting the better of him.

Mannix rolled a quarter around his fingertips. "If you ask me, it was way too schmaltzy, even for a keep-the-home-fires-burning picture. But brother, did it ever mint money at the box office. That's what we're shooting for here, but we don't want no copycat."

Taggert strummed the table. "A tearjerker, but not an American family doing it tough on the home front."

"Exactly."

"So instead of an American family, we could have a group of American friends—"

"We need an *international* story."

Mayer's owl eyes and Mannix's ex-bouncer glower stared expectantly at Jim, who continued to tap the table like it was going to conjure the story they needed. The silence grew more painfully awkward as each second passed.

Mayer turned to Marcus. "Feel free to jump in at any time, Adler."

If I'm free to jump in, he wanted to ask, why have I been rotting away on fillers while my original ideas are shot down faster than kamikazes? Still, he wondered how many chances he would get to bend the ear of the big boss.

"I do have an idea," he said.

Mayer's mouth twitched. "Let's hear it."

"It's about a bunch of neighbors who live on the same street, and how they each deal with the war. I conceived it as Anytown, USA, but what if we set it in Europe? Remember that picture we were going to do with Garbo? *The Girl From Leningrad.*"

Jesus! What part of my ass did I pull that out of?

Mayer snapped his fingers. "Where she was going to play a Russian resistance fighter?"

Mannix planted his elbows on the table and bunched his fists together. "I like that. *Song Of Russia* did well for us, but I thought it was too highbrow. All that Tchaikovsky crap went on and on."

"We could set it during the Siege of Leningrad." Marcus could feel his mind churning with possibilities. "The picture opens just before the siege starts and climaxes at the height of the Soviet offensive, driving the Germans out. I have a whole bunch of characters — baker, doctor, mechanic, dressmaker — all I need to do is change their names and some of the dialogue."

"You're talking like you've already written it," Mayer said.

Marcus nodded. "In my spare time. Sort of a side project. I was calling it *The Street,* but now I'm thinking a better title might be *Free Leningrad.*"

"This is a great idea," Mannix said. "Why haven't you pitched this?"

"I thought I was on the outs."

Marcus doubted that Mayer's "Oh?" was as genuine as it sounded. Unsure at how honest he ought to be, Marcus glanced at Jim. The two of them had worked together long enough to be able to read each other's faces. Jim's was saying, *It's your career. Fight for it.*

"At the *William Tell* premiere, Edwin Marr called me a murderer."

Mayer wiped his brow with a starched handkerchief he'd pulled from his pocket. "Christ almighty, what a night that was."

"I know that you two go back a long way," Marcus said, "and I got the impression he'd told you something about me." Mayer nodded, noncommittal. "My guess is that he either told you I was a murderer or a Commie."

Mayer didn't even blink. "Both. I know all about his son's death, and that you were there, so I didn't pay much attention to the murderer nonsense."

"But the pinko issue, you're not so sure. Especially when *William Tell* came back from the Breen Office. Am I right?"

Mayer nodded slowly, his beady eyes narrowing. "I'm starting to realize you're sharper than I gave you credit for."

Marcus could feel a layer of clamminess break out across his forehead and he wished he could borrow Mayer's handkerchief. He said, "I'd like to state for the record that I'm no Commie. My political preferences may lean left of center, but I can assure you they don't tilt anywhere near that far left."

"Adler," Mayer said, "I will admit that I allowed my opinion of you to be swayed, so I appreciate your honesty."

Marcus offered Mayer a reverential bow and then looked at Jim. *We should exit stage right.*

"So," Jim said, "Adler here has come up with the goods with this Leningrad picture. All we need is a deadline."

"Is a week too soon?" Mannix asked.

In all the time he'd worked at the studio, Marcus had only ever heard Mannix bark out orders like a drill sergeant, and now he was asking if a deadline he was suggesting was enough time? This meeting really was one for the books. He said, "I can do it in a week."

The four men rose to their feet, then Marcus and Jim started the long walk out of Mayer's office. They were halfway out when Mannix's rough New Jersey voice shot at them.

"By the way," he said, feigning nonchalance, "I understand you're friendly with someone inside the Breen Office."

I knew it, Marcus thought. I'm not here for my ideas.

In a way, Marcus was almost relieved this moment had come. He'd been half expecting the Sword of Damocles to drop ever since Doris told him what happened that night at the Oscars. Marcus could see Jim slowly turn his head. He didn't need to look at his boss to know what he was thinking: *You are?*

"Oliver Trenton, right?" Mannix asked.

Marcus and Taggert returned to the conference table. "Yes, that's right," Marcus replied.

"How did that come about?"

Marcus hesitated. Their standard story about meeting at the HWM left a sour taste now that the Motion Picture Alliance for the Preservation of American Ideals had labeled it a hornet's nest of subversives. "At a fundraiser for the USO canteen at the Beverly Hills Hotel. I knew the girl running the kissing booth and so did he. We got to talking and struck up a friendship."

"You went out of your way to strike up a friendship with someone from the Breen Office?" Mayer asked. The afternoon sun shone directly through the window behind Mayer, striking Marcus directly in the eyes, blocking him from seeing Mayer's expression.

"In a manner of speaking," Marcus replied evenly.

"Outstanding!" Mayer took Marcus' hand and pumped it. "Tremendous initiative!"

"Okay, Adler, this is what we need you to do." Mannix handed Marcus two scripts: *The Thin Man Goes Home* and *Meet Me In St. Louis.* "These are two of our biggest new movies, but we're having huge problems with the Breen

Office. They're objecting to all the booze being swilled in *Thin Man.*" He let out a snarl. "We keep telling them, 'It's a *Thin Man* movie, for chrissakes. Drinking is the whole goddamned point.' But they keep jabbering on about rationing and keeping sober for the duration, so we want you to fix that."

Fix it? Marcus thought. How am I supposed to—

"And with *St. Louis,* they're all pouty because of the Halloween sequence. We plan on shooting it from low angles to give the audience Margaret O'Brien's point of view. She's seven, so of course she's going to be scared. But they keep insisting that scary movies have no place during wartime. It's our job to lift public spirits, blah, blah, blah. So we need you to see what you can do about that, too."

Marcus looked up from the pair of scripts in his hand.

"This Trenton character, is he a drinking man?" Mayer asked.

Oliver had proven a number of times that he could out-drink anyone at the Garden, which was no mean feat. Marcus nodded.

"Terrific!" Mayer enthused. "We're going to set you up with an expense account. Nothing huge, so don't go hauling him off to the fancy places around town. Stick to the middle of the road. Nice enough to impress, but not enough to make him suspicious." Mayer held up a cautioning finger. "Discretion is key. I can tell from the look on Taggert's face that you even kept it from him. That's good, very good. Shows me you know how to keep a secret. Tell me, who else knows about this friendship of yours?"

Marcus thought about the gang at the Garden of Allah. Pretty much everybody knew. He said, "Nobody," and received a solid slap on the back.

For once, Marcus was glad for the sixty-foot walk to the walnut wood doors leading out to reception. He needed that time to catch his breath.

Taggert waited until they were alone in the elevator. "This Trenton guy," he said, keeping his eyes on the sliding doors. "You sleeping with him?"

"Yep," Marcus replied.

"Casual, or something more than that?"

"A whole lot more than casual."

Jim let out a world-weary grunt. "As your friend, I couldn't be happier for you. As your boss, I'd say you're screwed."

CHAPTER 34

Bette Davis strode into Kathryn's NBC dressing room. "Tell me I wasn't atrocious!" she commanded, and helped herself to one of Kathryn's cigarettes.

As she lit it, Bette took in her surroundings and frowned when she spotted Gwendolyn on Kathryn's loveseat. "I know you," she said. "From the Canteen, right?" She offered her hand. "And who's this fine specimen?" When Kathryn introduced Linc, Bette's face lit up. "As in 'Tuxedos'?"

Linc nodded. Over the months Gwendolyn and Linc had been dating, Kathryn had noticed how awkward he became when his family entered the conversation. He had this way of ducking his head, as though the Tattler name was a Molotov cocktail.

Bette sat on the chair next to Kathryn's vanity table and propped her feet up on the wooden coffee table. "Oh, but that *song!*" she yelped. "How the hell I let Jack Warner talk me into singing it, I'll never know. I'm a lot of things, but singer is not one of them."

Earlier in the year, some bright spark at Warners got the idea of turning the Hollywood Canteen into a movie, and Bette shot it over the summer. It was now time to promote it, so Warners had sent her onto *Kraft Music Hall*, where she was forced to sing a ditty called "They're Either Too Young Or Too Old" that she sang in a movie the previous year.

"What makes you think you were atrocious?" Kathryn asked.

Bette ignored her. "What's with all these flowers?"

Bunches of bright yellow tulips and daffodils and vases of red and pink roses had been arriving all evening. Kathryn's mother sent an aquamarine dahlia with bright orange tips.

"Tonight was Kathryn's first anniversary on the show," Gwendolyn explained.

Bette smelled the roses from Wilkerson. "I'd have brought champagne if I'd known."

The studio page, Sonny, appeared in the doorway and held up a business card. "A guy from *The New York Times* is requesting an interview."

Kathryn took the card from Sonny. "Have you ever met—" She silently read the name and smothered her reaction, then fixed her eyes on Gwendolyn. "Nelson Hoyt."

The night Kathryn walked all the way home from Cole Porter's birthday party, she found Gwendolyn still awake, and relayed her conversation with Louella and Hedda. They spent the rest of the summer and the entire fall paranoid that the guy would come knocking on their door, but the passing months brought no such appearance—until now. "Tell him I've already left."

"WHAT?" Bette jumped to her feet. "A girl knows she's really getting places when she comes to the attention of the *Times*. Of course you're going to see him. We should all clear out and give you some room—"

"The thing is," Sonny broke in, "he's not the only one asking to see you. Humphrey Bogart's in the building. Although he's not so much asking; more like demanding."

"What do you mean?"

"He's kinda plastered."

"Oh, boy," Linc said.

A woman's scream shot down the corridor, followed by a crash of falling cymbals. Sonny peeked out into the hallway. "Speak of the devil."

Kathryn turned to Gwendolyn. "We need to get him out of here. We can't let the *New York Times* see him like this." She still hadn't figured out why Louella and Hedda were so interested in Bogie's connection with a Hollywood bookstore, but her journalist's nose could smell trouble from a thousand paces.

Bogie swung into the room and waved a flask-sized bottle of Heaven Hill black bourbon in Kathryn's direction. "You miserable bitch."

Kathryn could feel a furious blush take over her face. She eyed Bogie's juddering bottle.

Bette Davis stubbed out her cigarette. "Steady on there, bucko."

If Bogie heard Bette, he gave no sign. "Mayo and me, we're announcing our separation at the end of the week. It was going to be all very civil and adult. Then Hedda Hopper jumps on us at Chasen's and starts jabbering on about my 'captivating new costar.'"

Bette stood up. "For chrissakes, Humphrey, everybody knows about you and Betty Bacall. You can't blame Kathryn if Hollywood's worst-kept secret reached Hedda."

"I didn't tell her about the *Sluggy*!" Bogie yelled. He swilled a mouthful of bourbon and took a step closer to Kathryn. She could now smell it on him. "I only told you about taking Betty down to my boat."

"I swear I never breathed a word to anyone," Kathryn said.

"Not even to me!" Gwendolyn put in. "And I'm her best friend!"

It took Bogie a moment to tunnel through his alcoholic fog. His bleary eyes widened when he recognized Gwendolyn's face. He went to say something, but it evaporated on his lips. Linc seized the moment, crossing Kathryn's dressing room in two strides.

"Okay, Mr. Bogart," he said gently. He towered over Bogie by at least a foot. "We're going to take a walk now. The fresh air is going to do us all a world of good." He nodded to Sonny. "Perhaps you could clear us a path to the nearest exit that doesn't involve the main foyer?"

Gwendolyn kissed Kathryn on the cheek and told her she'd see her at home, then disappeared up the corridor behind the guys. Bette shook her head. "Hitching himself to Mayo was the worst thing he could have done, but teaming up with a rookie half his age? Sounds like frying pan and fire stuff, if you ask me." She hugged Kathryn. "I'm going to leave you to prepare for your *New York Times* caller."

Kathryn realized Sonny had never made it back to the reception desk to tell Nelson Hoyt to get lost. She was still scanning the corridor for an usher to deliver her message when she heard a voice behind her.

"Miss Massey, I presume?"

The voice was rich and cultured, ripe with the charm of a Southern gentleman out of *Gone With The Wind,* just like Hedda said. When she turned around, the first thing she saw was that deep, deep cleft in his chin.

"Mr. Hoyt, I'm sorry, but you've not caught me at a good time."

He walked into her dressing room and parked himself on the loveseat, placing his dark beige homburg next to him. "This won't take long."

Kathryn closed the door behind her. "You're not with any newspaper, are you?"

"I assume Miss Parsons or Miss Hopper forewarned you about me. That is unfortunate, but to be expected from a couple of old gossips."

She sat at her vanity and started freshening her mascara. Diffused as they were by the light bulbs around her mirror, his eyes were an indeterminate color, but intelligent in a knowing sort of way. He had Clark Gable's impressive jawline, too. His cheeks lacked Gable's dimples, but that cleft in his chin was arresting.

"I really am pressed for time, Mr. Hoyt, so let's skip the niceties. Exactly what do you want?"

"I'm here on behalf of the US government to request that you serve your country."

"When you say 'US government,' can I assume you mean 'FBI'?"

Hoyt sat up more formally. "Miss Massey, you have access to all levels of persons engaged in the entertainment industry. All we ask is that you keep your eyes and ears open as you move about in the course of your work."

Kathryn tossed her mascara wand onto the vanity and turned around. "Keeping my eyes and ears open *is* my job."

"Exactly." Hoyt went through the motions of displaying a smile, but it had all the sincerity of a dime-store mannequin. "We just ask that you do your job and share with us anything you feel might possibly compromise the security of the country."

If Kathryn still had the brush in her hand, she would have thrown it at this implacable phony. "What you want is for me to become a squealer, but I value my friendships and relationships far too much to rat them out. Thank you for giving me the opportunity to serve my country, Mr. Hoyt, but I must decline."

He maintained the smile. "Miss Parsons and Miss Hopper—"

"You've already recruited Louella and Hedda. I'm sure those two are supplying you with all the *sharing* you need."

"I was going to say that Miss Parsons and Miss Hopper are more than eager to work with us, but they both lack your powers of discernment."

"You have a talent for gift-wrapping."

A smile stole out from between his lips with a trace of candid honesty, but only for a moment. "You remember the Hollywood Anti-Nazi League, don't you?"

Kathryn stared at the man's cleft chin while her mind spun through the possible reasons he'd bring up an organization that hadn't existed for five years. By the mid thirties, Hitler's Nazi party was no longer bothering to hide its long-term plans, and Hollywoodites responded by forming the Hollywood Anti-Nazi League. Dorothy Parker helped put the League together, so it was a hot issue around the Garden; her husband, Alan Campbell, was secretary, and their neighbor Donnie Stewart became chairman. Kathryn hadn't put much stock in the whole endeavor. What would Adolf Hitler care what a bunch of self-absorbed movie people ten thousand miles away thought about him? It wasn't like he'd get a letter of protest from the Hollywood Anti-Nazi League and think, *In that case, I won't invade Poland after all.* But the League petered out well before Pearl Harbor, leaving Kathryn to wonder why Hoyt was bringing it up now.

"Of course I remember it," she said. *And you know it.*

"Were you aware it was a Communist front?"

She regarded him coolly. "I don't keep current with that sort of thing."

He responded with a bland nod, difficult to interpret. "Do you know what Robert Benchley, Lillian Hellman, Dorothy Parker, Ginger Rogers, and Donald Ogden Stewart all have in common?"

All five people he mentioned had lived at the Garden of Allah, and Kathryn counted them as friends. She said nothing.

Hoyt continued. "As well as Joan Crawford, George Cukor, and Bette Davis."

Those three never lived at the Garden, but she knew them all. Then it hit her. "They were all members of the Anti-Nazi League, weren't they?" Hoyt nodded. "Which you think was a Communist Party front."

Hoyt nodded again, this time not so mildly, and crossed his legs. "Therefore we have a file on each of them."

Kathryn stiffened and looked away. Back in the maid's room at Cole Porter's house, this seemed silly and unlikely, but now she felt a noose tightening around her with agonizing determination. She forced herself to look at him. "Are you trying to scare me, Mr. Hoyt?"

"What I'm trying to do, Miss Massey, is paint you a picture of the real world, in contrast to—" he waved a hand around her dressing room, "—worlds of make-believe."

Kathryn Massey had long considered herself one of the most pragmatic people she knew. If this FBI guy was so smart, she decided, he ought to know that his approach was entirely the wrong way to go about recruiting her.

She got to her feet. "My answer is no, Mr. Hoyt." When she pulled open the door, the theme song of *The March Of Time* program filled the room.

Nelson Hoyt grabbed his hat and took his time joining her in the doorway. He put his face so close to hers she could smell his shaving cream. "Do you know who I report to?"

"I haven't the slightest idea."

"J. Edgar Hoover."

For the first time that night, Kathryn's nerve failed her. It's one thing to say no when the FBI wants you to become some lousy snitching stool pigeon fink, she thought, but saying no to the director is a whole different rat's nest.

He took her silence as vacillation, and pressed his argument. "Mr. Hoover takes particular interest in Hollywood, so he set up a special task force to observe what goes on here. I head up that task force."

Kathryn thought about Bette Davis, or more specifically the sort of women she portrayed on the screen. What would Julie in *Jezebel* do? She'd play it smart and call his bluff. "Your mother must be very proud."

As he dropped his hat on his head and retreated down the hallway, she expected a departing stink eye, but he disappeared through the swinging door that led into the foyer without looking back. She counted to ten before lurching back into her dressing room. It was then that she discovered she still had his business card in hand, crushed and folded, and dank with sweat.

CHAPTER 35

When Marcus pushed open the door to the Sahara Room, a racket engulfed him. In Hollywood, there was never any shortage of places to usher in a new year, but Garden of Allah residents always knew the best party in town was in their backyard. Or more specifically, in the main bar next to their backyard.

It was just past nine o'clock and already the room was half full with neighbors and their spouses, boyfriends, and girlfriends, drinking buddies, poker buddies, and a sprinkling of last night's leftovers. Marcus saw that Kathryn and Gwendolyn hadn't arrived yet, nor had Linc. He suggested to Oliver they get a drink while the getting was good.

These days, whenever Marcus approached the Sahara Room's bar, his eyes shot automatically to the Glenfiddich bottles on Seamus' shelf. For the longest time, three of them stood there, but now only one remained. "Jesus, Seamus," Marcus said. "I hadn't heard."

Seamus looked paler than Marcus had ever seen him. "We lost one in the Leyte Gulf under MacArthur, and the other in the Battle of the Bulge." His smile trembled at the edges. "Glenfiddich is a comforting drop, I can promise you that." He clapped his hands together and rubbed them. "If we can break the bulge and get those Huns on the run, this'll be the last holiday season of the war, and that's worth celebrating. What'll it be?"

Double whiskeys in hand, Marcus and Oliver spotted Alla with Glesca. By the time they pushed and squeezed their way over, Kathryn had joined them.

"Where's Gwennie?" Marcus asked.

Kathryn shot him an apprehensive look. "She and Linc are taking their time. Something's going on with those two."

"What kind of something?" Alla asked.

"I get the feeling there's an elephant in the room. Damned if I can see it, though."

There seems to be a plague of elephants, Marcus moped. He hadn't noticed any chords of discontent between Gwendolyn and her handsome boyfriend; he was too preoccupied with the elephant crowding him and Oliver.

He longed to feel Oliver's hand slide up his back. He'd always do it so casually, so discreetly, never failing to make Marcus feel wanted and needed. But it had been weeks since he sensed the warmth from Oliver's hand drifting up his spine, weeks since Oliver used their secret three code. In the year and a half they'd been dating, Marcus had come to realize that he liked who he was around Oliver. He brooded and drank less heavily, and laughed and forgave more easily. He felt more confident in his abilities and slept more deeply than ever.

But these past couple of months, Oliver had begun to pull away. Even when he was around, he seemed preoccupied. It hadn't escaped Marcus' notice that Oliver's withdrawal started around the time Marcus left the scripts for *The Thin Man Goes Home* and *Meet Me In St. Louis* lying around his villa.

He spent the week following his meeting with Mayer and Mannix stewing over how to bring up the subject in conversation, but failed to come up with any sort of likely scenario that Oliver wouldn't see through.

In the end, Marcus left the scripts out for Oliver to stumble across, which he did, and then improvised an exasperated — and, Marcus feared, overly melodramatic — speech embellishing the points Mayer made. Oliver agreed to take a look, and by week's end both movies were passed by the Breen Office. *Meet Me In St. Louis* opened a month ago to unanimous acclaim and enormous box office, and management had every expectation that *The Thin Man Goes Home* would repeat the success of its predecessors. Meanwhile, Mayer put *Free Leningrad!* into priority preproduction, and Marcus was suddenly the golden boy again.

But Oliver was no dummy, and Marcus was sure he'd seen through his B-movie performance. Marcus kept expecting to be confronted, and it was slowly tearing him to shreds.

Alla said, "Gwendolyn and her Mr. Tux make a fine couple. I'm sure they will resolve whatever's going on between them. Ah!" She lifted her champagne flute. "Here they are now."

Glesca gave an approving sigh. "How does she do it? These days, I can't seem to find enough decent material to stitch together a hausfrau bathrobe, and she comes up with this!" Gwendolyn's dress was the exact same shade as her honey-blonde hair, with a subtle pattern of tulips silhouetted in gold. "I guess it doesn't hurt when your boyfriend's in the rag trade. But still."

"Hey, everyone!" Gwendolyn called out. "Look who I found wandering around in search of company."

Humphrey Bogart appeared in the doorway, hatless and tieless and sucking the last half inch out of his cigarette. He was also conspicuously wifeless, which was surprising. Three days ago, Hedda Hopper reported in the *LA Times* that the "Battling Bogarts have signed a truce."

"So much for the ceasefire," Kathryn murmured before she crossed the room and prodded Bogie toward the bar.

"Talk about tense relationships," Oliver said. "Why doesn't he just get it over and done with?"

Oliver had barely looked at Marcus all day, and the thought struck him that Oliver may not have been talking about Bogart and his drunkard wife. *If you're going to pull the pin on us,* he thought, *I'd prefer you did it now so I can be plastered by the time we all launch into "Auld Lang Syne."*

"It's getting mighty crowded in here," Marcus announced. In the last few minutes, fifteen to twenty more people had shown up. The pandemonium of increasingly plastered cocktail chatter had jumped up a notch, and a thunderhead of cigarette smoke already filled the top half of the room. "Let's go find some corner where we can hear each other."

The two men reached the Sahara Room's heavy wooden doors just as Taggert and Hoppy arrived, already half tanked on a previous party's offerings. Marcus had invited them to tonight's celebration, but Taggert was noncommittal. The thought that Oliver might guillotine their relationship at any minute left Marcus apprehensive, so he was glad the two men had appeared. Taggert held up a bottle of whiskey. "You're leaving?"

"It was getting too loud and crowded in there." As though to prove Marcus' point, a shriek of laughter exploded from inside the room. A second wave followed closely, spilling out into the hotel foyer.

Hoppy ducked inside to borrow some glasses while the others found a quiet nook to settle in for a round or two. Taggert eyed Oliver's stern face. "I gotta say, Trenton, it's unnerving to fraternize with the Breen Office. I never know if I can speak freely around you."

Marcus nudged Oliver's knee and tried his friendliest smile. "Maybe you should give him your 'working from the inside' speech?"

Oliver's face remained inert. He said nothing, looked at nobody, until Hoppy joined them with a quartet of shot glasses. He aimed a dark look at Marcus. "Who is Edwin Marr?"

Marcus held out his shot glass for Hoppy to fill. "Do you remember me talking about one of our screenwriters, Hugo?"

"The one who shot himself?"

"Edwin is his father. Why are you asking?"

"A few weeks ago, I was at a meeting of the Motion Picture Alliance."

"You mean 'For the Preservation of American Ideals?'" Taggert asked. He and Hoppy looked like they wanted to throw their drinks in Oliver's face.

Inside the bar, someone had flipped on a radio and the brass section of Glenn Miller's band burst into "Tuxedo Junction" in tribute to the bulletins that Miller's plane had been reported missing over the English Channel.

"Listen, buddy." Taggert jabbed a finger in Oliver's face. "When Marcus told me about you, I had my reservations. You're the Breen Office and you know how that plays at the studios. I was prepared to loathe you, but then I met you, and you seemed like a regular guy, so I was happy to give you the benefit of the doubt. But those Motion Picture Alliance crackpots are a bunch of jingoistic — " He shook his head and lobbed Marcus a chilling glare. "Jesus Christ."

Marcus didn't know what to make of this news. Oliver had never even hinted that his political inclinations leaned rightward. *How can we have so much in common if you're an archconservative?* "You haven't mentioned attending any Alliance meetings."

"Can you blame me?" Oliver retorted. "The first time I mention it, look at the reaction I get."

"So why were you there?"

"The Alliance is running around screaming into the faces of anyone who'll listen that Hollywood is packed with Commies, and that some are screenwriters who are trying to sneak the Communist message into their scripts. Mr. Breen decided that somebody from the office should attend the meetings and report back."

"But why you?" Hoppy asked.

"It was a case of 'the guy who isn't in the room gets the job.'"

"What are they like?" Hoppy asked.

"You should hear the blowhard rhetoric! It's enough to give me ulcers. At the end of each meeting, I'm the first one out the door." He laid his hand on top of Marcus.' "I'm not there because I want to be. But as studio screenwriters, you guys need to start taking those so-called crackpots seriously. They have no intention of stopping when the war is over."

"But what does this have to do with Edwin Marr?" Marcus asked.

Oliver bugged his hazel eyes out while he chugged some whiskey. "At the last meeting they were in the middle of a discussion about lobbying the House un-American Activities Committee—"

"The HUAC is supposed to be rooting out Nazi sympathizers, not Communists."

"Not if the Alliance has anything to do with it. Anyhow, they were discussing it, and this old codger bursts into the room and announces he has a list of people he thinks the Alliance should investigate."

"Was he sober?" Marcus asked.

"Did anyone take him seriously?" Taggert added.

"He seemed quite sober, and he was preaching to the choir, so yes, they took him seriously."

"Who was on his list?" Marcus asked.

Inside the Sahara Room, somebody turned up the radio just as the Andrews Sisters started singing, "Is You Is Or Is You Ain't?" The roar of approval that followed had a ragged edge to it, and Marcus wondered how many of them would still be upright by midnight.

"I was so thrown by the first name he read out that I didn't hear any of the others."

"Whose name was it?"

Oliver faced Marcus. "Yours."

The word punched Marcus in the gut. He took *Free Leningrad!* as evidence that Edwin's campaign against him had failed. It never occurred to him that Edwin would widen his crusade past the MGM gates. "It's not true," Marcus told his lover. "You do know that, don't you?"

Oliver's response was the warmest and most genuine smile Marcus had seen in weeks.

"Tell me something," Taggert said. "Do these screwballs know what you do for a living?"

Oliver nodded. "I'm starting to wish I hadn't been quite so open about it. Some of them are trying to use my influence inside the office to get their pictures through."

Marcus resisted the urge to look at Taggert.

"This list of suspects," Taggert said. "Was it written down?"

"Yep."

"Did you see him give it to anyone?"

"He gave it to James McGuinness." This time, Marcus stared right at Taggert; McGuinness was a producer at MGM. "He was taking the notes that night. Edwin insisted his list be entered into the minutes." Marcus pulled at his collar, wishing he could loosen his tie.

None of the four men said anything, letting the roar of the party on the other side of the wall buffer the awkward silence.

Taggert shook his empty bottle. "After news like that, I reckon we're going to need some more of this." He pulled at Hoppy's elbow and led him back into the Sahara Room.

Oliver waited until they were gone before he took Marcus' hands in his. "I know I've been distant lately." He paused, but not long enough to give Marcus a chance to reply. "It's because of what I witnessed at that meeting."

"But you must know that I'm not—"

Oliver hushed him. "Here's the thing: at work I pretend to agree with the Production Code's ethics, and at those horrible Alliance meetings, I have to pretend I'm a conservative. To nearly everyone else, I have to pretend I'm some bachelor who just hasn't met the right girl yet. Everywhere I go, I have to pretend to be something I'm not."

Oliver was never one easily given to tears, but Marcus could see his eyes tear up. "What are you saying?"

"It's taken me a month to work up the courage, and maybe it's this damn fine whiskey we're drinking, but I'm ready to ask you now."

Marcus felt Oliver's hands squeeze his. "Ask me what?"

"I'm asking if I can move in with you. Here. At the Garden of Allah."

CHAPTER 36

When Gwendolyn opened the door to her villa, she was still bewildered. She didn't notice Kathryn sitting in their easy chair reading until Kathryn said, "You're both back early. I figured you'd stick around for some dinner and dancing."

"Ritchie didn't show," Linc said, removing his overcoat.

Kathryn cast aside her copy of *A Tree Grows In Brooklyn.* "That's odd, isn't it?"

Ever since Bugsy Siegel muscled in on Linc and Gwendolyn's operation, Kathryn and Gwendolyn had implicitly agreed that Kathryn should distance herself. Kathryn no longer asked what was happening, and Gwendolyn volunteered no information.

Gwendolyn slung her cashmere wrap over the back of the sofa and sat down. "Mr. Siegel is awfully fond of his money. Ritchie wouldn't dare not keep our appointment."

Siegel's initial cut of thirty percent only lasted a few months, then he raised it to forty. Two months ago he jacked it up to fifty. Any higher and it would hardly be worth their while at all. But getting out of the game wasn't an option. She kept telling herself she should be thankful that she wasn't leading the life of second-rate gun molls and bloodstained drapes she'd envisioned that day at Virginia Hill's house. In fact, it had all been quite civil.

On the first Monday of each month, Ritchie placed a classified ad in the *Hollywood Citizen News* telling them where they were to hand over Siegel's cut. It was never down some back alley or skid row hotel room, but always surrounded by masses of people. Gwendolyn didn't understand Linc's "hiding in plain sight" explanation, but it seemed to work. Last month, they met at Union Station, and the month before that, at Earl Carroll's on Sunset, where they handed over six hundred dollars in front of thirty beautiful showgirls. Tonight it was a lively bar called La Conga on Vine Street. Even though Ritchie was always prompt, they stayed an hour past their agreed time, but no Ritchie.

"Maybe he had car trouble?" Linc suggested.

Gwendolyn threw her roommate an unconvinced look and started fidgeting with the fingers of her gloves. "You really think Ritchie went to Siegel and said, 'Sorry, boss, I couldn't make the drop-off. I had trouble with my carburetor."

"You're right," Kathryn conceded, "but if you look in the *Times* tomorrow, I can guarantee you'll see an ad telling you where and when to meet him tomorrow night." She glanced at the clock above the sink; it was going on eight thirty. "I still have yesterday's coffee grounds. If I add one fresh scoop, I could probably make a halfway decent pot." She got up to walk toward the kitchen. "If I add some Sanka, it might not taste like dirt."

Gwendolyn nodded absently and stared at a spot on the wall opposite her, trying to tell herself not to fret over Ritchie. There were a hundred possible explanations for why he failed to show. She paid no attention when the telephone rang.

"Gwennie, that was the front desk," Kathryn said, hanging up. "A visitor asked for you by name, so he sent him up here."

"Old guy?" Linc said, standing. "When the old mobsters get too ripe to shoot straight, they turn them into messenger boys."

"I don't think so." Kathryn sounded puzzled. "Manny said he was some old geezer with no jacket, no tie, and no hat. No mobster would be caught dead in public without putting on the Ritz."

Just then, there was a knock on the door. Linc made a gesture, offering to open it for her, but Gwendolyn shook her head. When she pulled open the door, she found a lanky fellow, well into his sixties, unshaven and hunched over and looking for all the world like Walter Huston's older brother.

"Gwendolyn Brick?" he asked. "I was Ritchie Pugh's landlord." He looked down at the envelope in his hand before he thrust it toward her.

Gwendolyn took it and read the shaky handwriting on the front.

Please deliver this to Miss Gwendolyn Brick at the Garden of Allah Hotel in the event of my death.

"Oh, God!" She lurched a step backward into Linc. He wrapped an arm around her chest.

She lifted the envelope and felt Linc's body jolt. She closed her hand around his and heard Kathryn say, "Won't you please come in?"

The man seemed reluctant, but Kathryn gently insisted he join them on the sofa.

"You're Ritchie's landlord?" she prompted.

The man's wizened expression turned wary as he studied their faces one by one. Gwendolyn held her breath. He let out a quiet groan. "Like I said, I'm—was—just his landlord, so I never went stickin' my nose into his business. He seemed like a good lad, but kinda on the secretive side. Never knew what to make of him. 'Bout a month ago, he knocked on my door—just like that, outta the blue—and he says, 'If anything should happen to me, do what you like with my stuff, but there's an old metal saltine cracker box in back of the cupboard next to the stove.' He told me there were some odds and ends and instructions on what to do with them if it came to that." He gestured to the envelope in Kathryn's hand. Gwendolyn didn't remember letting it go. "So when the cops came and told me they'd identified Ritchie as the body all the papers've been talking about—"

All week, the appearance of a body in the foothills of Mandeville Canyon near the Pacific Palisades end of Sunset Boulevard had kicked news of the war from the front page. Playing up the fact that the murder had been "gangland style"—a clean shot directly between the eyes from a close distance—ensured the story had gripped the city.

Gwendolyn pressed her hands to her eyes. *And all this time it was poor, poor Ritchie.* She felt Kathryn's arm slide around her shoulders and press their heads together. "Ritchie was one of the good ones," Kathryn told the man. "He didn't deserve to go like this."

"Nobody does," Linc said.

"I'm sure sorry to have been the one to bring such sad tidings."

The man was on his feet now, so Gwendolyn rose to shake his hand. "Thank you." Her voice was barely above a croak. "I appreciate you going out of your way to deliver this to me."

The guy mumbled, "You're welcome, miss," and followed Linc to the door.

The three of them listened to him shuffle down the stairs and up the flagstone path to the main house. Eventually, Linc asked, "You want me to read it?"

Gwendolyn shook her head and opened the envelope. As she pulled out the folded paper, her hands started to shake. She rested them on her knees as she opened Ritchie's letter.

"You sure you want to read this out loud?" Kathryn asked.

Gwendolyn cleared her throat.

"Dear Gwendolyn, I'm writing this letter in the hopes that you'll never have to read it. But these days nothing's for certain and life is cheap, especially when you hang out with tough guys. And lately I've been getting the impression that certain tough guys are trusting me less and less. It's just a feeling, but it ain't a good feeling so I want to set this down in writing in case I don't get the chance to tell you.

"I've gotten pretty good at eavesdropping, and yesterday I was outside S's office and I overheard S and C talking about you two. I've heard him call you his 'one that got away' and how much he's always wanted to get you into the sack but knew that you were different from the usual broads he bangs, and so he's had to tread more careful. Be more respectful and say all the right things. And that he wasn't going to stop trying until he got you.

"I always assumed that this whole thing about S taking over your operation was more about the fact that S wanted you but never got you. But turns out this whole black-market business was only an excuse. You're just a bystander in all this. It's your boyfriend they want."

Gwendolyn looked up at Linc, who was staring at her, slack-jawed.

"What do they want with you?" Kathryn asked; a mite too sternly, Gwendolyn thought.

"I—I dunno!" Linc said. "Before that day at his house, I never met the guy. And I've never spoken to him since."

Gwendolyn returned to Ritchie's letter. "It's all about a set of three brothels up the hill, off the Sunset Strip." She looked up at Linc again.

He was slowly turning red. "I know *of* them," he admitted, "but that's it. I've never actually been to them. Or any brothel," he added quickly. "Not ever. *I swear!*"

Gwendolyn wanted to believe him, but that was a discussion for another time. She went back to Ritchie's letter.

"They're real classy, professionally run, and very profitable. The guys know that when the war ends, the black market will dry up so they're looking for another moneymaker. From what I can gather, they think Linc runs them."

"JESUS!" Linc started pacing the room, running his fingers through his hair. "This is nuts. Me? Run a brothel?"

"A chain of brothels, apparently," Kathryn said, crossing her arms.

"Linc," Gwendolyn asked quietly, "why would they think that?"

"I DON'T KNOW!"

"I'm not accusing you, I'm just posing a question. Why would the mob think you run brothels?"

Linc joined Gwendolyn on the sofa and took her right hand. "I swear to you I have no idea. This has come from way out in left field." He jutted his chin toward Ritchie's letter. "Keep going. Maybe there's a clue."

Gwendolyn lifted the paper. "If I learn more, I'll add it to this letter, but if not, just remember, these guys play for keeps. Getting away from them ain't easy. They're always looking for bigger fish to fry and from what I can see, they're greasing up their frying pan for your beau. Take care of yourself Gwendolyn. You and Kathryn have always meant a lot to me. Sincerely, your friend, Ritchie."

Gwendolyn laid Ritchie's letter on the table in front of her and let out a long breath.

"Screw the coffee," Kathryn announced. "I'm having a drink. Anyone want to join me?"

No one responded. Gwendolyn and Linc looked silently into each others' faces while Kathryn busied herself in the kitchen. Suddenly Linc grabbed Gwendolyn's hand and pulled her onto the landing outside. He closed the door and turned to her, his pale face silver in the moonlight.

"Have you ever wondered why I've been bothering?" he asked. "With the black market, I mean?"

"I figured you had your reasons, and if you wanted me to know, you'd tell me."

"I'm telling you now."

Gwendolyn wrapped her fingers around Linc's arm to show him she was listening.

"I think my father's been laundering money through the business."

"Are you sure?"

"It's more of a hunch. Whenever I look at the books, the figures all balance, but I'll be damned if something doesn't sit right. I'm no accounting expert, but the whole thing's made me feel uneasy. So just in case everything falls into a heap and I was left with nothing, I started making money separate from anything my dad's involved with."

Gwendolyn squeezed harder on his arm. "A guy needs to look out for his own best interests."

Linc gazed out across the deserted pool. "Clem O'Roarke has a side business. Real estate."

"They say after the war ends, LA is going to experience a boom —"

"But it's way out past the Mojave Desert. Why would anybody buy land in the middle of Nevada? Primm Valley Realty." It was as though Linc was talking to himself now. "That's the name of O'Roarke's company. It comes up on the books over and over. Primm Valley Realty and Tattler's Tuxedos keep lending and borrowing money to and from each other. Back and forth, over and over. Now this brothel business comes up."

"You think Clem O'Roarke's running those places?"

"There must be some reason why Bugsy thinks it's me. It must be a pretty good reason to go to all this trouble to drag me into his net."

"So you think your dad's helping O'Roarke launder brothel money? We need to figure out what we're going to —"

Linc grabbed Gwendolyn by her arms, his eyes darting back and forth. "This whole thing stinks, and I don't want any part of it. I'm going while the getting's good."

"Oh, God, Linc, you're going to try and sign up again?"

He scoffed away her fears. "After they knocked me back on account of my flat feet, I appealed. That's when they found out Dad's three factories were converted for making uniforms and suddenly I found myself officially deemed vital for the war effort, and was permanently excused. I'm so sick of him interfering in my life."

"Where are you going? Do you even have a plan?"

"There's this place in Mexico, on the coast, about halfway to Costa Rica. I saw an article on it in the *Saturday Evening Post*. It looks like a slice of heaven. Come with me."

That last sentence knocked the wind out of Gwendolyn. She began to pull away, but he jerked her closer to him. "It's so cheap down there. With what we've socked away, we could live for fifteen years, maybe twenty. I love you,

Gwendolyn. I truly do. You're the most wonderful girl I've ever met, but I can't stay here. Not anymore. Come with me, Gwendolyn. Come with me to Mexico."

CHAPTER 37

The opening notes of "Moonlight Becomes You" floated out of Mickey Rooney's house, greeting Kathryn as she walked up the brick path.

Beside her, Kay Thompson cocked an ear. "He's got someone playing live. Judy's going to love that."

Kay seemed to exist entirely on cigarettes, cocktails, and black coffee, which explained how she remained so thin. Always dressed in bright colors, white, gold, orange, highlighted with beads or diamantes, and always in ridiculously high heels. At five foot five, she was barely an inch taller than Kathryn, but she often made Kathryn feel short, plump, and dowdy. Kathryn was very pleased Kay was her neighbor, but today the last thing she wanted to feel was short, plump, and dowdy.

The aroma of roses engulfed them as soon as they stepped inside. A matching pair of enormous crystal vases sat on a table in the vestibule, holding two dozen blood-red roses. "It smells like the fucking Rose Parade in here!" Kay declared.

"It *is* St. Valentine's Day," Kathryn pointed out. The memories of past St. Valentine's Days she'd spent with Roy had been haunting her all day.

To their right, Mickey's living room stretched long enough to hold four large sofas, several coffee tables, a sideboard and a wet bar, and a piano surrounded by a dozen people. On every available surface were bouquets of roses, some red, some white, some pink, all in vases identical to the ones in the vestibule. The fragrance was overwhelming.

Kay picked up two champagne coupes from a tray sitting on the hall table and handed one to Kathryn. "Judy won't be able to breathe, let alone sing," she tut-tutted.

It was generally acknowledged that Judy Garland's success at MGM was thanks in large part to Kay Thompson's ability to dream up superlative vocal arrangements that brought out a singer's best qualities. When Mickey Rooney announced he was throwing a St. Valentine's Day party to celebrate the success of his latest picture, *National Velvet*, he asked Judy if she'd come along and sing a few songs. Judy was still riding high on *Meet Me In St. Louis*, and knew that every decision-maker at MGM would be at Mickey's party. Wowing the crowd would help consolidate her position as their biggest female star.

"I better go find her." Kay plunged into the crowd, blowing air kisses at every other person she came to. Kathryn watched Kay work the room, scrutinizing everyone she greeted.

You're obsessed, she told herself, and it's starting to drive you batty.

Since the visit from Nelson Hoyt last December, Kathryn found herself looking around tree trunks, double-checking waiters and cab drivers, and eavesdropping on conversations at restaurants. Everywhere she went, she searched for signs the FBI was watching.

Kathryn drained her champagne and dipped into a zebra-striped ceramic bowl for a heart-shaped chocolate. The first one was filled with creamy strawberry fondant that made her think of Marcus and how happy he was these days. Oliver's declaration that he wanted to move in was sweet, but unrealistic. There was no way the Breen Office would approve of one of their staff moving into a place as louche as the Garden of Allah, so he rented a cheap studio apartment as his official address and shifted all his clothes, books, and records into Marcus' home. The sweetest pair of lovebirds in all creation couldn't be happier than those two.

And then there was Gwendolyn. Kathryn gnawed into another chocolate and let bitter orange spill over her tongue. Linc hadn't made good on his Mexican getaway, but Gwendolyn wasn't sure how much longer he'd stick around.

Kathryn spotted a familiar figure across the far side of the living room. Her boss' meticulously groomed lawyer, Greg Bautzer, had been in the *Reporter*'s office more often lately. She decided it was time for a fishing expedition.

From the way his eyes darted around the room, it was obvious he would welcome the distraction from small talk with Ann Rutherford and Roger Edens. She was about to make her move when a fresh glass of champagne appeared in front of her face. She turned to thank her savior, but froze mid word when she saw the deep cleft in his chin.

She was reluctant to accept the champagne, but her mouth had gone dry. She grabbed the glass. "How did you talk your way into this party?"

His smile widened. "I'm with the *New York Times*, remember?"

She hit him with her haughtiest expression, and turned back to Bautzer, catching his eye and raising her glass. He did the same, mouthing the word *Help!*

"I was hoping I'd bump into you here," Hoyt said.

Kathryn kept her eyes on Bautzer. "I'm so flattered." She felt his hand on her arm and looked at him expectantly.

"We need to talk about my offer."

"Here's what I think about your offer. *You* get someone to snoop on her friends, and *I* get—hmmm. What do I get out of it? Oh, yes, that's right: nothing." She wanted to cold-shoulder him, but decided an unblinking glare might serve her purpose better.

To his credit, he didn't blink either. "I agree. You deserve more out of this than the chance to serve your country." He smiled at her withering pout. "How would you like to know the name of your father?"

It took her several heartbeats to grasp the implications of his question. "You've seen my birth certificate?"

"We do a background check on everyone we're thinking of approaching. Not only did yours turn up an unnamed father, but also a recent request for a copy of the birth certificate. Return address: the Garden of Allah Hotel."

And did your background check include the fights I've had with my mother?

What Francine failed to acknowledge was Kathryn's greatest fear. She was on the air now all over the country. There wasn't anything she could do about the circumstances of her birth, but if there was a skeleton lurking in the back of her closet, she wanted to know.

In a succession of carefully spaced intervals, Kathryn had initiated a series of casual conversations with her mother. They never started on the subject of her conception, but Kathryn found ways to maneuver them around to the subject, approaching it from different angles. Francine always saw through Kathryn's tactics, but it didn't stop Kathryn from trying again to dig deeper into a story she found difficult to swallow. The most recent attempt was when she treated Francine to a snazzy birthday luncheon at the Town House Hotel's Zebra Room on Wilshire.

She should have known better than to keep pushing her mother — especially in a public place. But something inside her drove her to hurl one last hammer against the thick pane of glass Francine had put up. Francine got defensive,

Kathryn got strident, the Bordeaux got knocked over, the fellow diners got a terrific story to tell their friends, and the waiter got a monumental tip. It would be a while before Kathryn Massey could show her face at the Zebra Room again.

And now, after all that, the person Kathryn liked the least was offering what she longed for most.

The hoards of people around her broke into enthusiastic applause, giving her an excuse to look away. Mickey Rooney stood with Judy Garland on a pair of footstools, which raised them over the heads of everybody in the room. "Ladies and gentlemen, we have a treat!" He grabbed Judy's hand and kissed it. "We're the luckiest bunch of so-and-sos because our own Judy has agreed to sing for us!" The crowd cheered while Roger Edens slid onto the piano seat and played the opening chords of "I'll Be Seeing You."

As Judy started to sing, Kathryn could smell Hoyt's aftershave. It had a metallic scent, rather like a smoking gun, she imagined; it contrasted sharply with the cloying roses. It was remarkably masculine and on anyone else, she might have found it appealing, but not on an FBI agent who thought he was entitled to stand this close to her.

She left the party the way she came, through the front door and right onto the brick-paved patio, leaving Hoyt to follow her. The streetlights dotting the sidewalk were all out. After three years of wartime dim-outs, Kathryn had gotten used to darkened streets, but now they gave her a sinking feeling. "You're a real piece of work," she told him.

"Aren't you curious about who your father is?"

"Of course I am! But I'm not sure I want to hear it from you."

"I didn't say I knew his name, I just asked if you'd like to learn it." His voice had turned softer now. "I'm willing to make inquiries on your behalf." She didn't know what to say. The two of them stood in the half shadows of Mickey's porch, listening to Judy wind her voice around the song.

"I was talking to Mr. Hoover about you, expressing your reluctance."

"I bet he didn't take it very well."

"He asked to see your file."

The FBI has a file on me? Kathryn recomposed her poker face. Happy now, Little Miss Smartypants? See what you get for being ambitious? "Did he find anything of interest?"

"He was very interested in the fact that you've lived with the same woman for eighteen years."

"That's it?" She felt relief drain away. "The fact I have a roommate? That's hardly—"

"There's a word for two women who live together, and it isn't *roommate*." He said that last word with unsettling deliberation.

"Hoover thinks I'm a dyke? Just because I've—oh, for crying out loud!"

She turned away and leaned on a wrought iron pillar for support. It was times like this that she really missed Roy, and that stalwart and dependable way he had about him. When they were together, more than once she'd woken in the middle of the night and watched him breathing his long, slow deep breaths—even the way he breathed was reassuring. If Roy were here now, he'd be punching this clown in the face and tossing him into Mickey Rooney's daisy bushes. But if Roy were here, she realized, she wouldn't even be having this conversation with the FBI.

She spun back to face him. "Tell me, Mr. Hoyt, what do *you* think?"

An evening breeze wafted across them, blowing his smoking-gun aftershave toward her. "It's what Hoover thinks that matters, and more importantly what he can do with information like that."

She opened her handbag and fished out a cigarette; it was a delaying tactic to consider her options. Within the protective walls of the studios — and places like the Garden of Allah — people were generally left free to live as they pleased. But being publicly branded a homosexual was as devastating to one's career as being branded a Communist, a bigamist, or a rapist. As far as the world at large was concerned, homosexuals were degenerates on the level of child molesters, and their acts considered prison-worthy.

They've got me, she thought, lighting up. Right where they want me. Cornered like a goddamned rat.

"Would you like some good news?" Hoyt asked.

She blew cigarette smoke in his face. "Got any?"

"We only want you until the end of the war."

The newspapers were full of conjecture about how long it might take the US Pacific forces to capture an island called Iwo Jima. It was only 750 miles from Tokyo and, once secured, they'd have Japan within the reach of medium-range bombers. Meanwhile in Europe, the Allies were converging on Germany's borders.

He risked a step closer. "We have our eye on a particular person of interest, and we need someone to do a little digging."

"Who?"

"Humphrey Bogart."

"You guys must have your wires crossed. I like to think I know Bogie reasonably well — "

"Why do you think we've approached you?"

The crowd inside erupted into applause for Judy, who responded with "Thank you! Thank you! Thank you!" Then

Roger started playing "They Can't Take That Away From Me."

"We suspect he's a member of the Communist Party."

"Are we back on the Anti-Nazi League? Because let me tell you, it was a frequent topic of conversation around the Garden before the war, and I do not recall anybody mentioning his name."

"He wasn't a member, not as far as we know."

"*Please* tell me you're not referring to that ridiculous dust-up Bogie had with the Dies Committee," Kathryn demanded. "That whole thing was a load of bunk. Humphrey Bogart is as American as Betsy Ross' recipe for apple pie."

"It's not our only evidence."

She stubbed her cigarette out on the brickwork. "What else you got, mister, because so far it seems to me you got bupkis."

"Last February, there was a meeting in the Book of the Day bookstore in Hollywood. We know it was a Communist Party meeting, and it's been alleged that Humphrey Bogart attended."

Kathryn thought about that confrontation in the maid's room at Cole's party. "Alleged by who?"

"All we need you to do is establish his whereabouts on the last day of February."

"A *year* ago? You expect me to find out where Bogie was—"

"You interview people for a living."

"These people are actors. They're in the business of making things up."

"I'm confident you know bullshit when you smell it. This is all we're asking of you, Kathryn."

"It's Miss Massey to you."

"If you can confirm where Bogart was that night, you'll have been of great service to your country . . . Miss Massey."

Speaking of smelling bullshit. "You go to this trouble to recruit me, and yet all you want is this one thing. There must be a lot at stake."

A lone car rounded a curve in the road, momentarily filling Hoyt's face with light, but he'd retreated behind a mask of professional detachment. "I need an answer, Miss Massey."

"To what?"

"Are you willing to work with us?"

She thought about the folder sitting in some FBI filing cabinet with her name neatly printed across the top. It probably sat next to the ones for Ginger, Joan, Bette, and George. *We only want you until the end of the war.* She nodded, curtly, silently, hoping to telegraph her resentment.

"Thank you," Hoyt said, then melted into the darkness beyond the porch light, leaving the racket of the party to fill the space he left behind.

CHAPTER 38

Yesterday's *LA Times* lay on Gwendolyn and Kathryn's dining table with a sobering headline in three-inch capitals:

ROOSEVELT DEAD!

CEREBRAL HEMORRHAGE PROVES FATAL;

PRESIDENT TRUMAN SWORN IN OFFICE

A cello played a slow dirge while a commentator described Roosevelt's hearse threading through Washington, DC.

"Does anybody know that tune?" Bertie asked.

Alla sipped the last of her tea. "'Adagio For Strings' by Samuel Barber.'"

"Apparently the troops are just outside of Berlin now," Bertie said. "Gosh, but it's a crying shame he won't be around to witness those last fifty miles."

"Gwennie," Marcus said, "where's Linc? He's not sitting at home alone, is he?"

The kettle on the stove next to Gwendolyn started whistling. She turned off the gas and poured boiling water into the teapot. "He had to run up to San Francisco for a problem with their satin supplier. He took off on Monday saying he'd only be gone a couple of days, but now it's Friday so I guess it turned into a crisis."

She set the full teapot on the table while they listened to the commentator.

"The crowds are lining Constitution Avenue from here to the White House, where this procession ends. The sound alone can describe the solemnity of this occasion. Let's listen."

As the mournful music filled the villa, Gwendolyn thought about how Linc would hate being stuck in a hotel room with nobody to share this awful moment.

She was so glad he'd decided not to go to Mexico, and liked to think that her refusal to run away had something to do with it. "Stick around," she'd urged him. "Study your father's books more closely. If you can get to the bottom of what's going on, maybe you can find a way to protect his reputation." Thankfully, he listened to reason and there had been no more talk of Mexico.

"Wait," Bertie said, "Linc left for San Francisco on Monday?"

"He took the Southern Pacific first thing."

The scowl on Bertie's face looked out of place. "But he was here on Tuesday."

"Here? At the Garden?"

"He knocked on my door about nine A.M., which means of course he got me out of bed—"

"What did he want?"

"To get into my safe."

"You mean the one in my old room?" Alla asked.

Bertie nodded. "I handed him the key and busied myself in the bathroom to give him some privacy. I couldn't have been in there more'n a minute before I heard him close the safe door."

Gwendolyn didn't like the way Kathryn was staring at her now. She looked at Marcus for reassurance, but his face held a rising panic. "And then?"

"He kissed me. On the cheek, like a big brother." She was still scowling, as though puzzling through something. "He told me not to take guff from anyone. I thought that was strange. Since when do I take guff?"

A flourish of trumpets announced the funeral procession's arrival at Fifteenth Street. "And so it is," the commentator resumed, "our former, late, great president makes his final journey to the White House."

Both Kathryn and Marcus were staring at Gwendolyn. She knew what they were thinking, but didn't want to acknowledge—not even for a moment—that their suspicions had any merit, so she stared at the steam rising from the teapot nobody had touched.

Thirty seconds that felt like three hours crawled past before Kathryn jumped to her feet. "If you're not going to check, then I am."

Gwendolyn listened to Marcus' chair scrape against the linoleum before she stood up.

"Bertie," she said, her voice guttural, "may I borrow your safe key?"

* * *

Bertie's apartment—Nazimova's old master bedroom— consisted of a living room and a bedroom, with a private bathroom. Its three windows looked into the Hollywood Hills, but Bertie kept the blinds drawn, ensuring it remained in semitwilight.

In Nazimova's day the safe was hidden behind a bookshelf, but that was impractical, so Bertie hung a William Morris Hunt print of Niagara Falls over it. She pulled the painting off its hook and handed Gwendolyn the key.

Gwendolyn listened to the tumblers drop into place, then pushed the handle down. *Please let me see Linc's cardboard box.* She opened the safe door and peered inside.

"Dammit! Dammit! DAMMIT!" she exploded. "I only got into this because banks won't lend money to single girls. So I figured, Who needs those small-minded men? In fact, who needs a man at all? I'll do this myself. And who ends up screwing me over? A MAN."

She let out a heavy sigh just as the edge of Bertie's bed grazed against her legs. She let herself drop onto it.

Kathryn pulled a folded-over note from the empty safe, with Gwendolyn's name on the front. "Aren't you going to read it?"

Gwendolyn curled her lip. "I don't care what his reasons are."

"I think you should," Kathryn persisted.

"Then *you* read it," Gwendolyn said. "Let's all hear how well Mr. Lincoln Tattler justifies taking my dream away from me."

Kathryn unfolded the paper and cleared her throat.

"'My dearest, darling Gwendolyn. I guess you've discovered I've flown the coop. This business with Siegel and the O'Roarkes and my father has made me realize I wanted to be anywhere but LA. Please don't think me a coward. If Siegel comes after you' — OH!" Kathryn looked at Gwendolyn, her eyes wide with alarm.

Ritchie's death three months earlier was still a sore spot. The news of the unsolved gangland killing had filled the front pages for a couple of days, then kicked off when Roosevelt was inaugurated for a fourth time. Officially, the murder went unsolved, but everyone standing in Bertie's room knew who was behind it.

"Go on," Gwendolyn insisted.

"'If Siegel comes after you, go to Mrs. O'Roarke. Tell her everything we talked about that night Ritchie's landlord came to see you. She'll help you. In fact, she's probably the only one who can. Try not to hate me, but I'll understand if you do. With all my love, Linc.'"

Gwendolyn took in the gaping faces around her. "You see what's happened, don't you? I spent all that time trying to become Scarlett O'Hara, but it turns out, I'm just Rhett Butler. A war profiteer. This is what I get for breaking the law. They were right—crime doesn't pay."

Bertie sat down beside Gwendolyn and brushed aside her Wild Man of Borneo hair. "Crime, schmime," she mocked. "In the first place, it's not like you've been peddling dope. Nobody's died, okay? And in the second place, it's not like you're Bugsy Siegel. That guy's been pilfering ration coupon books and selling them for obscene profits. *That* is what you call criminal. All you've been doing is what my dad calls 'responding to market demands.' For the first time in history, women have been earning more than they ever thought possible. They have money and need nylons; you have nylons and need money. A simple business transaction."

"You have made nearly four thousand dollars in three and a half years," Alla pointed out. "That makes you one hell of a businesswoman, if you ask me."

"The question is," Kathryn said, "what are you going to do about it?"

Gwendolyn thought for a few moments. To her surprise, she felt a blister of anger swell inside her. She jumped to her feet and plucked the note from Kathryn's hand.

* * *

Gwendolyn rapped on the wrought iron knocker. The timid black maid who opened the door confirmed that Leilah was home but doubted that she was receiving visitors. Gwendolyn shoved past her.

She stood at the bottom of the stairs. "LEILAH? LEILAH!"

"For heaven's sake, child!" Leilah stood in a doorway to the right.

"I need to speak with you." Gwendolyn glanced at the maid. "In private."

Leilah ushered Gwendolyn into the library and closed the pocket doors behind her, then snapped on a Tiffany table lamp with a butterfly pattern, lighting her face with greens and reds. She said nothing until they were seated on a pair of stiff-backed chairs. "Whatever is the matter?"

Gwendolyn thrust Linc's note toward her and ran a fingernail along the studded edges of the leather upholstery while Leilah read it.

"My goodness! No wonder you're steaming mad." She handed back the note. "He always seemed like such a nice boy."

"He is a nice boy." *Why am I defending him?* "Linc said you're the only one who can help me. So here I am."

"Why would Ben Siegel come after you?"

"A few months ago Siegel informed us that he was taking over our black-market business for a fifty percent cut."

"Fifty percent? That's outrageous."

"We were hardly in a position to say no. Then we discovered that the black-market thing was only a lure. Siegel thinks Linc runs a bunch of brothels above the Sunset Strip and—"

Leilah burst out laughing. "He thinks *Linc* runs those brothels?"

"You know about them?" Gwendolyn dug her nail into the tip of her thumb to keep her apprehension at bay.

"Those brothels are west of Crescent Heights, which puts them outside the LA city limits, and therefore beyond the reach of the vice squad." She gave a so-what-can-you-do shrug. "Does he really think Linc runs the most profitable brothels in LA County?"

Gwendolyn wondered how Leilah knew so much about these places.

"You, my dear, need Benjy to back off."

You call LA's most notorious gangster "Benjy"? Gwendolyn thought of Bette Davis' warning: Those O'Roarkes put themselves first every time.

"It's all in the approach," Leilah continued airily. "Something like this is best handled via the side door. In other words, his girl, Virginia. Lucky for you, I got Mayor Fletcher to do her a favor a few months ago, so now it's time to reciprocate."

* * *

The front door of 810 North Linden Drive opened. In place of Virginia Hill's sour face, Gwendolyn saw Mickey Cohen's thuggish puss with the scar below his left eye. He looked her up and down, then smiled at Leilah, who didn't seem the least bit intimidated.

"We're here to see Virginia."

"Went shopping." He opened the door wider. "Come on in."

Leilah stepped back onto the porch. "Some other time."

Cohen's mouth hardened. He stretched a hand toward the living room on his right. "He saw you come up the driveway."

Leilah hesitated. It was only for a moment, but long enough for Gwendolyn to sense a crust of uneasiness. *Oh no, if Leilah is losing her nerve . . .*

Cohen ushered them into the living room, where Ben Siegel was seated on the sofa. He was in shirtsleeves — no jacket, no tie. On a round table in a bay window was a wooden Emerson radio tuned to the same station they'd been listening to at the Garden. The commentator was saying something about the laying to rest of a mighty soul. Siegel let the women stand like forgotten toys until the broadcast ended.

"Take a seat, ladies," he said, looking at them for the first time. "Leilah, good to see you. And the charming Miss Brick. Always a pleasure."

"Benjy," Leilah said firmly, "Gwendolyn came to me this afternoon to seek my advice on an unexpected development. I told her, let's go straight to the top and sort it out like civilized adults."

Gwendolyn doubted she knew anyone who could match Leilah's bravado. She could see why Bette Davis warned her against the O'Roarkes, but it was different when you needed her in your corner. Siegel, however, was not as impressed. He regarded her for a moment, then turned to Gwendolyn.

"Where is he?"

For a split second, Gwendolyn thought he meant Ritchie. The image of Siegel raising his gun flashed in her mind, then disappeared when she realized who he was asking about. "You mean Linc?"

"Of course I mean Linc." His eyes were sapphire hard.

Gwendolyn squeezed her fingers around her pocketbook. "If I knew where Linc was, don't you think I'd be there with him?"

"Would you?"

She went to snap back, *Of course I would,* but realized how hollow she'd sound. Her heart was still catching up with what her head knew. *You slimy rat bastard,* she told Linc. *You stole my future and left me to deal with the biggest mobster this side of Lucky Luciano.*

"Where is he, Gwendolyn?" Siegel's voice had lost its measured civility.

"Benjy," Leilah broke in, "I'm sure if Gwendolyn knew — "

"I wasn't talking to you."

Leilah let out a huff. "Need I remind you of the less than inconsequential favor I convinced the mayor to do for Virginia?"

"And need I remind you that favor was payback for something I did for the mayor? We both know what that was, and we both know we need not speak about it here and now."

Leilah went pale beneath her makeup.

Movement off to one side caught Gwendolyn's eye. Mickey Cohen had a dark gray revolver in his left hand. In his right was a blue handkerchief. He was using it to slide his hand up and down the barrel, polishing it with a slow and deliberate rhythm.

"Honey," Leilah said slowly, "you need to share everything you know with Mr. Siegel."

Gwendolyn attempted a smile while she scrambled together a story that might hold water. "I only found out about Linc this morning, so the best I can do is guess."

"Now we're getting somewhere."

"Linc got his supply from South America. Mostly Argentina, but Brazil and Uruguay as well. Linc is no dummy, so I think Argentina is too obvious. My guess is Uruguay. He talked about it once. Said there was a lake. Lake Rincón something-or-other."

"Lago Rincón del Bonete?"

Shocked that Siegel could name any lake in South America, let alone one in Uruguay, Gwendolyn fought to keep the astonishment out of her eyes. "He said it was the perfect place to run away to." In truth, Linc had told her that the two most miserable weeks of his life were the ones he spent recovering from dengue fever in a bug-infested hotel on the shores of Lago Rincón del Bonete. "If I were looking for Linc, that's where I would start."

Siegel arched an eyebrow. "I take it you're not looking for him?"

"He left me high and dry, and took—" She was going to say that he took all her money, her hopes, and her dreams, but decided Bugsy Siegel didn't need to know that. "He took my heart with him."

"So screw him, right, honey?" Leilah patted Gwendolyn's hand.

While Cohen continued to polish the shaft of his gun— up, down, up, down—Siegel stared at Gwendolyn, unblinking and unreadable. "Here's what's going to happen. Lincoln Tattler has information I need, so he must be found. You're the person most likely to accomplish that for me. Locate your boyfriend, and our arrangement comes to an end."

"But our boys are less than fifty miles outside Berlin, and they've taken Iwo Jima," Gwendolyn pointed out. "Once the war ends, so does the black market. What if I can't find him before then?"

"Our arrangement only comes to an end when you deliver Tattler to me."

"And if I can't?" Gwendolyn asked.

"There is no can't."

CHAPTER 39

Marcus stopped typing. He had to. Every tendon in his fingers throbbed. He let his hands drop to his side and started counting to sixty.

Sixty seconds was all he could afford. The rewrite had to be on Taggert's desk by Friday lunchtime. It was now eleven thirty Wednesday morning. With enough black coffee, Camels, and Benzedrine, he could make it.

He heard the clack of a single typewriter belonging to one of the new guys several offices away. These days, half the desks in MGM's writing department were filled with fresh-faced twenty-year-olds who'd maneuvered their way out of the draft or jaded fifty-year-olds too ripe for service. The one with the clacking typewriter belonged to the former group: talented and he knew it, ambitious but didn't care who knew it.

Marcus interlaced his fingers and stretched his hands over the Remington until he heard the joints in his wrists crack. His eyes fell on the words across the top of the page inserted in his typewriter:

FREE LENINGRAD! – REWRITE – MAY 2, 1945 – MARCUS ADLER

It was difficult for Marcus to stop and think about his life and not feel some measure of guilt at how smoothly it flowed nowadays, and the irony that at a time when war roiled across the globe, his own little world was like a still pond in spring.

Oliver had moved in without officially moving in, and the four of them now dined out on Marcus' expense account. He was still glowing from reconnecting with sweet Doris, and he'd come up trumps with his *Free Leningrad!* idea.

Mayer loved it so much that he made an unspoken promise that the studio would fully support an Oscar nomination. In an unprecedentedly short space of time, the movie was cast, old sets were transformed into Russian streets and homes, and filming progressed without incident. A quality movie soon emerged from the editing room.

But then the sneak preview in San Diego happened. That day, the radio was filled with the news that Mussolini and his mistress had been executed near Lake Como, and the German forces in Italy were laying down their guns. As *Free Leningrad!* unfolded on the screen, it became obvious that if the movie had been released when the real siege was ending, it would have been a hit. But now it felt like last month's news. *Free Leningrad!* was a disaster.

The Marcus of three years ago would have crumpled under the disappointment, but he sent word through Taggert that the movie was fixable. The order came back in less than an hour: the release date for *Free Leningrad!* was set in stone, so the rewrite had to be on Mayer's desk by the end of the week. "Not a problem," he told Taggert. "I've got it all worked out." He would shoehorn into the story a fictional American GI who — implausibly but bravely — helps break the siege. Ta-da! Movie fixed, boss happy, Oscar nomination guaranteed.

Marcus' fingers had started to send Lieutenant Charlie Walters crawling along a secret tunnel underneath the blockaded walls of Leningrad to meet his love interest, Veronika, when a roaring cheer filled the department.

"GODDAMN COWARD SON OF A BITCH!"

Marcus emerged into the corridor to see Taggert rushing toward him.

"It just came over the wire," he said. "Hitler has shot himself." Taggert gripped Marcus by the shoulders, tears welling up. "The Ruskies have got Berlin surrounded."

Marcus felt all his strength drain out the soles of his feet. "So it's all over?"

"Not officially, but close." A deafening cheer boomed down the corridor from the conference room. "I've only got half a bottle of gin in my office." He pulled a ten-dollar bill out of his wallet. "Scoot down to the commissary and pick up as much booze as this'll buy."

Marcus glanced back at his typewriter.

"Screw Leningrad!" Taggert barked. "We're getting roaring drunk, and that's an order."

Outside the building, Marcus spotted knots of people gathered around open windows and doorways—anywhere that put them within earshot of a radio. As he dashed past soundstage 18, he heard a chorus of voices singing, "Ding, dong! Hitler's dead! Mean old bastard, let's get plastered! Ding, dong! The German prick is dead!"

The commissary was already more than half full; the din of a hundred excited voices engulfed him.

"Let me guess," the woman behind the beverage counter said. Her mascara had left two thick trails down her cheeks. "You want booze."

Marcus waved Taggert's money at her. "How much will ten bucks buy me?"

"I got Pabst Blue Ribbon and some whiskey. It ain't top drawer, but it's palatable—especially after the third go-around."

Marcus watched her disappear behind a swinging door and realized he'd much rather be with Oliver and Kathryn,

Gwendolyn and Alla at a moment like this. But they were scattered all over the city and wouldn't be home for hours. He smiled at the thought of the humdinger of a celebration at the Garden tonight.

"Marcus, my boy!"

Those three words were all Marcus needed to recognize the voice of George Cukor. The two men embraced.

"It's a great day!" George declared. He watched the woman set six bottles of Pabst and two of whiskey on the chrome counter, then shifted his gaze to Marcus. "I hope that's for later."

"About ten minutes later, I'd say." Marcus went to pick up the bottles until he felt the weight of George's hand on his arm. "Something wrong?"

"I had a meeting this morning," George said, speaking more carefully than usual. "With L.B. and Mannix. It was about *Free Leningrad!*"

"Oh?"

"Clarence Brown is already knee-deep in *The Yearling* and I'm between projects, so they want me to direct the new sequences. The deal was no screen credit, but double pay. Plus, it's your picture, so I wanted to help out."

With his revised script and George at the helm, Marcus was sure *Free Leningrad!* could be saved. "That's great!" he exclaimed, but George didn't seem thrilled. "Isn't it?"

"Yes, but haven't you got a deadline? Mayer and Mannix stressed that never has an MGM project had less time to waste. They promised me they'd deliver the script in forty-eight hours." He cast around the tumultuous commissary. "Marcus, I don't mean to be a killjoy, but do you really have the time to sit around drinking?"

Slack-jawed, Marcus gaped at his friend. "Hitler is DEAD. I think that deserves *some* celebration."

"And I think you need to look further than the next two days. We have a lot to reshoot for a picture whose release date cannot be moved. A lot hinges on this movie, and your new version needs to be done. By Friday. This whole project—to say nothing of the future of your career—hinges on this deadline. Hitler will still be dead on Saturday; go celebrate then. But meanwhile, you've got a Russian city to liberate."

* * *

Living at the Garden of Allah for eighteen years should have taught Marcus that the biggest *Ding Dong Hitler Is Dead* party in town would be around the swimming pool forty feet from his place. But his head was too filled with Lieutenant Charlie Walters and Leningrad to think about that on the streetcar ride home. It wasn't until he stepped out of the Garden's main building and onto the path to the pool that he realized he should have gone someplace else.

The huge gathering around the pool was already three drinks ahead of him. Kay Thompson's husband, Bill, was playing bartender at a patio table littered with a haphazard collection of booze—though he seemed as half-smashed as everyone else.

Alla's face lit up. "There you are, my darling!" It was encouraging to see her smile. She'd done three movies in the previous year and was excited that her acting career was back on the upswing. But no more offers materialized, and her soulful face seemed more lined, weighed down by the advances of age. "This glorious day has arrived!" She hooked her arm through his. "A drink to celebrate, yes?"

"Later." He patted her arm. It felt thin and fragile through her cotton blouse. *Hitler will still be dead on Saturday.* "I'm battling an impossible deadline. *Free Leningrad!* is—"

"Bill!" Alla called. "Some punch for my boy!"

Marcus accepted the cup she thrust into his hand. She clinked her glass against his and winked one of her violet eyes. "Here's to happy days!"

"MADAME!" Kay Thompson's strident voice shot through the crowd. "That's a marvelous suggestion!" She elbowed her way to the side of the pool. As she clambered onto the diving board, the sun slipped out from behind a cloud like a spotlight and picked up the gold thread in her shot-silk pantsuit. She held up her arms. "Two, three, four, and . . . Happy days are here again, the skies above are clear again . . ."

Sober or drunk, Gardenites were really just a bunch of hams at heart, and never needed much prompting. By the end of the second line, every last one of them had joined in.

Marcus offered Alla a vague I'll-be-back gesture. Halfway to his villa, he was captured by Dorothy Gish happily sandwiched between Artie Shaw and her current live-in lover, Louis Calhern. Marcus never understood how Louis could be so happy with Gish when his ex-wife, Natalie Schafer, lived right next door. But that was the Garden of Allah—no rules, no expectations, no problems. Marcus lingered for a verse, then broke away. He made it through his front door without being ambushed a third time.

He figured if he could bang away until the halfway point where Veronika reveals to Charlie the hoard of Nazi grenades hidden beneath her father's bakery, then maybe he could finish for the day and rejoin the celebrations. Once they were over, he could Benzedrine his way through the rest of the night.

It didn't take him long, though, to realize that his plan to hide away and concentrate on the Siege of Leningrad was delusional. The singing and laughter, plus the chatter and shrieks of new arrivals, bled through the walls, windows, and doors.

He thought about Bertie's room in the main house, where the walls were thick enough to buffer the loudest noise. Bertie was probably several drinks in by now and unlikely to need her room for the next few hours, but getting access meant going back out there, typewriter in hand, and risking recapture.

A squeaking floorboard drew his attention.

"Sweetheart!" Marcus stepped forward to embrace his lover. "Your office as nutso as mine? Everybody's crazy drunk and singing and carrying on—just like here. Hard to believe, huh? We can't be more than a couple of days away from the end of the war!"

But Oliver didn't return Marcus' embrace. He stood rigid as a toy soldier, his arms by his sides.

"What's wrong?" Marcus asked.

"I'm here to pick up my things." Oliver's voice was low and restrained.

Marcus went to grab his hand, but Oliver pulled it away. "What's going on?"

Oliver headed for the closet. He yanked the door open, but stopped. When he turned around, his eyes were filled with hostility. "*The Thin Man Goes Home*, and *Meet Me In St. Louis*."

Oh, crap. Oh, no. Oh, jeez. Marcus feigned a blank look.

"Don't even bother." Oliver yanked a fistful of shirts off the rack and threw them onto the bed. "On second thought," he spun back, "I want to hear you deny that you developed our relationship so you had an insider at the Breen Office."

Outside, Bertie's hoarse laugh burst through the window, chased by a shockingly loud champagne-bottle pop. The distraction gave Marcus a moment to sort through his options. *Do I finagle my way out of this, or just come clean and hope to hell he understands?*

"You're the one who suggested we talk over drinks," he said.

"Stop skirting the issue!"

"What *is* the issue?"

Oliver stepped forward, and poked a finger into the air over Marcus' chest. "I got hauled over the coals by the entire executive committee this morning. They had the scripts for *The Thin Man Goes Home,* and *Meet Me In St. Louis,* and they demanded to know why I approved them."

"Why did you?"

"I DID IT FOR YOU!" he exploded. "I figured if I rushed them through, you'd score big points with the boss. Once scripts are approved, nobody goes back and takes a second look. There are too many coming down the pipeline. I figured I'd just push 'em through and that'd be that."

Marcus sat on the bed and looked up at Oliver. "But somebody did go back?"

"I kept hoping it was a coincidence, but then Breen made me swear—on a Bible, no less—that I wasn't doing someone at MGM a favor. It was the way they said it. *Someone. A favor.*"

Marcus gripped the chenille bedspread. The soft material folded between his fingers. "Mayer and Mannix dragged me into a meeting and asked if I had deliberately cultivated the friendship of someone inside the Breen Office."

"Why didn't you tell me this?"

"Because I didn't want you to think exactly what you're now thinking. They'd just handed me *Free Leningrad!* then made me feel like I owed them. I didn't know what to do."

"So you just leave the two scripts sitting around and figure if I pick them up myself . . . " Oliver let the rest of the sentence mingle with the voices outside singing "We'll Meet Again."

"Something like that," Marcus admitted. "I am so, so sorry. I was stuck; I didn't know what to do. I know I handled it badly—"

"Badly? Marcus, you handled it *atrociously*."

Oliver turned back to the open closet and pulled out more clothes. Marcus got to his feet and clutched at Oliver's arm, but Oliver pulled away; the heat behind all that hazel-flecked green was gone.

"I feel like everything's in limbo," he said. "Hitler's dead. Berlin's surrounded. Maybe the Krauts'll hold off the Ruskies, maybe Goering will take Hitler's place. Whatever happens, there's still Japan. It's like the whole world is holding its breath."

"The whole world *is* holding its breath."

"It's how I feel about you and me. If you'd come to me that day and told me what you were faced with, I wouldn't have been happy, but at least I'd have known what was going on."

Shame burned Marcus' chest. "But I didn't do that."

"No, Marcus, you didn't. And now I don't know how I feel." Oliver reached under the bed and pulled out his suitcase. "Until I do, I need to get away."

It felt like only last week that he'd arrived with his luggage in hand and they'd laughed while they made room for him. Marcus withdrew to the living room. He stared at the typewriter on his dining table and realized that getting any more work done today was beyond even the help of Benzedrine. He became so mired in his thoughts that Oliver had to clear his throat before Marcus noticed him standing at the front door, case in hand.

"Will you call me?" Marcus asked.

Oliver didn't nod, nor did he shake his head. He simply lowered his eyes and disappeared through the door.

Marcus crossed over to the kitchen window to watch Oliver skirt around the pool as discreetly as he could and hurry up the path. As he rounded an azalea bush, the radio started playing the Duke Ellington tune, "Do Nothing Till You Hear From Me."

Marcus wrapped his fingers around the window latch. "Screw you!" he told Ellington, and slammed the window shut.

CHAPTER 40

Sitting alone at the center table of La Rue on the Sunset Strip, Kathryn picked up the red and gray Hollywood Canteen matchbook and started tapping it against the black lacquered tabletop, trying to ignore her nerves. *This isn't my pitch. I'm not here to impress Howard Hughes. That's all up to Wilkerson. I'm just here to be a cheerleader. Billy! Billy! Rah, rah, rah!*

Both Wilkerson and Hughes were late, so she looked around the restaurant in case a story appeared. She spotted Ida Lupino with her husband, Louis Hayward. *How interesting! I thought they were on the verge of announcing their divorce.* Randolph Scott and Cary Grant were lunching with their wives, Patricia Stillman and Barbara Hutton. Kathryn made some notes on the back of next month's Canteen volunteer schedule.

When Ciro's burned down, Kathryn assumed it portended the last of Wilkerson's foray into upscale dining. He'd opened the Trocadero, Vendome Café, and Ciro's, and they'd all done very well until he lost interest and moved on to something new. But Kathryn had underestimated her boss. His latest "something new" was a classy lunch spot he'd called La Rue, and in typical Wilkersonian style, he'd gone all out.

La Rue sported gold leather booths and two enormous crystal chandeliers so elaborate that Wilkerson claimed he'd hired specialists to come down from San Francisco to keep them clean. Kathryn had never seen these cleaners, so she wasn't convinced they actually existed, but it made for great copy. And it seemed to do the trick — the Master of Hype's latest eatery had become popular with celebrities by the end of the month.

Hughes came dashing into the restaurant like he was three hours late. He slid into Kathryn's booth and ordered a large tomato juice, room temperature, no ice.

The man was still gangly thin, but his face had filled out since the USO tour.

"Nice to see you again." He scanned the room, for kewpie cuties, Kathryn guessed, and then settled in to focus on her. He smiled when he noticed the bracelet on her wrist.

She'd managed to talk Melody Hope into being realistic about the Hughes situation by admitting that she'd had an abortion herself. It took Kathryn several days to track down Dr. Harrison, the doctor she'd seen, but by the end of the week everything had been taken care of. The MGM brass never found out, and everybody accepted Kathryn's tonsillectomy story at face value. Several weeks later, a spectacular bouquet of yellow Oriental lilies arrived at the Garden of Allah with a silver charm bracelet whose nine tiny letter-shaped charms spelled out "HOLLYWOOD." Attached to the bracelet was a note: *To Kathryn, a friend indeed, H.H.*

"I'm glad you like it," he said. "Choosing jewelry for women is a tricky business."

Kathryn lifted her wrist and jiggled it so the silver letters caught the chandelier light. "I get compliments whenever I wear it."

"It barely begins to express how grateful I am, especially seeing as how I got nowhere with Gwendolyn's brother. I tried all my contacts in the armed services, but they stonewalled me. The guy must be in the thick of things; I've never seen the brass so button-lipped."

"Thanks for trying, anyway."

A wave of anticipation rolled through the crowd, and all eyes darted to the front door where Bogie and Bacall were strolling in with a humility bordering on shyness. Kathryn was glad to see them dispense with the over-wide smiles, the showy waves, and the too-loud laughter.

A couple of months ago, Bogie's wife announced that their marriage was over, but everybody at the Garden already knew; Bogie had moved into villa number eight. He had confessed to Kathryn the date of his impending marriage to Betty Bacall, and told her that if she kept it to herself, she could have the exclusive. It was a big scoop that garnered a lot of attention, but it also meant that Bogie trusted her again, which struck Kathryn as sadly ironic, considering what the FBI was asking of her. She wondered if it was too late to weasel out of her agreement.

Kathryn hoped for a moment with Bogie, but he was intent on avoiding all eye contact, so she gave up and turned back to Hughes. He wore a bemused smile in his dark eyes.

"What?" she asked him.

"I assume this is some sort of pitch meeting." He took Kathryn's silence as a yes. "Now that this place is up and running, your boss has something new in mind?"

It was time to go for broke. "He's got this screwy idea that he wants to build a casino."

"That's not so screwy." Hughes motioned to a waiter for a refill. "If you run them right *and* keep out of the clutches of the mob, they can be a bonanza."

"That must be why he's been talking about the desert."

"Which desert?"

"Out past the Mojave, into Nevada. But you've seen the way he plays poker. Putting a guy like Billy Wilkerson in charge of a casino is like making W.C. Fields foreman of the Johnnie Walker factory."

"So you want me to knock him back?"

Kathryn leaned forward. "You're here because he's four hundred grand short on capital. Last week he went down to Agua Caliente to win it—and ended up losing two hundred grand." For years now, Kathryn had kept the betting cage supervisor of the Agua Caliente racing track on retainer. He cost her a pricey $50 per month and had provided her with all sorts of tips, but never had he come in as handy as he had last week. "I'm just saying that if you're going to put money into this absurd venture of his, do it with your eyes open."

Wilkerson chose that moment to make his entrance, all smiles and nods. He stopped by several tables—Bogie and Bacall's included—before approaching the booth with his hands outstretched, ready to "greet and grip," to use his own words.

When Hughes ordered butterflied steak and green beet salad, Wilkerson unhesitatingly followed suit, so Kathryn told the waiter to make it three. Wilkerson didn't even bother with niceties, and jumped into his spiel. That morning, Wilkerson had coached her on her role for tonight. Lots of smiling, lots of "Oh my goodness, yes!" and precious little else.

Wilkerson made no secret of what he wanted: $600,000 to meet his budget in return for a substantial stake in his Flamingo Club. As Wilkerson laid out his plan, Hughes posed no questions and made no interruptions. The steaks arrived just as Wilkerson was winding up.

"That's the deal, plain and simple," Wilkerson concluded. "Now let's enjoy these steaks and talk of better things, like the end of the war. They've gotta capture Goering soon. The Huns can't hold out much longer, don't you think? Then this whole blasted mess will be over and we can all get back to business as usual."

Another wave of excitement swept through the crowd as Judy Garland and Vincente Minnelli walked in. The couple had just announced their plans to marry. The talented star falling in love with the sensitive director was a classic Hollywood fairytale, and the press had run with it from coast to coast.

"Excuse me," Wilkerson said, getting to his feet, "but I have some glad-handing to do."

As soon as he was out of earshot, Kathryn asked Hughes, "What do you think?"

"Gambling's legal in Nevada," Hughes said. "It's got that going for it."

Kathryn thought about Gwendolyn's dilemma with Linc and his suspicions about his father cooking the books and transferring money to and from Clem O'Roarke. On a whim, she asked, "Ever heard of an outfit called Primm Valley Realty?"

Kathryn loved it when she surprised big-time businessmen. "As a matter of fact, I have."

"Clem O'Roarke, right?"

"Uh-huh." Hughes' tone had turned cautious.

"What can you tell me about it?"

"What do you need to know?"

"Ever dealt with them?"

"Not directly."

"They on the up-and-up, you think?"

Hughes selected a toothpick, but didn't start using it right away. "Depends on what you mean by 'up-and-up.' We're talking Clem O'Roarke here, so . . . " His eyes drifted to

Wilkerson's attention-grabbing conversation with Judy and Minnelli, but Kathryn could see his mind lingered elsewhere. "What's your interest in Primm Valley Realty?"

"Long story," Kathryn said. "A friend of mine is involved with someone who does business with them. It all smells like last month's garbage to me, but I want more information."

"I can make inquiries." Hughes turned his dark eyes back to her. "Tell me what your connection is with Nelson Hoyt?"

His question took Kathryn by such surprise that she missed her mouth with her fork by an embarrassing margin. "What makes you think—?"

"Apart from the way you stabbed yourself in the face just now? First of all, the FBI has recruited Louella and Hedda, and I assume they've approached you as well. Secondly, Hoyt's at the table nearest the kitchen door. And number three: his eyeballs keep bouncing back and forth between you and Bogie."

"How do *you* know Nelson Hoyt?" Kathryn asked.

Hughes finished picking his teeth, snapped the toothpick in two, and dropped it into the glass ashtray. "He and I tangled over a thorny issue back when I was remaking *Hell's Angels* for sound. Prohibition and all that jazz. He got the better of me—a rare occurrence, I can assure you." He watched Bogie and Bacall giggle over some sort of private joke. "I like Bogie. I like the kind of man he is." He pulled his gaze away from them and looked at her expectantly.

"They think Bogie's a Commie," Kathryn admitted.

"Because of that idiot who testified in front of the Dies Committee?"

Kathryn nodded. "He'd be a real big catch for them. They want me to bring them verification and I want to prove them wrong."

"How are you going to do that?"

Kathryn shrugged. "Beats the hell out of me. I'm supposed to find out where Bogie was on the night a Communist Party meeting took place at the Book of the Day."

"Your boss know about any of this?"

"Are you nuts?" Kathryn scoffed. "Have you read his editorials lately?"

Billy Wilkerson had appointed himself a mouthpiece for the fervor of anti-Communist sentiment that was gathering momentum in Hollywood. Over the past months, he'd used his "TradeView" column to expound his theory that the Screen Writers Guild was on its way to becoming a principal Communist stronghold, and had taken it upon himself to expose what he saw as a plot. Using increasingly hysterical language that suggested the Guild was only the first step in a Communist takeover of Hollywood, he'd transformed himself into a topic of water cooler conversation in studios across the city. Secretly, Kathryn suspected he was only doing it to increase circulation. She was for anything that improved her job security, but it worried her that he'd started to believe his own bluster.

"Keep him in the dark," Hughes said, "otherwise he'll get drunk one day and blab everything. I'm going to say yes to him, by the way."

Kathryn felt her heart drop. "To his casino deal?"

"He's made a success of every establishment he's opened. Take a look around you. Now throw in the declaration of peace, the lifting of rations, and the post-war boom every economist worth his weight in rolled pennies is predicting. It's all up from here." She started to say something, but he cut her off. "This Primm Valley Realty has me intrigued. What kind of garbage are we talking here?"

"Possible money laundering."

"I'll look into it for you and let you know if I find anything. And this Book of the Day meeting? When was that?"

"Last day of February."

"Ah, the twenty-ninth."

Kathryn felt like she'd been kicked in the stomach. *How did I not make that connection before now?* "Leap Year Day! Maybe my job just got a whole lot easier."

"It certainly did," Hughes told her. "That was the first day of shooting on *To Have And Have Not.* All you need do is look at those two lovebirds to know that Bogie's going to recall what he did the first day of shooting on that picture."

"But how do *you* know when shooting on that movie started?"

Hughes permitted a glint of sheepishness to flicker across his face like a moth before he caught it and brushed it away. "I'd heard about this Betty Bacall girl from Hoagy."

"Hoagy Carmichael?" The unexpected friendships in this town never ceased to amaze her.

Hughes nodded. "He's in the movie. Anyway, he was blathering on and on about this spectacular new skirt Bogart was going all baboon-crazy over, so I decided to go see for myself. You can't use me as proof, but you can take this to the bank—on Leap Day last year, Humphrey Bogart wasn't in any damned bookstore."

CHAPTER 41

It was four in the afternoon when Gwendolyn walked into the Zephyr Room. You may not be the world's greatest actress, she told herself, but you can pull this off. Even with a sharp tack like Ben Siegel.

The bar was decked out in white paint and chrome mirrors, curved surfaces and ornamental plaster flourishes. Not too fussy, just enough to please the eye. To her left stood a semicircular bar with padded stools spaced around it, half of them filled. None of those would do for today, she decided.

The last booth tucked away in the corner was free, but might be tricky if she needed a quick getaway. The booth next to it fell in less shadow but it'd do. She slid across the dark green upholstery and popped open her bag. She didn't need to double-check if the map and the sailing schedule were in there, but her nerves forced her to. By the time she looked up, she found Siegel striding toward her. He wore the jacket with the large black-and-white checks he'd had on the day he coerced her and Linc inside Virginia's house.

A waiter appeared at the table. Siegel ordered a scotch and soda; Gwendolyn asked for iced tea.

He lit up a cigarette and opened his gold case to her. Gwendolyn was dying for a smoke, but accepting one felt like giving in. She thought of Ritchie and how she was sitting next to the guy who ordered his execution, or perhaps even pulled the trigger. *I've heard him call you his "one that got away."* She swallowed hard and shook her head.

"So," he said, "what have you got for me?"

She prayed her hands wouldn't shake as she pulled out her "evidence" — a schedule of ocean liners between Miami and Buenos Aires and a timetable for trains to Uruguay's capital city, Montevideo. She'd underlined the name *Allemannia* and scribbled in a date, cabin number, and the fare. She pointed to the date and steeled herself. "That's the day after the last time I saw Linc."

Siegel nodded slowly. "What else?"

She'd purchased a map of Uruguay and spent twenty minutes folding and unfolding it, along the creases, bending it every which way, sprinkling coffee on it and throwing it on the floor. She opened it to Lago Rincón del Bonete and tapped her fingernail on a small town called San Gregorio, where she'd gotten Marcus to write *Hotel Los Medanos*. "I'd bet my last dime that you'll find Linc in that hotel."

Siegel finished his drink with his eyes glued to the map. "I knew you could do it if you put your mind to it."

Gwendolyn wondered — again — why she was risking her neck for someone who'd stolen so much from her. But she refused to believe Linc was just a cheap thief. Whatever his reasons, she suspected they had to do with Tattler's Tuxedos and Primm Valley Realty. Especially in light of what Howard Hughes had told Kathryn after he'd gone digging.

"So there you have it." She snapped her purse shut. "And he can rot in hell's sewer as far as I'm concerned."

Siegel eyed Gwendolyn's untouched iced tea. "I hear it takes three weeks to get a passport, faster if you pay more."

Look him in the eye, she told herself. Wolves can smell fear. "Going somewhere?"

He shifted his eyes to the map laid out in front of him. "One of us is taking a trip, and it ain't me."

Gwendolyn felt the alarm spread up from her chest. "You said, 'Locate Linc, and our arrangement comes to an end.' That was the deal."

"The deal's changed. I need him here, and you're going to bring him back to me because you're the only one he'll listen to."

It was in that moment Gwendolyn realized that she never did get away from Bugsy Siegel that night at the Hollywoodland sign, six months before Pearl Harbor. He'd just let her go for another day. *These guys play for keeps.*

"A gentleman doesn't change a deal," she told him.

Before Siegel could reply, the bartender yelled out "JESUS!" He leapt onto the circular bar and cupped his hands to his mouth. "THE HUNS JUST SURRENDERED. IT'S OVER, EVERYBODY! THE WAR IN EUROPE IS OVER!"

A primitive roar filled the place as though someone had thrown a switch. The two well-dressed ladies in the booth next to Gwendolyn hooted like owls and a trio of navy officers at the bar threw their caps into the air and started hugging each other. Everybody jumped to their feet laughing and hollering, whooping and embracing every stranger they could seize.

Gwendolyn snatched her handbag and went to slide out of the booth, but Siegel stopped her. "Where do you think you're going?"

"They just declared peace," she yelled over the din. "You think I'm going to just sit here with you and—"

"We haven't finished our business."

Gwendolyn pulled her arm free and threw herself into the revelry, declining every hug and kiss as she wormed her way to the door. She kept expecting Siegel to wrench her back, but she reached, unmolested, the white swinging doors that led out to Wilshire Boulevard.

The uproar inside the Zephyr Room was magnified a hundred times outside. The traffic on Wilshire had ground to a halt. People switched off their cars and jumped onto the road, leaping and dancing with whoever happened to pull alongside them. Horns blared over and over while somewhere someone was playing "Chattanooga Choo Choo" on a trumpet. Along the sidewalk, a conga line started heading toward Gwendolyn, twenty or more people gripped hip to hip, chanting: "War is over, yeah, yeah! War is over, yeah, yeah!" Halfway down the line, a tall guy in a ridiculously outsized sombrero invited her to join in. Gwendolyn glanced behind her in time to see Siegel emerge from the bar.

She ducked across the side street and into the Brown Derby. It was bedlam in there, too. This time, however, she accepted every embrace that came her way and let the tears spill down her cheeks. The conga chant got taken up inside the Derby, too. Gwendolyn knew the war wouldn't be over for her until Monty was back on American soil, but meanwhile, Europe was finally at peace! She could scarcely believe it.

Back at the Derby's front door, she looked out across the mayhem choking Wilshire. Still no Siegel. She ventured outside and picked her way through the maze of stopped cars. If she could make it across the street to the Ambassador Hotel and into the Cocoanut Grove where she knew Chuck would be setting up the bar, she'd be safe.

She reached the southern side of Wilshire and was barely five steps from the Ambassador's gates when she felt herself being whipped around. "Don't ever do that to me again!" The chords in Siegel's neck stood out; his face was brick red.

She stared at him. These guys play for keeps.

"I've pussy-footed around you too damned long," he told her. "Enough is enough."

I've heard him call you his "one that got away."

"We're going back to my place—" Siegel tightened his hold, "—and celebrate."

Gwendolyn broke away from his hypnotic scrutiny. She could picture Ritchie's words on the page—*He's always wanted to get you into the sack*—and knew she had to play her sole ace.

"All this nickel and dime hooey, why are you bothering?" He gaped at her. Nobody spoke to Benjamin Siegel like this. "What if I were to tell you about something going on right under your nose that will make all this black-market nylons and perfume look like kids' stuff?"

His eyes ran down her and up again, cool but intrigued. "Like what?"

She waited until the conga line, now more than fifty people long, chugged past.

He released her arm but his twitching fingers showed that he was ready to grab her again.

"Ever heard of a place called Las Vegas?" He shook his head cautiously. "It's in Nevada. Billy Wilkerson plans on building a casino there. And you know what moneymakers those joints can be, especially in a state where gambling is legal."

A trio of car horns burst to life, accompanied by a roaring cheer. Gwendolyn let them die down. "But Wilkerson's a reckless gambler, so nobody trusts him with this idea. Except for one person: Clem O'Roarke." The light of recognition ignited Siegel's face. Gwendolyn silently blessed Howard Hughes for the information Bugsy Siegel was about to receive. "He's got this company called Primm Valley Realty, and he's using it to buy up cheap land in and around this Las Vegas place. Wilkerson's willing to pay a bundle for the right plot, and O'Roarke's company now owns nearly all the land from there to the state border."

Gwendolyn prayed Kathryn would understand. After all, when Kathryn told her and Marcus what Hughes had reported, she did say, "We need to get him out of the casino business!"

"Wilkerson's not the right person to build a casino," Siegel said.

"But *you* are," Gwendolyn prodded. "You, with all your experience. Imagine the fortune you could make if you took over."

She took a long, slow step back and turned to face Wilshire again. The conga line had looped back onto the northern side of the boulevard, a hundred people long. Even from this distance and over the clamor of the horns, she could hear their chant. "War is over, yeah, yeah! War is over, yeah, yeah!"

"Look at that thing," she shouted over the ruckus. "It just grows and grows." She paused for a moment, then gauged his mood from the corner of her eye. He seemed somber and preoccupied, barely aware now of the commotion around him. "See you around," she told him.

He nodded with a slight jut of his chin, and she blended into the pandemonium.

CHAPTER 42

When Nelson Hoyt's note arrived, Kathryn was arguing with Artie Shaw over which song would play best when Bogie and Bacall arrived. The Garden of Allah was throwing a party for them before they headed east for their wedding, and Artie wanted "Speak Low" on account of Bacall's deep voice, but Kathryn preferred "How Little We Know," which Hoagy Carmichael had written for Bacall to sing in *To Have And Have Not*.

She didn't recognize the handwriting on the front of the envelope: *Miss Kathryn Massey, c/o the Garden of Allah Hotel, Sunset Boulevard.* She told Artie to pick whichever song he thought best and retreated to her place.

Both the envelope and the note inside were made of expensive paper: thick and yet slightly translucent.

It read: Your father's name was Thomas Danford. See? I'm not all bad. And I do keep my word. Now it's time you kept yours.

She stared at the perfectly formed letters in dark brown ink. *Thomas Danford.*

"I thought you were helping to set up." Gwendolyn stood in the doorway leading from the bedroom. "I'm glad you're here, though. This dress is a beast to zip — what's wrong?"

Kathryn felt like one of those actresses from the silent screen, mouth open but no sound. She held out Hoyt's note and watched Gwendolyn's eyes move across the page.

"So you're really Kathryn Danford." It felt as though Gwendolyn was talking about someone neither of them had ever met. "It does have a nice ring to it."

"Say it again."

"Kathryn Danford. Kathryn Danford. You sound like one of those blue-blooded ladies with permanent waves, the ones who lunch in the Bullocks Tea Room three times a week."

"I am not Kathryn Danford." She slid the note back into its envelope. "Kathryn Danford is someone who grew up in a nice part of Boston with doting parents, then went to Vassar or Bryn Mawr before she married a well-mannered patent attorney and joined the country club where she learned to play a thoroughly decent game of bridge."

Kathryn needed time to understand her bitter reaction. She'd expected to feel the final piece of a jigsaw puzzle falling into place. But instead, she felt detached from the stranger in Hoyt's note.

"Aren't you the teensiest bit curious about who this Thomas Dan—"

"Kathryn Danford never happened. Kathryn Massey is alive and well. And besides, Mother said she didn't even know who my father was, so how can Mister FBI come up with this sort of information? I bet he just plucked a random name out of some old Boston city directory."

"He's probably got some FBI tricks up his sleeve," Gwendolyn said, "so there's a chance this name is legit. And if it is, maybe this Hoyt guy's not so bad after all."

Kathryn started to grapple with Gwendolyn's obstinate zipper. "There's something I probably should have told you," she said. "The FBI has a file on me."

"If they were going to recruit you—"

"And in that file is a report about how I have lived with the same woman for eighteen years."

"It's the truth, isn't it?"

Kathryn hooked the fastener at the top of Gwendolyn's black-and-white polkadot swing skirt and spun her around. "Not 'shared with' or 'roomed with,' but '*lived with.*'"

Gwendolyn's mouth formed a perfect O. "You mean like Alla and Glesca?" She started to laugh. "And I always assumed the FBI was smart."

"We're both over thirty and neither of us have ever been married."

Gwendolyn stopped laughing like she'd been slugged. "But that hardly makes us lesbians. Besides, I've been seen in public with Linc, and before him Alistair and Eldon."

Kathryn sat down at the table and stared at Hoyt's note. "Meanwhile, I've been sneaking around with a married man. No dinner and dancing, no movie premieres. As far as the world is concerned, I might as well be dating Marcus."

Gwendolyn joined her at the table. "This Hoyt guy sounds like a smart cookie. I'm sure he doesn't think you're some sort of skirt chaser."

"Evidently, my living with the same woman for eighteen years is of particular interest to J. Edgar Hoover."

Gwendolyn grimaced as she pulled on her white glacé kid pumps.

"Hoyt promised me they only want me until the end of the war."

Gwendolyn let out a scornful "Pffft!" and then added, "We both know what those 'until the end of the war' promises are worth."

When Gwendolyn arrived home late on V-E Day, she hyperventilated herself into a fluster telling Kathryn what she'd done to get out of her obligation to Siegel. As far as Kathryn was concerned, even Wilkerson couldn't fend off the mob if they wanted to muscle in on his casino project. Gwendolyn had done Wilkerson—and by extension, Kathryn—the biggest favor possible.

"So what now?" Gwendolyn asked.

Kathryn shrugged. When she reported what Howard Hughes told her about Bogie being on the first day's shooting of *To Have And Have Not*, Hoyt pointed out that filming finished at six P.M. and the Book of the Day meeting started at eight.

"Japan can't hold out much longer," Kathryn said. "The whole thing might be over before Humphrey and Betty get back to LA. I don't want to risk the F-B-goddamned-I saying to me, 'Well, Miss Massey, our agreement was to bring us the proof we need before the end of the war. You didn't do that, so . . .'"

She got to her feet and picked up the platter of bacon rolls she'd spent a month's meat rations on. "I need to speak to Bogie before they leave."

* * *

When Humphrey and Betty stepped outside, the two dozen neighbors gathered at the pool burst into applause as "How Little We Know" floated over their heads. When Bacall heard it, her hands flew to her face in horror, but then she burst out laughing. "If I never hear that song again, I'll be one happy girl!"

No wonder Bogie fell for you, Kathryn thought. As arresting as she was on screen, Betty Bacall was even more in real life. Her hair was a warm chestnut brown; she kept it parted at the side and let it fall loosely to her shoulders.

Dorothy Parker—back in town for the summer with her husband, Alan—handed them each a drink and proposed a toast:

Here's to Bogie and Bacall,

Eastward ho their asses haul,

Leave us here? What cursed gall,

Quel dommage she's so damned tall!

A raucous cheer went up. Ever since V-E Day, Kathryn had noticed how buoyant everyone was. With hopeful eyes now turning toward Japan, ear-splitting cheers had become a daily event. Combine that with a marriage between a major movie star and his exquisite ingénue, and optimism was running through the Garden at feverish levels.

Dottie sidled up to Kathryn. "Those two glow with so much love, it's enough to inspire even us steadfast misanthropes."

"I'm not a misanthrope when it comes to love," Kathryn rejoined, aware of how defensive she sounded. Dottie lobbed her a skeptical eye. "Really, I'm not." *Nobody would accuse Kathryn Danford of being a misanthrope.* A second thought assailed her. *But you're not Kathryn Danford, are you?* "I'm a career girl, whose priorities may differ from the standard—" Kathryn broke off when Dottie started to laugh. She'd been had. "Please tell me you brought your Pineapple Surprise punch."

Kathryn was at the punchbowl when she sensed Humphrey by her side. He wore the wily grin he usually reserved for double-crossing gangsters.

"You've been on my mind," he said earnestly. "I never apologized to you. Not properly, at any rate."

She handed him a cup of punch. "Apologized for what?"

"That day down at NBC when I called you a miserable bitch."

"Don't be silly," Kathryn told him. "That's all water long under the bridge. I haven't given that day a thought since—"

"I'm heading into a whole new life tomorrow, and I want to leave a clean slate behind me, so just shut up and let me do this." A smile surfaced. "I want to apologize. I don't think you're a miserable bitch at all. Whatever the opposite of 'miserable bitch' is, that's you in my book."

He was looking at her with those droopy hound-dog eyes of his. The camera never picked up the depth of them, not even in close-ups.

Jesus Christ, Kathryn thought, *I just can't do it.* "You and I need to talk," she whispered hoarsely.

"I'm listening."

"It needs to be in private." Robert Benchley, Charlie Butterworth, and Kay Thompson let out a volley of laughter boisterous enough to wake Sleeping Beauty. "Tonight."

Humphrey looked around to see his bride-to-be trapped mid conversation with Dorothy Gish and John Carradine. He caught her eye, and mouthed, *I'll be right back.* Kathryn followed him into the villa he shared with Betty and closed the door. Their apartment was laid out differently from hers and Gwendolyn's — their living room was bigger but their kitchen looked like it'd been jammed into a tight corner. There also seemed to be less light. When Bogie shut the door, it threw the place into a deep murkiness leavened only by the smell of fresh-cut gardenias.

Hoyt's voice filled Kathryn's ears. *Tip Bogart off and this lesbian thing will only be the start.* Now that she finally had him in front of her, sober and ready to listen, her courage faltered.

"The FBI!" Kathryn pushed the words out. "They approached me a while ago. I thought it was to be an informer, like Louella and Hedda."

"Louella and Hedda are FBI informers?" He let out a long whistle.

Kathryn started pacing the floor toward shelves loaded with books on sailing and yachts. "Turns out they had me in mind for a special assignment. They want to know where you were the night of the Book of the Day meeting."

"What meeting? And why do they think I was there?"

"It was a Communist Party powwow, and apparently every big Hollywood name who's a member of the party was there that night."

He pounded a fist against a dark wooden lowboy. "Jesus goddamned Christ. Is this the whole Dies Committee thing again?"

"I suspect their plan is to make you name the names of everyone else who was there."

"Otherwise what?"

"Otherwise they'll drag you through the mud, just like they've threatened to drag me if I didn't."

"They're not fooling around, huh? So when was this meeting?

"Last year. February twenty-ninth – Leap Day."

"The day we started filming *To Have And Have Not*."

"You remember that?"

"Our director had the commissary bake us a cake. It had this black frosting with white lettering that said, 'Once every four years. To Have And Have Not.'" Relief washed over Humphrey's face. "That's it, then. I'm in the clear. We were filming all day."

"You finished at six and the meeting started at eight."

He stubbed out his cigarette with enough force to choke a seagull. "So I'm screwed."

"Not necessarily." Kathryn pulled him onto the sofa. "You just need to account for your time from six till midnight."

"Like I said, I'm screwed."

"Why?"

"That was the first night I took Betty to go see the *Sluggy.* The marina's deserted at night. We took separate cars off the lot, but met up down the street, a few blocks away in North Hollywood."

"So you have a corroborating witness!" She caught the dark look on his face. "No?"

"There's a clause in my divorce agreement. I had to swear my relationship with Betty didn't start until later. Any admission that we got together earlier, it gives Mayo grounds to renegotiate. I can't go through that again."

"It looks to me like the FBI is looking to hold something over you, so I doubt—"

"I will *not* take that chance, you hear me?"

"Okay," Kathryn said, thinking fast, "so what did Betty do with the car she drove that night after she jumped into yours?"

Bogie snapped his fingers. "Peter Lorre. I drove us down to the *Sluggy,* and Lorre drove her car to where she was staying with her mom."

"So he didn't tag along too?"

He threw her a pained look. "The point was to be alone with her."

"What I'm getting at is, would he be willing to swear that he was with you on the *Sluggy* that night?"

"Peter Lorre is the best pal a guy could ask for."

"I'm talking about swearing to the FBI." She let him think about what she was proposing.

"Yeah," he decided, "I think so. But we've gotta keep Betty out of this."

"Okay, so here's the story: You finished shooting at six, swung past the soundstage where Peter Lorre was working. Then the two of you motored to the *Sluggy* and did whatever it is guys like you do when you're sitting around a boat."

Bogie grinned. "Drinking, mainly. Maybe some poker."

"Get specific; get your stories straight."

Bogie nodded just as Artie Shaw and the three-man version of his orchestra started playing "Moonglow" a notch or two louder than they had been. Benchley yelled, "Where the hell did Bogie get to?"

Bogie took Kathryn by the hand and kissed it. Kathryn wondered if that was the tactic he'd used with his fiancée; it was dizzyingly effective. "I can't thank you enough for what you're doing," he said.

"Thank me by going out there and make Betty Bacall bless the day she met you."

He escorted her through the door, and then broke into a jog as he approached the crowd. They let out a cheer when he appeared.

Kathryn hung back, content to watch the good will envelop Bogart. Her eyes sought out Marcus' face in the crowd, but couldn't locate him. Instinctively, they went to his kitchen window where she could see the light of his reading lamp. He'd been putting on a brave face since Oliver packed his things, but she knew he missed him terribly. He'd handed in the new version of *Free Leningrad!* and the MGM executives flipped their toupees over it, reigniting talk of an Oscar nomination. But even that failed to put a genuine smile on his face.

When he spotted her at his door, he said, "Not tonight, Josephine."

She stepped inside anyway. "You know what this place needs? Fresh flowers. I was just over at Bogart's place and Betty's got it filled with gardenias. It smells divine."

"You were at Bogart's?"

"Pour us some whiskeys," she told him, and pulled Nelson Hoyt's note from inside her bra strap. "There's somebody you need to meet."

CHAPTER 43

It had been three days since *Free Leningrad!* had had its big, shiny premiere at Grauman's Chinese. The thunderous ovation still rang in Marcus' ears; the shock of Mayer acknowledging Marcus' contribution still thrilled him: "And I want to mention a member of our staff whose contribution to this motion picture was essential. I refer to our screenwriter, Mr. Marcus Adler."

Moreover, at the post-premiere party, Mayer took him aside and practically guaranteed him an Oscar nomination. Guarantees like that were as cheap as confetti in Hollywood, so Marcus took Mayer's promise as a "possible maybe, subject to change."

Marcus' one regret was that Oliver wasn't there to share it with him. But that was okay, because Oliver and Marcus had become pen pals over the past three months.

Not long after he packed his things, the Breen Office sent Oliver (or perhaps he volunteered) on a nationwide fact-finding mission to take the nation's temperature on the job they were doing to secure the country's morals. His assignment took in twenty cities in four months, his days filled with civic leaders, church groups, and women's associations, with names like the High Plains Coalition for the Preservation of Public Morality, New England Mothers' Intemperance League, and — Marcus' favorite — Teachers of Religion Against Motion Pictures, whose acronym spelled TRAMP, but nobody seemed to notice.

The first time Marcus heard from Oliver was a picture postcard of the Lambert Gardens in Portland, Oregon. His message was brief and included no address. Similarly ambiguous cards from Seattle and Boise followed. But then came one from Omaha, telling Marcus he'd be staying at the Curtis Hotel in Minneapolis the second week of May, and hinted that if Marcus wanted to write him, he'd welcome it. Marcus knew a white flag when he saw one, and mailed back a picture postcard of Hollywood and Vine.

Their correspondence evolved into one- and two-page letters, which soon grew to four and five pages as Oliver journeyed from Chicago to Boston to St. Louis, then all points south. Their second courtship, tentative and hesitant at first, bloomed into a love that Marcus feared had died. Oliver wasn't sure when he'd land back in Los Angeles, but Marcus didn't mind so much. It gave him something to look forward to.

The Monday after *Free Leningrad!*'s triumphant premiere, Marcus walked into the writers' department. Even in his euphoric state, he could feel the tension in the air. He stopped at the front desk and asked the receptionist what was going on.

"Rumors are flying around like buzzards," Dierdre told him. "Jim Taggert—we think he's gone."

"You mean fired?"

She curled a finger to draw him closer. "Word is that Mayer caught him screwing someone on his desk."

Hoppy and Taggert had been together longer than anybody Marcus knew. Taggert had a number of qualities Marcus wouldn't want in a partner, but Marcus never figured infidelity would be one of them. "But the mountain never comes to Mohammed, so what was Mayer doing in Taggert's office?"

"No!" Dierdre's pale green eyes bugged as though the four horsemen of the apocalypse had just come out the elevator. "Not on Taggert's desk. ON MAYER'S!"

* * *

The summons from Ida Koverman, Mayer's chief secretary, came about an hour later.

When Marcus started the long walk toward the mogul's raised desk, Mayer got to his feet and greeted him with a handshake heartier than Marcus would have credited him capable of.

Marcus looked around for Eddie Mannix, but Mayer's ever-present second-in-command was nowhere in sight. He took the chair offered him.

Mayer sat down again and arranged his face into a serious veneer, and clasped his hands together. "I don't know what you've heard, but the thing is, I've had to give Jim Taggert his marching papers."

"I see."

"There was a situation, and his dismissal was the only course of action."

"I'm sure you did what you thought best."

"Your department is left without a rudder. We need to fix that—pronto—so I've decided to promote you."

"Me?" The word popped out like a Ping-Pong ball.

"Your work on *William Tell* and *Free Leningrad!* made it clear that you know how to tell a story for the screen better than anyone else here. Congratulations."

The air around Marcus seemed suddenly thin, like he was flying at 20,000 feet. He ducked his head in a vague half-nod. "Thank you, sir." Then Mayer's eyes hardened.

"It is important you behave like a model employee. You are an example to your staff. You represent MGM everywhere you go."

* * *

What was Jim thinking? And who had he been screwing? And why on Mayer's desk? Marcus had been aware of friction between the mogul and his top script guy, but had it gotten so bad that he deemed it necessary to execute a revenge hump on the lord and master's desk?

Marcus stood in the shadow of the writers' building and looked up at the window of what was now his office. The war had seen a regrettable departure of talented writers— not only from MGM, but from studios all across town— whose replacements were wiseass wunderkinds who were impressed with their knack for snappy dialogue and couldn't understand why they weren't pulling in a grand a week already.

Marcus took the stairs to the first floor and strode into the foyer like MacArthur walking onto Palo Beach. Dierdre leapt to her feet. "So? Is it true?"

"Give me five minutes," Marcus told her, "and then tell the staff to assemble in the conference room."

He headed into Jim's office. *This is MY office now.* He pulled open one drawer after another until he found a bottle of Kentucky Tavern bourbon at the bottom of the filing cabinet. There were, however, no glasses. He could've just slurped from the bottle, but Mayer's instructions to be an example to his staff came back to him. He headed for the break room and was only a couple of steps away when he heard one of the guys say, "What's the bet Adler gets the top job?"

"What's the bet Taggert was screwing Adler on the big guy's desk."

Marcus stepped back.

A third voice spoke up. "I heard Adler's a Commie. And that he blackmailed someone at the Breen Office to sneak some pinko speech into *William Tell*."

"Pinko faggots, the lot of them."

"Ever hear of a guy called Hugo Marr?" the first guy asked. "He was another one of those queer-ass writers. The pissant shot himself before the war, and the way I hear it, Adler was in the room. No charges or anything, but it makes you wonder. My ol' pa always said it's the quiet ones you gotta watch."

"Maybe Adler set Taggert up knowing Mayer would walk in," the second guy said. "Talk about your *coitus interruptus*."

"More like coitus interrupt-ASS."

They erupted into hard-edged laughter. Marcus had never said much more than "Good morning" or "Nice weekend?" to the new guys, so he couldn't positively identify the voices. He was still leaning against the wall when Dierdre appeared, frowning.

"Kathryn Massey from the *Hollywood Reporter*, she's a friend of yours, right?"

"If she's on the line, tell her I'll call her back."

"Okay, but my women's intuition tells me this is a call you should take."

In Jim's office, Marcus picked up the telephone. "You won't believe the day I'm having."

He could hear Kathryn take a jagged breath. "Marcus, honey, you need to brace yourself. I've got—"

"Not right now. There's a lot going—"

"It's Alla; she's had a heart attack."

Marcus fell back in Jim's chair, gripping the receiver as though it was a life preserver. "Is she . . . ?"

"Not last I heard. She had it at home. Glesca called for an ambulance and it took her to the Good Samaritan. That's all we know. I'm about to jump into a taxi and pick Gwendolyn up at work."

"I'll meet you there."

He couldn't feel the homburg on his head, the carpet under his feet, or the summer sun probing through Jim's window. All he was aware of was the sinking feeling in his chest.

* * *

The emergency department of the Good Samaritan Hospital smelled overwhelmingly of chlorine. A nurse with red hair starched more stiffly than her cap directed him to room 711.

Kathryn and Gwendolyn stood on the far side of the bed, holding hands. Glesca was on the side closest to Marcus, holding Alla's. Alla lay between them, as pale as the bed linen tucked tautly around her and frail as a sparrow. Her hair, once thick and dark, lay in damp clumps like the fraying bristles of a scorched broom. Her eyes were closed and her breathing so light he could barely discern the rise and fall of her chest.

Glesca, almost as drawn as her companion of sixteen years, stepped back to allow Marcus near. He picked up Alla's right hand. It felt warm but heavy, like a rock left in the sun. He stroked the back of it, his fingers navigating each distended vein. Alla opened her eyes. She looked tired and distracted. "My boy," she whispered, "my sweet boy. I fear it's time we said our goodbyes."

"No, no." Marcus choked on each syllable. A couple of weeks earlier, Alla had been taken to this same hospital for coronary thrombosis. She'd recovered, but not as well as Marcus had assumed. "You'll be back in your Garden before you know it." Her face blurred and distorted as tears collected in Marcus' eyes. He bit down on his lip, determined not to buckle like an accordion.

Alla shook her head weakly. "I'm bound for a different garden." She looked over at Kathryn and Gwendolyn. "Be good. Be strong. Be loving." Her voice faltered on the last word, losing her breath and her focus. Her grip loosened.

"Marcus, honey?"

He looked up at Kathryn. She gestured toward Glesca. He didn't want to let go of Alla's hand, but it was Glesca who was losing the love of her life, not him. He laid Alla's hand on the coarse hospital linen and joined the girls on the other side of the bed, Gwendolyn to his left, Kathryn to his right.

"Would you like us to leave you alone?" Gwendolyn asked.

Glesca shook her head. "She considers you all family." She bent down until her lips were almost touching Alla's ear and whispered delicate words. Marcus couldn't hear what she was saying, but it was the same long sentence over and over. It made Alla smile. It was a fragile smile, the ends of her lips barely curling upward, but a smile nonetheless.

Then, suddenly, the smile wilted and Alla gasped. She held her breath for three, maybe five seconds, then let it out so slowly it seemed to take an eternity. Eternity came to an end, and Alla Nazimova was gone.

Marcus felt Gwendolyn and Kathryn pull themselves into him. He closed his eyes, squeezing them so tightly he saw geometric patterns kaleidoscope. *Hold on,* he told himself, *hold on.* Marcus Adler unraveled like a rag doll coming apart at the seams.

* * *

There was a time when Alla Nazimova's star blazed so bright, the Shuberts named a Broadway theater after her.

Her incandescent presence earned her more money per week than Mary Pickford, and her name conjured images of dramatic poses in elaborate costumes from the Orient, France, and Arabia. The American public had never seen anybody like her, and it adored her.

And then there was the time when she died, and barely a dozen people showed up at her funeral. It was a brief service, the preacher appropriately respectful but clearly with little idea who he was burying. His role fulfilled, he limply shook the hands of each person who'd bothered to show and made his way down the slope.

Dorothy Parker and her dark-haired husband, Alan Campbell, approached Kathryn. Robert Benchley trailed after them, unsteadily dragging his feet across the lawn. "We're taking Glesca with us back to the Garden," she told Kathryn. Glesca stood at Alla's graveside with her cotton dress flapping in the breeze. Behind her, the leafy sprawl of Glendale braced itself for the baking July heat.

Marcus felt George Cukor's hand squeeze his. "She deserved better," George said.

"She deserved a funeral as big as Valentino's," Benchley announced.

"She certainly did." Franklin Pangborn dabbed at his eyes. "I'm going to miss that old gal so very, very much."

"Come on, Pangy," George threw his arm around Franklin. "I'll take you home."

As the group made their way down the grassy slope toward a pair of cars parked against the curb, Marcus kept his eyes on the mound of newly turned sod covering Madame's coffin. The damp earth smelled fresh, like it was bursting with potential life, an irony that Alla would have found amusing.

"I'm glad so few people showed up," Marcus said. "If there'd been five thousand people here, I'd have walked away." He snaked his arms around the girls' waists and drew them close with what little strength he had left. "I feel like I just buried my mother."

"She was mother to all us Gardenites," Kathryn said.

"Looks like we have a straggler." Gwendolyn pointed to a lone figure trudging up the steep hillside.

"Who shows up an hour late to someone's funeral?" Marcus asked bitterly, not even looking.

"Is that . . . Oliver?" Gwendolyn asked.

Marcus shaded his eyes from the glare of the sun. He didn't dare hope Gwendolyn was right until Oliver drew up to the gravesite.

"I was in Santa Fe yesterday when I heard the news." He looked at Marcus, his eyebrows crinkling upwards. "How are you doing?"

Marcus let go of the girls and threw himself into Oliver's arms. If he had any tears left, Marcus would have shed them now. Instead, he pressed his face into the man's neck and breathed in his smoky aftershave balm. The two men hugged until the strength in Marcus' arms gave out.

"Your tour of duty," Marcus tried to fight off the early tremors of a throbbing headache. "It's over?"

"The good folks of Albuquerque won't be happy, but I suspected I was needed elsewhere. I'm so sorry I missed the service."

They stood around Alla's grave for a few moments, lost in their own thoughts.

Then Oliver said, "I have an idea." He pointed to a late-model Chevrolet Styleline, bottle green and new-dime shiny. "Let's go raise a toast to the great Madame Nazimova. The Sahara Room, perhaps? I'm sure Seamus could rustle up some quality Russian vodka."

Marcus faced the girls. "Give us a minute." He watched them head toward the Chevrolet, then ran his fingers down Oliver's arm. "My little pen pal. I've enjoyed our long-distance courtship, but I'm so glad you're back." He stared into those hazel eyes he'd missed so much. "You are back, aren't you? I mean, *we* are back, aren't we?"

Oliver smiled and nodded. They gazed at each other for a long, quiet moment, then he gestured toward his rental car. "Shall we?"

"I'll be right there."

Oliver left to join the girls. Marcus knelt down beside Alla's grave. "You told me the first time we met that it's important to have good friends, especially when I was so far from home. You gave me a home when I had none, and you gave me friendships when I needed them most." He picked up a handful of dirt and pressed his fingers around it, imagining she was already a part of it. "Thank you."

He let the damp, cool earth drop through his fingers as he stood up and turned to join the others.

CHAPTER 44

It was Bertie Kreuger who sent Gwendolyn, invitation in hand, heart in throat, to The Players nightclub two weeks after Nazimova's passing.

Gwendolyn, Marcus, Kathryn, and Oliver were still in the Sahara Room after returning from Forest Lawn cemetery when Bertie pinwheeled in, shedding apologies in all directions. "I'll never forgive myself for missing Alla's funeral! What a dunderhead I am! Such a terrible person!"

She calmed down after Gwendolyn ordered her a double gin, and listened attentively while Marcus, Kathryn, and Gwendolyn reminisced about how over the years their friendship had deepened into something closer and dearer, and how she'd become a mother figure to them, each in different ways.

Alla was the one who pushed Marcus the hardest to write back to Doris and embrace his sister fully. It was Alla Kathryn turned to when seeking advice at how best Kathryn might pry the details of her father from a mother who preferred to leave that part of her life behind. And it was Alla Gwendolyn deferred to with questions about style and sewing when Gwendolyn realized she'd taken on a dress that was beyond her skills.

When the conversation touched on Alla's encouragement about Chez Gwendolyn, Bertie piped up.

"If you ask me, I think you should go after Linc's father for your money. I know the Tattlers from all those stuffy society parties, so trust me when I tell you that Tattler Senior is *loaded*. To you, four grand is everything, but to someone like that? Ha! He won't even miss it."

Gwendolyn didn't think anything of it until Bertie appeared at her door a week later, invitation in hand. "Take this," she insisted, "get back what's rightfully yours, and don't take no for an answer!"

* * *

It was a perfect Angeleno summer evening. The last of the afternoon's warmth mingled with the jasmine and was tempered by the hint of a sea breeze drifting in from Santa Monica. Gwendolyn read the sign at The Players' front door.

PRIVATE CHARITY FUNCTION

FOR THE EUROPEAN FOOD DROP COALITION

TO ASSIST WAR VICTIMS

SPONSORED BY TATTLER'S TUXEDOS & PRIMM VALLEY REALTY

She flashed Bertie's invitation to the burly marine decked out in his dress blues at the door.

The Players' foyer led directly onto its main room, whose tables had been cleared away for two hundred people gussied up in their finest: silk-lapelled dinner jackets, gold-braided military epaulettes, midnight-blue chiffon, and ocelot fur evening wraps.

Gwendolyn scanned the faces, hoping to see a familiar one. If Primm Valley Realty was cosponsoring this bash, chances were good that she'd see — *bull's eye!*

She picked her way through the crowd until she moved into Leilah O'Roarke's peripheral vision. The week before, Gwendolyn found an old reticule in a vintage clothing store downtown. She relined it with her last scraps of decent satin and stitched black and silver beads in alternating stripes across the outside. It glittered in the spotlights that dotted the ceiling, and she held it to her face now, pretending to be searching for something until she wrested Leilah's attention.

Leilah excused herself from her conversation and took a moment to admire Gwendolyn's blue moiré silk gown. "Don't you pop up in the most surprising places?"

Gwendolyn leaned in for a melodramatic whisper, laying it on thick. "I'm in pursuit of a particular certain someone, and I need your help."

"Sounds thrilling. Who's your target?"

"Horton Tattler. My problem is I don't know what he looks like."

"Linc never introduced you? Very poor form, I must say."

Gwendolyn offered up her best *Men! What-can-you-do?* shrug.

Leilah pointed out a stout gent standing alone at the bar, ordering a drink. Gwendolyn thanked her and beelined it before anybody else had a chance to commandeer him. "Mr. Tattler?"

The enormous handlebar moustache protruding several inches punctuated a round face; it made him look like he'd stepped out of a Dickens novel. She got over her shock in time to take in his eyes. They were Linc's: sea-blue flecked with sky. It was disconcerting to see those eyes she knew so well on someone else.

"May I help—ah!" he exclaimed. "Miss Gwendolyn, isn't it? Bullocks Wilshire?"

With a poorly concealed gasp, she realized he was one of her sweetiepies, the well-heeled gentlemen whose purchases for their mistresses had contributed substantially to her monthly sales totals. Moreover, he was one of her favorites. He took his time stroking the silks and satins, making observations on the quality of the lace and commenting on hues. Somewhere out there was a beautifully adorned and expensively scented young lady, and now she knew why.

Oh my heavens, Linc's father has a mistress! The thought made her blush, which in turn made Linc's father blush. His alarm—*Holy smoke, she knows who I am!*—was broadcast across his otherwise genial face.

"Isn't it funny, the coincidences that crop up in life?" Gwendolyn laughed.

"Why, yes. I, er . . . "

"Mr. Tattler," she said gently, "you probably weren't aware of this, but your son and I were dating."

He cast an appraising eye up and down her, then broke into a twinkling smile. "How very fortunate for him."

She thought of the nickname Linc often used: Parentasaurus Rex. She'd always imagined Linc's father to be some wheezing old coot; part Scrooge, part Quasimodo, all horrible teeth and bleary eyes, jaundiced with disapproval. That he turned out to be this Victorian sweetiepie left Gwendolyn blindsided.

"Thank you. Now, about Linc—"

His eyes turned glum. "Miss Gwendolyn, if you've approached me in the hope that I shall tell you where Linc is, I'm afraid you've let yourself in for disappointment. My son's disappearance has left me completely in the dark. If you have any information, I would be most grateful if you shared it with me."

Oh, Linc, how could you up and leave without telling your father anything? "I don't know where he went, either. All we can do is wait until he reappears."

Tattler harrumphed. "Just wait till he does!" He squinted at Gwendolyn, suddenly suspicious. "Exactly why did you seek me out tonight?"

"Mr. Tattler, you might want to prepare yourself." *Here goes nothing.* "Were you aware that your son — very successfully, I might add — dealt in the black market?"

Horton Tattler huffed at her like a blowfish. "The years I've put into building a sterling reputation for myself. The Tattler name means quality, perfection, class. He was set to take over the whole operation upon my retirement. Why would he risk it all for the — the —?"

"Because he doesn't want it." Gwendolyn softened her tone. "He wants to open an electronics store: radios, gramophones, and some newfangled thing called television."

The handlebar moustache twitched. "The black market, of all things."

"It's not as bad as it sounds. Just nylon stockings, perfume and lipstick, and some scarves. And besides," she flicked his lapel with her nail, "you should be very proud. Your son has quite the head for business. Okay, so maybe he was operating in a legal gray zone, but he was very, very good at it."

Horton pulled out a Romeo y Julieta Cuban cigar. Gwendolyn used to sell them when she worked at the Cocoanut Grove, but only to the connoisseurs. "If you don't know where my son is, can you at least tell me why he disappeared?"

Gwendolyn looked around the packed room and decided that she couldn't count on Xavier Cugat's music to drown out the names she was about to drop. She guided him through a labyrinth of cocktail tables and down a tiled staircase to an intimate basement bar. It held seating for maybe thirty, but it, too, was crowded with well-heeled society chatter and military bravado. So then she led him to a door painted a dark maroon, the same color as the walls. She whipped it open and prodded Linc's father inside. A line of sporadically spaced lightbulbs lit the corridor ahead of them like a landing strip.

"Where are we?" he demanded.

"It leads to the Chateau Marmont."

She watched him recalibrate his assessment of her. "What you're about to tell me can't be good if you need to bring me in here."

Gwendolyn leaned up against the tunnel wall. The cement was unpainted but pleasantly cool. "We came to the attention of Bugsy Siegel." Gwendolyn waited for another wail of disappointment to burst out from under the old-fashioned handlebar, but Horton stared at her, unmoved.

"Go on."

"We were so successful that he decided to take a large piece of our pie."

"In exchange for what?"

Gwendolyn had never stopped to consider the specifics of turning Siegel down. "The luxury of keeping our kneecaps intact, I suppose."

A wry smile emerged from the shadows cloaking Horton's face. "In other words, the standard arrangement."

It took Gwendolyn a moment to comprehend the man's indifference to the news that his son had become entangled with the mob. "You mean—you too?"

Horton leaned up against the wall opposite Gwendolyn and pulled on his cigar. "It's the price of doing business in this city of so-called angels," he sighed. "The LAPD are a pack of paper tigers."

"You have more in common with your son than you thought."

Gwendolyn snuck a peek at Linc's father from the corner of her eye. He wasn't at all the Parentasaurus Rex his son made him out to be. A little behind the times, perhaps, and a tad too stern in an antiquated sort of way, but nothing like the ogre she'd been picturing.

"Tell me, Miss Brick," Horton said. "Linc was saving for his gadget store, but what about you?"

"I'm not too shabby with a sewing machine—"

"I can see that." He cast a seasoned eye over her outfit. "Admirable work."

"I had plans to open a dress store. Nothing grand, but something to call my own."

"And is that what you'll do now?"

Gwendolyn stepped away from the wall, her resentment rising again. "No," she replied with a curtness designed to capture his attention. "I had close to enough money to finance my store, but when Linc went on the lam, not only did he take all his money, but all of mine, too."

Horton took this news like a punch to the sternum. "My son *stole* your money?"

"Everything I've done, every dollar I've earned has been about opening my store. But Linc snatched all that away."

"Miss Gwendolyn, I'm truly horrified to hear this. I thought I raised my son to be a better man than that."

Gwendolyn wanted to give Linc's father a chance to do the right thing without her having to nudge him, so they stood in the semidarkness for a few moments. The chill of the tunnel was starting to seep through her silk, so she crossed her arms for warmth. She heard "The Trolley Song" muffled through the concrete and wood; the smell of burning dust from the lightbulbs filled the air.

"Miss Brick," Tattler said at last, "may I ask how much Lincoln took?"

"Of my money, four thousand."

"And when you approached me this evening, was it your intention to get your four thousand dollars out of me?"

"It was."

"But I didn't steal your money, Lincoln did. He's of age, which means I am not responsible for his debts."

So you're like all those other moneybags. Tight as a bug's butt when it comes to parting with your cash. "Four grand is a hell of a lot of money to me, but you probably spend that every month on your cigars and brandy, and presents for your 'friend.' I assume all those camisoles and teddies you bought from me weren't for Mrs. Tattler?"

"Are you threatening me with blackmail?"

The crisp, sour way he said the word *blackmail* made Gwendolyn realize she didn't have the nerve for something like that. She fell back against the wall. "No. Your secret's safe with me."

"I'm going to share information with you that I haven't even told my wife. The truth of the matter is, I'm broke. Flat stony broke."

"You're not!"

"It's true, I'm afraid. All three of my clothing factories were converted to making uniforms. I was happy to do my bit for the war, and if only two of them had been requisitioned, I'd have made enough money to break even. But all three has sunk me. Each one was taken over by a different branch—army, navy, and the marines—and they do not talk to each other very well. They each told me to take my case to someone else. They've been giving me the runaround for four years."

"But the war's nearly over. Surely you can convert them back —"

"That takes money. Before the war, I invested heavily in Japanese silk and Italian linen. I don't need to tell you how those investments worked out." He let out a poor-little-me sigh. "I'm selling Linc's house on San Ysidro, plus the one I live in with my wife. At least my mistress has disappeared, so I don't have that expense anymore."

The man I came to retrieve my four thousand from is worse off than I am. The pensive silence that followed gave Gwendolyn time to piece things together. "But if you're so broke," she said, "how come you could afford to sponsor this shindig tonight?"

"Don't be fooled by that sign out front." Tattler ground the end of his cigar into the bare concrete. "I'm sponsoring this shindig, as you call it, in name only. The whole thing is being underwritten by Primm Valley Realty."

"Clem O'Roarke, huh?"

Horton Tattler sported a pair of bushy eyebrows every bit as oversized as his moustache. Gwendolyn watched them rise to their maximum height. "How in the world would you know about that?"

"Linc was studying your company's books. He noticed a lot of money flowing back and forth between Tattler's Tuxedos and Primm Valley Realty."

"O'Roarke has been propping up my business for the past year now. Although I fear it's all been a waste of time. We can't go on much longer."

"It hasn't been a waste of time for Clem O'Roarke," Gwendolyn said.

"What do you mean?"

"I don't know how he's managed it, but Clem O'Roarke has bought up all this land in and around some podunk nowheresville called Las Vegas."

"Why would he do that?"

"Because Billy Wilkerson plans to build a casino there."

Horton's eyes lost their focus as his gaze drifted down into the murky end of the tunnel. "You old fool," he murmured.

"What is it?"

"I'm not good with ledgers, so when I started to become successful it was the first task I handed over to someone else. I asked Clem if he knew of a good accountant and he said, 'Use mine, he's terrific.' So I did." He paused to think things through. "I haven't repaid Clem one thin dime of the money he's lent me. Those books should have only shown money going from his business to mine."

"Linc suspected money was being laundered. He thought it was you."

Tattler scoffed. "I don't have any left to launder." He took Gwendolyn's hands in his. Despite the chill and damp of the tunnel, they were warm and dry. "I'm very sorry my son left you in such a bind. I'd like to think he had good reason."

Gwendolyn nodded. "Me too."

"Clem O'Roarke and I go back thirty years." Even in the dim light, Gwendolyn could see the betrayal cutting into him. He let go of her hands and turned to leave, but then turned back. "What was the name of that podunk town?"

"Las Vegas. It's in Nevada."

She watched Horton Tattler trek down the tunnel. The darkness buried him foot by foot until she was left alone with the notes of a Hoagy Carmichael tune filtering in from the bar.

CHAPTER 45

Marcus stirred the ice cubes in his Mai Tai with a yellow paper umbrella. Normally he wasn't big on cocktails that came with umbrellas, but he figured if you're standing in a bar called the Seven Seas Club, you might as well drink like a native. The orange curaçao was a bit sweet but the lime juice cut it to a tolerable level. He took another swig; it tasted better the second time around. He felt his body relax and realized it was the first chance he'd had to unwind in the month since Madame died.

His questions about the story behind Taggert's departure remained unanswered, so he kept calling Taggert and Hoppy's house until someone finally picked up the phone. Taggert commanded Marcus to meet him at the Seven Seas and be prepared to settle in for a long night.

Marcus parked himself at the end of a row of vacant barstools, closest to the bamboo wall, and listened to a ukulele playing over the loudspeakers. He was halfway through his Mai Tai before Taggert and Hoppy walked in. He waited until they'd ordered Fijian Fireballs before he said, "Out with it. I want the whole story, starting with Mayer's desk. Is the rumor true?"

Taggert maintained his poker face. "What's the rumor?"

"That you were fired because Mayer walked into his office and caught you on his desk. Mid schtup."

The two men burst out laughing.

"That's not what happened, then?"

Taggert leaned up against the bar. "Oh, there was some schtupping going on when I walked into Mayer's office, but it wasn't me with my Brooks Brothers down."

"Mayer?"

"Um-hm."

"But doesn't he have that secret room behind his office?"

"Um-hm."

Hoppy let out a groan. "Go on, Jimmy," he said, "don't make him beg."

Taggert lowered his voice, forcing Marcus to lean closer. "We'd been hashing out story problems on Garland's new *Harvey Girls* picture, and Mannix told me I couldn't leave the studio until I had finished the latest revision. So I stayed late, got the damned thing done, went to Mannix's office, but he'd gone. His secretary told me he left word to take it to Mayer, no matter how late it was. So I did."

"And you caught him going at it?"

"The door to his office was open. He only had one light on, so I couldn't really make anything out until I was halfway there. You should have seen the look on his face. Talk about your blueballs caught in a vice."

"So who was he banging?" Marcus had his money on Melody Hope.

Taggert screwed his nose up in disgust. "One of Miss Leilah's girls."

Marcus nearly choked on his Mai Tai. He set the glass down on the cherry-red bar with a thump. "Do you mean the Leilah I think you mean?"

"How many Leilah O'Roarkes you think we got in this town?"

"Leilah O'Roarke is a—" Marcus was so astonished he could barely push the word out, "—madam?" *Does Gwendolyn know this? Does Linc?*

Marcus gazed down the bright red bar. The place was starting to fill up. Floyd Forrester walked in with a guy around his age with unruly red hair and watery eyes; Marcus recognized him as head of casting at Republic Pictures. Behind them tottered a couple of uniformed sailors. Marcus motioned the bartender for another round.

"But that's not the funny part!" Hoppy insisted. "The hooker was a dead ringer for Katharine Hepburn."

"Spitting image," Taggert said. "That long face with those cheekbones, exactly the same hair, and those young-boy hips of hers. For a minute there, I thought it actually was her. Until she opened her mouth. Out came this feeble attempt at a New England accent via the South Bronx."

"But how did you know she was one of Leilah O'Roarke's girls?" *Did Leilah try and recruit Gwendolyn?*

"She used to be Kate's stand-in at RKO back when I was a dialogue sharpener over there. But she got in trouble passing bad checks—she ain't the brightest ornament on the Christmas tree—so she dropped out of sight. I bumped into her about a year ago at the Florentine Gardens, bombed out of her noodle. She greeted me like a long-lost brother and blurted out everything. It wasn't hard to put two and two together when I walked in on them. Hepburn—the real one—is probably one of his few stars he hasn't tried to pull something on, which I bet has frustrated the bejesus out of him."

"So you walked in on him," Marcus said, "and he fired you?"

Taggert laughed again. "I negotiated my way out."

"He's been wanting to leave for a while," Hoppy said. "Thinks he's got the Great American Novel inside of him."

Taggert shrugged as he lit up a Camel. "So I made my demands. He keeps his secret and is free to spin whatever story he wants about my departure. Meanwhile, I get an immediate exit, a termination check big enough to live on for a year, and the right to name my successor. The bastard couldn't say yes fast enough."

Marcus blinked. "Name your successor?" He could feel a blush charging up from his chest and flooding his face. "You mean—?"

"Let me guess: Mayer made it seem like it was his idea. Phuh! He wouldn't have the first idea who to appoint."

Marcus grabbed Taggert by the hand and pumped it. "Jim, I don't know what to say. Thank you. Thank you!"

"Ah, cut it out." He elbowed Marcus away. "Who else was I going to give it to? One of those know-it-all punks we've got now? They're all Dorothy Parker with the snappy lines, and maybe—*maybe*—one or two of them know how to put a story together." His eyes turned earnest. "You've had some shitty stuff happen to you, but it's the shitty stuff that gives you something to say. No storyteller worth his weight in typewriter ribbons can tell a decent yarn unless he's fallen into a ditch or two." He clinked his Fijian Fireball against Marcus' Mai Tai. "So good luck, my friend." He motioned to the bartender for another round. "You're going to need it. Those Young Turks aren't too broadminded when it comes to guys like us."

"I've encountered that already," Marcus admitted.

"Did you square off with them?"

"Not yet."

"Good," Taggert said. He tapped his right temple. "Use the ol' noggeroo. Psychological's the way to go." He clinked Marcus' glass again. "Here's to screwing with people's minds."

By the time he'd drained his second Mai Tai, Marcus began to realize how they could sneak up on a guy. He hadn't been this loose-limbed in a while, and it felt good. He leaned back in his bamboo stool and looked over at Forrester's table. He and his friends were already slouched over their chairs, pie-eyed to the gills and not looking to slow down. Forrester met Marcus in the eye, tilted his head into a slight nod, and mouthed the word *congratulations*.

Hoppy moaned. "Oh Jesus, look out."

Edwin Marr, bloodshot eyes fired with rage, came at Marcus from a dark corner of the bar. "YOU!" He sounded like he'd been scraping his voice box over a cheese grater. He gripped the back of a bamboo barstool with gnarled knuckles to steady himself. "Everywhere I turn. Now I open the *Hollywood Reporter* and have to read you head the writing department." He jabbed a claw at Marcus. "That job should have gone to my boy! Hugo should be running the show, not—not—you!"

Hoppy got to his feet. "Mr. Marr—Edwin, please, calm yourself." He stepped closer, but stopped when Marr threw him a caustic look.

"I don't know who the hell you are," Edwin said, "but this has nothing to do with you."

"Edwin," Hoppy persisted, "you know me. It's Vern. Vernon Terrell. You remember? With the wooden leg? I wrote *Forty Acres And A Mule*; it was our biggest success."

Realization dropped onto Marr's face like a punching bag. "Hoppy," he croaked.

"That's right. Hoppy. Now you got it." Out of the side of his mouth, he murmured to Marcus, "Scoot."

But before Marcus could collect his hat, Marr exploded again. "Why the tarnation are you hanging around this bucket of scum?"

"Now just hold on a minute," Marcus began, but Marr was too worked up.

"You may have L.B. fooled, and you may have everybody fooled, but I know the truth, and you know it. *You killed my son.*"

"You got one thing right," Marcus spat back. He felt Taggert's placating hand on his arm, but he pushed it off. It was time to have this out. "The real truth is you gambled your way so deeply into debt that you had to sell out your own son."

"Marcus," Taggert whispered, "what are you talking about?"

Marcus ignored him, keeping his focus on Marr. "Industrial espionage, isn't that what it's called?"

Edwin Marr let out a tortured screech wrenched from somewhere deep and spiteful. He raised his hands and lunged at Marcus. "You son of a goddamned bitch!" Hoppy tried to grab Marr by the arm, but the old crank sidestepped him. "You and your wicked lies. You profited by my son, my poor innocent son. He trusted—"

Marr gasped and reached out for the nearest bar stool to catch himself, but missed it by barely an inch. He seemed to hang in midair at an impossible angle, trying to say something but finding only air caught in his throat. His gaunt body collapsed on itself as he dropped to the mottled red carpeting.

Marcus heard Hoppy yell, "Someone! Call emergency!" and the sound of running feet.

First Hugo, then Alla, and now Edwin?

He turned to Taggert. "I just wanted to clear the air. Set the record straight, you know? He's been running all over town, accusing me of murder and—" He looked down at the figure sprawled on the floor. "Oh, jeez, look at him."

He bent down and loosened Marr's firmly knotted necktie. "Help's coming. Try and relax. It won't do any good to—"

Edwin's eyes were open, still so blazingly defiant and so sure of his facts that any argument Marcus could muster evaporated on his lips.

CHAPTER 46

Anticipation draped over Los Angeles like a low-hanging cumulus, heavy with hope. Another bomb had been dropped, this time on a city called Nagasaki. The end was so close people could taste it. To Kathryn, it tasted like French champagne, real *pâté de foie gras*, and chocolate cake with frosting made from genuine sugar.

Meanwhile, she had a radio show to record. Normally, *Kraft Music Hall* was broadcast live, but Bing Crosby was set to entertain troops on the USS *Missouri* battleship currently steaming into Tokyo Bay, so they'd taped an entire show pretending that the news had been announced. Kathryn found the experience a surreal rehearsal for the real thing. When Dinah Shore finished singing "Thank Your Lucky Stars," even the radio crew, normally the most dry-eyed bunch of guys this side of an undertakers' convention, was dabbing at wet cheeks.

Kathryn stepped out of the NBC studios bursting with pep and ready for her four o'clock shift at the Hollywood Canteen. As arranged, she met Gwendolyn on the corner of Sunset and Vine.

"I thought I'd be exhausted," Kathryn declared, "but I'm ready to dance with every serviceman in the whole Canteen!"

A familiar voice called out her name.

Kathryn and Nelson Hoyt had an arrangement. If she needed to speak with him, she placed a classified ad in the *Reporter*. She was "Paul," he was "Eric," and they had a list of coded meeting places. After telling him where Bogie was the evening of Leap Year Day, she placed three successive ads in an attempt to meet with him and formalize the end of their association, but had heard nothing back.

Now you show up? Kathryn thought. She turned to Gwennie. "I'll meet you there."

"Gwendolyn, isn't it?" Hoyt stepped forward.

Kathryn waved a hand in his direction. "This is Mr. Hoyt."

"I have some news for you," he said, "regarding your brother, Monty."

"Oh?" Gwendolyn's eyes glinted with expectation. Kathryn felt something in the back of her neck cramp up.

"He was involved in the Battle of Okinawa."

Gwendolyn gripped her purse more tightly.

"He wasn't active in the fighting, so don't you fret. He's on the USS *Iowa*, somewhere off the coast of Japan. Miss Brick, you have every reason to believe you'll see your brother again."

Kathryn watched her roommate's face dissolve with relief and joy.

You slimy ingratiating little toad.

"This shouldn't take long," she told Gwendolyn. "Just tell them I got unavoidably detained."

She watched Gwendolyn cross Vine Street, then spun around. "What the hell was that?"

"I think she appreciated the information —"

"I know, I know, you're Mister Special Insider Information. You made that quite clear when you came up with my father's name." He winced, then looked away, and she realized she'd hit a nerve. But somehow she didn't feel like she'd scored a point. "Not that I'm not grateful," she was curiously compelled to add. "In fact, I was thinking that perhaps when things settle down after the war, I might look into his whereab—"

"Don't bother," he snapped, and pressed his lips into a thin line.

"Hey, I didn't ask you to track my father down. You're the one who opened that door, and now you're telling me to close it?"

"It was my job to woo you." Hoyt met her gaze, glare for glare. "Persuade you to join us in our fight against Communism. I figured if I did you a favor and tracked down information you wouldn't normally have access to, then you'd trust me. That didn't seem to work. So I dug further and eventually found him."

Kathryn's heart jolted. "You found my father? How . . . ? Where . . . ?"

He raised his hands as though to push her away. "I know you won't want to, but on this, you have to trust me. This is not something you want to take any further. Drop it, okay?"

FBI be damned! "I think I've had all I can take," she hissed. "You come barging into my life, just about blackmail me to snoop on my friends, you try and worm your way into my good books by using my dearest friend's brother, and then to top it all off, you dangle my father's identity in front of me, then whip it away like it's some cheap little sparkly bracelet. What kind of person *are* you?"

"Miss Massey, you're a public figure, you're known coast to coast. You don't want this skeleton escaping the closet—"

Her heart jolted a second time. "It's that bad?"

"Sing Sing."

"My father is—"

"In prison. *Now* will you drop it?"

Kathryn's mind fogged over. Through the roar of traffic, she heard him say, "Can we please now focus on the issue at hand?"

"What issue is that?"

"Humphrey Bogart."

"Yes," she said, facing him more squarely now, "let's talk about Humphrey Bogart." I've given you what you wanted, so I assume this is where we bid each other *sayonara*."

"I'm afraid it's not," he replied coolly.

"Don't you dare welsh on me now." Kathryn pulled her elbows in to cloak her shaking.

"Our deal was for you to provide us with accurate information on Bogart's whereabouts on the night in question."

"Which I did."

"February twenty-ninth was also the final night of the Clover Club. I'm surprised you weren't there. Lots of celebrities. And photographers. Taking photographs. Of celebrities. Like Peter Lorre."

Kathryn stepped back until she felt the wall of the NBC studios against her back. The afternoon sun had heated the bricks, and it now seeped through her clothes.

Hoyt said, "And while I'm glad to know that Bogart considers Lorre the best pal a guy could ask for, I must question whose side he's on."

Kathryn saw only one path left: go on the offensive. "What the hell did you expect?" she demanded. "You asked me to spy on my friends, my colleagues, my neighbors."

"You agreed to—"

"You're barking up the wrong tree. As far as Bogart is concerned, you're not even in the right forest."

"Your job was to bring me the evidence, not analyze it."

"So what if he got Peter Lorre to cover for him?" She pushed herself off the brick wall. "The point is, he wasn't at your damned Communist meeting, he was—"

Something shifted inside Kathryn's head, like a half-forgotten dream falling into place. "Peter Lorre is the best pal a guy could ask for? That's what Bogie said when we were in his living room." She stepped forward, within slapping distance. "You quoted him word for word."

"Miss Massey! It is you, isn't it?" A pair of middle-aged women approached her. From the conservative cut of their lacy outfits, Kathryn guessed them to be Pasadena society matrons.

"We were in the audience just now," the nearer one said. "My daughter is such a fan of yours. Works for Universal. Just the typing pool, but she has ambition." She thrust her audience ticket toward Kathryn, along with a fountain pen. "Would you mind?"

Kathryn could barely see three inches in front of her. *You FBI sons of bitches bugged Bogie's villa. You were listening to us the whole time.* She uttered some inane platitude of thanks. *If they bugged Bogie, have they bugged other people?* She waved the women goodbye.

"Why even rope me into this whole ugly business if you were just going to bug Bogie anyway?"

"I didn't know about the bug until afterwards." An involuntary tic started twitching Hoyt's right cheek. It was the first chink she'd seen in the guy's armor. "Hoover sent the order without telling me."

"What about my place?" she threw back. Oh my God! All those conversations about Gwendolyn's black-market business! "You got that bugged too?"

"No, just Bo —"

"Who's to say you cretins haven't broken into every villa in the Garden of Allah and —"

"I promise you, Miss Massey, only Bogart's —"

"Promise me? HA!" She slapped Hoyt across the face with every last scrap of strength she could muster. Her palm landed flat against his cheek, the *thwack* ringing louder than she expected. It caught him off guard and sent him stumbling across the sidewalk. "Your promises aren't worth spitting on." She went to cross Sunset, but he jerked her back from the curb.

"You were right about Bogart," he said. "He's not the Commie we suspected him to be. But his was only one of many names on our list. We have every reason to believe that the reestablishment of peace will give rise to a deliberate attack on our democratic process from Communist influences." She wished she could summon up a gob of spit, even just a few drops, but her mouth was like parchment.

"We're going to need your services after the war has ended. Mr. Hoover instructed me to let you know that if you refuse to cooperate with us, a lot may be accomplished with a whisper campaign."

Kathryn watched the traffic — motorcars, bicycles, delivery vans, pedestrians — make its way along Sunset and up Vine. She envied the people and their untroubled lives while hers was sinking into quicksand. "Whisper campaign?"

"Remember that lesbian thing we talked about?"

He let go of her hand, then tipped his hat. She closed her eyes to pull herself together. By the time she opened them again, he was gone.

* * *

Kathryn's innards felt like a cement mixer, churning anger with fear, outrage with frustration, disappointment with bitterness. Danford . . . Sing Sing . . . Bogart . . . Okinawa . . . bugs . . .

She stood in front of the Canteen's cloakroom mirror and found she needed an overhaul. Her lipstick was all but gone, blotched mascara sat in tiny puddles under bleary eyes, and her hair was sticking out like broken sticks of cactus. She was already late for her shift, so a patch job would have to do.

She dove into her purse and pulled out the stub of her last good lipstick. *You must know somebody who can pull strings or lean on*— She paused to stare at herself. *And just who do you think you're going to find to lean on J. Edgar Hoover? Even the president's scared of that jackass.*

Her eye caught the hand-lettered sign above the mirror. Bette Davis had written it herself the day the Canteen opened.

> *WHATEVER TROUBLES YOU MAY HAVE, LEAVE THEM AT THE DOOR.*
>
> *YOU ARE HERE FOR THE BOYS.*
>
> *SMILE, LAUGH, DANCE, AND BE GAY.*
>
> *GIVE THEM A MEMORY TO LAST THEIR WHOLE LIVES,*
>
> *HOWEVER LONG THAT MAY BE.*

She dropped her lipstick back into her purse, swiped away the smudged mascara, and ran a quick brush through her hair. When she walked into the main room, she sensed an intense hum permeating the crowd.

Dozens of men, excited to be on shore leave and eager for female company, always kept the Canteen contagiously buoyant. But tonight the enthusiasm seemed to border on manic. On stage, Gene Krupa's orchestra was hammering out "No Name Jive." Kathryn had seen them perform often through the war, but this night they were playing louder, faster. The couples on the floor danced with rousing frenzy, their arms and legs reduced to flickering blurs.

Kathryn walked to the coffee station and joined Alexis Smith. "Sorry I'm late."

"Don't worry about it," Alexis replied. "This crowd needs cold drinks tonight."

Kathryn jacked a thumb toward the dance floor. "What gives? Did someone drop Benzedrine in their soda pop?"

Alexis smiled. "Word's out among the troops that Japan's made an offer of surrender. They're saying the announcement's just a matter of time." She grabbed Kathryn by the arm. "We're nearly there."

Kathryn watched the couples hurl each other around the dance floor. In the center was Betty Hutton, her golden hair glowing in the lights. She wore a full skirt, black and studded with jet beads, and was dancing with a muscular, sandy-haired sailor who resembled Monty so much it gave Kathryn a start. *Monty's on the USS* Iowa *somewhere off the coast of Japan. What a manipulative ploy.* She felt a hand on her back.

"You didn't tell me he was so attractive!" Gwendolyn said.

Kathryn planted her hands on her hips. "You know what that devious little fink just admitted to me? They snuck in and planted a bug in Bogie's villa. They were listening in on our conversation. They know we made it all up!"

"They didn't!" Gwendolyn exclaimed. "Do you think we've all been bugged?"

Onstage, Krupa launched into a prolonged drum solo to the cheers of a hundred sweaty bodies.

"He said no, but screw him if he thinks I'm going to take his word for it." She thwacked the coffee table with her hand. "Oh, and because I lied to him with my Bogie and Peter Lorre story, he says I violated our agreement, so they will continue to require my services after the war."

"Can they make you do that?"

"If I don't cooperate, Hoover himself plans on starting a whisper campaign to spread the word that I'm a lesbian." Kathryn watched the implications filter through Gwennie's mind. "Sweetie," she said, "I think it's time we each got our own place."

"I always assumed we'd be roomies until one of us got married, or die there a couple of cantankerous old biddies." Gwendolyn's voice sounded thin.

"I feel like I'm being dragged deeper into something that I don't want you to get caught up in."

Gwendolyn winced.

"And don't forget Leilah," Kathryn persisted.

The girls were still recovering from Marcus' news about Leilah's brothels. They had concluded it must have something to do with Linc's disappearance, and that Linc had discovered the O'Roarkes had used Tattler's business to launder their brothel money in order to buy up land around Las Vegas. It would explain why he took off with his and Gwendolyn's money before O'Roarke or Siegel got their hands on it. But they'd never know until Linc resurfaced, if he ever did.

But it was also possible Linc's Mexico story was a red herring. Who's to say he was even there? He could be in Timbuktu for all they knew. The night Marcus revealed Taggert's news about Leilah, Gwendolyn declared that she'd written Linc off as "a casualty of war" and needed to move on.

Kathryn asked, "Do you really want the FBI to discover a direct connection between you and someone who runs a bunch of brothels?"

Gwendolyn shook her head.

"We can talk about all this later."

"Speaking of talking, Bette sent me to fetch you. She's in the back."

Kathryn wound her way to the office, where she found the boss at her desk. As usual, it was littered with bills and correspondence.

Kathryn knocked on the doorjamb. "Sorry I was late. We taped a special show tonight and — "

Bette came around from behind her desk. "There's something I want to ask you. Something personal."

"Does this have anything to do with my being a lesbian?" The question spilled out of her like yolk from a broken egg.

Bette stared at her, open-mouthed. "I was going to ask you what your relationship with L.B. Mayer was these days. I know you and he used to go dancing, and I've been having problems with Melody Hope. She's become so unreliable and — "

"Do you think I'm one? A lesbian, I mean? Because I'm not, you know."

Bette blinked with heavy-lidded deliberation. "Oh?"

Her "Oh?" had a ring of surprise around it. Kathryn sank into one of the two chairs facing Bette's desk. "IS that how I come across?"

"I'm a tough-minded broad trying to stake my claim in a man-centered world. You think I haven't weathered my fair share of accusations?" Bette let out a chuckle. "If I had a dollar for every time 'that Davis dyke' is said out loud in this town, I could finance this Canteen single-handedly — and buy a beach house in Malibu with the change."

"You really thought I was a dyke?"

"I shouldn't speak for everyone, but I suspect it's safe to say most people have made the same assumption."

"THEY HAVE?"

"My dear, you're in your, what, mid thirties? And you aren't married. Apart from those Orson Welles rumors a while back, you've never been publicly linked to anyone. *And* you've lived at the Garden of Allah with the same — "

"I'm not that way. And neither is Gwendolyn."

"Oh, Kathryn," Bette said, more tenderly now, "I don't really care one way or the other."

"I just wanted you to know, in case it ever came up."

"Why is it coming up now?"

Those huge Bette Davis eyes pierced her. Kathryn was starting to feel more than a little foolish and wished she'd clamped down her big fat mouth. "Somebody recently brought all this circumstantial evidence to my attention. You and I don't know each other terribly well, so I was just curious to see what you thought."

"Okay then," Bette said, suddenly sounding like one of her take-charge characters, "why don't you just start dating around? LA's simply swarming with men. Get out there and sample the buffet until you're fit to burst."

Kathryn shook her head. "That's not really my style. I can barely juggle one man, let alone a whole battalion. At any rate, I just wanted you to know — "

Bette waved away the rest of Kathryn's sentence. "My dear, it's quite immaterial to me who you — " Her telephone jangled to life. "That blasted thing never stops!" She reached over and picked up the receiver.

What if the FBI is serious? One whisper into the ears of those hard-core right-wingers at the Motion Picture Alliance for the Preservation of American Ideals and my life could go to blazes.

Kathryn became aware that Bette was sitting quite still, barely breathing. She tried to say something but her voice had disintegrated into a raw croak. The telephone receiver lay dead in Bette's hand.

"Who was that?" Kathryn asked.

"My contact at the war department. Truman was just on the radio. Japan has accepted the terms of surrender." She dropped the telephone and gripped Kathryn by the shoulders. "It's over! Oh my God, Kathryn. It's all over!"

They hugged each other tightly, spattering each other's shoulders with tears until Kathryn was shaking. Bette pushed her away to arms' length. "I don't know what to do first!"

Kathryn pointed toward the stage. "You get yourself in front of that microphone, and you tell everybody in the room the greatest news they will ever hear."

Out in the packed barn, Bette shouldered her way through the dancers, then climbed the steps to the stage. By the time Kathryn rejoined Gwendolyn at the coffee table, Bette had interrupted the band and was gripping the microphone stand with both hands to steady herself.

"Sailors, soldiers, marines, all you wonderful, brave boys! And all my marvelous volunteers, I have an announcement. President Truman has announced that Japan has surrendered. THE WAR IS OVER!"

A deafening cheer erupted and military caps and hats flew into the air. Kathryn turned to find Gwendolyn weeping into her hands, repeating Monty's name over and over. Kathryn wrapped her arm over Gwendolyn's shoulder. "Monty's made it through," she shouted over the tumult. "We're all going to be okay." Gwendolyn nodded. They stayed huddled together until other arms pulled them apart, needing hugs of their own.

The next hour hurtled by in a blur: a tumultuous, unrestrained chaos of tears and Tarzan yells; a carnival of navy blues and army greens; kisses to the cheek, the forehead, the lips; bear hugs and singing, conga lines and wolf whistles. The place emptied fast—booze wasn't served at the Hollywood Canteen, and these men needed something stronger than coffee and pop. The volunteers had families and friends to celebrate with, so Bette closed the Canteen, declaring, "We can clean up tomorrow!"

It was six o'clock when Gwendolyn and Kathryn hit the streets and found the same scene playing out along the length and breadth of Sunset Boulevard. Radios blared from open windows—"Happy Days Are Here Again," "Boogie Woogie Bugle Boy," "Ac-cent-tchu-ate The Positive." Paper streamers rainbowed the air, strangers danced, and lovers loved.

The girls could hear the party at the Garden of Allah from half a block away. Artie Shaw's clarinet was unmistakable.

The two dashed through the main building and burst into the pool area. Paper lanterns of red, white, and blue dotted the trees like patriotic fireflies. The communal booze table was twice its usual size, piled with every type of hooch: from whiskey to wine, beer to Dottie's punch. Dozens of bright orange and green balloons bounced over the heads of the crowd; every now and then one burst from a cigarette butt.

Bertie emerged from the crowd and reached her arms around Kathryn and Gwendolyn. "Oh, sweet Jesus!" Her breath was already ripe with the tang of beer. "Our boys are coming home. Our boys are co-o-o-ming ho-o-o-me!"

Kathryn hugged her. "Is Marcus around?"

"Uh-huh." Bertie broke away, wiping her eyes. "Last I saw, he and Oliver were fixing themselves something at the bar."

When Kathryn shouldered her way to Marcus, he was holding an unopened bottle of Glenfiddich.

"Is that from Seamus?" she asked. "The last one from his family made it, huh? I'm so glad."

Marcus shook his head. "His youngest son was in Okinawa, a gunner on the USS *Bunker Hill*. Kamikazes got him." He cracked open the bottle. "Poor Seamus wasn't up to being here, but left word to drink it in good health." He poured out four shots and handed one each to Kathryn and Oliver. "Where's Gwennie?"

They spied her in a shadowy tête-à-tête with Errol Flynn.

Seamus' Glenfiddich was a buttery smooth mouthful, but it was only a mouthful. Kathryn pointed to an unopened bottle of Gordon's Orange Gin. "Make me a gin-and-something," she told Marcus. "I don't care what, just as long as there's a lot of it." Artie and his band started playing an up-tempo version of an old Irving Berlin ditty, "I'm Putting All My Eggs In One Basket."

"Dance with me!" she commanded Marcus.

She handed him the tumbler of bourbon he'd just poured himself and led him into the thicket of dancers tangled around the pool. Robert Benchley was dancing with Lillian Hellman while Dorothy Parker allowed Louis Calhern to twirl her around like a music box dancer. Dorothy Gish was there too, with Kay Thompson's husband, Bill, while Kay was standing with Artie's band belting out the lyrics.

Kathryn took a deep swallow from her drink — Marcus had made sure he'd added only a splash of pineapple juice and seltzer to her orange gin — and pressed her head against Marcus' chest. "It's like waking up from a nightmare, isn't it?"

"Mmm."

She lifted her head to look at him. "Well, isn't it?"

His eyes were on Oliver, but he shifted his gaze to her. "Absolutely. I was just thinking about tomorrow morning."

"What's happening tomorrow morning?"

He pressed her head back against his chest. "Oh, you know, life goes on."

She thought of Nelson Hoyt and the way his lips disappeared when he said, *Remember that lesbian thing we talked about?* "Let's leave tomorrow for tomorrow."

Marcus grabbed her left hand, twisted it around the back of her waist, and pivoted her into a spin so fast it sent half her drink flying onto Dottie Parker.

Dorothy ran a finger along her wet arm and tasted it. "At last, my prayers are answered! It's raining gin! There is a God!"

The crowd roared and soon everybody was dipping fingertips in drinks — their own and their neighbors' — baptizing each other with booze and tonic and juice and soda and ice cubes and pool water and paper umbrellas and anything else that came to hand.

In the middle of this ritualistic shower, Kathryn grabbed Marcus by the chin. "Happy peacetime to you," she said.

"And to you," he replied. "To all of us." He paused. "Including those no longer here."

CHAPTER 47

Marcus sat on the diving board and watched Kathryn perform the Dance of the Seven Veils for Errol Flynn, Charlie Butterworth, Arthur Sheekman, and some guy in an army uniform nobody seemed to know. Instead of seven veils, Kathryn was making do with a mismatched pair of silk opera gloves and three wilted calla lilies.

The party to celebrate the declaration of peace was six hours in now; Marcus guessed it was past two A.M.

He felt Oliver nudge his shoulder. "Having second thoughts?"

"Why do you ask?"

Oliver glanced down to the paper cocktail napkin in Marcus' hand. He'd reduced it to shreds.

Marcus balled up the paper and stuffed it into his shirt pocket. "You are okay with our plan, aren't you?" He twisted around so he could see Oliver's face. "She'll probably say no, and she probably should. But once I've asked her . . . " He let the rest of the sentence float away on the night air.

"I've already told you what I think," Oliver said. He called out to Kathryn, who'd finished her dance of the gloves and lilies. "OVER HERE!" As she picked her way among the revelers, Oliver said, "She doesn't look too drunk. The time has come. I'll find Gwendolyn."

Marcus scrambled off the diving board and took Kathryn by the hand. "I need you to come with me."

She squinted. "What's going on?"

Marcus said nothing, but led her around the periphery of the partygoers and into his living room. He switched on the corner lamp, but it made the place seem murky. He was aiming for a romantic tone, so he lit the two candles he kept on his bookshelf and moved them to the side table by the sofa.

She sat down just as Oliver and Gwendolyn appeared at the door. Marcus pointed them to the two chairs on the other side of his coffee table, and sat down beside Kathryn. "Gwendolyn told me what happened tonight outside NBC with that FBI guy."

Kathryn blinked but said nothing.

"And about the whisper campaign he threatened you with."

"Ah." She nodded. "Did she tell you about the conversation I had with Bette?"

"About how everyone thinks you're a dyke?"

She rolled her eyes and strained for a smile. "I guess I'm going to have to find myself a very public beau."

Marcus wished he'd had the chance to slug some bourbon before they sat down. "I think I've got a solution to both our problems."

"What problem have you got?" Gwendolyn asked.

In the time he'd headed up the writing department, Marcus had pushed through a number of pet projects: a love story set in a London air-raid shelter; a reworked version of his *Pearl From Pearl Harbor*, now renamed *Hannah From Havana*; and a Jerome Kern biopic called *Till The Clouds Roll By*. It would all be going swimmingly, but the comments from his junior screenwriters were becoming more vocal and more public, and he needed to do something drastic.

"Certain members of my staff don't respect me because I'm a homo," Marcus told Kathryn. "People do respect you, but if the FBI follows through with their threat, that might change."

"You think this is news to me?" Kathryn set her elbows on her knees and her chin on her palms. "But what can I do about it?"

Marcus took the deepest possible breath and let it out slowly. "You could marry me."

Gwendolyn let out a yip and clapped her hands together.

Kathryn's face didn't register the surprise Marcus expected. Instead, he saw all the implications and possible outcomes spinning through her mind like reels in a slot machine. With restrained deliberation, she lifted her head from her hands. "You're serious, aren't you?"

"I've put a lot of thought into this. Let's be honest, it wouldn't exactly be the first lavender marriage that ever took place in Hollywood."

"Or at the Garden of Allah, for that matter," Gwendolyn added.

Kathryn reached out and took him by the hand. "Are you sure about this? I mean, are you *sure* you're sure?"

"It'd solve some problems," he pointed out. "The war's over now, which means we get to start our lives again. I'd like to start it minus the biggest difficulties facing us both." He paused for a few moments to give her the space to think, then slowly slid off the sofa and onto one knee. "Miss Massey, or Miss Danford, or whoever the heck you are, will you do me the honor—"

"YES!" Kathryn threw her arms around his neck and hugged him, but only for a moment. Abruptly, she pulled them apart. "That was a proposal, wasn't it?" She turned to Gwendolyn. "He did just ask me to marry him, right?" Gwendolyn nodded. She pulled him back into a bear hug. "In that case, my answer stands."

"You're not drunk, are you?" he whispered.

She laughed and released him. "At about eleven o'clock, I realized I was going to have to write about tonight in the morning, so I've been pacing myself." She jutted her head to one side. "So when do you want to do this, dearest husband-to-be?"

Oliver cleared his throat. "There's a twenty-four-hour justice of the peace on the corner of Sunset and Fairfax. We could be there in ten minutes."

"Ten minutes?" Gwendolyn asked. "Isn't there something about blood tests . . . ?"

"Not in the state of California," Oliver said. "We checked already."

"Let's do it," Kathryn said. "I just need to fix my face and change my shoes." She grabbed Gwendolyn. "We'll meet you boys out front." They were gone before either man could say anything.

"I was laying fifty-fifty odds she'd say no," Marcus said to Oliver. He rapped his knuckles on the coffee table three times. "Of course, I'd rather be marrying you."

Oliver gave him a me-too smile. "So you do what's practical." He patted his jacket pocket. "I've got the rings. Who knows if they'll fit, but we can deal with that later. Anything else before we go?"

Marcus walked up to his bookshelf and picked up an old wooden toy rocking horse, ten inches tall, its paint job peeling away.

"I've often wondered about that," Oliver said.

He blew the dust off its head and ran a finger down its spine. "It belonged to Alla." He nestled the horse into the crook of his arm. "Since she can't be here tonight, this will stand in for her."

He picked up the latest letter he'd received from Doris: *I told them EVERYTHING about my trip,* she wrote, *and guess what. The sky didn't fall in. They even asked questions.* It wasn't until the letter arrived that he'd realized Doris' visit had pierced what he had assumed to be dead tissue of the past and revealed it to be very much alive. He slipped her letter into his back pocket.

The girls were waiting on the sidewalk outside the Garden of Allah. They linked arms—girl, boy, girl, boy, rocking horse—and headed east toward Fairfax Avenue.

The celebrations along Sunset were still in full swing. Streamers and confetti littered the boulevard. Stray hats and mislaid neckties sat atop streetlights, and underneath, a line of partygoers—too drunk to even conga—snaked their way through a jumble of cars parked haphazardly across the sidewalk. A couple of chorus girls dressed in layers of white chiffon were Charlestoning on the roof of a red Duesenberg.

The neon sign was about two feet square, with amber letters blinking:

JUSTICE OF THE PEACE

OPEN 24 HOURS

NO APPOINTMENT NECESSARY

"How come I've never noticed this?" Kathryn asked.

"Maybe because you've never been in the market for a husband before."

Marcus faced Oliver and Gwendolyn. "We'll be there in a moment." He waited for them to disappear inside before turning to his bride.

He was still afraid she'd say no—there were a heap of reasons they shouldn't head through the door in front of them. But instead, she reached up and stroked his cheek. A carful of drunken sailors hooted and hollered as they roared past, screeching around the corner on two wheels.

"It's not too late to change your mind," he said.

Her smile dropped away. "I can't think of anybody else in this world I'd rather marry."

They looked at each other for a moment, then burst out laughing.

"As far as the honeymoon night goes," Marcus said, "you might want to lower your expectations."

"And as far as the whole cooking, cleaning, mending, and white-picket-fence-wifey situation goes, you might want to lower yours."

"Duly noted, and officially lowered." He swept his hand in front of them. "Ladies first."

Kathryn ran her manicured finger along the back of the toy rocking horse, her brown eyes brimming with emotion. She grabbed his left arm and hugged it closely against her body. "Let's do this side by side."

They stepped through the open door and into an office the size of Marcus' living room, the lights dimmed to a suitably solemn level. Two large sprays of artificial roses in white wicker baskets banked the back wall.

In front of them, a bushy-browed justice of the peace in a dark blue suit, matching bowtie, and benevolent smile waited patiently. Oliver stood to his left, Gwendolyn to his right.

The justice appraised the couple in front of him. "Are the bride and bridegroom ready?"

Marcus passed Nazimova's rocking horse to Gwendolyn and took Kathryn's hands in his. For a long, silent moment, he stared directly into her eyes, searching for signs of hesitation or doubt. Then he shook his head.

"No, sir, we are not." He let go of Kathryn's hands.

"Oh?" Her lips trembled in surprise.

Marcus glanced over his shoulder at the open front door, then pivoted and marched toward it. He wrapped his fingers around the black wrought iron handle and pulled the door closed with a thud, leaving the rowdy chaos on Sunset Boulevard behind them. Returning to his place, he took Kathryn's hand again and flashed her a knowing wink.

"Now we're ready."

THE END

~oOo~

Did you enjoy this book? If you did, could I ask you to take the time to write a review on the website where you found it? Each review helps boost the book's profile so I'd really appreciate it. Just give it the number of stars you think it deserves and perhaps mention a few of the things you liked about it. That'd be great, thanks!

Martin Turnbull

ALSO BY MARTIN TURNBULL

Book One: *The Garden on Sunset*

Book Two: *The Trouble with Scarlett*

Book Three: *Citizen Hollywood*

ACKNOWLEDGMENTS

Heartfelt thanks to the following, who helped shape this book:

My editor, Meghan Pinson, for her dedication, perseverance, guidance, and professional nitpickery.

My cover designer, Dan Yeager at Nu-Image Design who thinks in images the way I think in words.

Bruce Torrance at HollywoodPhotographs.com for the Hollywood Canteen image used on the cover of this book.

My advance readers: Jerry McCall, Matthew Kennedy, Vince Hans, Royce Sciortino, Allen Crowe, and Gene Strange for their invaluable time, insight, feedback, and advice in shaping this novel.

My proofreader, Bob Molinari whose keen eyes never miss a trick.

VISIT MARTIN TURNBULL ONLINE

www.MartinTurnbull.com

If you'd like to see photos of Los Angeles and Hollywood back in its heyday, be sure to visit the Photo Blog on MartinTurnbull.com where old photos are posted daily.
http://www.martinturnbull.com/photo-blog/

Facebook.com/gardenofallahnovels

The Garden of Allah blog:
martinturnbull.wordpress.com/

Goodreads: bit.ly/martingoodreads

If you'd like to keep current with the Garden of Allah novels related developments, feel free to sign up to my emailing list. I do NOT send out regular emails so I won't be clogging your inbox. I only do an email blast when I've got something relevant to say, like revealing the cover of the next book, or posting the first chapter. Go to http://bit.ly/goasignup

9309383R00245

Printed in Great Britain
by Amazon.co.uk, Ltd.,
Marston Gate.